THE THEATRE OF GLASS AND SHADOWS

Also by Anne Corlett

The Space Between The Stars

THE THEATRE OF GLASS AND SHADOWS

Anne Corlett

Black&White

Black&White

First published in hardback in the UK in 2024
This paperback edition published in 2025 by Black & White
An imprint of Bonnier Books UK
5th Floor, HYLO, 103–105 Bunhill Row, London, EC1Y 8LZ
Owned by Bonnier Books, Sveavägen 56, Stockholm, Sweden

Hardback ISBN: 978-1-7853-0552-8
eBook ISBN: 978-1-7853-0555-9
Paperback ISBN: 978-1-7853-0554-2

All rights reserved. No part of this publication may be reproduced, stored in a retrieval system, or transmitted in any form or by any means, without the prior permission in writing of the publisher, nor be otherwise circulated in any form of binding or cover other than that in which it is published and without a similar condition including this condition being imposed on the subsequent purchaser.

A CIP catalogue record for this book is available from the British Library.

Typeset by IDSUK (Data Connection) Ltd
Printed and bound in Great Britain by Clays Ltd, Elcograf S.p.A

1 3 5 7 9 10 8 6 4 2

Text copyright © Anne Corlett, 2024

The right of Anne Corlett to be identified as the author of this work has been asserted in accordance with the Copyright, Designs and Patents Act 1988.

Every reasonable effort has been made to trace copyright-holders of material reproduced in this book. If any have been inadvertently overlooked, the publisher would be glad to hear from them.

Black & White London is an imprint of Bonnier Books UK
www.bonnierbooks.co.uk

For Rob, who loved music, stories, and all the worlds beyond this one.

1669: The Second Great Fire of London was in full flame, and the slums of the city's south bank were alight.

As the fires came close to the Theatre District, burning away the tight-packed clutter of tenements that clung to the fringes of the place, Zekiel Danes, twenty-third Director of the district, smiled his trademark crooked smile and said, 'The show must go on.'

Chapter 1

SOMEONE HAD COVERED THE oxygen machine in a floral throw.

Juliet had hated its mechanical wheezing, but now it had been turned off, the resulting silence was a stark reminder of how little time was left.

She took a small step towards the bed.

Her stepmother sighed. 'He can't see you from there.'

He can't see me anyway. Juliet didn't say it out loud.

She found it hard to speak in this room. It had something to do with the way the nurses looked at her, all with the same expression, as though it had been bulk ordered from some medical supplier, along with everything else needed for the business of dying.

Gauze.

Antiseptic.

A precise tilt of the head.

An acute and specific sympathy.

'Juliet.' Her stepmother's voice was sharp, jolting her into movement.

Walking over to the chair beside the bed, she sat down. Her father's bleached-bone face was framed by the crisper white of his pillows. He was supposed to be propped up to ease his breathing, but he kept slipping into a slack-shouldered slump, as though there wasn't enough Stephen Grace left inside his skin to give him structure. His eyes were open, but focused on nothing.

'I'll give you a few minutes.' Her stepmother's heels clicked away, leaving Juliet staring at her dying father.

Should she take his hand? That was what you were supposed to do, wasn't it? She'd seen it in films. You sat forward, gripping their hand in both of yours, as though you'd never let go. There was a distracting drama to the image. Juliet could see herself, dressed in black, tendrils of dark-red hair falling about her grief-hunched shoulders.

The chair was too far from the bed, and she had to drag-shuffle it closer, then couldn't work out how to fit her fingers into his. Had she ever held his hand before? She couldn't remember. She was about to give up when her father took a scraped, shuddering breath.

'Madeleine.' His voice was a tight rasp, and he strained to lift his head from the pillow, face knot-tight with effort. 'Do you remember? Do you . . .' His voice snagged on whatever he'd been about to say, and when he coughed, it went on for a long time, ending in a horrible liquid gargle. He clutched Juliet's hand, his grip urgent. 'Madeleine.' His eyes rolled back. 'Mad . . . e . . . leine.'

As Juliet scrambled to her feet, footsteps clattered, and her stepmother appeared in the doorway, the nurse behind her.

'What's going on? Did he say something?'

'No. I mean it didn't make sense.'

Stephen was scrabbling at the sheets with clawed hands, his coughing a heaving haul, and Juliet took a sharp step back, colliding with the nurse.

'For goodness sake.' Clare's face creased with irritation. 'Go downstairs and stay with the girls.' It was always *the girls*. Never *your sisters*. When Juliet didn't move, her expression tightened into something so close to dislike that you'd struggle to tell the difference. 'Today would be good, Juliet.'

*

Juliet found her half-sisters in the playroom. Ten-year-old Rebecca was in the window seat with a book, while eight-year-old Elizabeth was arranging the furniture in the dolls' house. Juliet noticed that the father doll was tucked under the stiff covers in one of the bedrooms.

She tried for a smile. 'It's all right,' she said, although neither of them had asked.

There was a pause, and then Rebecca did ask. 'What's happening?'

'It's all . . .' No, she'd already said that. Juliet felt a twist of sadness as she realised she couldn't remember how to talk to them. When they were small, they used to follow her about the house, calling her *Dul'yet*, but as they grew older, her stepmother had found ways of sliding space between them. 'Everything's fine. Your father . . . I mean our father . . .' It sounded as though she was praying. 'He . . .'

Footsteps echoed in the hallway, and then the door opened. Walking straight past Juliet, her stepmother held out her arms to her daughters, who scrambled to their feet and ran to burrow against her.

Holding them close, she addressed Juliet over their heads. 'I need you to listen for the doorbell. The doctor should be here soon. I don't know how long . . .' She broke off, lips tightening, then gave her daughters a final hug, detached herself and walked quickly out of the room.

*

The doctor arrived and went upstairs. Shortly afterwards, the mother of one of Rebecca's friends collected the younger girls, who left without protest. When they were gone, Juliet drifted aimlessly about, listening to the muted creak and scuff of people moving above her. In the sitting room, there was an uncharacteristic pile of post on the sideboard. She was leafing through it vaguely when she heard voices in the hallway, then the sound of the front door closing. The silence that followed was broken by footsteps, then the sitting room door opened and her stepmother entered.

Her gaze went straight to the envelopes in Juliet's hands. 'What are you doing?'

'Nothing.' Juliet put them down. 'What's happening?'

'Your father's dead.' The older woman walked over and picked up the post, tucking the letters away in her pocket, before turning to Juliet. 'Did you hear what I said?'

Juliet's throat felt tight, as though she'd breathed in dust. 'Yes.'

The older woman nodded. 'I have to go and see the girls. They'll stay with Jane tonight, and she'll take them to school tomorrow.'

'School?'

'It will be better if everything stays as normal as possible.' Her stepmother headed to the door, then looked back. 'I'm sorry. This must be difficult for you.'

'Who is Madeleine?'

Her stepmother stopped, hand resting on the door-knob. 'Where did you hear that name?'

'He said it. Just before you came in.'

There'd been another stepmother before this one, and a clutch of other, more fleeting faces to which Juliet could probably put names if she tried, but there was one woman she knew nothing about. Her father had told plenty of stories over the years, shedding the older versions as carelessly as his worn-out relationships. For the starry-eyed romantic, she was his first love. For the world-worn cynic, she was the one who had reeled him in, broken his heart. She was a dancer, a girl from a bar, a gypsy. He'd lost her to an accident, another man, an incurable disease. When she was very young, Juliet hadn't registered the inconsistencies. It was only later she realised other people had parents who were one thing or another. No one else she knew had a mother who shifted and shape-changed like something from a Greek myth. By then, though, the stories were so tangled she could barely find her way through to the things she needed to ask. And if she did ask, her questions were met with an uncharacteristic bluntness. It didn't matter. Her mother was dead and he didn't want to talk about it.

There'd been times when she'd thought about pushing the point, but the truth was her father was an expert at leaving, a Houdini of the heart, and, deep down, she was frightened that one day she'd be the one left behind. So she'd let him spin his tangled web of stories until she could hardly remember what she'd heard him say, and what she'd woven out of her own desperate longing.

'I don't know any Madeleine.' Her stepmother pulled open the door. 'I have to go.'

She walked out of the room, and a few minutes later, Juliet heard the front door close.

As she stood there, feeling her way around the edges of the misshapen thing inside her chest, the phone shrilled. It rang a few times before it occurred to Juliet that she should answer it.

She walked out to the hallway and picked up the handset. 'Hello?'

The line was a haze of static. Through it, she could just make out the burr of a voice.

Stephen? Stephen?

She pressed the receiver closer. 'Who's there?'

There was a pause, whether in response to her words or not, she wasn't sure, then the voice came again.

Stephen? Stephen?

Juliet felt a rush of angry impatience. 'He's dead.' She raised her voice and said it again. 'He's dead.'

A memory flickered. Her stepmother standing where she was standing right now, her voice sharp with something Juliet hadn't heard there before. *He doesn't live here. Don't call again.*

Through the scrape of the static, Juliet thought she could hear someone crying. Then there was a loud crackle, and a voice flared through the earpiece, tinny with the distinctive tone of a recorded message.

. . . on the line. Please hang up. There is a fault on the line. Please hang up. There is a fault . . .

The connection snapped off, leaving a silence so sudden and complete that it set Juliet's heart beating hard against her ribs. She stood there for a moment, then replaced the handset and walked upstairs to her room, that voice still echoing in her head.

Stephen? Stephen? Stephen?

Chapter 2

DEATH SEEMED TO BE a busy thing.

Juliet loitered in doorways, watching the comings and goings, until her stepmother asked her if she couldn't for goodness sake find something useful to do. The playroom needed tidying, and she could change the girls' beds. The cleaner wouldn't be in today, for obvious reasons.

As she headed upstairs, Juliet tried to summon some resentment for her stepmother's edict – *Anything else? Scrub the kitchen floors?* – but in truth she was rarely asked to do anything. She thought she might have preferred to be treated like a skivvy. At least that would have given her a tangible grievance, as well as fitting with almost every story told about stepmothers. But how were you supposed to feel about someone who made sure all your material needs were met, while withholding everything else?

Juliet gave the playroom a cursory tidy, but took a little more time over the girls' beds, making sure their favourite teddies were tucked against the pillows. She'd just finished when her stepmother called her name.

The older woman was standing at the bottom of the stairs, her coat slung over her arm. 'I have a couple of appointments.

I'll need you to collect the girls. There's a key on the table, and I've made sandwiches for their tea.'

As the front door closed, Juliet went straight to her room and pulled a small bag from under her bed. Back downstairs, she picked up the key she wasn't normally entrusted with and headed out, pausing behind the entrance pillars for a moment to avoid the questions that would follow if her stepmother saw her. Why was she leaving so early? Was she going somewhere first? Why couldn't she follow a simple instruction?

It was strange, Juliet thought, how someone could care so little about you, but so much about what you were doing.

*

Miss Abbeline's Academy for Young Ladies was a stately, square-fronted building at the end of a street of expensive shops, not far from St Albans cathedral and its gardens. Juliet had been a pupil there before her father and stepmother met. She'd left a few months ago, after her stepmother had decreed that she needed to let go of her pipe dream about ballet school, and get some *sensible* qualifications.

As she walked up the front steps now, to ring the brass bell, she felt a drag of anger and resentment. Everything she cared about had been swept away in the space of a few calmly delivered words. All her dreams for the future replaced with something so dull and grey and stifling that sometimes she could barely breathe when thinking about it.

The door was opened by one of the assistant teachers. 'Juliet,' she said. 'I haven't seen you here for a while.'

Juliet wondered what explanation her stepmother had given, along with her carefully-timed-so-as-not-to-incur-fees notice. 'I've come to collect my sisters. I'm a bit early.' She pinned on a hopeful smile. 'Can I wait outside the studio?'

'Checking we're teaching them properly?' The assistant smiled back. 'We're supposed to put family in the salon, but seeing as it's you . . .' She moved back to let Juliet inside. 'Miss Lawrence will be pleased to see you.'

The dance studio was at the end of a panelled hallway. Through the window, Juliet could see a group of girls in pink leotards and gauzy skirts, arms raised above their heads. Rebecca and Elizabeth were among them, and Juliet felt a twist of envy as she retraced her steps to another door.

This studio was smaller and more utilitarian, with a stack of scores in the corner. Closing the door, Juliet slipped off her shoes and tights, before pulling her ballet shoes out of the bag. The hard pointe toes felt stiff and tight after not wearing them for so long. She'd tried to dance in her room a few times, but there wasn't enough space. The hallway would have been better, but until the last couple of days, she'd rarely been alone in the house.

Juliet ran through a swift series of warm-up exercises at the barre, then moved to the centre of the room, and stepped into a dance she knew well enough that she didn't have to concentrate on the steps. She could just relax into the lilt of it, letting her mind drift to a stage, somewhere glittering and glamorous. Beyond the lights, there was the blur and rustle of a vast crowd, awed by the clear line of her arabesque, the spark and dazzle of her leap.

Juliet finished that dance, and moved into a more challenging piece, pushing herself further, reaching for something beyond perfection. For her, dancing wasn't something to be written on a certificate and framed on a dining room wall. When she danced, the world felt as though it was turning around her. She was exactly where she was supposed to be.

Something flickered at the edge of her vision. Startled, she stumbled out of the dance to see Miss Abbeline watching her from the door.

'I'm sorry.' Taking a couple of swift steps, Juliet snatched up her tights and scrunched them into her pocket. 'I was early. I didn't . . .'

'No need to apologise, Juliet.' Miss Abbeline was tall and slim, with the smooth hair and upright posture of a ballerina. 'It's been a while since I've seen you dance.'

Coming from anyone else, that comment would probably have been accompanied by a smile of regret, but the expression on Miss Abbeline's face was one Juliet had seen before – cool, appraising, with a hint of something more complex behind it. Whenever the principal of the Academy looked at her that way, Juliet had a niggling fear that the older woman didn't actually like her.

'I didn't want to stop my lessons,' Juliet said.

'You're at college now.' The comment was delivered entirely neutrally, and Juliet wasn't sure whether it meant *time to grow up and move on* or if it was just an observation. Miss Abbeline glanced away. 'I heard about your father. I hadn't realised he was so ill. I'm sorry.'

I'm sorry for your loss.

It was one of those things everyone said, but there was genuine sadness on Miss Abbeline's face. A few times, Juliet had seen her father talking to the principal – not like how most of the fathers talked to her, with their backs very straight and their chests pushed out, but leaning against the wall, as casual as if they were old friends. It was rare for Stephen to show much interest in anything Juliet did, so she'd sometimes tried to weave a narrative out of those encounters. Miss Abbeline had been in love with her father; he'd chosen the wrong woman and now regretted it. Miss Abbeline was her aunt; her dead mother had asked her to watch over Juliet, and she had to pretend that their relationship was no more than teacher and pupil. Once, another thought had tried to take form, but there was something unyielding about Miss Abbeline, and Juliet knew, with an instinctive certainty, that she had never been anyone's mother.

'Thank you.' Juliet cast about for one of the correct responses. 'It was a shock.'

'What will you do now?'

'Do?' Juliet wasn't sure what her old teacher meant. Her father had never been much of an active presence in her life. It was her stepmother who made sure that the household ran as it should, and everyone ate and washed and visited an appropriate number of museums and stately homes.

'Your college course finishes soon, I think?' Miss Abbeline said. 'What are your plans after that?'

'I'm not sure.'

Miss Abbeline nodded. 'If you need anything, please do ask. I mean it, Juliet. You can always come to me.'

Juliet's throat tightened. As she swallowed, the principal gave her another brisk nod, and left the room.

Chapter 3

AT HOME, THE YOUNGER girls disappeared upstairs, leaving Juliet to lay out the tea Clare had left for them.

She was just taking the foil off the plate of sandwiches when there was a knock at the front door – probably some well-wisher bearing yet another casserole. Juliet brushed crumbs off her skirt as she crossed the hallway. There were a couple of neighbours who would feel it their duty to tell her stepmother she'd answered the door looking as though she'd dragged herself out of the laundry basket.

When she opened the door, there were two men outside, both dressed in suits. The older of the pair had steel-grey hair, and the deep creases at the corners of his eyes and mouth didn't look as though they'd been put there by laughter. The other looked to be in his late twenties, with dark hair and broad shoulders.

'We're looking for Mrs Clare Grace,' the older man said. 'Is she home?'

'I'm afraid she's out.' Juliet wondered which of the many death-related tasks they'd come to deal with. They didn't look like florists or caterers. 'Can I help you?'

'What's your name, please?' the man asked bluntly, his gaze raking over her in a swift appraisal that made her spine stiffen a little.

'I'm sorry.' She echoed the tone her stepmother saved for people she didn't want to talk to. 'Can I ask who you are?'

The man pulled out a wallet, flipping it open to reveal a metal badge. 'I'm Detective Inspector Mansfield. This is Detective Constable Lambert. We have a few questions regarding Stephen Grace. Are you a relative?'

Juliet felt a flutter of irrational guilt, and pushed back against the feeling. This was probably part of what happened when someone died. In a minute, he'd say something about *just procedure, routine questions*, like detectives did in the films.

'I'm his daughter.' Juliet tried to sound grown-up and sure of herself. 'What is this about, please?'

'Just a few questions.' No *routine*. No *procedure*. 'Can we come in?'

As she showed them to the sitting room, she wondered whether she should offer tea. The etiquette for dealing with police officers hadn't been covered in her final year finishing lessons. Before she could decide, Mansfield sat down in one of the armchairs and nodded towards the sofa opposite, as though this was his house, and she the guest.

With another brush of resentment that felt borrowed from her stepmother, Juliet sat down, tucking her knees to the side and folding her hands in her lap, as she'd been taught. Over by the door, the younger officer leaned against the wall, the drift of his gaze around the room too pointedly casual for her to miss the intent behind it. By contrast, DI Mansfield was studying her openly, his head turned slightly to the side. He seemed in no hurry to disclose the reason for their presence.

'I'm sorry, I . . .' Juliet felt about for a polite way to say *What do you want?* 'How can I help you?'

'Your father was Stephen Grace, recently deceased.' Mansfield paused. 'I'm sorry. For your loss.' He didn't wait for a response. 'I assume Mrs Grace is not your mother, though. How old are you?'

'She's my stepmother,' Juliet replied stiffly. 'I'm almost twenty.'

'Can I ask about your mother?' Mansfield said.

There was a flush rising on the back of Juliet's neck. Whenever any of the girls at school asked, she'd always had an answer to hand, but she couldn't use any of those extravagant, made-up stories now. *Of course, Officer, she was a film star in Hollywood.* Or *I'm sorry, I can't talk about her. Government orders, I'm sure you understand.*

'She died.' Juliet fell back on the brief, official version her stepmother used if someone was gauche enough to ask. 'When I was born.'

'What was her name?'

'I . . .' There was something about the situation that was making Juliet's head feel fuzzy, like the time one of the guests at a dinner party had insisted on topping up her glass with wine, while her stepmother smiled through gritted teeth and never invited him back. 'My father wouldn't talk about her.'

Mansfield raised an eyebrow. 'You don't know her name?'

Juliet felt a shift of anger. He had no idea what it was like, living in a family where you weren't wanted. You walked on ice every day, stepping as lightly as you could, waiting for the sudden plunge into cold disdain and being loved even less.

'What is this about?' Her voice was too loud. Miss Abbeline would have given her one of her looks. 'Why are you asking about my mother?'

'How long have you lived here?' Mansfield moved on to the next question, as though she hadn't spoken.

Juliet wanted to push the point, but she didn't know how. This wasn't *just procedure* or *routine questions*. She was sure of it. 'Since I was nine.'

'Did your father own this house?'

She shook her head. 'It belongs to my stepmother. We moved here when she married my father.'

'And where did you live before that?'

Juliet's skin prickled, as though charged with static electricity. They weren't here about her father's death. They were here to talk about something that no one ever let her ask about. They were here about *before*. It was a struggle to keep her voice steady as she ran through a brief summary of what she could remember of the pre-stepmother years. Her father's first marriage. The woman they'd stayed with for a while, who used to let Juliet play with her make-up.

Mansfield listened silently, his expression giving nothing away, and when she finished, he moved straight to another question. 'Where were you born?'

'I don't know.'

'Have you seen your birth certificate?'

It was sufficiently removed from their stated purpose for Juliet to risk a challenge. 'What does that have to do with my father's death?'

'Can you answer the question, please, Miss Grace?'

Over by the door, DC Lambert shifted. He was uncomfortable, Juliet realised. Did he think they shouldn't be here, pestering her with questions so soon after her father's death, or was there something else?

'No,' she said. 'I haven't seen it.'

'Do you know where your father was born?'

'No.'

It was getting harder and harder to take a clear breath. All the *no*s and *I don't know*s were merging inside her. They'd never been pushed together like this before, and it was as though the negative space around them was forming a picture, like that vase that turned into two faces if you stared at it long enough.

'You've never needed any of this information?' Mansfield said. 'Not for a job?'

'I'm at secretarial college,' Juliet said. 'My stepmother arranged it.'

'What about school?'

'I went to Miss Abbeline's.'

'Miss Abbeline's?'

'Miss Abbeline's Academy.' Juliet left off the bit about *young ladies*. 'It's a girls' school, with an emphasis on drama and dance.'

It sounded as though she was advertising the school to an unlikely pair of prospective parents. If she was, she hadn't done a good job, as Mansfield moved on to another matter.

'When will your stepmother be home?'

'I'm not sure,' Juliet said. 'She had some appointments.'

The detective stood up, reaching into his pocket to pull out a card. 'This is my number.' His tone was suddenly brisk. 'Please ask her to call me.'

'That's it?' Juliet was thrown by the abrupt termination of the interview.

'Thank you for your time, Miss Grace.' Mansfield moved towards the door, then stopped and turned back. 'You said the Academy teaches dance and drama. Do many of the pupils go on to work in those fields? I had the impression there weren't many jobs to be had these days. Not outside the Theatre District, anyway.'

His tone was casual, but Juliet had a sense of a finely honed intent behind the question. Or perhaps it was just a poor attempt at small-talk by a man not used to small-talk.

'No, they don't.' She didn't add that not many of the Academy's pupils would work at all.

'Have you ever been to the Theatre District?'

The Theatre District. The mysterious, glittering Theatre District. It was one of the most famous places in the world, a vast labyrinth of wonders, wound around a show that had played for centuries. A place where nothing was dull and ordinary. A place you could only belong if you were special, and then you'd belong so hard you'd never have to wonder what your life was really about. For a while, one of her favourite daydreams was that she'd go to the district and somehow finish up in the Show, dazzling the audience with the brilliance of her dancing. She'd never been able to work out exactly how it would happen, though, given no outsider ever joined the district's notoriously secretive resident cast and, in the end, the allure of the imperfect fantasy had faded. As for Mansfield's question, of course she hadn't been. She had about as much chance of being permitted to visit a place like that as she did of flying. Museums, galleries, appropriately staged performances of appropriately improving plays – they were the cultural currency in which her stepmother dealt.

She shook her head. 'No.'

Mansfield seemed about to ask something else, but his colleague spoke up, a warning note in his voice. 'Sir.'

The older officer gave a curt nod. 'Thank you, Miss Grace.'

Juliet had once read a fairy tale about a girl who had to finish some task – spinning, perhaps; it always seemed to be spinning – but it kept multiplying. There had always been things Juliet didn't know, but now there was a great tangled mess of additional unanswered questions, and Mansfield was walking away, leaving her trying to claw her way out.

Driven into movement by a surge of anger, Juliet caught up with the officers in the hallway.

'Why did you come?' she demanded, as Mansfield opened the door. 'What do you want?'

'Just procedure, Miss Grace.' Mansfield didn't react. 'Routine enquiries.'

There it was, but it was far too late. 'I don't believe you.'

'I'm sorry about that.' He stepped out.

As DC Lambert followed, he gave Juliet a small nod, which might have held a hint of apology.

Impulsively, Juliet touched his arm. 'What's going on? Please, I need to know.'

The young officer hesitated, but Mansfield spoke his name, his voice sharp.

He shook his head. 'I'm sorry.'

Juliet watched as he followed his colleague down the steps, and then she closed the door, and leaned against it, her head a blur of half-formed questions. She was sure of only one thing: whatever had brought DI Mansfield to the door, it wasn't *routine* or *procedure*.

Through her frustration, Juliet was aware of something else. There was a prickle across the back of her neck. It was a feeling she got every now and then – a tension; a sense that *something* was about to happen. It could be triggered by anything – a stranger catching her eye in the street, a half-familiar scent, even the doorbell ringing unexpectedly. Her scalp would tingle, and she'd find herself straining every sense. *This is it*, a voice would whisper in the back of her mind, breathless and urgent. *This is it*. But nothing ever happened, and the feeling would fade, leaving her sad and dull, as though some wonderful opportunity had been missed.

'Who was at the door?' Elizabeth was standing at the top of the stairs, looking down.

'No one.' Juliet pushed herself away from the door. 'Tell Rebecca tea's ready.'

*

'Elizabeth said someone came to the house.' Clare never knocked before opening Juliet's door. 'Who was it? Why didn't you tell me?'

'It wasn't important.' Juliet fiddled with the bulb of a bottle of perfume on her dresser. She'd almost told Clare about the police when she'd arrived home, but as she'd reached for DI Mansfield's card, she'd felt a push of defiance. Everyone else had their secrets. Besides, if she told her stepmother about the visit, whatever lay behind it would slip away into the world of closed doors and private conversations and become yet another question she'd never know the answer to. 'Just someone selling something.' She embellished. 'Dishcloths. I told them to go away.'

The older woman's lips tightened – she disapproved of cold callers, certain that most of them had been in prison – and she changed the subject.

'I need you to run some errands tomorrow. I've booked the funeral for two weeks' time. I'm having notices printed.'

'Miss Abbeline will probably want to know the date,' Juliet said. 'I saw her today. She said she was sorry.'

'It will be a small ceremony,' her stepmother said. 'Just people who were close to Stephen.' She turned away, straightening a couple of things on the shelf. 'Did she say anything else?'

There was an odd note in her voice. She'd always been somewhat distant with the principal of the Academy, never indulging in any of the jostling for position that went on among the other parents.

'No.' As soon as she said it, Juliet wished she'd shaped a clever lie, something to draw out whatever her stepmother had turned away to hide. But the moment had passed, and

Clare was moving towards the door, satisfied that Juliet had nothing to say that was worth her time.

*

It must have been around midnight when Juliet was woken by a sound from along the hallway. Getting up, she made her way to Rebecca's room. It was quiet, but that stretched kind of quiet that meant someone was keeping very still, trying to hold back a tell-tale ragged breath.

'Are you all right?' Juliet kept her voice low.

Silence.

'I thought I heard you crying.'

Silence.

Juliet was about to turn away, when the sound came again, faint and stifled. She hesitated, then stepped inside. Walking across to the bed where Rebecca was a huddled bump beneath the covers, she slid in behind her, folding herself around the younger girl. For a moment, Rebecca was rigid in Juliet's arms, and then she let out a tear-puckered breath and curled against her sister.

Juliet held her tightly, feeling the suppressed shudder of her ribcage, and remembering how they sometimes slept like this. Rebecca used to have nightmares, and she'd slip into her sister's room and Juliet would hold her until the shivering stopped.

'Do you miss him?' Rebecca said, suddenly.

If she'd been asked that question in the daytime, Juliet would have said, *Of course I do.* But there was an honesty in the darkness. 'I don't know. Do you?'

A long pause. 'I don't know.'

Juliet waited, but her sister didn't say anything else, and after a few moments, her breathing smoothed into the steady rhythm of sleep. Juliet's arm was in an uncomfortable position, but she didn't want to disturb Rebecca, so she lay still, staring into the darkness.

When she'd first come to live here, she used to find it hard to sleep. There was something brittle about the house at night, and lying there, stiff and sleepless, she'd distract herself by imagining another version of herself – like those princesses in fairy tales who were only themselves in the cold hours beyond midnight, trapped by day in swan feathers or the cold flanks of a monstrous snake. Night after night, she'd woven those stories, until that other self had a clear and constant form, and an existence distinct from her creator. She was Juliet's lost twin, a darker, less compliant version of Juliet. She didn't need a family, didn't need people to like her. She lived in the dark, in the shadows, at the tattered edges of ordinary things, and she was happy there.

Now Juliet could feel her stirring once more.

There's something, she thought. *Something I don't understand, and I don't know how to find out.*

Yes, you do, came the answer, trailing an idea with it, like a gift.

Juliet felt the soft click of a decision. Turning her face on the pillow, she tightened her arms about Rebecca, and let sleep claim her.

We're cogs in a machine. We play our parts and the world keeps turning.

The girl in the silver shoes can't remember who said it, but the words have stayed with her. She knows what a cog is. There's a clock on the mantelpiece with a clear glass dome, so you can see the metal workings. She isn't troubled by the idea of being a little piece of something big. She is little. But when she grows up, she'll be one of the stories that runs through this place, carrying everyone along with the force of its telling. But that's all in the future, and for now she has an errand to run.

The girl in the silver shoes slips through a medley of alleyways, the parcel tucked under her arm. As she climbs a flight of steps onto a path that runs along the top of a crumble-topped wall, a couple of stones shift beneath her feet, but she knows this place too well to ever stumble. A short way along the wall, she turns and steps up to the edge, looking down onto the street below. There's a small crowd gathered there, staring along the lane with a sort of yearning she's seen many times before. She knows what it means, what she's just missed. A Wanderer has picked someone out of the crowd and led them away, leaving the others bereft, because it wasn't them.

The girl smiles. Never mind, *she thinks*, tender as a mother comforting a child after a bad dream. Never mind, I'm here for you.

It's a few seconds before someone looks up and sees her. The knowledge of her presence runs through the crowd as a rustle, an indrawn breath, a ripple of black as, one by one, the masked faces turn up towards her. She makes sure she's wearing that tilted, mysterious smile that says I know something you'll never understand, *and then she fixes her gaze on a narrow gap between the upper floors of the buildings across the street, stretches out her free arm and steps off the edge.*

There's a gasp from below as the girl curls her toes around the wire that's stretched beneath her. You can barely see it, but she doesn't need to. She's been walking the wires for as long as she can remember. Her mother doesn't like it. She's afraid the wire will snap, or the girl's foot will slip, or someone will shout out and startle her. She's afraid of the fall that lies beyond those things, but the girl doesn't understand why. This is part of who she is. This moment, with the masked faces turned towards her, and the wire taut under her feet, this is the moment when the girl in the silver shoes becomes The Girl in the Silver Shoes.

She heads for the gap, her steps neat and precise, the parcel clutched tight against her side. She knows the crowd will have seen it, that they'll be trying to figure out what it means, where it fits into whatever story they've spun about her. They'll never know it was simply that someone had a parcel to deliver and she was the quickest of the children to stick up her hand and claim both the errand and the shiny coin waiting at the other end.

As she steps off the wire into the narrow space between the walls, she can hear the scramble and clatter of feet down below. Some of them will know this place well enough to predict where she'll come out. Sure enough, when she emerges, there's a breathless huddle gazing up at her. She doesn't look at them as she descends, and they part before her, then fall in behind as she turns along the street.

Her destination is just ahead – one of the smaller theatres. The crowd stops at the bottom of the steps, but she can feel them watching as she slips inside. Then the door closes behind her, and The Girl in the Silver Shoes becomes the girl in the silver shoes again, with a package to deliver, and a coin to claim.

Chapter 4

Two days passed before Juliet was able to put her plan into action.

There was always something to be done, and on the occasions she was left alone in the house, it was never for long. By the third day, though, it seemed Clare had decided it was time for the household to return to its usual routine.

'You can put the key I gave you in the hallway drawer,' she said, after breakfast had been cleared away. 'I'll be back by the time you get home from college.'

Juliet's heart sank. Last night, as her stepmother had reeled off a list of today's appointments, she'd felt a sharp nip of anticipation.

Her resolve wavered briefly, then hardened.

'I don't have classes today,' she said.

Her stepmother's gaze narrowed. 'It's Monday.'

'The timetable has changed.' Juliet dug her nails into her palm. 'They phoned yesterday.'

Her stepmother stared at her for a moment, then gave an irritable shrug and turned away. Juliet ducked her head to hide a flush of nervous triumph. She knew her stepmother would check, and her deception would come back upon her tenfold, but in that moment, she didn't care.

*

When the front door closed, Juliet waited until she was certain no one had forgotten anything, then went up to the bedroom her father had shared with his wife. With no clear sense of what she was looking for, she would have to look everywhere. Despite her nerves, she was conscious of a tremble of guilty excitement at the thought of peering into all the places that usually fell under the labels of *None Of Your Business* or *You Don't Need To Be In There*.

She searched with methodical defiance, leafing through the notebook on Clare's nightstand, sliding her hand into the pockets of the clothes in the wardrobe, inspecting each key in the bundle inside her father's bedside drawer. Finding nothing, she made her way up to the top floor. The spare room drawers were kept empty for visitors, but there was a wooden chest in the corner, packed with sentimental items relating to her half-sisters. Old school books. Pictures they'd drawn. Their first shoes. There was nothing of Juliet's in there and an old pain scraped inside her, dull and slow, but still enough to make her chest ache.

Heading back downstairs, she went into the study. Ostensibly, this had been her father's, but his wife used it more than he had, sitting at the desk with her meticulous log of household finances. The bookcase was packed tight with notebooks and reference texts. Stephen had been writing a book about the history of English theatre. It was once something he'd fitted in between lecturing jobs, but shortly after marrying Clare, he'd declared himself a full-time writer. As far as Juliet could tell, this hadn't involved any increase in productivity, just a dramatic reduction in his inclination to take on other work.

She pulled one of the notebooks off the bookcase. Notes covered every page, broken by the occasional sketch or diagram. She tried to read a few pages, but Stephen's writing was cramped and small, so she gave up and turned to her father's piano. He hadn't played very much, but she'd sometimes heard a drift of music, halting and uncertain, as though he was trying to remember something he'd once known. On a page of manuscript paper, he'd written down a simple melody, with a few chords in the left hand. Here and there, he'd scribbled out a wrong note, replacing it with another.

Juliet spread her hands on the keys, trying to remember the single term of lessons she'd had at school. Her attempt was clunky and slow, but she recognised the tune as the one she'd heard Stephen trying to play. It was in an odd key, with a yearning lilt to the melodic line that caught at Juliet, making her wish she could have heard the whole piece.

Turning away from the piano, Juliet moved behind the desk, where she opened each of the drawers in turn. Paper clips. Pens. An old invoice from a tailor. Her stepmother's lips would purse when she found that, and she'd dig out a page of accounts that had never tallied. The cupboard to the left of the footwell was locked, and Juliet's thoughts went to the bundle of keys in her father's nightstand. Hurrying upstairs, she retrieved them and took them back down to the study.

The third one she tried worked. Inside the cupboard she found some papers, haphazardly stacked, and a battered, brass cash-box. Juliet picked up the top page. It was a letter addressed to her father – official-looking, with a discreet header.

Marlowe & Co Solicitors
Inner Temple, London.

It was dated a few months earlier and referenced a payment of some sort. Behind it were several others, identical save for the date – one each year. At the bottom of the stack, however, Juliet found something different: a handwritten letter in a scrawled, lopsided script, smudged here and there, as though the writer had been in too much of a hurry to let the ink dry. It was dated over fifteen years earlier, and there was an address at the top, nearly illegible.

3 Pal . . . din Str . . .
Lond . . .

The first few lines were entirely incomprehensible, but further down the page, the writing settled a little, allowing Juliet to pick out a few words.

What parent . . . their child . . . sorry . . .

She took a quick breath in and leaned closer, trying to force meaning from those uneven letters.

If you . . . see her . . . girl . . . silver shoes . . .
Silver shoes.

Juliet could feel the prickle of that special tension, and it wasn't fading this time. Instead it was growing more urgent, aching after the sense of something hovering just out of reach.

Silver shoes.

As Juliet turned the words over, a memory shook loose. She was younger, perhaps eight or nine, standing at the sitting room door in her nightdress, driven downstairs by the throbbing ache in her ear. Inside the room, Clare was focused on Stephen, brandishing a piece of paper. Her voice was tight with anger, and Juliet's stomach twisted with that unsettling sense of the grown-up world gone wrong. As she slipped away, she caught the end of an odd little volley.

. . . silver shoes.

Juliet stared at the letter, trying to match the pattern of creases to the memory of her stepmother's white-knuckled grip. Had she really heard those words, or was her mind trying to piece something together from fragments of nothing?

No. This was something. She could *feel* it.

Putting the letters aside, Juliet turned to the cash-box. The smallest key in the bundle fitted, and it opened to reveal an odd collection of objects. A black silk mask with ribbon ties. A tarnished chain twisted around a bundle of silver charms. A key on a velvet ribbon. An old photograph.

The mask was trimmed with tiny feathers, like the belly of a black swan. On the back, there was a brush of what looked like make-up around the bridge of the nose. The fabric smelled musty, but with a trace of something else too – the merest hint of what might have been perfume.

The photograph showed a young woman. There was something faintly familiar about her smile, although Juliet had no idea who she was. Her father's voice echoed in her mind, wracked with the final desperation of the dying.

Mad . . . e . . . leine.

Juliet put the photo down and picked up the chain. It was a cheap-looking thing with a flimsy catch, the charms too light to be real silver. There was a mask, like a miniature version of the one lying beside her, a ballet shoe – *silver shoes* – a rose, a feather, a lantern, a crown and a bird.

Unlike the charms, the key was solid and heavy, with an odd, ridged face. It was threaded onto a purple ribbon, fraying at the ends, like the ties on the mask. Juliet placed it beside the other items, feeling as though she was trying to draw the pieces of a puzzle together without knowing what the picture was supposed to be.

Mask. Photo. Charms. Keys.

An indecipherable letter, smudged with what might have been tears.

A name she'd never heard.

Police officers asking questions about the unknown *before.*

At school, they'd studied a poem about a sea monster, sleeping at the bottom of the ocean. Miss Abbeline had said it was about secrets, forgotten things. Every line had been heavy with menace – except the last.

In roaring he shall rise and on the surface die.

Juliet could still remember the disappointment of that ending. All that dark promise, that slow, drifting threat, coming to nothing. What if this was the same? What if this tangle of confusion, this sense of *something* hovering just beyond understanding, fell away, leaving her alone and ordinary once again?

Lost in her thoughts, it took Juliet a second or two to register the scuff of sound from the front door. When she did, panic flared – the all-encompassing, vision-blurring fear of a child caught doing something forbidden. It turned her hands clumsy, and she dropped the necklace twice as she tried to fumble it back into the box. She got it in and scrabbled for the key, but it was too late. Footsteps approached, and her stepmother appeared in the doorway.

With a drag of resignation, Juliet sat back on her heels and waited for the storm to break.

The older woman crossed to the desk and leaned over to look down. 'Stephen always kept that cupboard locked.' Her tone was almost conversational. 'What was in there?'

When Juliet held out the mask, Clare took it, turning it over in her hands as she studied it.

'Do you know what it is?' Juliet found her voice.

'A memento, I suppose. Of some other woman.' Clare handed it back, nodding towards the photo. 'That one, perhaps.'

Juliet brushed her fingers over the woman's face. 'Do you know who she is?'

Her stepmother gave a brief, cool smile. 'Madeleine,' she said, and then, as Juliet's heart contracted, 'or at least that's what you're thinking, isn't it?' Juliet bit the inside of her lip.

Her stepmother had always been able to read her like a book. It was a particularly acute humiliation. Before she could reply, Clare sighed and brushed some non-existent lint from her sleeve. 'You asked if he ever mentioned that name. He did. Once. When we were first married. It was when . . .' Her face tightened. 'Never mind. He called me Madeleine. I don't think he realised, and I never spoke of it.'

'Who was she?'

'I said I never spoke of it,' her stepmother repeated sharply.

'Was she my mother?' Juliet's fingers were trembling. Maybe one of her father's stories of heartbreak was true. Maybe he couldn't talk about her because it hurt too much. Maybe . . . she felt a lift of hope . . . maybe Juliet reminded him too much of his lost love.

Her stepmother's gaze narrowed. 'Don't do that.'

'What?'

'I know that look. A photo, a name, and off you go, spinning some tale about how you're a stolen princess and *she'll* come and whisk you away to her castle at the end of the rainbow. I used to hear you telling the girls your stories. Made-up nonsense, for the most part. But every now and again, your voice would change, and you wouldn't be talking to them anymore. You'd be telling yourself things you thought might be true.'

'But it's not just a story,' Juliet said. 'He kept her photo all these years.'

The older woman shook her head. 'There you go again. You have no idea whether that's even your mother in the photo.'

Juliet remembered something Mansfield had asked – another of those questions that had ended in an *I don't know.*

'My birth certificate,' she said. 'It will have my mother's name on it, won't it?'

She could write off for it, to whoever dealt with that sort of thing, and it would arrive in an embossed envelope. She'd open it and smooth it out, and it would say . . .

Her thoughts snapped off. Her stepmother was moving towards a cabinet in the corner. She unlocked it and pulled out a folder. Extracting a piece of paper, she walked back to hand it to Juliet. 'I needed your birth certificate to enrol you at college. This was all I could find.'

It was a letter on headed paper. The address at the top was Somerset House, London.

Dear Mrs Grace,

Thank you for your enquiry. Unfortunately, I am unable to fulfil your request for a copy birth record. While there is an index entry matching the details you provided, the birth was registered within one of the London liberties. The liberty in question retains its own records and, while there is a statutory requirement for the registrar to provide an annual list of entries for inclusion in the central index, this information is limited to the name of the individual, and the quarter in which the event took place.

For more information, please write to the following address:

The Registrar
Kilner Street
The Liberty of the Southern Hallows
London

Yours faithfully,
E Halliday
Chief Registrar

Juliet read the letter twice through, trying to understand what it meant. 'Did you write?' she asked. 'To the place he said?'

The older woman shook her head. 'I managed without it in the end. From what I've heard about that place, I wasn't likely to get a reply, so I didn't waste my time.'

'That place?'

The Liberty of the Southern Hallows. The name rang a faint bell.

Her stepmother looked away. 'The Liberty of the Southern Hallows is the real name for the Theatre District.'

It was strange how soundless an explosion could be. Juliet's thoughts shattered into shrapnel, flung into the far reaches of her mind. For a moment, she struggled to drag them back together, and then she felt a great winged lift of the purest joy she'd ever known. She was from the Theatre District. This was it. *This* was the secret she'd sensed all these years.

'What did he say to you?' She tried to focus. 'About where he came from?'

'He told me he'd spent time in the Theatre District,' Clare said. 'He told me your mother was someone he'd only known for a while, that she died when you were a baby, and there was no one else to take you. That's all.'

'You never wanted to know more?' Juliet couldn't wrap her thoughts around that idea.

'I was satisfied he wasn't a drunk or a criminal, or bankrupt. That was my main concern. Not where he grew up, or what he did with some other woman years before he knew me.' There was something in Clare's clipped tone that made Juliet look more closely at her.

You're jealous, she thought, with swift certainty.

Not jealous of her stepdaughter, or another woman. Nothing that mundane. But Juliet wasn't just the unwanted product of some undesirable union. She was something rare and wonderful, and her stepmother would never be either of those things. That was why she'd tried to crush Juliet's bright dreams. That's why Juliet had found herself enrolled in college with girls whose only ambition was a typing speed of eighty words per minute.

Those stories she'd told herself *weren't* just stories. She must have known, somewhere deep down, that she'd never been meant for this dull and loveless life. She belonged in the Theatre District, and now that she knew, she could go back there and find out the truth and maybe . . .

'You're doing it again,' her stepmother said. 'If you'll take my advice – although I know you won't – you won't waste time thinking about what may or may not have happened in the distant past. You'll focus on the future.'

'It's not the distant past,' Juliet said sharply. 'It's my life.'

'Then I suggest that you get on with living it,' her stepmother replied, equally sharply. 'And I don't mean in some fantasy world where you walk up to the Theatre District, and trumpets sound, and flights of angels sing you through the gates.'

'That's not what . . .'

'It is.' Her stepmother cut across her. 'That's exactly what you're thinking. That you'll go there, and they'll all come rushing to give you everything you've ever wanted.'

'Why not?' Juliet felt anger rising. 'Why shouldn't I get what I want for once? Other people do.'

'No one gets everything they want,' her stepmother replied flatly. 'Most people just figure out how to settle for what they have.'

'Is that what you did?' Juliet flung at her. 'When you married my father?'

Her stepmother gave a small, tight smile. 'I always knew what kind of a bargain I was making. I kept my end of it, and he kept his. For the most part.'

'A bargain? That's all your marriage was?'

'That's what every relationship is,' the older woman replied. 'It always comes down to the same thing – what you're worth to someone. What do you think you're worth to whoever is running the show . . .' Her mouth twisted, '. . . quite literally, in the Theatre District?'

'Why do you care?' Juliet said, with a flare of resentment.

'Honestly?' Her stepmother met her gaze levelly. 'I don't. I have my girls to worry about. But I'm telling you, Juliet, there's nothing for you in that place. Your mother is dead. She died years ago.'

'You don't know that,' Juliet said. 'He lied about everything.'

'It has nothing to do with your father. Women don't leave. Mothers don't leave. Men seem to find it easy enough.' She gave Juliet another straight look. 'Tell me, do you honestly think he would have taken you if he'd had a choice?'

It should have hurt. Perhaps it did, in some muffled, hidden place, but Juliet had wrapped so many things around that old pain she could barely feel it.

'We don't know what happened,' she said. 'Maybe it wasn't meant to be forever.'

'Then why did he say she was dead?'

'He said a lot of things.' *He probably told you he'd love you forever.*

The older woman's gaze hardened, as though she'd caught that unspoken thought. 'Yes,' she said. 'He did. But do you really think that if there was any chance of being free of being a father, he wouldn't have taken it?'

Juliet looked up at her. 'Does that include his other children?'

Her stepmother gave her a wintry smile. 'Probably. But he stayed anyway. Who else could have afforded him?' She paused, as though considering the question. 'Maybe he would have left, eventually. But not women. Women stay. Mothers stay. They do whatever it takes to protect their children.' Something brushed across her face, and she gave a shake of her head. 'You'll carry on spinning your fantasies, no matter what I say.' She held her hand out. 'The letter.'

'No.' Juliet held on to it. 'I'm keeping it. And the other things.'

She'd never openly defied her stepmother before, but the knowledge that she didn't belong here – that she'd never belonged here – gave her courage. For a moment, the two of them stared at one another, and then Clare shrugged.

'Fine.' She nodded at the lawyer's letters. 'I'll take those, though.'

Juliet's hands were shaking as she handed them over. Victory should have left her triumphant, but she felt as though she'd reached out to lean on something, only to have it fall away. Somehow she found herself looking up at her stepmother again and asking, 'What now?'

Clare gave a tight smile. 'I'm working on it.'

ANNE CORLETT

From The History and Architecture of London's Theatre District *by S L Corran*

First published 1942

The architecture of the Theatre District is as complex as the show that lies at its heart. It is generally accepted as consisting of two semi-distinct parts – the inner district, and the outer – also known as the district precincts. The inner district is generally held to include all the streets falling beneath the shelter of the main roof. The boundary of the outer district has long been in dispute, as has the exact nature of the area's relationship to the inner district, and the surrounding metropolitan area.

The front wall of the district is a free-standing construction, formed of large, precision-cut blocks, and curving away from the main gate in both directions. At intervals, iron girders rise out of the concourse and up to the central dome. An inscription on the girder to the right of the gates commemorates the construction of the dome and front wall under the supervision of the great British engineer, Isambard Kingdom Brunel, who also oversaw the renovation of parts of the existing roof and its extension to the new outer wall. Mr Brunel was, by all accounts, initially reluctant to undertake the task, but was eventually persuaded. The exact sums involved have never been disclosed, but it is well accepted that the remuneration allowed Mr Brunel to complete the project closest to his heart – the Clifton Suspension Bridge.

Viewed from the front, there is nothing to indicate that this grand aspect does not continue all the way around the district. However, like many things in the Southern Hallows, this is an illusion. If you walk along the embankment in either direction, you will see that the wall curves back only a short distance before merging into the surrounding clutter of buildings. Behind the wall there is a wide avenue, lined with shops, coffee houses and bars, these establishments being the descendants of the stalls and sideshows that clung to the district fringes during its early history. There is little uniformity of building style or materials, with some structures giving the distinct impression that their collapse has only been staved off by the efforts of generations of unskilled hands.

Once through the turnstiles behind the main gate, visitors can follow the central parade to the main plaza, or turn off to explore the streets, squares and passageways that form the greater part of the inner district. In many places, newer infrastructure has been built directly on older foundations, leaving a maze of hidden subterranean spaces, some of which may date back almost a thousand years. There are references to a Glíwesgaderung or 'Play-Gathering' as far back as the ninth century, and in 1083, Arnuld of Billingsgate, a monk and historian, wrote disapprovingly of the activities at the 'Glíwesburg' on the south bank of the Thames: 'A sanctuary for fools and pretenders and charlatans. A place of lies, designed to lead men astray and cause them to forget their duty to God and their masters.'

The earliest reference to the House of Doors theatre can be found in a twelfth-century gazetteer, while several fourteenth-century accounts describe 'the great show' and refer to the fact that the actors were 'not contained' by the walls of the theatre, but ventured out into the surrounding streets. By the fifteenth century, the district was not too far removed from its current form, with a central part consisting of the House of Doors, several smaller theatres, and various inns, hostels and shops, surrounded by a warren of tiny streets, with cramped dwelling-houses providing accommodation for the actors and other workers who had made their homes in the district.

The central plaza was the brainchild of Zekiel Danes, District Director from 1651 to 1672. He was vocal in his dislike of the haphazard layout of the district and the press of poor tenements around its edges. This latter problem was solved in drastic manner, when the Second Great Fire of London burned away a large swathe of the surrounding slums.

In the aftermath, Danes commenced a large-scale project in the district. This included the relocation of all residents to dwellings outside the centre, as well as the levelling of two theatres, the foundations of which are believed to be located beneath the present-day plaza. At this point, the project stalled, presumably due to a lack of funds, visitor numbers still being low after the ravaging of the city by plague and fire. In time, the central space was paved, but the results were a far cry from Danes' ambitious vision.

In 1693, Prince Henry of Wales came to visit the district, now under the Directorship of Zekiel Danes' successor, Byron Ballard. The prince was, by all accounts, greatly enamoured with the place and became an unofficial patron.[1] *He persuaded his father, King James II, to make the district a generous financial gift, as well as sending the royal architect, John Boyd, to discuss plans for improvements, including an expansion to the House of Doors. In 1695, work began on a covering roof, intended to turn the centre of the district into one unified performance space, and, by the end of the century, the centre of the district began to resemble the main square that modern visitors see today.*

In 1699, the king, presumably at the behest of his son, passed a decree known as the King's Gift, confirming as an independent liberty 'all the dwellings and establishments which fall beneath the cover of its roof' and granting substantial tax relief for the same. At this time, there were a number of theatres and other commercial properties outside the assigned area. As a result of the decree, several independent construction projects commenced, bringing six more theatres and various other establishments under a newly expanded roof. At the same time, some residents living on the outskirts used

---

[1] *Much has been written about the affiliation between the Theatre District and Prince Henry, particularly in relation to the period immediately following his legitimisation, when rumours abounded as to his proclivities. For a balanced and scholarly treatment of this complex and ill-fated prince, see* Henry Villiers – Bastard, Prince and Patron, *Samuel Connington, 1915*

whatever materials they could find to bring themselves into the fold. Some of these projects were successful, with the houses and streets beneath them forming part of the current inner district, while others were abandoned, leaving the areas they had been intended to cover as part of the outer district.

Around this time, the Board of Directors began to introduce restrictions upon those permitted to live and work in the district. By the end of the century, all non-performers had been forced to give up their resident leases, with most of them relocating to the dwellings.[2]

---

[2] *This relocation marked the establishment of the district precincts as an area distinct in character and, some argued, legal status, from the surrounding area, which was then part of the ancient parish of Lambeth. Much of the regeneration work that followed the destruction wreaked by the Great Fire was apparently carried out by labourers working for the district board, but the resulting structures stood upon land that had historically formed part of the manors of Lambeth and Kennington North. It would appear that the Archbishop of Canterbury, who had held these manors since the restoration, was entirely content for the fire damage to be put right at the district's expense – until, of course, it became apparent that the residents no longer considered themselves under any financial obligation to the largely absent lord of the manor, preferring to affiliate themselves to the Theatre District. The resulting legal proceedings were abandoned at an early stage, but formed the foundations for various other legal challenges over the following centuries. Despite the lack of clarity over its status, the outer district continued to expand until it occupied the entirety of the fire-damaged area to the east and south of the district, and a fairly substantial strip of land to the west. At time of writing, the status of the precincts remains unresolved, with one issue of particular concern being the tendency for precinct residents to register births, marriages and deaths in the district registry. The result of registration within an independent liberty is*

built to replace those destroyed in the Great Fire. In relation to commercial premises, many of these appear to have remained under the control of their original proprietors, now living in what would become the outer district.

Under the terms of the king's decree, the Board of Directors was now the uncontested authority within the district.[3] This was not something which sat well with king's successor, Queen Anne. This may have had something to do with the well-known connection between the Theatre District and the queen's disgraced and disinherited nephew – Anne refused to speak of the former Prince of Wales by name, purportedly referring to him in private as 'that twice-damned bastard' – but is more likely to have been due to straightforward resentment about the loss of tax revenue from such a large area of the city.

Despite the loss of its royal patronage, the district continued to grow and thrive. Its reputation spread across the empire and beyond, and by the nineteenth century, it saw increasing numbers of wealthy foreign visitors. It entered a new era of affluence, with the

---

that the only accessible record of the event in question will be a short form index entry at the Central Record Office, and the availability of even this limited information is entirely dependent upon the liberty complying with its statutory duty.

[3] The district was not wholly exempt from the laws of the land, with the police retaining powers to carry out certain criminal investigations, but for the most part the district was self-governing.

productions growing ever more lavish[4], and many famous dance and theatre companies being eager to perform in the district's smaller theatres and halls, despite the heavy levies and restrictions placed upon visiting artists.

By 1843, the roof was in need of extensive repair work. The Director at this time was Garrard Blythe, and it was he who secured the services of Isambard Kingdom Brunel.

[Cont]

---

[4] *It is worth noting that the financial standing of the district has always been something of a mystery. There have been a number of high-profile patrons, but it is generally assumed that there are, in fact, many more financial backers, with most preferring to remain anonymous.*

Chapter 5

IT WAS ALL DONE quickly and smoothly, Juliet had to give her stepmother that.

Between the tight clauses outlined by the pinstriped lawyer, Juliet caught the echo of Clare's cool efficiency. The offer was full and final. In exchange for a one-off payment, Juliet would waive any claim against the estate of her late father or the assets of his widow, although nothing in the agreement should be taken as an admission that any such claim existed.

'I just need a signature.' The lawyer extracted a silver pen from his breast pocket. 'Here.' He tapped the paper. 'And here.'

The pen was cold, as though he kept that pocket chilled. Juliet rubbed her thumb over it as she stared at the page. That was what you were supposed to do, wasn't it? You didn't just sign any old document stuck in front of you. But she had no sense that anything was being renounced. Her whole life here had been borrowed from someone she'd always known would want it back one day, and fair compensation was not something she'd considered. She'd never had to deal with money, but the figure on the page was bigger than anything she'd imagined owning.

She scrawled her signature on the dotted line. As soon as she'd added the date, the lawyer whisked the document away, holding his hand out for the pen, as though he thought she might pocket it. Equally swiftly, the woman who was once her stepmother moved in, ushering him to his feet and out through the door.

Exit stage left, Juliet thought, trailing them into the hallway, where the lawyer was lacing up the shoes he probably hadn't expected to be asked to remove. As he straightened, his gaze fell on a picture on the wall.

'Your daughters?'

Clare opened the front door. 'Thank you so much for your time.'

With the door closed behind the lawyer, Clare stood still for a few seconds, then turned to look at her former step-daughter. 'Well, that's done. Have you made any plans? No hurry, of course.'

'Of course.' Juliet couldn't keep the edge out of her voice.

If the older woman noticed her tone, she gave no sign. 'Someone Mary Hallam knows in London is looking for a mother's help for a few months from January – board included. It would give you time to find something more permanent. Shall I tell Mary you're interested?' A pause. 'You're welcome to stay till then.'

Juliet had no idea which of Clare's identically respectable friends was Mary, and no interest in any job she might have heard about.

'That would be lovely.' She pinned on an insincere smile. 'Thank you so much.'

As she turned away, that smile gave way to another, small and secret. Very soon, none of this would matter.

She still hadn't mentioned the police visit. She knew all hell would break loose if DI Mansfield came back, but over the last couple of days, she'd thought of little else but piecing the puzzle together. She'd found an old *London A to Z*, although there was nothing in the index that might fit the address in the smudged letter, and the Theatre District was greyed-out, broken only by a small, labelled square marking the central plaza.

Clare picked up her coat. 'I want you to go to Rossiters after college and get a black dress for the funeral.' She counted some notes from her purse. 'Make sure you get a receipt.'

Juliet took the money, her pulse quickening. She had a plan, but hadn't been sure how long it would take for the lawyer's payment to appear in her newly opened bank account. Now she didn't need to wait.

Once Clare left, Juliet hurried up to her room. Changing into a silvery-grey jumper and a black skirt with a hemline just slightly shorter than had been deemed acceptable, she retrieved her college bag, then packed the mask, photo, necklace, key and, after a brief hesitation, the letter from the record office. On top, she added a change of clothes, her washbag and her new bank book. She would be back tonight, of course, but it wouldn't hurt to take a few things. Just in case.

*

When she got to the station, it was busy; a cancelled train, according to a disgruntled elderly woman. The next train was full, leaving half of the would-be passengers – including Juliet – on the platform to wait for the following one, and it was early afternoon by the time she got to London. It took her another half hour to navigate the maze of the Underground, her impatience rising with every passing minute.

When she eventually emerged onto the embankment, a vague drift of rain blurred her vision, and the river was unsettled, boats swaying fitfully on their ropes. But there, on the far bank, the great curved roof of the Theatre District rose from the dull clutter of the city. As she crossed the river, the feeling of *almost* and *so close* was like electricity, sparking through her. This was every Christmas, every birthday, every magical thing that only happened to other people, all rolled together, and she could hardly breathe with the press of it inside her.

On the opposite bank, Juliet fell in behind a middle-aged couple in wine-coloured coats, a little like robes. Anywhere else, they would have drawn glances or smirks, but here, it simply made it seem that they knew something others didn't. Juliet glanced down at her own clothes with a renewed sense of dissatisfaction. Furtively, she folded over the waistband of her skirt to shorten it, but it still didn't look right. She felt a lurch of something close to panic. The first time she set foot in the Theatre District should be perfect and special, and this *wasn't* special. *She* wasn't special. She was just another person in the crowd. Ridiculously, after her earlier impatience, she now wanted to pause, but the steady flow of people was sweeping her along. All around, she could feel anticipation, excitement, like a pulse beating through the crowd.

Hurry. Hurry. Hurry.

The district's front wall rose ahead of her, ribbed by great steel girders. And there were the famous gates and everyone was moving faster – too fast. She wasn't ready but the gates were rising in front of her, above her, and then she was through, jolted and jostled on all sides as the crowd bottle-necked towards a series of entrance barriers.

Juliet took a deep breath, trying to steady herself. The air smelled of coats and hair and other people's perfume, but through it, she caught a hint of something indefinable and enticingly different. The roof was low here, and hung with lanterns, their warm glow reflected in the windows of the shops and coffee bars that nestled against the wall. The crowd thinned slightly, as some people peeled away, but most joined the queues for the turnstiles.

Juliet joined too, craning her neck to see ahead, as the line inched forward. She could see attendants handing out plain black masks, but not everyone was accepting one: some seemed to have brought their own. Juliet felt a tug of regret for the feather-trimmed mask tucked away at the bottom of her bag. If she'd had it to hand, she too could have smiled a satisfied, secretive smile and shaken her head at the gate attendant, like the girl in the queue to her right, whose sequinned mask trailed ribbons down her back.

Instead, Juliet accepted a plain mask, tying it in place as she emerged onto a paved thoroughfare, lined with more shops, ticket offices and various other establishments. Great iron lamps hung from the girders, with strings of flimsy paper lanterns twisted around their chains. Up ahead, there was a faint scatter of music, a distant descant to the low, close hum of the crowd. The chatter had dropped significantly, as people turned away from their conversations to stare about them. Most visitors seemed to be heading straight on, towards the centre of the district, but some disappeared through doors or into narrow alleyways.

Anxiety scuffed the edges of Juliet's anticipation, as she realised how little she knew about the district. Was there an administrative centre? She couldn't exactly walk up to the counter of a ticket office and announce herself. As she looked around, her gaze was caught by a flurry of movement near the entrance to a side street where a group of visitors were hurrying after a tall woman with greying hair. She was striding swiftly along, apparently unaware of her followers, and she was unmasked.

A performer, Juliet realised with a thrill. One of the mysterious denizens of the Theatre District whose real identity would never be known to anyone who wasn't part of this place. For a moment, she thought of hurrying to catch that eager group, but she hesitated too long, and they turned the corner and disappeared. Juliet shook away a pang of regret. That wasn't what she'd come for. She wasn't one of those ordinary visitors, seeking nothing more than an afternoon of diversions.

Turning into another side street, Juliet closed her eyes, breathing in the multi-layered smell.

I've been here before. She articulated each unspoken word inside her head, trying to make the idea feel real. *I've been here before.*

Nothing stirred. No forgotten memories surfaced. No echo of voices called from the past to tell her this was where she belonged. She opened her eyes, shrugging off the disappointment. It didn't matter. When she found her way to the heart of this labyrinth, all of the confusion and uncertainty would fall away, and she wouldn't just know: she'd *know*.

Juliet set off along the street. It was narrower than the main route, and most of the shops were old-fashioned, with low doorways and leaded windows. There was a confectioners with jars of brightly coloured sweets packed onto shelves behind the counter, a jewellers, a clockmaker's workshop, a haberdashery selling nothing but black buttons and trimmings, and various other shops and stalls, many with clusters of visitors peering at what was on offer.

When she reached a junction, Juliet picked a direction at random. The street she turned onto was narrower still, with little uniformity to the buildings. Some were top-heavy, their upper floors sagging forward, while others looked as though they'd been squeezed in between their neighbours as an afterthought. Her attention was caught by the elaborate ironwork entrance to a covered arcade, and she turned into it. Inside, she couldn't work out whether the paperweights, miniature kites, and telescopes on display were actually for sale. She couldn't see any shopkeepers, but a masked visitor in a long, jade-green skirt was standing beside one of the doors, as though waiting for something. As the woman glanced her way, Juliet realised, with a jolt of confused shock, that it might *not* be a woman. She thought she read a challenge in the blank gaze and made an awkward gesture that might have been an apology of sorts, then hurried on, a flush heating her cheeks.

She emerged from the arcade onto another street, turning from that onto another and another and another. The district was growing busier as afternoon eased into evening. Towards what must be the outer edges, the streets were still relatively empty, but when her wanderings took her close to the centre, she found herself weaving through throngs of visitors. In amongst the everyday clothes, there were more strange and wonderful outfits – floor-length ball gowns, kimonos, Arabian-style embroidered trousers – paired with elaborate hairstyles and beautifully decorated masks.

A couple of times, Juliet found herself at the edge of the famous plaza, with its bustling fringe of bars and coffee shops, and the great glass dome gleaming overhead. Dotted about the central space, there were various street performers. A woman with skin and hair the same silver as the folds of her long dress. The slight figure of a magician, cards rustling in his pale, slim hands. A dark-skinned man on stilts juggling lit torches.

More diversions filled the streets around the plaza. Imp-like faces peeped out from the shadows as Juliet navigated a silhouette maze of archways, trees and pillars. A green-eyed fortune teller beckoned from the drapes of a silk-hung entranceway, while an artist painted a scene that subtly shifted as Juliet moved, revealing a distorted image of the artist himself, his features twisting out of brick and stone and curving roof.

At the end of one alleyway, a flight of steps made from hot-air balloon baskets swayed gently as she ascended. On a platform at the top, a brass telescope looked out through a series of breaks in the rooftops to magnify another platform, where clockwork figures whirled slowly around one another. A tiled tunnel seemed to loop round in a circle, but when Juliet emerged, she wasn't where she'd come in at all. In a garden of silk flowers, flesh-and-blood visitors mingled with hazy projections of women in old-fashioned dresses. A pool lay at the centre of a maze of subterranean halls, flanked by crumbling statues, the silver fins of carp glinting in a dusty drift of light from an opening above. The door of a tower room opened onto a network of rope bridges, with visitors passing beneath, never noticing Juliet balanced high above them. On the far side, a winding staircase hung with wind chimes led down into another impossible tangle of alleyways.

*

Juliet had been wandering for some time when she found herself back near the main entrance. As she stopped to catch her breath in a paved square, her gaze fell on a wooden noticeboard, covered in flyers, posters and what looked like timetables, all overlapping in a hodge-podge of information. Around the edges were layers of notes, handwritten and incomprehensible.

Will be at TSN for an hour at seven o'clock. JG.

SBN – Gone on ahead. Meet me at south end of Crossways. K.

On the other side, Juliet found a map of the district, carved directly into the wood. She felt a beat of excitement, but as she leaned closer, she saw that it was incomplete. In the centre there were road names and diagrams of theatres and bars, but further out, the names disappeared, streets giving way to large blank spaces. There was no index, and no sign of any office or information point.

As Juliet looked around, wondering if she should ask someone for help, she noticed a small crowd gathered nearby. For a moment, she thought they were staring at her. Then she realised they were looking past her, and she turned to see a strange figure standing a little way away.

He – if it was a he – was cloaked and hooded, and his face was entirely covered by a mask constructed from all manner of metallic odds and ends. Cogs and gears, nuts and bolts, wire mesh, twisted together into the contours of an unnervingly realistic face, currently turned towards Juliet.

The figure raised its arm, metallic fingers unfurling, and a tension spread across her shoulders and down her spine. It was that feeling again, but a thousand times stronger and more urgent than ever before. As she took a step forward, responding to that wordless summons, the moment seemed to pull tight around her, oddly intimate, despite the watching crowd.

Without warning, she was knocked aside, as a young woman with a black flower in her hair pushed forward to take the outstretched hand. Righteous outrage swelled inside Juliet and she waited for the figure to disregard the importuner. Instead, he drew the girl towards a nearby door, ushering her through. Before following her, he paused, turning that impenetrable gaze back upon Juliet.

Reaching up to his chest, he twisted his hand and tossed something towards her. She lurched forwards to catch it before it hit the ground. When she unfurled her fingers, she was holding a silver rose, a twin of the one on the chain of charms. And both man and interloper had gone.

The crowd surged forward, pressing around the closed door, some trying the handle, others pushing their faces close to a dark window at the side. Juliet stood still, not sure what had just happened, but conscious of a sharp chill of disappointment and loss.

'You'll have to be quicker than that.' A voice spoke from behind her, and she turned to see a small man smiling at her. He was dressed in an old-fashioned grey morning suit, which might have looked distinguished on someone taller. His mask was feathered around the eyeholes, giving him the look of a not-quite fully fledged owl, and there was a silver pin shaped like another feather at his lapel. 'First visit?' When Juliet nodded, his smile widened. 'You can always tell.'

She looked at the door. 'What was that?'

'A Wanderer.' The man somehow managed to articulate the capital *W*. 'You were about as close as you can get to one of the most coveted experiences in this place.' He grinned. 'Until you messed it right up, of course.' The flicker of annoyance must have shown in Juliet's face, because he gave a contrite grimace. 'Sorry. To be fair, there wasn't much you could have done. Some of the regulars can move like lightning when they see an opportunity.'

'An opportunity for what?' Juliet asked.

The man tilted his head contemplatively. 'What do you know? About how all this works, I mean.'

'A little bit,' Juliet said. 'Articles, that sort of thing.'

The man snorted. 'The newspapers won't tell you anything.' He lowered his voice. 'There's a place I can take you, if you want to understand the district. As much as anyone can, that is.'

'I was looking for an office.' Juliet glanced at the map. 'Somewhere I could find out . . .' She stumbled over what she couldn't say, the sentence trailing off into a vague ending, '. . . some things.'

'An office?' The little man chuckled. 'We should be so lucky. Nothing in this place is straightforward. Not even for the Followers.'

That last word was accompanied by a swift, lidded look. It was an obvious hook, but Juliet let herself bite. 'The Followers?'

The man held his hands up. 'I know, I know. But we've got to have a name to separate us from the ordinary punters.' His smile twisted into another grimace. 'That didn't come out right, but there are two kinds of visitors. The ones who come here, and the ones who *come back*. For most people, the district is just a night out. They'll go home and talk about how amazing it was and how they must come back sometime, but that's as far as it goes. The Followers are the ones who walk through those gates and realise nothing will ever be the same again. I'm not sure Followers is even the right name. *Searcher*s might be better. Although people don't usually know what they're searching for when they first come here. Most of us still don't. You'd think we'd have worked it out by now, given how much time we spend talking about it. That's one of the wonderful things about this place. It's all right to go on and on about things you'd never normally say. Like how it all makes you feel, or what it makes you believe.' His smile turned mischievous. 'Or the grudge you're still holding about that missed encounter with a Wanderer.'

Juliet glanced towards the door again. 'Who was he?'

The man gave an exasperated click of his tongue. 'Sorry. I'm rambling, as usual. The Wanderers are . . . well, they're like him. It's hard to tell them apart. Mostly, you know who is who from the places you see them. We call that one the Gatekeeper, because he's never too far from the entrance. You never know what they're going to do. Sometimes they'll just touch you, or point you in a particular direction. Sometimes they'll bar your way for no obvious reason.' His lips curled into a wistful smile. 'And sometimes they'll take you away for a private scene. That's what everyone hopes for.'

'What happens if they do that?' Juliet asked.

'I'm not sure about the Gatekeeper,' the man said. 'I don't know anyone who's been chosen by him.' He paused for a quick grin. 'You nearly changed that. Although, if you'd gone with him, we wouldn't be having this conversation. Anyway, some of them dance with you. Some take you somewhere you wouldn't normally be able to go. The one thing they have in common is that they all send you on your way with a token. There are seven, but I don't know anyone who's managed the full set.' When Juliet looked down at the rose, he leaned forward. 'Yes, that's one of them. They don't often give them out like that.' He touched his lapel pin. 'There's this one. Then a ballet shoe, a lantern, a cat. I can never remember them all.' *A crown*, Juliet thought. *A clockwork bird. A mask.* 'You've got that look.' He gave Juliet a knowing smile. 'I've seen it before.'

'What look?'

'The kind that says you'll be coming back.' He lowered his voice again. 'That place I mentioned . . . well, you should see it for yourself.'

Juliet could imagine her stepmother's cold disapproval. Going off with a strange man? Was she trying to become one of *those* girls?

'I don't even know your name.' She made a half-hearted effort at propriety.

'That's something of an occupational hazard here,' the man said. 'Not everyone is who they say they are.' He gave her an old-fashioned bow. 'I'm Eugene.'

'Is that true?' Juliet asked.

'You're a fast learner,' he said, with a grin. 'But yes, it is. This place isn't about pretending for me.'

'Then what is it about?' It was a strangely intense conversation to be having with a stranger.

'Understanding,' he said. 'There are layers upon layers of stories and secrets. I'm under no illusions that I'm going to be the one who pieces it all together, but I want to unpick as much as I can. And on the subject of unpicking, would you like to see the place I mentioned?' He hesitated, looking uncertain. 'Or do you have plans? I feel like I've waylaid you a bit. I haven't even asked your name.'

'It's Juliet.' This wasn't how she'd imagined her visit playing out, but Eugene could be her best chance of discovering how things worked here. And besides, she was enjoying talking to him. She couldn't remember anyone ever being nervous or uncertain around her, as though it was actually important what she thought of them. She smiled at him. 'And no, I don't have plans.'

Chapter 6

JULIET FOLLOWED EUGENE ACROSS the street and into a tiny passage.

After a few yards, a sharp turn plunged them into almost complete darkness.

'They really should replace the bulbs in here,' Eugene said. 'I mentioned it in one of the ticket offices, but they never respond to anything you say, so no way of knowing if it gets passed on.'

'Passed on?'

'To the District Board.'

'Do you ever meet them?' Juliet tried to sound casual.

Eugene laughed. 'Us mere mortals? Not a chance.' They'd emerged into a high-walled courtyard, where a shimmer of water fell into the lichened basin of a fountain, with a glint of silver and copper beneath the surface. 'District tradition.' He turned to smile at Juliet. 'A coin for a wish.'

Juliet slid her hand into her pocket. She knew it wasn't true, but what was the harm? Pulling out a coin, she tossed it in, then found herself struggling to shape a request concise enough to fit into a single wish. The resulting garble of *and . . . and . . . and . . .* left her with an irrational flutter of anxiety that she tried to brush away.

It wasn't real.

'You have to take one out as well,' Eugene said. 'You make a wish and take a wish. You might get your own, or you might get someone else's.'

Juliet didn't want someone else's wish, but she reached in and extracted a penny, wiping it on her sleeve and dropping into her pocket.

Eugene turned towards a gateway on the far side of the courtyard. 'Come on.'

'Aren't you going to make a wish?' Juliet asked.

There was a wry tilt to his smile as he glanced back. 'There are too many of my wishes in there already.'

He led her through a labyrinth of passageways, twisting steps and almost-hidden gaps. A kite-hung alley led to a mirror maze which he navigated with casual skill. A wood-panelled passage ended at a tiny squeeze of a doorway that opened onto a path lined with spindly evergreens. The ground was strewn with fallen needles, and when Juliet brushed against one of the branches, it released a tang of old resin.

At a humpback bridge spanning a stream, Eugene peered over the railing. 'You have to be careful here. One of the Wanderers sometimes hides under the bridge. He's the only one who shows any sense of humour. They're a fairly intense bunch for the most part. The same goes for the stagehands, who definitely do *not* see the funny side of life. There's a theory that the Wanderers serve a similar warden-type role out on the streets. They do often seem to pop up if someone is doing something they shouldn't.' He leaned out a little further. 'Or hanging about on bridges for longer than is wise.'

Eugene seemed entirely at ease in the district, despite its quirks and vagaries. Or maybe because of them. There was a similar quirkiness to him, and Juliet wondered how well he fitted into whatever place he occupied in the outside world.

They eventually emerged onto a narrow street, lined with lead-windowed establishments that looked as though they could be home to a Bob Cratchit or two. Eugene stopped at a building that seemed to have been cobbled together from several centuries' worth of materials and architectural styles.

'The Shipping News.' He gestured at the sign above the door, which depicted a stocky man, legs planted wide in John Bull style, with tall ships bobbing over the white-curled waves behind him. 'Come on in.'

The pub was much bigger inside than it looked from the street. At some point, someone had knocked through into the neighbouring buildings to create one large main room. There was a gallery running around the upper floor, and the bar was an island of stained counter-tops, with a black-painted canopy that gave it the appearance of a fairground booth. A vast wooden candelabra hung above, with bulbs where once there'd been candles, and a wire winding round the chain to disappear between the roof beams.

The place was fairly busy, and Juliet noticed that no one was wearing their mask. As they removed theirs, Juliet saw that Eugene was younger than she'd thought – perhaps only a few years older than her.

He smiled at her. 'So that's what you look like.' He hung his jacket on a chair, then turned towards some stairs in the corner. 'Come on. There's something I want to show you.'

At the end of the upper gallery, a door opened onto a long, narrow room. It looked as though it should stretch to the end of the pub, but archways ahead and to her left revealed two more rooms. Was everything in this place an illusion? Juliet glanced around. To her right, there was a row of wooden chests and battered filing cabinets, but the other walls were entirely papered in overlapping pages of writing and drawings, many of them stained and faded like old documents in museums. Tight lines of scribbled notes rubbed shoulders with pages of elaborately penned script, while pencil sketches vied for space with charcoal or watercolour renditions of dancers.

As Juliet turned on the spot, images leaped out at her. The blur of a dark forest. A man's face, his expression of tenderness so clearly rendered that it looked as though he might move and speak. The scarlet and peacock hues of a stained-glass window. A gunmetal grey sketch of a Wanderer, his cogs and gears picked out in metallic ink.

'Who did all this?' she asked, as she completed her rotation.

'People who loved the district,' Eugene replied. 'Generations of them. There's about a century's worth of papers on the walls – maybe more, given how many layers there are, and some of the stuff in the cabinets is even older. It's not clear whether the original Followers were given permission to use these rooms, or whether they just found them empty and moved in, but no one seems inclined to evict us. They'd have a fight on their hands if they tried it. This place is . . .' He looked around. 'Well, it's everything. Whatever secrets the district holds, this is the best chance any of us have of figuring them out.'

'Have you found any secrets?' Juliet asked.

'I should be so lucky.' Eugene smiled. 'Sometimes I wonder whether there's anything to the rumours at all, or whether it's just overactive imaginations. But other times, I have a feeling of being so close to something I can hardly breathe.'

Juliet knew that feeling. 'So close to what?'

'That's the problem,' Eugene said. 'No one is entirely sure. There are all sorts of stories – well, fragments of stories really – about some people being *let in* in some way. That the Show is just the tip of the iceberg, with the real mysteries hidden below the surface. That most things you see are part of a . . . what would you call it? A lobby? Something you have to work your way through, in order to get to the next level. No one ever admits to it happening to them, but everyone's heard about someone who knows someone who was sworn to secrecy by someone no one has ever met. Some people take it literally – they think there are secret routes into hidden parts of the district. Others think it's about the Show, that there are scenes most people won't ever see. There are stories about passwords, about doing certain things in the right order, about going to a particular place at a particular time. Clocks, mazes, hidden codes, mathematical puzzles. If you can imagine it, I can guarantee it's come up in some rumour or other.' He gestured at the sketch of the Wanderer. 'The seven tokens feature in several theories, which is part of the reason those private scenes are so coveted.'

Juliet's thoughts snatched briefly at the chain of tokens, tucked away in her bag, and she had to remind herself she wasn't an ordinary visitor. Still, there was something enticing about the idea of it – generations of people painstakingly piecing together everything that might be a fragment of a vast puzzle.

'What do you believe?' she asked.

Eugene shook his head. 'Honestly, I don't know. My sensible side wonders if it's just about a deeper level of understanding. The stories in this place are so complex that it would be a lifetime's work to even get close to seeing how it all fits together.' He grinned. 'My less sensible side is rather attached to the secret door theory. I thought I'd found it once. Which is very much a story for another time.' He turned towards the archway. 'There's more to see.'

'How do you find anything in here?' Juliet said, following him.

'With great difficulty. Papers from the same time frame tend to be grouped together, but there's not much of a system other than that, I'm afraid.'

Juliet was about to ask another question when something caught her eye. She stopped dead, staring at a large painting to the side of the archway, its corners curled around the pins that held it in place. It was an achingly detailed rendering of a young woman in a blue-grey dress. She was en pointe, her arms crossed in front of her. Her hair was a rich auburn, the same as Juliet's own, and her smile was so familiar that Juliet could barely breathe.

'Ah.' Eugene had turned to see what she was looking at. 'Beautiful, wasn't she? That picture really ought to be in the far room, but someone clearly thought it deserved a more prominent position.'

'Who . . .' Juliet swallowed. It was the woman from the photo. 'Who was she?'

'The Moonshine Girl,' Eugene said. 'There's been more written about her than any other character in the Show's history. It's like that sometimes. Something – a performer, a storyline – catches everyone's imagination, and it starts to feel like it means more than everything else. Of course, she was connected to so many of the Show's stories, going way back. And when she disappeared so young—'

'Disappeared?' Juliet's voice was sharp. When Eugene gave her a questioning look, she forced a smile. 'That sounds terribly mysterious.'

'It was,' Eugene said. 'There are plenty of things in this place that don't make sense, but this *really* didn't make sense.' He smiled. 'If that makes sense. Here, I'll show you.'

Juliet followed him over to a filing cabinet. From the bottom drawer, he pulled out a cardboard folder.

'Here.' He fanned some pages out on top of the cabinet. 'This is a list of all known characters since the Followers started keeping records. It's got their first and last known appearances, their connections with other storylines, and whether they've appeared in the Show or just out in the streets.' He peered at the last page. 'Looks like it needs updating. Some changes to the main Show cast haven't been written up yet. To be fair, the most recent was only a few days ago.' He gave Juliet a wry smile. 'The problem with puzzle-solving by committee is that there's no way of predicting when someone will get round to dealing with any given piece of it. Sorry, I'm getting distracted.' He tapped a name near the bottom of one of the other pages. 'Here's the Moonshine Girl, along with her last appearance in the Show.'

The date he was indicating was a few months after Juliet's birth, and she took a slow, careful breath, trying to steady the thudding of her heart. 'Does anyone know where she went?' She had to force out the next question. 'Did she die?'

'We don't think so.' Eugene indicated a note at the bottom of the chart. 'She was apparently seen in the district a handful of times over the following few years.'

'What happened to her after that?' Juliet stared at those few scant lines of writing, as though there might be some secret hidden between the words.

Eugene shrugged. 'No one knows. There are still references to her story in the Show, but no one ever saw *her* again.'

'But she could have still been here.' Juliet was struggling to hold on to her composure. 'Couldn't she?'

'I don't know,' Eugene replied. 'There was something strange about the whole situation. It wasn't just that she left the Show. It was *how* she left.' He led Juliet through to the next room, stopping in front of a tattered newspaper clipping. 'This is apparently the only piece that appeared in any of the papers.'

Juliet squinted at the tight lines of newsprint, trying to make sense of what she was reading. An actress fell from a gallery, and then it turned out she hadn't fallen at all. The police were investigating, and then it turned out they weren't investigating after all. 'I don't understand.'

'Join the club,' Eugene said. 'Even at the time, there were different versions of events doing the rounds. Quite a lot of people saw her fall. Some said they'd heard a scream, and a man's voice shouting a name. One or two even claimed to have seen a body. Others said they'd seen her play out the rest of the loop, and had no idea that anything had happened, until the police turned up.'

'The police?' DI Mansfield's face rose in Juliet's mind.

Eugene nodded. 'Someone must have called them. It was chaos, by all accounts. The Show was still going, of course, and when the police arrived, a lot of the audience thought they were performers.' He gave a rueful smile. 'That must have been fun. A bunch of uncooperative theatre-goers, convinced you're part of some exciting new storyline, while you're trying to round up witnesses and take statements. The next day, everything was normal, with the Moonshine Girl there, playing her loop as usual. But that was the last time she appeared in the Show.'

'A name,' Juliet said. 'You said someone shouted a name.'

Eugene nodded. 'Not a character name – just an ordinary one.' There was a pinch of pain in Juliet's palm, where her nails were digging in. 'Madeleine.'

The world pulled in close, and when it receded once again, it was a different shape. The edges of the things she knew were sharper, throwing the things she didn't know into clearer relief. Madeleine was the Moonshine Girl, and she was Juliet's mother. Juliet belonged here. She was the daughter of the district's most beloved performer, and this was her true home.

'There's a lot to take in, isn't there?' Eugene was watching her. 'I remember my first time here. I was all over the place, trying to work out how it fitted together. And here I am now, still trying. Mind you, I've figured out a few things along the way. Maybe I'll tell you, someday.' His smile was clearly meant to be arch. 'If you come back, that is. Do you think you will?' When Juliet gave a distracted nod, his face lit up. 'I knew you would. As soon as I saw you, I knew you were one of us. And speaking of *us*, we should head down.'

There was still so much Juliet didn't know, but she couldn't begin to make sense of the evening's revelations while she was still reeling from them. At some point, she had to go home, but she'd return and find her way to where she needed to be, and there'd be people waiting, smiling and opening their arms.

We've missed you. We love you. We've found you at last.

Chapter 7

BACK DOWN IN THE bar, they found a group seated at their table.

A crop-haired woman of about fifty looked up as they approached. 'Saved your seat.' She pushed Eugene's chair out. 'If you keep leaving that pin of yours unguarded, I'll have it off you. Then I'll only have two tokens left to get.' She looked at Juliet. 'Friend of yours?'

'This is Juliet,' Eugene said. 'I found her after a near-miss with the Gatekeeper.' He ushered her into a chair and took the seat next to her. 'Introductions,' he said. 'This is Macy.' As the older woman lifted her glass, Eugene gestured towards a fair-haired girl of about Juliet's age. She was slightly built, with the kind of natural glow that doesn't need make-up, and her dark-blue dress showed a lot of shoulder. 'And Esme.' The other girl gave a brief smile as Eugene ran through more names, finishing with the young man at the end of the table. 'And this is Jan. He's editor of our newsletter.' He looked around the table. 'So what are we talking about?'

'Ghosts,' Jan said, with a small grin. 'Or rather, what we'd do if we came back to haunt the Show.'

Esme tilted her head thoughtfully. 'I'd go to the top floor, to that space between the pillars, and I'd dance there. When visitors passed, they'd almost see me, but when they looked properly there'd be nothing there. But they'd walk on with a feeling that they'd been close to something wonderful.'

'That's a lovely idea.' Eugene turned to Juliet. 'Esme dances beautifully.'

'I'm a dancer too,' Juliet said. 'I wanted to go to ballet school, but—'

'I went to the London School of Ballet.' Esme's voice was sharp. 'I was there for three years.'

There was a flicker of hostility in the other girl's eyes, and Juliet was conscious of the beginnings of an answering chill of dislike. She searched for something to say, but Eugene stepped in, shooting a look at Esme as he turned the conversation back to the original subject.

'I'd go to the gangway above the ballroom,' he said. 'I'd float right through the locked doors for a proper view of those scenes you can never see properly.'

'What about you?' Jan said to Macy.

She smiled. 'I'm not planning on keeling over just yet. And besides, if I was a ghost, I wouldn't be able to hold a pen to add what I saw to the walls.'

'But *you'd* have seen it,' Esme put in. 'It's all very well reading about it, but it's not like having those moments for yourself.'

Macy shook her head. 'I'm not sure that's true. On my first visit, I had no idea what was going on. I somehow managed to get picked by the Architect, back when he did the private scene in that hidden passage. It was wonderful, but I came out with so many questions, and no one to talk to about it. Once I found *this* place, it stopped being just a strange experience I didn't understand, and became part of something much bigger. It's about seeing where your own little piece of it fits in.' She smiled. 'And leaving a bit of yourself behind when you're gone.'

There was a pause, then a sudden clatter of noise as people all over the room started pushing their chairs back.

'The ballot.' Esme scrambled to her feet and dashed away.

'Come on.' Eugene stood up. 'We'll need to be quick. It's busy in here tonight.'

Juliet followed him to the bar, where people were crowding around a wooden box, waiting for their turn to reach in and pull out an envelope.

'What is it?' she asked.

'Tickets to the Show.' Eugene's attention was fixed on the box. 'The powers-that-be send a few down here each evening. It's too expensive for most of us to go as often as we'd like.' He gave a quick smile. 'By which I mean every day, obviously.'

Juliet hung back. 'I don't think I have time.'

'No, no, no.' Eugene hustled her forward. 'You can't come to the district and not try to see the Show.'

Stepping up to the counter, he reached into the box to pull out an envelope. When Juliet followed suit, the envelope was heavier than she'd expected. As she tilted it, something slid inside. Back at the table, Eugene grinned and made a cross-fingered gesture. As Juliet peeled the envelope open, her hesitation gave way to anticipation. Meeting Eugene, coming here, finding her mother's picture – everything was falling into place, as though it was meant to be. Her fingertips tingled with certainty, as she reached inside and pulled out two flat metal tags.

'Oh, bad luck,' Eugene said. 'Blanks.'

'Blanks?'

'The Show tickets are keys,' Eugene said. 'The blanks stop people trying to pick the right envelope by feel.'

A hollow of disappointment formed under Juliet's ribs. The other Followers were shaking their heads – all except Esme, who gave a squeal, dangling a pair of silver keys from her fingertips.

'Well done,' Jan said, with a hint of envy. 'That's twice in a row, isn't it?'

'Twice this week, and once last week,' Esme said. 'Someone must like me.' She scanned the group. 'Now, who's been particularly nice to me recently?' She glanced at Macy. 'Not you. You got the last envelope a few days ago, leaving me out.'

'I'll live,' Macy said drily.

Esme turned to Jan, wagging a finger. 'And *you* didn't print that last piece I gave you.' As her gaze flitted to Juliet, her lips tightened and she turned away. Juliet felt that stirring of dislike harden as Esme pointed towards the remaining Followers. 'Eeny Meeny Miny Mo . . .'

Eugene stepped back with a shake of his head. 'Count me out.'

Esme continued without missing a beat, dragging out the final *Miny Mo,* before settling on a young man with floppy dark hair. 'It's your lucky night, Henry,' she said, with a dazzling smile. 'Shall we go?'

As Juliet watched the other girl sashay out with the young man trotting eagerly behind, there was a pressure behind her ribs, pushing her close to tears. She belonged here.

Surely some fate or guardian spirit should have intervened to guide her hand to the right envelope.

Eugene nudged her arm. As she turned, he smiled, and opened his hand to reveal a pair of keys.

'Looks like you've brought me luck. I haven't won the ballot for ages.' He dipped at the waist in a little bow. 'I'd be honoured to escort you to your first Show.'

The weight of Juliet's disappointment lifted, as though someone had tied balloons to it. Perhaps there *was* something at play here, working through Eugene.

'Thank you.' She smiled at him. 'How long is the Show?'

'However long you want it to be,' he said. 'The evening is when you have the most performers on set together, but even if you go to the theatre at five o'clock in the morning, there'll be someone there. The Show never stops. With the keys, you can arrive and leave whenever you like, but once you're out, you can't go back in. Four hours is usually my limit, but I know some people who've pulled twelve-hour stints. I don't know anyone who's managed longer than that.'

'Sascha did,' Jan put in. 'Of course, he made the mistake of lying down for a rest on the bed in the Red Widow's room and woke up several hours later with a crowd staring down at him. A few people have tag-teamed to try and work out if there's any pattern to the schedule, but no one ever gets it right. The last attempt had the Willow Woman on set for eighteen hours straight, and neither of the people involved would concede they might have made a mistake.'

'Some of them do spectacularly long shifts, to be fair,' Macy said. 'I don't know how they manage it, day after day.' She smiled. 'Eighteen hours might be pushing it a bit, though.'

'What if you buy a ticket and the performers you want to see aren't there?' Juliet asked.

Eugene shrugged. 'That's how the Theatre District works. You might see all your favourites, get picked for every private scene going, and have an encounter with a Wanderer on your way out. Or you might drift about for hours, feeling like you're invisible. When it comes to the Show, you have to take your chances. I don't know what would happen if you tried to complain, but somehow I don't think it would be a heartfelt apology and a complimentary ticket. What time do you need to be away?' He paused. 'Where do you live, anyway?'

'St Albans.' Juliet hesitated before adding, 'But I'll be moving to London when I've found somewhere to live.'

'St Albans?' A dark-haired girl who'd just arrived spoke up. 'You weren't planning on getting the train back tonight, were you?' When Juliet nodded, she grimaced. 'Sorry to be the bearer of bad tidings, but there are no more trains out of St Pancras tonight. I think there was a derailment or something.'

'No more trains?' Juliet felt her stomach drop. 'But what do I do?'

'We've got a spare room,' the girl said. 'You can stay with us tonight, if you like. I'm Sally.'

Juliet's panic subsided slightly, but there was a sick feeling in her stomach. She couldn't imagine how her stepmother would react. Her less compliant secret self was whispering that it didn't matter, but Juliet had spent years trying to avoid the older woman's disapproval, and the fear was deeply ingrained.

'That room is still free?' Eugene said. 'I'm surprised. Rooms in the district precincts aren't exactly two a penny.'

'I didn't think outsiders could live in the district,' Juliet said.

'The precincts are a bit of a no man's land,' Eugene said. 'Not quite district, not quite . . . not district. Not many houses come up for rent.'

'How come you've got a spare room?' Jan said.

'Millie moved out a couple of months ago,' Sally said. 'Didn't you notice she hadn't been around?'

Jan shook his head. 'She was always so quiet. Did she move back home? I don't remember her ever saying where she came from.'

'I don't think so,' Sally said. 'She was a bit vague, but I had the impression she was moving on, not back, if that makes sense.'

'It's like that with the Theatre District for a lot of people,' Macy said. 'They come, stay for a while and seem to love it. Then you never see them again.' She shrugged. 'I suppose people find new interests.'

'Interests that aren't the Theatre District?' Eugene pantomimed shock. 'That's blasphemy.' He looked at Juliet. 'So will you be all right staying at Sally's place?'

'What do you think we're going to do to her?' Sally said. 'Other than indoctrinate her, obviously.'

'You may not need to,' Eugene said. 'I think she's hooked already.'

'I can meet you by the gates around eleven,' Sally said to Juliet. 'That should give you enough time at the Show.'

'Thank you.' When Juliet eventually got home, all hell was going to break loose – if hell was a cold, relentless picking over of everything you'd ever done to make someone not love you – but that was a problem for tomorrow. 'Yes, please.'

'Come on,' Eugene said. 'We'd better get going.'

He hurried Juliet out of the pub, and through the winding streets of the district, until they reached the back of a queue of people filing slowly into a high-walled alleyway. As they shuffled forward, he handed Juliet a key. 'Keep it safe. I don't know what happens if you lose it, but I can't imagine the doormen being particularly helpful. You might never get to leave. You'd become part of the Show. *The One Who Lost Her Key*, they'd call you.' He tilted his head. 'Actually, that's a bit prosaic. Maybe the *Lost Girl*.'

A shiver went down Juliet's spine, but there was no time to let her imagination chase that idea. They'd reached a turnstile and Eugene was sliding his key into the slot. There was a clank, and it dropped back into his hand. With a quick grin at Juliet, he pushed through the turnstile. When Juliet followed suit, he led her through a high doorway, into a hallway. At the top of a short flight of steps, there was a midnight-blue curtain, which fell back behind them, plunging them into complete darkness. Up ahead, there was music playing, low and faintly ominous.

As Juliet took a cautious step forward, a brief shaft of light broke through the darkness behind, and someone muttered and pushed past her.

'Keep walking.' Eugene said, in a low voice. 'You won't hit anything.'

'Shh.' A disapproving hiss came from up ahead.

Eugene gave a faint snort, but dropped his voice to a whisper. 'There's no talking inside.'

Pushing through more drapes, they emerged into a room papered in stripes of dark-red velvet, with several doors leading off. Two were made of wood, dark-panelled and set into heavy frames. One had an odd metallic surface, reflecting a distorted image of the room, while another was formed out of Bakelite. Eugene led her through one made of Chinese silk, set in a surround of burnished brass. It opened onto a tight passage, from which they emerged into a wider space, dimly lit and wreathed in a faint haze of smoke or dust. There was an odd scent to the air, like a fraying perfume – something masculine and old-fashioned – and Juliet felt a brush of what might have been recognition.

Eugene led her through a narrow gap, into a square, surrounded by walls of rough-hewn wood, in which stained-glass windows glinted from elaborately carved frames. They were lit from behind, and a small crowd was gathered, watching a girl dance in the intersection of those multicoloured drifts of light. Her collarless shirt fell to a couple of inches above her knees, and was unbuttoned almost to the waist, the curve of her small breasts visible each time she lifted her arms. Juliet drew a sharp breath, then felt a squirm of embarrassment at such a predictable response.

As more visitors joined the crowd, she looked around, caught in a cross-pull of anxiety. All over the theatre, scenes like this must be unfolding. What if she was missing out on something important, something that would help her understand everything? Eugene's attention was on the performer and, as someone squeezed in between them, Juliet slipped away.

S J Hanson Esq
7 Greendale Avenue
Kingston upon Thames

Dear Mr Hanson,

Thank you for your letter. I am indeed the author of A Guide to the Mechanics and Mysteries of the Theatre District. *I am sorry to hear that you have had difficulty locating a copy. Sadly, the book is not currently available through commercial sellers. Following discussions with mainstream publishers, it became clear to me that this was a project that would appeal to a specific and discerning readership.*

I therefore took the decision to publish the book myself. I have a small number of copies still available and I enclose one as a gift to you. I would be grateful if you would recommend the book to anyone of your acquaintance who might be interested in making a purchase, and I would be prepared to offer a discount to anyone mentioning your name.

In your letter you spoke of a particular interest in the characters known as Itinerants. I refer you to chapter three of the book, and I have marked the relevant section for ease of reference. With regard to your question concerning the rumours that private performances may be purchased for a fee, my extensive research has uncovered no evidence of any such arrangement.

I hope you enjoy my humble offering and I remain

Yours sincerely,
J D Heathley

Chapter Three

It is generally accepted that the residents of the Theatre District fall into four main categories: Principals, Itinerants, Nomads and Ancillaries. I should make clear that I use the accepted terminology for these groups with some caution, as the performance hierarchy is not a static structure. While the fundamental nature of a resident's unique role remains unchanged throughout their lifetime, its manifestation and relative importance may change considerably over the years. It is my firm belief that all residents start out as nomadic characters, with no formal scripted activity. This is supported by the fact that none of the activities of the vanishingly small number of child performers who have been seen in the wider district have appeared to follow any regular pattern or loop.

While some individuals appear to remain nomadic throughout their lifetime, most see some career development, by way of promotion to Itinerants or Principals. Both of these groups have scripted loops which are part of the district's great mesh of connected stories, with the role of the Itinerants differing from that of the Principals only in that their storylines are played out on the streets of the district, rather than in the House of Doors. The usual path to Principal status appears to involve a period of Itinerancy, possibly to test the popularity of a particular character or storyline before they are promoted to the Show itself, but it is not unheard of for a nomadic character to be elevated directly to Principal status.

In relation to the final category of non-Principals, the Ancillaries are, in simplistic terms, all those individuals who carry out specific tasks not directly related to the Show. There has been considerable debate over the years as to the exact parameters of this group. Some commentators argue that it should include only those whose role is to entertain, such as those involved in the self-contained shows that take place at various locations within the district, and those engaged in the provision of more intimate diversions, such as fortune-telling or street performance. These commentators would seek to exclude those individuals who carry out the more mundane activities necessary for the continued functioning of the district. However, given that there is no way to be certain as to whether any encounter, with a shopkeeper or bartender, for example, is actually straightforwardly transactional, as opposed to serving some purpose within the interconnected stories of the district, I prefer to take a catholic view as to the parameters of the Ancillary category. I would therefore define it as including all individuals who are not Principals, Itinerants or Nomads.

I would also include the stagehands within this category. There is a tendency among commentators to treat the stagehands as an entirely separate group, due to the fact that they operate primarily behind the scenes, and interact with visitors only where strictly necessary. This may be due, at least in part, to a lingering and somewhat bourgeoise prejudice, with its roots in the history of the stagehands as a group. They are generally believed to be the descendants of the circus families who were permitted to lease winter quarters in the outer district from the late seventeenth century onwards, in exchange for the provision of services to the recently expanded Show. The fact that the stagehands are still believed to reside in the outer district, rather than in the hidden enclaves of the inner district, may also allow more narrow-minded commentators to perpetuate this distinction.

[Cont]

Chapter 8

As she crossed the space where they'd first come in, Juliet could make out the outlines of tall shapes up ahead.

As she drew closer, she realised they were the brittle limbs of bare-branched trees – a whole forest of them. A narrow path wound between the trees, and Juliet followed it, ducking beneath the spindly branches until she reached a clearing. White light drifted down from above, dust motes shifting in the pale gleam. It had the stiff, artificial look of a spotlight, and Juliet waited a moment or two, before giving up and moving on, not sure whether she'd missed a scene, or whether the light was there all the time, illuminating the slow dance of the dust.

On the far side of the clearing, silver ornaments hung from the branches of some of the trees. When Juliet reached up to touch one, it turned on its thread, the benignly smiling face of an old man giving way to a gnome-like visage, puckered with spite. As Juliet pulled her hand back, it turned again, bringing the old man back round. Now she knew what was on the other side, that gentle smile seemed to have taken on a hint of mockery, and she walked on, slightly unsettled, leaving the ornament spinning behind her, smiling and glaring by turns.

Emerging from the trees, Juliet found herself at the end of a row of shops with leaded windows. An ordinary-looking haberdashery stood next to a store full of broken household items, while the next contained nothing but three elaborately framed portraits on easels behind the counter. The subjects – an elderly man and woman, and a little girl with a high, stiff collar – glared out like a trio of indignant shopkeepers.

The last window revealed a warmer, more reassuring scene. In a shop lit by amber light, a white-haired man was polishing the brass weights from a set of old-fashioned scales. When a woman in a ribbon-trimmed mask stepped past Juliet to open the door, he looked up, his expression delighted, as if he had seen his oldest, most beloved friend. Hurrying forwards, he grasped the woman's hand, leading her away through the back of the shop. Juliet waited for them to reappear, but when the door behind the counter stayed closed, she moved on.

At the end of the street, Juliet found a white-painted door, set into a wall of heavy stone. Through it, she could hear a scatter of notes, brighter and closer than the music that had been playing since she stepped onto the set. When she opened it, she found herself in a small club, with masked couples sitting at little tables, nursing drinks and listening to an old man playing a battered piano. He looked like something out of a Hollywood movie, with a fedora hat pulled low over his face, and a cigar dangling from his lips.

A door on the far side of the room opened, and a woman stepped through. She was dressed in a blue beaded dress, and carrying a cage in which a metal bird whirred on a wire perch. At the piano, she put the cage down and picked up the melody in a dark, husky voice.

Part of Juliet wanted to stay, soaking in every nuance of the scene until she could work out what it meant, but she could still feel the spark and pull of a thousand other unseen moments. Crossing to the far door, she stepped through into a train carriage. The doors to the compartments were covered by blue velvet curtains, and a flight of steps at the far end led up to what looked like the entrance to a church. When Juliet turned the handle, only a tiny panel of the heavy door opened, and she had to duck to climb through into a gallery full of snow globes.

In an artist's studio, a woman sketched a young girl, naked beneath a drift of gauzy fabric. A clock ticked behind them, the second hand snagging endlessly. In a wide space with an elaborate parquet floor, a dark-haired girl wept in the shadows, as a young man walked away. A gallery gave a view of a ballroom, hung about with diaphanous curtains, through which a pair of shadowy figures danced and twirled, as masked faces watched from other balconies and windows set high in the walls.

Room after room, staircase after staircase. The levels didn't quite seem to line up, and there were passageways that Juliet was sure didn't follow the rules of physics. There were doors that wouldn't open, steps that went nowhere, windows overlooking rooms she couldn't find. Some looked as though the occupant had just left, with books lying open on unmade beds. Others looked as though they had been abandoned for years. There were walls covered in photographs and sketches and pages ripped from children's books, while letters and scribbled notes spilled from drawers onto cluttered floors. Portraits hung in unlit corners, the faces of their subjects ghost-vague in the darkness.

She'd see a performer at the far end of a corridor, or through the loose-woven walls of a maze, but by the time she got there, they'd disappeared. She was always on the wrong side of a two-way mirror, or looking out from a balcony at unmasked faces glinting palely in the distance. Whenever she stumbled across a scene, it always seemed to be just as the performers were moving away, followed by a crowd of visitors. And all the time that unsettling music played, always seemingly building to a crescendo that never came.

At the end of a vaulted passageway, as Juliet paused beside a trickle of water running down a wall into an iron grate in the floor, she heard swift footsteps. A dark-haired young man in a grey shirt came into sight, followed by a crowd of masked figures. Juliet stumbled out of the way as he stepped up to the water, pressing his palm against the wall and then to his brow, as though baptising himself. As he turned round, droplets of water glinting on his face, the crowd pressed closer, and Juliet only just managed to hold her place at the front.

The man scanned the masked faces, as though searching for something. As his gaze lingered on Juliet, her pulse began to pick up, anticipation sparking through her. It was clear from the urgency all around her that this was something important, something to be coveted and claimed, like the encounter with the Wanderer. The moment swelled like a bubble, and then he turned to hold his hand out to the young woman next to Juliet. She stepped forward, stumbling in her eagerness, and the two of them disappeared along a side passageway, followed by a ragged trail of some of the rejected. Others turned to walk away, their shoulders a slump of disappointment, leaving Juliet wrapped in a sudden aching misery.

Everything here was an *almost*, a *not-quite* and her steps were heavy as she moved on, eventually finding herself at the bottom of a flight of stairs. It was dark, and as she fumbled her way forward, she felt the smooth brush of velvet on her fingertips. Pushing the curtain aside, she stepped into a small room with bare, white walls, the plaster crumbling in places. There was a cabinet to her left, its drawers open to reveal tight-packed reels of film, and on the far wall, an image played, ghost-thin, with a vague, soundless flicker.

The girl, dancing with the precision and poise of a classical ballerina, was achingly familiar. Juliet felt another swell of sadness, ragged at the edges. The tilt of the Moonshine Girl's smile seemed like a conspiracy.

Don't tell her. Don't let her in.

Turning away, Juliet stumbled out of the room and back up the stairs. The ever-present music had taken on a menacing lilt, and she'd lost all sense of direction.

Eventually, she found herself at the edge of the dead forest. Ducking beneath the snag of low-hanging branches, she followed the path through the trees and made her way out of the theatre.

Chapter 9

THERE WAS A LOW ache in Juliet's back, and she could feel an answering drag in her chest, threatening to swell into tears.

You're being a fool, her other self told her, with sharp impatience. *What did you think was going to happen?*

Another voice echoed, sharp with disdain. *You think flights of angels will sing you through the gates.*

Juliet took a steadying breath. There was no conspiracy against her. No one in the Theatre District had the slightest idea she was here. As her composure slowly returned, a glance at her watch confirmed she was an hour early to meet Sally. She looked up at the rise of the roof, trying to get her bearings, then headed in what she thought was the direction of the Shipping News. She could use the time to search the walls for more references to the Moonshine Girl.

The streets, however, seemed as determined as the theatre to thwart her at every juncture, with dead-ends, and sharp hairpin bends that led her back the way she'd come. As she turned into a cobbled lane, her gaze landed on the street sign, one of only a handful that she'd seen.

Kilner Street.

The name rang a faint bell, and halfway along the street, Juliet stopped, staring at a sign beside a heavy wooden door.

District Record Office

Any requests for information must be in writing and will be reviewed by the District Board.

Through the fanlight above the door, Juliet could see a lamp burning. On impulse, she tried the handle, her heart giving a thump when the door swung open. The hallway was narrow, with just one other door leading off. When she stepped through, she found herself in an untidy office. The shelves were crammed with leather-bound volumes, the floor covered with precarious towers of files, lit by haphazardly placed lamps.

Through an archway, Juliet could hear rustling. She hesitated, before lifting her voice. 'Hello?'

There was a pause, and then an elderly man appeared. He had to be at least ninety, with a shrunken, loose-cheeked look, as though his skin didn't fit properly anymore.

He squinted suspiciously at Juliet, one hand patting vaguely at his breast, as though in search of his spectacles. 'Who are you?'

'I'm . . . I was looking for the registrar. I'm sorry . . . it's late . . .'

'The what?' The patting took on an impatient, irritable rhythm.

'The district registrar. This is the record office.'

'Of course it's the record office,' he said, sharply. 'It's got a sign, hasn't it?'

'I'm sorry,' Juliet said again. 'It's just . . . there was a record I wanted to see.'

The old man's hand fell still. 'What sort of record?'

'My birth certificate.'

The man gave a throaty sniff. 'No certificates here. Everyone knows who they are, don't they?'

Juliet hesitated. If she agreed with him, he might take that as acceptance she had no need to access the records after all, but if she argued, he might take offence and not help her.

She risked a question. 'If there are no certificates, then what does the record office hold?'

The man looked at her as though she was very stupid. 'Records, of course. Beginnings and endings, and some of what happens in between.'

'I'm looking for my birth record. Somerset House said I should ask here.'

'What did you say your name was?' As she started to answer, he made an impatient gesture. 'Take your mask off.' When Juliet complied, he squinted at her. 'Name?'

'Juliet Grace.'

He pursed his lips. 'Don't remember registering you.'

'Would you remember?' Juliet asked. 'How long have you worked here?'

'Here?'

'At the record office.'

The man's brow creased. 'The record office?'

An uneasy suspicion stirred. Did this scene play out every time anyone set foot in here? But if the old man was playing a role, it was one he'd drawn so closely about himself that there was no hint of where it ended and he began.

She tried again. 'Is there a time I can come back to check the records?'

'Come back?' he said. 'You're here now, aren't you?'

Hope ignited, but Juliet was careful to keep her voice level. 'If I could look now, that would be very helpful.'

The old man frowned. 'I'm not sure you're authorised,' he said. 'Can't just have anyone coming in here.'

'Do many people come?' Juliet looked around the untidy office.

'Wouldn't matter if they did,' he said, with a hint of satisfaction. 'I know who's who round here.' Then his certainty seemed to falter. 'At least I did once. Back when . . .' His face twisted. 'I can't remember. Someone told me they didn't need me anymore, but they didn't send anyone else. Besides, you can't just pick it up, and off you go. You have to *know*. I know district, and I know outside.' He peered at Juliet. 'You're district, aren't you?' Then, even as her heart contracted, doubt crept into his expression. 'Are you? There's something else there. You remind me of someone, but I can't quite remember.' He was silent for a long moment, then gave a brisk shake of his head. 'It doesn't matter. Long time ago now.'

Juliet wanted to shout at him that it did matter, that he had to remember, but she forced herself to smile. 'So can I see the records?'

The old man blinked. 'What date?'

When Juliet told him, he picked his way towards a door in the far corner. Juliet skirted stacks of files to follow him into a storeroom, crammed with filing cabinets. The old man rummaged in a drawer, humming tunelessly to himself. When he pulled out a cardboard file, the loose pages inside shifted, and his humming gave way to an irritable tut as he shook them straight.

When he had them lined up to his satisfaction, he leafed through for a moment, then shook his head. 'Nothing here for that date.'

A line of chill unfurled. 'There must be. I was born here.'

'What did you say your name was again?'

It was getting harder to hold on to her composure. 'Juliet Grace.'

The old man flicked through the pages again. 'No, nothing there.'

'Could there . . .' Something snagged in her throat, and she cleared it and tried again. 'Could there be a mistake?'

He shrugged. 'Who knows what goes on out there that no one tells me about.' His expression turned contemplative. 'Still, that lot in charge always want things done properly. The district might be a hurdy-gurdy merry-go-round on the surface, but there's clockwork and steel underneath. Stops the powers-that-be, the ones out *there*, poking their noses in.' He smiled, sly and gap-toothed. 'The board like to think they're the only gods in the sky, but there's a whole other panoply out there. So we keep our records, even if we keep them hidden.'

As he started to close the folder, the pages slid loose, landing in a haphazard scatter on the floor.

'I'll get them,' Juliet said quickly, as the old man began a slow, painful stoop.

Dropping to her knees, she gathered the papers into a rough stack. As she climbed back to her feet, her gaze snagged on a word.

Grace.

Juliet's heart gave a hard thump of relief. The page was headed with the year of her birth, and her name was right there, in the first entry. The old man had just missed it.

At Paladin Street, Olivia, daughter of Stephen Grace, born on . . .

Before she could read more, the stack was snatched from her hands.

'You're not authorised.' The old man glared at her. 'I *told* you, you have to be authorised.'

'But it was there,' Juliet said. 'I saw . . .' She broke off, registering what it was that she'd read.

Olivia.

But it was her father's name, and the right year. And Paladin Street – that had to be the address on the smudged letter.

So who was Olivia?

The answer came with a dizzying wrench of vertigo.

She was. When her father took her away from here, he'd changed her name. Had he stolen her from her mother? Was that tear-stained letter a desperate plea for the return of her child?

Olivia.

She sounded the name in her head, hoping she'd feel it swell to fit the lines and curves and hollows of everything that was *her*.

Olivia. Olivia.

As she felt her way around the rise and fall of it, it started to lose its meaning. She'd been Juliet all her life. It was like a watermark, stamped across her thoughts and memories. She couldn't expect to shrug it off and pick up another, as easy as changing her clothes. When she found her way into the district, they'd call her Olivia, and she'd have to remember to answer to it. She'd forget sometimes, and someone would be left saying her name over and over, and then she'd remember and they'd laugh. Perhaps they'd say, *You can be Juliet if you like. All that matters is that you're home.* But when they thought about her, she'd be Olivia. Their lost girl who'd now been found.

The old man was watching her, his brow creased in suspicion.

She forced a smile. 'Please may I see it again? My name is there.'

'If you're there, then you're there,' he said. 'Nothing more to it. Nothing more to see.' His frown deepened. 'Did they send you to check up on me?'

'They?'

'The board.' He shoved the file in the drawer, shooting looks back over his shoulder at Juliet, as though she might make a grab for it. 'You can tell them I keep everything right here. And if that's not good enough, they can come down here and see for themselves what a job it is.'

Closing the drawer, he turned the key with a click of finality.

Juliet bit back the argument she'd been about to make, realising the futility of it. 'The board,' she said instead. 'Could you give them a message?'

He shook his head. 'I won't remember. I try, but I can't keep hold of things. Not anymore. The old memories, they're hard to lose, but the new ones don't cling on as tightly.'

There was a wistfulness in his voice, and through her frustration, Juliet felt a pang of sadness for the old man with his fraying mind, in this office that wasn't his anymore, clinging to a purpose that didn't seem to exist.

'That's all right,' she said. 'Thank you for your time.'

He smiled. 'Time. I've got nothing else. Until it runs out. That's the thing, isn't it? You have too much, until you have none at all.'

Juliet didn't understand, so she just smiled back at him, then turned away, picking her way out of the storeroom and across the office.

She was almost at the door when he spoke from behind her. 'Grace.' Juliet twisted back round to find him staring at her. 'Full of grace. That's what I thought when I saw her. She came in with a man and a baby.' He tilted his head. 'Red hair, like yours, but more colour in her cheeks, I think. Are you getting enough sun? It's hard in this place. Vitamins. That's the secret. You should get yourself some.'

'Do you remember her name?'

The old man shook his head. 'Names don't mean anything. They're just something for people to hold onto.'

'But do you know what it was?' Juliet's nails dug into her palms.

An irritable expression flickered across the old man's face. 'I'm tired. What time do you call this, to be coming in here? All requests in writing. That's the rules. There's paper by the door. And envelopes. Put it in writing.'

With that edict, he turned and made his way across the office, disappearing back through the archway.

Juliet walked over to the desk he'd indicated, where she found some notepaper, a pen and a stack of envelopes. She decided to make her approach as business-like as possible. She had in her possession a letter from the central record office, confirming she had been born in the Theatre District. Her father was Stephen Grace, and she believed her mother was a performer named Madeleine, known in the district as the Moonshine Girl. She would be grateful for any information they could provide, especially pertaining to her mother, who she believed may have tried to locate her.

She hesitated before signing the letter, but there was nothing she could add that wouldn't sound desperate and childish.

Tell me I'm special, that I'm part of this place.

She paused again over her contact details. After a moment's thought, she wrote, *Any reply can be left at the Shipping News.* It felt like a suitably dramatic way of doing things. It felt like the *district* way of doing things. But more than that, it felt like a promise to herself.

I'm coming back.

Chapter 10

Juliet found Sally waiting for her by the entrance.

'Did you enjoy the Show?' she asked, as she led Juliet out onto the embankment, where a light drizzle was falling.

'It was lovely.' Juliet forced a false brightness into her voice.

Sally gave her an amused look. 'I've heard that tone before. By *lovely* I assume you mean *I have absolutely no idea what any of it was about, but I will sell all my closest relatives to pay for another ticket.*'

'Something like that.' Juliet changed the subject. 'I thought you lived in the outer district.'

'We do,' Sally replied. 'But it's quicker to go round the edge from here.'

Two uniformed police officers were walking slowly along the embankment, collars up against the rain. Guilt pricked at Juliet as she remembered DI Mansfield's card, tucked in her purse, and she looked away, following Sally into a narrow alley that led into the clutter of buildings between the outer wall of the district and the bridge.

The outer district was shabbier than Juliet had expected, and seemed deliberately uninviting, its buildings packed close together, the flagstones and cobbles cracked and uneven. In a few places, she saw what looked like the remains of a makeshift canopy or roof clinging to a ridge or chimney pot, or bridging a gap between two houses. Most of the streets were lined with cramped-looking tenements, but they also passed a row of workshops with wire mesh over cracked windows and barn-style doors sagging against heavy chains. There were no signs advertising the wares of the handful of steam-glazed shops, and the pub that stood at the junction of two of the wider streets looked as though someone had designed it with a view to deterring all but the most determined and least discerning customers.

'Do the performers live here?' Juliet said, as they passed an old phone box, tucked furtively behind a jutting wall at the edge of a cobbled square.

'Sadly, no,' Sally said. 'If you could run into your favourite performer in the local pub, people would be biting our hands off for the room. We think they have their own enclaves at the edges of the main district, although they're very good at not being spotted going in and out. People are also fairly sure they wear masks when they want to move about in peace.' Juliet thought of the mask tucked into her bag right now and felt a secret little thrill of realisation. 'You do occasionally see someone who could be a performer – although it's hard to be sure without the stage make-up – but you just pretend you haven't noticed them. It's part of the deal.'

'The deal?'

'There's a sort of unspoken agreement that comes with living in the precincts.' Sally gave a small grimace. 'You're very much here on sufferance. I've been here two years, and the lady in the corner shop still looks at me as though I've come to steal her corned beef.' She tipped her head contemplatively. 'Still, the barman in the pub looked as if he might smile the other day. He thought better of it in the end, but it's progress.' They turned another corner. 'Here we are. Glover Street.'

'So who does live in the outer district?' The narrow street was lined with tenements, with no discernible order to the patchy numbering.

'It's mainly people who work in the district in some capacity. Most houses have been in the same families for generations. The stagehands live here, although you'd never recognise any of them. Here, this is us.'

She nodded at a house in the middle of a short terrace, set back from the rest of the street, and overhung by what looked like the crumbling remains of some taller building. Juliet could see the ghost-outline of an old room – ragged edges of a cupboard and a boarded-up doorway – and she wondered whether it had ever been part of an actual house, or if it was just another illusion.

The front door opened onto a narrow flight of stairs, and Sally led Juliet up to a kitchen where another girl was drinking tea at a cracked wooden table.

'This is Anna,' Sally said. 'Anna, this is Juliet. Eugene adopted her after a near-miss with a Wanderer, and I offered her a bed for the night after it turned out she was stranded. She's just come from her first Show.'

'Sounds like you've had a bit of a day of it.' Anna pushed out a chair. 'Grab a seat. Kettle's just boiled.'

Sally made tea, then joined Anna in quizzing Juliet about her visit to the district. Both girls listened intently to everything Juliet said, and she felt herself warming under the unaccustomed attention. As the conversation moved to Juliet herself, she remembered Eugene saying people didn't always tell the truth about themselves in the district. Why should she be the same old Juliet? One day she'd disappear into the secret heart of the district, and all that would be left behind would be the remnants of whatever role she'd briefly played here. Why not make it something better than the truth?

Her family lived in St Albans, she told them. Her father was a teacher, and her mother a dressmaker. She had two younger sisters, and they lived in a small house near the town centre. They didn't have much money, but her parents worked hard to give their children everything they could. Juliet had been offered a job in London, and she'd come to the city to look at rooms. She'd had a frustrating day, viewing unsuitable places, so she'd decided to fulfil a long-standing wish to visit the Theatre District.

'You were looking for a room?' Anna said, then raised her eyebrows at her housemate.

Sally turned to Juliet. 'I don't know where you were hoping to live, but we've got the empty room here. You'd be welcome to take it, even if it's only until you find something else.'

It was an enticing idea. Juliet had no idea how long it would take for her letter to reach someone in authority, and she couldn't exactly travel here every day. Besides, even if it was only for a while, it would be nice to live with people who seemed to like you, people with whom you could sit around the table, and talk and laugh and feel part of things.

'I'd love to, if you're sure that's all right?'

'Of course,' Anna said. Then she grinned. 'And I promise, my enthusiasm has nothing to do with having someone else to split the rent with.'

'When do you want to move in?' Sally asked.

Juliet thought about her college course, and her stepmother's oh-so-generous offer of board and lodgings until January. There was a flutter of nerves in her stomach and she could feel all sorts of *what ifs* crowding at the edges of her thoughts – but she ignored them. What better way to mark the end of that old Juliet than with a dramatic gesture, leaving one day and never coming back?

'I can move in straight away.' Even as she said it, Juliet remembered Rebecca, cuddled into her that night after their father died. She made a reluctant concession. 'But I'd better phone home and let them know I'm all right.'

'We don't have a telephone here,' Anna said. 'The phone box down the road is your best bet, although it might not be working. The phone system round here is only a couple of steps up from carrier pigeons.'

'I'll go now,' Juliet said, pushing her chair back and standing up, before she could change her mind.

*

The phone box smelled of cold metal and damp. The glass panes were almost opaque with dirt in places. It took Juliet three attempts to get a dial tone, and when the call did connect, the phone rang twice, then cut off in a crackle of static. She replaced the handset, and was about to open the door, when she heard the murmur of low voices nearby, and two figures stepped around the jutting wall. It was dark, and the dirty glass obscured Juliet's view, but the figures were clearly female, both slightly built, with one just a smidgen taller than the other. There was an intimacy to the way they were standing close together, and Juliet stayed where she was, not wanting to be found intruding on a private moment. As she watched, the taller of the two put her hands to the other girl's face, and leaned in to press a slow kiss onto her lips.

A flush of shocked heat flooded Juliet's cheeks, and she held her breath, not daring to move. The girls kissed for a long moment, and then, with what looked like reluctance, the taller girl pulled back. As she turned and walked away, the other girl lingered for a little longer, then leaned around the wall, as though checking the coast was clear. Then she too stepped out into the square and disappeared.

Back at the house, Anna and Sally had been joined in the kitchen by a third girl who was at the sink when Juliet walked in. When she turned, Juliet's heart sank. It was Esme.

'You two met earlier, didn't you?' Sally said. 'Juliet's staying tonight – she missed the last train – and she's going to take the spare room.'

'Lovely.' Esme gave an unconvincing smile.

'Did you put the chain on the door?' Anna said.

'Why? Worried the Lambeth Stalker is going to get you?' There was a derisive note in Esme's voice.

'No,' Anna said. 'I'm worried about the fact that a body was found in the river just a couple of minutes away from where we live.'

'A body?' Juliet asked uneasily.

'A young woman,' Anna said. 'About a month ago. And she wasn't the first.'

'Not the first person to be found in the river?' Esme said. 'That's not exactly surprising. The city's been here a long time.'

'You know perfectly well what I'm talking about,' Anna said sharply.

'Yes, I do.' Esme's voice was equally sharp. 'Because we've had this conversation before. The Lambeth Stalker doesn't exist. Nor does the Knockerman or the Night Walker or the Southbank Ripper or whatever we're currently calling this non-existent murderer. It's a load of rubbish, like nine-tenths of the rumours and stories floating around the district.'

'Well, this one has been floating around for a long time,' Anna said mutinously.

'Decades,' Esme said. 'He'd have to be a pretty elderly murderer by now. He's not going to be doing much jumping out of dark alleyways. He'd probably do his back in.'

'And what about that poor girl?' Anna said.

'What about her?' Esme replied, then made a sharp gesture. 'You know what I mean. Yes, it's very sad, but I hardly think we need to be barricading ourselves in the house. There's nothing linking her death to the Theatre District.'

'Putting the chain on is hardly barricading ourselves in,' Anna said.

'Speaking of locked doors . . .' Sally spoke up, clearly keen to steer the conversation to a less contentious subject.

As talk turned to the route taken by one of the district's more elusive performers, Juliet saw an opportunity to slide in a question.

'I saw a map just before I met Eugene,' she said. 'But not all the streets were labelled. How do you find a street that isn't marked?'

'Depends what you're looking for,' Sally said. 'There are some maps upstairs in the Shipping News that are about as complete as they can be. If a street name is missing on there, then it's missing in real life.'

'Missing?' Juliet said.

Anna nodded. 'There are lots of streets with no signs. Part of the district's ongoing plan to make us spend every last minute obsessing about all the things we don't know.'

'Or to stop us getting to the places they don't want us to go,' Sally said.

'I thought you could go anywhere,' Juliet said.

'In theory, yes,' Sally replied. 'But there are plenty of locked doors and gates, and a fair few blank spaces on the maps. There are rumours about what's on the other side, but there are rumours about all sorts of things in the district. You have to take them with a fairly hefty pinch of salt.'

'Some of them are true,' Esme said. 'I don't mean the kind about centuries-old murderers, or hidden safes containing the meaning of life or an unlimited supply of Show keys. There are some stories that come from something real. You can feel the difference, once you get close enough to it all.' She gave Juliet a sideways look. 'Anyway, best not to go poking about in too many dark corners. The Knockerman might be waiting for you.'

'I'm going to bed.' Anna stood up, pointedly turning her back on Esme. 'Shall I show you to your room, Juliet?'

Chapter 11

JULIET SLEPT LATE, WAKING to an empty house, and a note with details of how to pay the rent tucked under a door key on the kitchen table.

After a quick breakfast, she found some paper and an envelope and wrote a letter – defiantly addressing it to Rebecca, rather than Clare – telling her not to worry, that she'd found somewhere to live in London and decided to move in straight away. She paused, wondering whether to ask for some of her things to be posted on. Then she remembered – she would have to go back for the funeral.

Juliet's stomach twisted slightly at the thought of what her stepmother would say to her. It shouldn't have mattered, but it did. Did she really have to go? She could stay in London and let the day pass like any other. That thought fell away, barely formed, resignation taking its place. He might not have acted much like one, but he *had* been her father.

She would return for the funeral and to collect some of her belongings, she wrote. Then she added a couple more sentences and signed it.

The precincts were no less of a maze by day, and it took Juliet a while to find a shop. The proprietor was a small, thin woman whose entirely blank gaze managed to convey a whole spectrum of negative opinion. Juliet paid for a dog-eared stamp she wasn't entirely sure hadn't already been used, and left, uneasily conscious of that flat stare following her.

She dropped the letter into a postbox on her way to the Underground station, where she caught the Tube to Oxford Street, following the memory of a long-ago shopping trip. There, she withdrew some cash – the money from Clare had clearly gone through, and Juliet felt rich – and went into one of the department stores to buy clothes and other necessities, feeling a tiny thrill at every purchase of which her stepmother wouldn't have approved.

Back at the house, she changed into one of the new outfits. The velvet dress was embroidered along the hem, and the little velvet jacket was a slightly different shade of grey – matching wasn't right for the Theatre District. Fastening her hair, Juliet left a few strands loose about her face. Then she tucked the feathered mask into her pocket and headed down to the front door, her heart already beginning a thump of anticipation.

At the entrance barriers, Juliet shot the attendant a swift glance as she tied her mask into place, but his gaze slid over her. It didn't matter. It was just a mask. Perhaps one day they'd laugh about the time she walked past him, and he had no idea who she was. *It's fine*, she'd say, smiling and touching his arm. *It all worked out in the end.*

She'd intended to go straight to the Shipping News, but as she passed a ticket office, she stopped, a thought taking shape. There was a price list in the window. On-the-day Show tickets were eye-wateringly expensive, but Juliet could still remember the hollow feeling in her stomach when she'd pulled the blanks out of her envelope. Besides, she had money now.

Pulling out her purse, she went inside.

'I'd like a ticket for the Show.' Then she thought of Eugene. 'Two tickets.'

The sum seemed even bigger when counted out in actual notes, but this wasn't frivolous spending. Her stepmother had told her the money was to set her up in a new life, and that's exactly what she was using it for.

It was still early when Juliet got to the Shipping News, and the place was quiet. She asked the barman if there were any messages for her, swallowing her disappointment when he gave a shake of his head. Upstairs, she found the maps Sally had mentioned – one a fairly complete representation of the district, albeit with blank spaces at the outer edges – and some detailed renderings of specific areas. When she looked more closely at the main map, Juliet could see it hadn't been completed in one go. Beneath the surface layer, faint, contradictory lines were visible, as though the ghosts of old streets still lingered there. It had clearly been a labour of love – and generations.

There was a neat index down the edge, and Juliet skimmed the street names until she reached the entries for *P*. There were only a few, and no Paladin Street. Returning to the map, she studied the streets around the edges of the largest blank space until she found the access point between the precincts and the main district. She spent a few moments memorising it, before making her way through to the room where Eugene had shown her the newspaper article.

References to the Moonshine Girl were scattered and disconnected, but Juliet read every one she could find. There were descriptions of her loop, with directions and timings all laid out methodically, as though someone had thought the key to understanding might lie in numbers and minutes. There were theories about the meaning of each interaction, step-by-step descriptions of her dances, accounts of the private scenes some Followers had been fortunate enough to enjoy.

It was odd how many discrepancies there were. Juliet had assumed that everything in these rooms was accurate, but the truth was that she had no idea whether there was a moderation process, or whether people could pin up any old nonsense. In some accounts, Madeleine seemed cautious, almost hesitant, while other writers described a much more sensual encounter, some descriptions giving Juliet a squirm of voyeuristic discomfort.

Aside from the Moonshine Girl, there were other pictures and accounts that rang faint bells of familiarity. There was the older man she'd seen hurrying away from a door that had been locked against him. A description of a dance she'd watched from above, looking down from a balcony onto a paved square scattered with dead flowers. The girl looking back over her shoulder was the one who'd wept as her lover betrayed her. *The Rose Singer*, the title said. Her strap was slipping down, to reveal a distinctive tattoo of a hummingbird hovering in front of a mirror, each inked line reproduced in meticulous detail by the unknown artist.

Near one of the archways, Juliet found a picture of Stephen. The jolt was less pronounced than when she'd seen that picture of the Moonshine Girl, but she felt an odd sense of dislocation, as though the world had shifted slightly. He was younger, but the cool, detached gaze was the same. She'd known he'd had a life before her, of course. That was what all this was about, after all. But there was a difference between knowing and *knowing*. She reached out and brushed her fingertips lightly over the sketched lines of his face. Her skin prickled slightly. Even touching his picture felt strange, as though someone might come in and say *that's not yours*.

The Rag and Bone Man, the title read. That name had been mentioned more than once in the descriptions of her mother's loop. Walking through to the first room, Juliet tried a couple of drawers until she found the character charts Eugene had shown her. The Rag and Bone Man was listed, a couple of entries away from the Moonshine Girl, with his final appearance in the Show not long after Madeleine's.

Back in the other room, Juliet noticed another picture. It stood out from those around it, because its subject was a child. She looked very young, perhaps only three or four, and she was walking along what looked like a tightrope, her arms outstretched. She was smiling a tilted, secret smile, her red hair escaping from her plait.

There was a title scribbled in the bottom corner.

The Girl in the Silver Shoes.

There was a high-pitched sound in Juliet's ears, making it hard to think clearly. Hurrying back to the filing cabinet, she pulled out the character list again. She found the Girl in the Silver Shoes on the page after the Moonshine Girl, and she held her breath as she read the neat columns of information. The Girl in the Silver Shoes hadn't been part of the Show, and no connections with other storylines had been recorded. She'd appeared for a relatively short period of time – about a year and a half, with her last appearance taking place fifteen years ago. That was almost five years after the Moonshine Girl's last appearance in the Show.

Juliet could see a couple of corresponding footnotes on the page, but nothing that told her anything of note. She was struggling to take anything in. She was the Girl in the Silver Shoes. She *had* to be. Somewhere back there in the blur of lost years, she had walked on a wire, high above the street. People had watched her and loved her and written her into the stories they told about the district. Then her father had taken her away, weaving a web of lies around her memories.

Juliet's lungs ached, as though she'd been winded. Her mother hadn't died when she was a baby. Juliet must have lived with her, here in the district. Somewhere in this tangle of streets was the house where she'd slept and ate and washed and played and known she was loved. Because that's what mothers did – they loved you. Her stepmother had been right about that much, at least. Juliet felt a sharp twist of hatred. Had Clare known the truth? Had she colluded with Stephen as he took a wire brush to Juliet's past, scrubbing away every trace of love and belonging, and leaving only a tattered yearning?

How had he managed it? How could she have forgotten something so important? If you had something like that inside you, surely you clung onto it so tightly that no lies, no muffling, suffocating *ordinariness* could steal it from you. She had a few memories she'd always assumed related to the first few years of her life, but they were isolated moments, fleeting and lacking context.

A bleak thought took shape. She could still remember the tight, stretched feeling she'd had when she was trying to please them – the sense that if she was good enough and quiet enough and compliant enough, they'd suddenly realise that they loved her after all. Had she colluded in erasing her own memories? Had she let go of the most precious thing she'd ever had, in the vain hope of winning her father's affection?

She took a shuddering breath. It didn't matter how it had happened. What mattered was that the memories had to be there, hidden somewhere inside her. She just had to find a way to draw them out, like picking at a roll of Sellotape until you felt the lost end beneath your fingernail.

Juliet walked back to stand in front of the picture.

This is who I am, she thought. *I'm the Girl in the Silver Shoes, and I once walked high above the district.*

She recalled standing on the rope bridge the previous day, suddenly sure there'd been something tugging at her as she'd looked down at those visitors passing beneath her. Not a memory, exactly, but a brush of a feeling, like when you hear a phrase of music or catch a scent that reminds you of something.

For the briefest of instants, she could see it clearly, and then the image faded, leaving her aching with frustration and loss.

Chapter 12

DOWNSTAIRS, THERE WAS A group at the Followers' table.

One of them glanced round and Juliet recognised Esme. The other girl looked swiftly away, launching into an animated story, with much gesturing and laughing.

As Juliet hovered awkwardly, one of the young men noticed her and smiled. 'Are you looking for someone?'

Esme gave an exaggerated start. 'I didn't see you there. Everyone, this is Julie.'

'Juliet, actually.' She took the seat the man pulled out for her.

Esme wafted a careless hand. 'I'm terrible at names. What were we talking about?'

'The Shadow Man,' someone said. 'You mentioned you got his private scene last night.'

'Oh, yes.' Esme took a sip of her drink. 'I should have had it on the loop before, but there was a whole crowd of people in my way. I couldn't get anywhere near.'

'That's unusual for you.' Macy appeared with a drink. 'So who got it? Anyone we know?'

'Some blonde girl.' Esme gave her wine a petulant swirl.

'I think I was there,' Juliet said slowly. 'I thought he was going to pick me. He stared at me.'

Esme made a dismissive gesture. 'That doesn't mean anything.'

'It did look like he was about to do something,' Juliet said. 'Maybe if I'd stepped forward . . .'

Macy laughed. 'I see you've fallen into the eternal trap of *what if?* It'll drive you mad if you let it. They choose who they want to choose, and that's all there is to it.'

Esme shook her head. 'That's not true. There are things you can do. I don't mean all that rubbish about standing on a particular spot, or wearing a particular colour. You have to make them *want* to pick you.'

'How?' a round-faced young woman asked. 'I've tried all sorts of things, but it's never worked for me.'

'No.' Esme's unspoken *it wouldn't, would it?* was clear. 'You have to make them see you're responding to the Show in a deeper way. They want someone real, someone special.'

Juliet felt a prickle of resentment. Esme was talking as though she was some sort of gatekeeper, with the right to decide who was worthy. But Juliet was the one with the *real, special* connection to the district.

'Do all the performers have private scenes?' she asked, trying not to let her irritation show.

Macy nodded. 'They don't always do them, though. During quiet times – late nights and early mornings – they tend to do simplified versions of their loops with fewer dances, and solo versions if the other performers aren't there.'

'Why do they have performers on set through the night?' Juliet said.

'To stop England falling, or the world ending, or the entire universe disappearing into a black hole,' Macy said. 'Or any of the other things people claim will happen if the Show ever stops.' She shook her head. 'It's just how it is. Whatever time you go, there are usually people wandering about. Maybe London has a big population of insomniacs.'

'Anyway.' Esme raised her voice pointedly. 'I might not have been chosen that time, but I made sure I was on the next loop.'

'How?' one of the men asked.

'Ah.' Esme wagged a finger at him. 'That would be telling.'

As the man gave a discreet eye roll and turned to speak to Macy, Juliet looked around the bar, wondering when Eugene might arrive. 'Will the ballot be soon?'

'It's already happened,' Macy said. 'It was early tonight. They like to keep us on our toes. If it's any consolation, none of us were lucky. I didn't even get an envelope. It's been busy recently. There's always a buzz after cast changes.'

'And now everyone's buzzing round here.' Esme's fingers drummed an irritable tattoo. 'Why can't they leave the ballot for the proper fans?'

'We don't have a monopoly on it,' Macy said mildly. 'We're lucky more people don't know about it.'

'Small mercies,' Esme said sourly. 'The Show will be heaving until it settles down again. Last night I saw the Silver Lady trip over some idiot who wouldn't give her space. A stagehand had to get involved. And don't get me started on all the people camping out in the lumber room.'

'To be fair, that's always been a popular spot,' Macy said. 'It's a crossing point for what, four loops?'

'Five now,' one of the men said.

'Oh yes,' Macy said. 'I haven't seen the new one yet.'

'I didn't see any stagehands on the set,' Juliet said.

'You wouldn't,' Macy said. 'They stay backstage unless they're needed, but they're always watching. If you overstep, they're there before you have time to blink.'

'Sounds like you're speaking from experience.' Jan had arrived. 'What have you been up to?' As Macy grinned, he turned to Juliet. 'Hello, again. How was your trip to the Show? Got it all figured out yet? Ascended – or descended, depending on which stories you listen to – to the next level of access?'

Esme snorted. 'Hardly. If anyone's going to manage that, it's going to be someone who's close to it.'

'You, for example?' There was a hint of malice in Macy's voice.

Esme shrugged. 'Why not? I've had almost all of the private scenes, and I've been chosen by four Wanderers. I've seen as many of the district's hidden places as anyone.'

Jan shook his head. 'I don't think it's a numbers game.'

Esme's gaze flashed a little. 'How many private scenes have you had?'

'A few.' Jan didn't seem troubled to find himself in competition.

'There you go then.' Esme pushed her chair back. 'Anyway, I'm off.' Her expression darkened. 'Not to the Show obviously.'

'There's nothing to stop you paying for a ticket.' There was a sardonic tilt to Jan's smile.

Esme raised her eyebrows. 'Do I look like I'm made of money? Besides, I don't think the district is something you should be able to buy your way into.' Esme managed to look both petulant and pious at the same time. 'That's why the ballot is so important. It's the powers-that-be recognising the true fans. Having money shouldn't mean you get more than everyone else.'

'Sorry to be the bearer of bad news, but that's exactly what it means,' Jan said. 'And we probably shouldn't get started on those rumours about extra access in exchange for a barrow-load of cash.'

'Now you're just stirring,' Macy said, elbowing him. 'Tell me, have you ever seen *Very Expensive and Extra-Special Private Scenes* advertised on any of the ticket office boards?'

'There'd be countless idiots willing to pay,' Esme said. 'Some people have more money than sense.'

'Don't worry.' Jan patted her hand. 'We're all in the same boat.' He grinned. 'The same leaky, shabby boat. No yachts or trust funds round here.'

Juliet felt a tight curl of embarrassment. When she was at school, she'd always been conscious of having less than her schoolmates. Then *having* meant belonging, but now everything seemed to have shifted, and *having* was somehow shameful.

'You came back, I see.' A voice broke into her thoughts. Eugene was standing behind her chair, a beer in each hand. There was a hint of shyness in his smile as he passed one to her. 'I saw you from the bar.'

'I don't remember you ever buying me a drink.' Esme gave Eugene a cool smile.

As a flush mottled Eugene's cheeks, Juliet felt a tug of protectiveness. A perfect lie unfurled itself – one that would wipe the self-satisfied look from Esme's face. Reaching into her pocket, she pulled out the Show keys.

'What are those?' Esme's gaze snapped straight to them.

'Tickets.' Juliet dangled them casually from a fingertip.

'You missed the ballot.' Her expression turned contemptuous. 'Did you buy them?'

Juliet shook her head. 'A Wanderer gave them to me.'

There was a second or two of silence, then everyone started talking at once.

Jan banged on the table. 'Order, order. Juliet has the floor.' He grinned. 'And with an opener like that, she can have the walls, ceiling and stairs as well.'

'Which Wanderer?' Esme's hands were spread flat on the table. 'Where?'

Juliet shrugged. 'I don't know how to tell them apart. It was near the alleyway with the kites.'

'What did he look like? What colour was his cloak?'

Juliet wished she'd worked out the details before opening her mouth. 'Dark green.' She made a show of screwing her face up in thought. 'Maybe dark blue. I wasn't taking much in, to be honest.'

Eugene laughed. 'They do tend to have that effect.'

'Dark green.' Esme hadn't taken her gaze off Juliet. 'That's the Missionary. He doesn't come out that far.'

'Enough of the cross-examination.' Macy flicked a hand in Esme's direction. 'You know what it's like when you get a private scene. You're lucky if you can even remember your own name when you come out.' She turned back to Juliet. 'So where did he take you?'

'To the square with the fountain,' Juliet said, inventing rapidly. 'He asked me for a coin—'

'He spoke?' There was something about Esme's interjection that put Juliet in mind of a predator about to pounce.

She shook her head. 'He just pointed. I realised what he meant and threw the coin in. When I picked one out, he took it from me. Then he pulled the keys out from somewhere and tucked the coin away.' Juliet was beginning to enjoy her story. 'He handed them to me, bowed, then gestured at me to leave.'

'Did he give you a token?' Esme's gaze narrowed when Juliet shook her head. 'No token?'

'Sorry, he did.' She needed to be careful not to tie herself up in knots she couldn't unravel. 'But he'd already given me the keys, so I dropped it in the fountain for someone else to find. That's when he bowed. Sorry. I'm not telling it very well. It was a bit of a blur.'

'It usually is.' Eugene let his breath out in an awed huff. 'Well, this is new and interesting.'

'I was waiting for you to come before I said anything.' Juliet held out one of the keys. 'Here.'

Eugene took the key, holding it reverently. 'Are you sure?'

'You took me.' As she spoke, Juliet remembered how she'd abandoned him, but he didn't seem to be bearing a grudge.

'That was just from the ballot,' he said. 'This is special.'

'It's just a ticket.' Esme stood up. 'No more special than any other.'

As she stalked away, Eugene turned back to Juliet.

'Thank you,' he said, that shy smile nudging at his lips once again. 'I'd love to go with you.'

*

'It's going to be busy tonight.' Eugene stepped round a dawdling clutch of visitors, as they walked to the House of Doors.

Juliet nodded, but was only half-listening. Her thoughts had circled back to what she'd discovered in the Shipping News. 'I saw a picture,' she said. 'A little girl on a tightrope.'

As she paused, feeling her way to the question she wanted to ask, Eugene smiled. 'Yes, that's the Girl in the Silver Shoes. She used to walk the wires between the rooftops. There's a whole network of them. You very rarely see the district children, but she was quite well-known for a short time. Then nothing for, what, sixteen years?' He side-stepped as someone stopped in front of him, lowering his voice to say, 'I wish they'd give people lessons in how to move efficiently about the place.' He returned to his normal tones. 'We had a few cast changes recently. The Show has cycles. You'll get a sense of things building up, and there's a countdown of sorts, using the clocks in the House of Doors and a few other places. There's apparently a way of working out when the peak will happen just from that, if you're a maths genius, but it gets clearer, with other clues appearing, not just about the *when*, but the *what* as well – which storylines are involved, I mean. Then there'll be a peak, a big performance, with most of the cast on set together. Some storylines wrap up or develop, and there'll be changes to the cast, and then it all carries on.' He'd got distracted, flitting away to an unrelated topic. As she wondered how to draw him back to the Girl in the Silver Shoes, he gave her a sideways look. 'Don't worry about Esme. She's not usually like this.' He paused. 'Well, she's not *always* like this. She can be lovely. I think . . .' There was a hint of red above his collar, as though his easily heated skin was reacting to some unvoiced thought. 'I think she's a bit jealous of you.'

'Jealous?' Juliet couldn't help but feel a small pang of pleasure at the idea. 'Why?'

'I don't know.' Eugene said. 'It's just . . . some things are important to her, that's all. She doesn't like it if someone else seems to be getting too close. In some ways she seems to understand the place better than a lot of us. I guess the stage is in her blood. She was supposed to join one of the big ballet companies, but she got injured and missed her chance. Anyway, don't worry about it.' He smiled at her. 'We all like you.'

Juliet felt a warmth spread through her. She couldn't remember anyone ever saying that to her before. Not even in the unfiltered early years of childhood, when everything was *You're my best friend* or *I don't like you anymore*. That pleasure was wound through with a thread of guilt, however. She liked Eugene, but not in that way. And she wouldn't be around for long. Maybe when she was part of the district, though, she would be able to redress that balance. She pictured him at the Shipping News, breathless with excitement, as he told the other Followers how he'd somehow been picked for every single private scene in one visit, and something else, something new, that meant he'd got *closer* than anyone else.

Yes, she thought, with another glow of warmth. *That's exactly what I'll do.*

*

The queue for the House of Doors was longer than last time, and it moved more slowly. As they edged along the alleyway, Juliet wondered where to go when she got inside. She'd find as many of the locations in her mother's loop as she could, she decided. Walking where Madeleine had walked, seeing what she would have seen, would be like knowing her, just a little.

When they finally made it onto the set, the smell and taste and feel of the place wrapped about Juliet, so instantly familiar there was no doubt in her mind that she was remembering it from some visit long ago – carried in her mother's arms, perhaps. As before, she slipped away from Eugene as soon as she could, not wanting to share the moment. She'd memorised the beginning of the Moonshine Girl's loop, but couldn't find any room matching the description in the Shipping News. She did find a couple of the other locations, but she couldn't pick up the loop, and eventually abandoned the attempt and simply wandered the set, looking for anything that might be a reference to the Moonshine Girl.

It was like looking for a needle in the proverbial haystack – if the haystack was actually a haphazard mix of grass and twigs and dead flowers, and the needle wasn't a needle at all, but something unspecified, that may or may not even exist. The whole place was a dense, multi-layered tapestry, and for the first time, Juliet had a real sense of just how old this place was. Open a bureau and you'd find paperwork going back decades, perhaps even centuries. Pick up a sketchbook and there'd be faded drawings on pages brittle with age. Some documents were almost entirely incomprehensible, the letter formation cramped and unfamiliar, the language stilted and archaic. Some pages contained references to storylines she'd seen playing out, while some were just lists of names and dates, or rambling diary entries.

She ran into various performers during her search, occasionally following one for a scene or two, before being drawn away by something else. She was starting to get some sense of the shape of the Show, aided by what she'd read in the Shipping News, but it wasn't something that could be easily summarised. There were various references to stories and myths that Juliet recognised, and a sense of a search – with most characters seemingly hunting desperately for something they couldn't find – that was both shared and fragmented. The various loops wove together to create a complex narrative, with a few main strands running through it all.

There was an intensity, even a darkness to many of the individual stories, but Juliet did see the odd lighter moment. At one point, she found one of the older male performers hiding behind a stack of boxes with an audience member. When Juliet came in, the pair of them ducked down, helpless with a shared laughter that gave Juliet a pang of unexpected envy.

At one point, she found herself back in a room she'd passed through a couple of times before, in a group following one of the performers. Deserted now, it was long and narrow, with trunks and boxes piled haphazardly around its edges. At one end, two vast frames faced one another across a spotlit patch of floor. She'd vaguely registered them earlier, but it had been too crowded to look at them properly. When she walked over, her heart thudded. She was looking at a pair of life-size oil paintings of the Moonshine Girl, elevated by the heavy frames, so she had to tip her head back to study Madeleine's serene, painted face.

When Juliet had imagined having a mother, this was how she'd always pictured it – looking up and thinking there was no one more beautiful, no one more important. Driven by an impulse borrowed from a much younger version of herself, she reached out and placed her hand over Madeleine's, pressing her fingers against the paint. The longing she felt in that moment was acute and painful, for a mother who was real, in a way she'd never been before. Madeleine had walked the streets of the district, danced through the strange spaces of the theatre. Her feet would have ached after hours on these hard floors. There would have been nights when she was tired and irritable, nights when she had a cold and wanted to be at home in bed. She was real, and Juliet was part of her.

Beyond the spotlight, the rest of the room was in darkness. The music playing was a lilting counterpoint to the low rumble of the Show's endless soundtrack, and it sounded a faintly familiar note. This was what it would be like to be in the Show. You'd barely see the audience. There would just be you and the music and the dust-drift of the spotlight.

An idea took shape, and Juliet shivered with the audaciousness of it. It was exactly the kind of bold, daring plan that felt right for the Theatre District, and it was so complete, so perfect, that it felt like a message from the secret gods of this place. It was her best chance. Her letter might languish in the box at the record office for years. The registrar might use it to light a fire, or to create a flock of origami birds if the fancy took him.

As she stared at the pictures, trying to fix every detail in her memory, her concentration was broken by the shift of a figure beyond the light. Ducking swiftly out from between the frames, she hurried away.

The Times *25 October* **Court Reports**

Sir Henry Knollys, Sheriff of the County of London, has dismissed the application of Sir John 'Blind Beak' Fielding, Chief Metropolitan Magistrate, for a warrant to permit the constables of the Bow Street Office to carry out investigations within the Liberty of the Southern Hallows, known colloquially as the Theatre District. The application cited various alleged instances of financial and administrative misconduct, although the particulars of these were not given, with the application failing to progress beyond initial arguments. The Chief Magistrate argued that the provisions of the 1697 act against 'pretended privileged places' were incompatible with the general acceptance that police powers were restricted to investigations into crimes committed by, or against, persons not resident within the district. This submission was rejected, on the grounds that the decree known as the King's Gift, granting liberty status to the Theatre District, was issued after the 1697 act took effect, indicating that King James intended it to supersede the earlier act.

Following this finding, Sir John spoke harsh words against the Sheriff, stating in open court that there are 'too many among us who serve other interests than those of Lady Justice', and vowing to continue his pursuit of the perpetrators of 'divers dark deeds'.

Chapter 13

THE NEXT DAY, JULIET went back to Oxford Street, eventually finding what she was looking for in a tiny boutique.

When she got home, she unwrapped the dress and put it on, before going in search of a full-length mirror. She found one in Esme's room, and when she looked into it, she felt a beat of excitement. The dress wasn't exactly the same as the Moonshine Girl's – it was longer, falling to just below Juliet's knees, with more fabric across the bodice and shoulders – but it was close enough. She went up on her toes, holding the pose from the pictures, closing her eyes a little, to blur her reflection. As she imagined herself in the drift of the spotlight, her pulse quickened.

This would work. It had to.

*

Juliet went out before the other girls got home. In the first ticket office she saw, she bought another Show key. Tucking it into her pocket, she made her way to the House of Doors, and the room with the film of the Moonshine Girl. It didn't take long to commit to memory, but she stayed, studying every nuance of it.

When she couldn't wait any longer, she wound her way back up through the theatre to the lumber room, finding it empty. She knew that the loops of several performers passed through this room. Surely there would be a stagehand somewhere nearby.

Juliet's bare arms were a prickle of goosebumps as she moved towards the pictures, dropping her mask to the floor and stepping into the haze of the spotlight.

Come on, she thought, rising up on her toes. *I'm here. Come and find me.*

Lifting one arm in imitation of the paintings, she held that pose for a moment, then stepped into the dance she'd memorised. Her movements were stiff at first, but after a moment or two, everything beyond that drift of white faded away. She felt light-headed, light-limbed, as though she wasn't quite real.

As she executed the second fouetté, she caught a blur of movement outside the spotlight. It resolved itself into the figure of a man, watching from the doorway, unmasked, and flanked by a small crowd. Adrenaline blazed through Juliet, and she almost lost the thread of the dance.

Focus. The voice in her head was sharp. *This is what you wanted.*

As Juliet turned again, the man moved forward, and she realised it was the dark-haired performer she'd seen on her first visit. The Shadow Man, Esme had called him. Juliet's nerve faltered, and she stumbled, colliding with one of the frames. With a swift movement, the Shadow Man reached out and caught hold of her shoulder, steadying her. A chill spread through Juliet's body as she stared up at him, mutely.

That other self was right – this was exactly what she'd wanted – but now she had no idea how to take hold of the moment and turn it into what she needed it to be.

The Shadow Man was studying her with an intensity that felt oddly impersonal. After a long moment, the corner of his mouth lifted in the barest suggestion of a smile, and he took her hand, wrapping his fingers into hers. As he drew her from the spotlight and towards the door, retrieving her mask on the way, the audience parted to let them through, before closing behind them. Juliet could feel the urgent press of them as the man hurried her out of the room and along to a door, which he unlocked with a key from his pocket. Placing his hand on her back, he gave her a gentle push. She stumbled into the low light of a tiny room, hung with faded drapes, with a cluster of candles guttering on a low table.

Locking the door, the Shadow Man leaned against it, that smile still tilting the corner of his lips. There was something in his gaze that made Juliet feel there wasn't enough air. The silence stretched, and then he spoke, his voice low, but resonating in the confines of the room.

'Once upon a time, there was a girl made of clockwork . . .'

The threads of the story wound about her, frayed and hard to follow. Girls of clockwork and moonshine. Stolen girls. Forgotten girls. Something lost for a long time. Something tarnished, then grown bright and beautiful once again. As the tale drew to an end that didn't feel like an end at all, he fell silent, watching Juliet, as though waiting for her to say something.

This was it. This was her chance. But her head was a blur of half-formed thoughts, and she couldn't draw out the words she needed to say.

'Tell me a story,' the Shadow Man said. 'Something real. Something of yours.'

With a glint of relief, Juliet thought she could see how to unfurl the truth.

'Once upon a time . . .' When she began, her voice was thin and shaky, but the story gathered momentum, the words crowding together.

Once upon a time there was a girl who lived with her father. She didn't know her mother. And there was a stepmother. And half-sisters. Then her father died and she found some hidden things and followed them to the Theatre District where she'd been born, and she saw a picture of her mother and . . . Juliet faltered. Even with everything she knew, she still didn't *know*. It was like something broken and pieced together, the joins not quite fitting, fragments missing. She drew in a slow lungful of air. *And she was the Moonshine Girl. Her mother was the Moonshine Girl.*

Juliet fell silent, staring up at the man in mute hope. There was an intensity in his gaze that made her shoulders tighten but then his expression shifted into another of those tilted smiles. Leaning down, he kissed her cheek, his lips a warm brush against her chilled skin.

'It's a good story,' he said.

Lifting her mask, he tied it back on, his fingers deft. He smoothed the ribbons, brushed his fingertips across the feathered trim, then turned to unlock the door. There was a tremor in Juliet's hands as she stepped out. This was the moment she'd look back on and remember how it had all begun.

The quiet *snick* of the closing door didn't make sense for a moment. Then Juliet's heart hurled itself against her ribs, and she twisted round, scrabbling at the handle.

The door was locked.

A bubble of shock swelled, then burst, sending a shiver of reaction through her. He'd sent her back onto the set, as though she was just an ordinary visitor. Had he thought she was just playing along with the scene?

Juliet fought for calm. Perhaps he'd gone to find someone, to tell them she was here. Or perhaps this was a test of some sort. Racked between hope and despair, she waited, but the door stayed closed. As her vision blurred, she turned and stumbled away. She shouldn't have spun that garbled story. He probably hadn't understood a word she was saying.

A darker thought took shape, and Juliet's breath shuddered behind her ribs. Perhaps he *had* understood. Perhaps they all knew she was here, and were laughing together at her desperation. As she made her way out of the theatre, a self-pitying resentment slid in. She'd go and never come back. The Followers would talk about her sometimes, and the Shadow Man would feel a brush of shame whenever he saw a red-haired girl in the crowd.

But he wouldn't, would he? Because he'd looked right at her and she'd hadn't been enough.

She'd never been enough.

Chapter 14

Juliet stepped around the edges of sleep until the early hours, eventually falling into a tangle of restless dreams she couldn't remember when she woke.

She felt flat and empty, but the night had scuffed the sharpness from her emotions, moulding her hurt and disappointment into something smaller and more contained. This wasn't the end. She'd just made a mistake. That particular moment was gone and it wouldn't come again, but there was another possibility she hadn't explored.

Juliet forced down a cup of tea, before getting dressed. A couple of things in her top drawer looked as though they'd been moved, and although she knew it was probably just paranoia, she slid the paperwork and photo under her mattress, along with DI Mansfield's card. The key and necklace she tucked into her pocket with the mask. Then she went out, aiming for the cut-through to the main district.

It was hard to identify where the precincts ended and the district proper began, but after a few wrong turns, Juliet found herself under the low edge of the roof. Here, it was a thing of odds and ends butted together, beams and rough-cut boards, braced by a few more solid struts. The layout of the streets was more confusing than she'd anticipated, scattered with passages and entrances that looked promising, but led nowhere.

After a little while, Juliet found herself on a street where all the windows and doors on one side were bricked up. A little way along, half hidden behind a toppled stack of crates, she found a small gap. Inside, there was a flight of steps, squeezed into a space so narrow that anyone broader-shouldered would have had to turn sideways. The walls pressed tight as she climbed the steps, emerging, with a relieved drag of air, onto a gallery lined with mirrors.

Judging from the dust, no one had been this way for a long time. The floor was cracked and splintered in places, and as Juliet picked her way carefully along, she could feel the sag of the boards. Her reflection flickered alongside her, leaping from mirror to mirror. It flared briefly in what looked like a converted church window, then stuttered like a flick-book image across a row of Art Deco mirror tiles, into an ornate round of brass leaves, where cross-eyed cherubs lurked in the tarnished folds.

At the mid-point of the gallery, two full-length mirrors faced one another, creating a playing-card array of Juliets curving off into the endless distance. She felt an irrational lurch of certainty that, any second now, one would break ranks, step forward and turn to smile at her.

The tilt of that imagined smile made Juliet think of her dark almost-twin.

Olivia? she thought.

There was no reply, but somewhere in the shadows at the edges of her mind, Juliet thought she felt that smile curl tighter.

As she looked away, a floorboard shifted, and Juliet threw out a hand, catching at the frame of one of the mirrors. It swung beneath her touch, sending the reflections into a twisting ripple that made her close her eyes against a surge of vertigo. Opening them again, she kept her gaze firmly ahead as she moved on.

At the end of the gallery, another flight of stairs led down to a cobbled street with a slight look of the precincts. To the left was a high, windowless wall, the stonework broken here and there by heavy beams, although Juliet couldn't imagine what they might have supported. Across the road, the district roof cut straight through the upper floors of the houses, leaving just the sills of the old windows visible. Juliet wondered if the rooms were still there, with the occupants required to bend double to access them.

As she walked along the street, she could hear music playing in the distance, and a blur of what might have been voices. Those sounds were occasionally punctuated by something closer – a scuff of footsteps, a door closing, the ripple of running water. At one point, Juliet heard children's voices, lifted in what sounded like some rhyme or chant, but before she could work out which direction they were coming from, the voices fell away.

Juliet felt an ache of loneliness. These were the sounds of a life she'd had taken from her, leaving her tiptoeing around the margins.

The street ended at a locked iron gate. To the side, an alley led to a short flight of steps and a basement door, also locked. Returning to the gate, Juliet gave the handle another pointless tug. The gate shifted slightly, before snagging against the lock. On a whim, she pulled out her father's key on its velvet ribbon and slid it into the lock. When it slipped in smoothly, she felt a faint flutter of excitement. She knew it wouldn't turn, but she couldn't help that little catch of *what if*.

As the key clicked round, Juliet snatched her hand back, shock arcing through her. She stared at the gate in disbelief. Of all the doors and gates in the district, what were the chances of her stumbling upon the one the key unlocked? She shot a look along the street, half-expecting to see someone watching, waiting for her to realise this was just a scene, another sleight of hand in a place full of tricks and illusions.

There was no one there, and Juliet turned back to the gate, pushing it open just far enough to step through into a tiny square. Hands still shaking slightly, she closed it and locked it behind her.

There was a prickle between her shoulder blades as she set off again, and she found herself stepping as silently as possible. Those sounds of life were closer now, and for the first time, she considered what she would do if she actually met someone.

The alleyway she chose ended at yet another locked gate. The key was still clutched tightly in her hand, and she felt a sudden lift of impossible possibility. As she slid it into the lock, she knew it was a hope too far, and when it turned, this time with a rusty scrape, her disbelief left her light-headed. She put out a hand, steadying herself against the wall.

The *odds* of it. All those doors.

Realisation dawned. All those doors for the performers to navigate, the stagehands to operate. They would have to carry huge bundles of keys. Huge bundles – or a single one that opened any door.

Juliet pushed the gate open, hands trembling again, this time with elation. This was a level of access that any visitor would give their right arm for. She might have borrowed it, rather than having been granted it, but soon that would change, the key becoming a reminder of how she'd fought her way to her birthright.

As she walked on, there was a lift of voices behind her. With a flare of guilty panic, she ducked into the entrance to a passageway, pressing herself against the wall. The voices came closer, furtive and punctuated by stifled laughter. To Juliet's dismay, they stopped just by the passage entrance, so close that she could see what looked like the edge of a sleeve, as though its owner was leaning back against the wall.

There was more laughter, low and breathy, then a pause for what Juliet was fairly sure was a kiss. The passage behind her was dark, the floor too uneven for her to be sure she wouldn't stumble if she tried to slip away. The voice in her head was sharp and impatient, telling her she *should* be revealing herself, not skulking here. But the idea of taking that step felt like falling, setting her heart beating hard.

'We should get back.' The voice was young and female.

'Not yet,' her male companion said, before lowering his voice to murmur something which drew another brush of laughter from the girl. 'What, you don't believe me?' he said. 'Maybe we'll be the district's next great storyline.'

'We might have to wait a while.' The girl's tone was dry. 'I think that vacancy has been filled.'

Whatever the boy might have said in reply was again too quiet for Juliet to catch –then smothered by what was clearly another kiss. Juliet shot another look along the tunnel. She couldn't reveal herself, not after eavesdropping for this long. Her eyes had adjusted to the low light and she could make out some stairs. She risked a step, and then another, and another. She trod as lightly as she could, but as she reached the stairs, the girl spoke.

'What was that?'

Juliet froze.

'What was what?' the boy asked.

'I heard something.'

Juliet didn't wait, tiptoeing up the steps, which wound back on themselves before emerging onto a pathway between two high walls. As she made her way along, she heard another ripple of laughter, this time above her. Something flashed overhead, and she glimpsed a figure leap across the gap and disappear.

Heart thudding, Juliet walked on. The path led round a sharp corner, and onto a high ledge. A few yards along, there was a wire, anchored to an iron ring in the wall and stretching across a paved street to another ledge.

A shiver of realisation ran through Juliet. Stepping cautiously along the ledge, she made her way to the wire and looked out along its length. It was an impossibly flimsy bridge, but she remembered the picture of the little girl, smiling as though the idea of falling was nothing more than a story.

Bending her knee slightly, Juliet dipped one foot to touch the wire. Her heartbeat seemed to resonate through her whole body, pulsing in her fingertips and echoing in her head, bringing with it a hard, almost physical, urge to spread her arms and step onto the wire. It would be as close to flying as you could ever come, with just the barest sliver of sensation against the soles of your feet. Somewhere out there, with no clutter or confusion around you, you might remember everything you'd buried deep inside you.

Juliet shifted a little more weight onto the wire, but she couldn't feel anything. Her shoes were wrong – hard and unyielding. Pulling back onto the ledge, she slipped them off, then stepped forward again, curling her toes around the edge. There was a crackle, like static in her head, with all sorts of thoughts caught behind it. Her body felt tight and stretched, as though someone was trying to pull it out from her control.

They'd had a special class once at school – a circus performer brought in to teach them juggling, walking on stilts and swinging on a low trapeze. There'd been a tightrope too, a rope stretched between two metal stands. Juliet had wondered why the other girls couldn't balance on it. All you had to do was walk along it, placing one foot in front of the other. Now she knew why she'd found it so easy. Her body had remembered, even if she hadn't.

I'm the Girl in the Silver Shoes, she thought. *And this is where I belong.*

As she stretched out her arms, the world pressed in close, as though it had taken a sharp breath. Fixing her gaze on the far side, she reached out with her foot, finding the wire.

As her weight followed, *Olivia* was saying something, but Juliet couldn't hear the words. The static had given way to something that sounded like high-pitched singing. The wire was taut beneath her feet, and her arms had found an instinctive, wing-like spread. For a fraction of a heartbeat, Juliet felt the world click into place around her.

She belonged. Here was the proof, in this perfect balance, this perfect moment.

Then she looked down.

The street seemed to leap up, ready to tear her down and savage her against the hard stones. As her head spun, she threw herself backwards onto the ledge, her fingers finding a crack in the stonework, her heart pounding. An image flared in her head – her body, broken and bloody on the ground. Swallowing against the bile in her throat, Juliet pulled her shoes back on, climbed to her feet and set off, slowly and shakily, along the ledge. Near the end, she found another flight of steps, winding back down to street level.

She wasn't the Girl in the Silver Shoes anymore. She wasn't *Olivia*. She was just Juliet, lost and lonely and afraid that there was no way back to the life that should have been hers.

Chapter 15

THE STREET ENDED AT another gate – which also yielded to Juliet's key – leading into a low-roofed passageway.

Near the far end, Juliet heard a discordant chime. A grandfather clock leaned against the wall, its face showing the wrong time and, for an irrational instant, she contemplated the possibility that time in the district ran differently. What if she made her way out to find that whole days or months or years had passed?

Don't be stupid. The voice in her head seemed to be gaining a sharper edge of impatience with each utterance. *It's just a stopped clock.*

The off-key chimes died away as Juliet emerged into a wide, high-walled space. On the far side, an elaborate metal sign hung over a door, the word *Market* picked out in dented scroll-work.

The place didn't look like any market Juliet had ever seen. There were no stalls, no hawkers calling her *my love*, just mounds of clothes and bric-a-brac, crammed haphazardly between pieces of old furniture. A pair of scarlet vases stood beside an upturned saddle and a set of yellowing antlers; scenery boards propped up a wooden platform, heaped with fabric.

At first glance there seemed to be no order to any of it, then Juliet noticed table legs beneath some of the piles, and what looked like narrow paths winding between. Stepping around a stack of crates, she squeezed between two trestle tables, shoulder-high with junk, and round a wheeled trolley on which more scenery formed a haphazard mix of crackle-glazed pillars and forest clearings.

As she turned through another gap, she knocked an Anglepoise lamp. Somewhere behind it, something shifted, then the whole stack began to slide. She threw out her arms, trying to stop it, but there was too much weight. The table leg buckled, sending books and crockery smashing to the floor.

As the echoes of the crash faded, Juliet heard a sound from behind her. She spun around to see a thin-faced man near where she'd come in. The low-hanging bulb behind him cast shadows across his skull, making it look almost fleshless and she imagined him, hunched and spider-like, scuttling through hidden twists and turns to grab her. With a surge of panic, she plunged between a rack of fur coats and a row of narrow metal lockers – but as she rounded an overloaded table, another figure appeared in front of her. For a second, there was just scuffled confusion, and then the young man she'd collided with managed to untangle himself.

'Steady.' He put a hand on her shoulder.

Juliet dragged in a lungful of air, fighting against the panic that had seized her. Her hair had come loose, and she pushed it back from her face and looked up at the man. He was young – perhaps only a few years older than her – and familiar.

The Shadow Man.

Juliet's mind went blank. There was something she was supposed to tell him, but in that moment, with her heart thumping and the thin man still staring across at her, she couldn't remember what it was.

'Ah.' The Shadow Man had followed the direction of her gaze. 'He does rather have that effect on people.' Raising a hand, he called over, 'There's no harm done.'

The thin man stared at them for another few seconds, before turning and disappearing among his jumbled wares.

The Shadow Man lowered his voice conspiratorially. 'He hates people cutting through. And he really doesn't like anyone trying to take anything away. They call it a prop store, but it's more of a prop museum.' His lips quirked. 'A prop graveyard, perhaps.' He tilted his head. 'I know you, don't I?'

'I . . .' Juliet found herself unaccountably close to tears, the frustration and disappointment of the last few days catching up with her just when she needed to be clear-headed. 'I was trying to . . .'

'It's all right.' The man's voice was gentle. 'I do remember you. I went back on the set to look for you, but you'd gone.'

'I wrote to the board.' Juliet felt out of step with the conversation, as though she'd learned the wrong part in some scripted scene. 'I didn't know if anyone would get it, but I didn't know what else to do.'

Her voice caught, and she took shallow breaths to try to stop her composure from cracking.

'It's all right.' He touched her arm. 'Just take your time.'

'I'm . . .' There was so much she needed to ask, but it all felt too much in that moment.

'It's all right,' he said again. 'I'm sorry, I've not even introduced myself. My name's Ethan.'

'I'm Juliet.' Then she remembered *Olivia*. 'Or that's what my father called me. I don't know if it's my real name.'

Ethan frowned. 'Why wouldn't it be?' When she told him about the old man at the record office, the frown gave way to a rueful smile. 'There's nowhere in the world like the district, but I do sometimes wonder what it would be like to live in a place where everything works as it should.'

'What do you mean?' Juliet stared at him. 'He showed me the records. My father's name was there.'

'Oh, I'm sure it was,' Ethan said. 'He kept the records diligently enough, from what I understand. The problem is that what he chose to record wasn't always exactly what was presented to him. This is the Theatre District, after all. Besides, names here don't mean quite what they mean in the outside world.' He tilted his head. 'Who do you want to be?'

Juliet didn't know how to answer him. There was just a vast, impossible tangle of longing and loss and hope and fear. Then everything seemed to spiral in close.

She looked up at him. 'I want to be who I once was. I want to be the Girl in the Silver Shoes.'

Ethan studied her for a long moment. 'I think you better tell me everything. How did you find your way here?' He glanced around the prop store. 'Not *here*, obviously. To the Theatre District.'

Juliet stumbled through an account of events since her father's death. She didn't mention the key, that furtive sortie into the residents' enclave feeling like an intrusion. Ethan cut in a few times, to ask questions, mostly concerning who else knew about her connection to the district. Only her stepmother, Juliet hastened to assure him. No, she hadn't told anyone she'd met here.

'I knew it had to stay a secret.' He needed to know she'd done everything right. 'I knew I couldn't say anything to anyone.'

Ethan nodded slowly. 'And do you think your father told anyone else?'

'I don't think so,' Juliet said. 'He never talked about it. Not even to me.'

'You knew nothing at all about the Theatre District?' Ethan said.

It was a neutral enough question, but it gave Juliet a little squirm of shame, as though forgetting was a betrayal. Once again, she wondered how she could have let her early life be so entirely erased. Then she recalled the way she'd felt when she looked at that picture of herself in the Shipping News, the way those almost-memories had glinted at the edges of her mind.

'I never quite forgot,' she said. 'When I came back here, there were some things I did remember. The smell of the theatre. Places that felt familiar. Being the Girl in the Silver Shoes, up on the wires. Up high and looking down.'

'You remember that?' The way he was looking at her made her uncomfortably aware how little substance there was to bolster that claim.

'They're not memories exactly.' She paused, gathering herself. 'More like a dream I once had.'

That sounded better.

Ethan's gaze was searching her face, and Juliet felt a panicked certainty that she hadn't done enough. That he would give her a polite smile, say it was nice to meet her and she really must visit again sometime, then walk away.

As though to confirm that fear, he glanced over his shoulder, before turning back to her. 'I have to go. I'm due at the theatre.' As misery began its cold swell, he reached into his pocket and pulled out a key. 'Here. It's for the Show. Give me a couple of hours, then head up to the third floor. I'll find you there.'

'Find me?' Juliet stared at him.

'Don't worry,' he said. 'I know the place must seem impossibly confusing, but you get pretty good at navigating it when you're there day in, day out. I'll track you down.' His mouth lifted. 'Just don't hide in a cupboard or anything like that.'

As he turned to lead her through the prop store, Juliet could feel hope trying to rise, but she was afraid she hadn't understood. He navigated the narrow aisles of the prop store with practised skill, leading her out beneath the scrollwork sign, and into a tangle of tiny streets.

At a small crossroads, he stopped. 'The plaza is straight on from here. I'll see you soon.' He took a few steps away, then shot a last smile over his shoulder. 'And remember, no cupboards.'

After he'd disappeared, Juliet stood still, light-headed with possibilities, replaying the encounter, trying to slide what he'd told her into the imperfect puzzle of her understanding. Most of her questions were still unanswered, but the Theatre District had its own way of doing, of *being*. If she was going to be a part of this place, she needed to let go of her ordinary world expectations.

Part of this place. She felt a leap of elation. After all those years of not belonging, all the things she'd had taken from her, or never had in the first place, she'd found her way home.

Chapter 16

THERE WAS NO QUEUE at the House of Doors.

Ethan had said to wait a couple of hours, and Juliet decided to use that time to explore. It might be the last time she'd come here as a visitor. After two loops, she turned her steps towards what she guessed was the third floor, hoping Ethan would be there. As though the thought of him had been a summons, she saw him coming towards her, trailed by a few early visitors. She waited for his gaze to find her, but he walked past without a glance, leaving her to tag onto his following crowd.

He moved swiftly along the passage and into a hallway that Juliet recognised, coming to a halt at the far end, and pressing his hand to the slick of water running down the wall. As he turned, Juliet could feel the straining anticipation of the audience.

Choose me it's me you want please choose me.

This time he didn't scan the crowd. Instead, he stepped straight towards Juliet, brushing between two other visitors, to take her hand: his fingers wrapped into hers, she felt a tiny squeeze that made her think of the smile he'd given her back at the prop store, secret, confiding, and feeling as though it was for her alone.

The rejected visitors moved aside, resentment written clear in their stances. Ethan drew Juliet to a door, which he unlocked, following her into a small room with a chessboard on a low table. He closed the door, flicking the catch back into place, just as the handle twisted in the grip of someone on the other side.

As he turned to look at her, Juliet felt an unexpected shyness take hold, and she felt around for something to break the moment. 'What happens in here?'

'Do you mean what usually happens? Well, I take this off you.' He reached out to remove her mask, sending a tiny shiver of exposure through her. As he leaned closer, she wanted to close her eyes. 'And then . . .' He pulled back with a quick flick of a grin, '. . . we play chess.'

'Chess?' Juliet was startled into a laugh.

'Just a few moves.' Ethan picked up a black knight and handed it to her. 'Unless I've chosen someone who can actually play. Then the loop rolls on, while they stare at the board, trying to work out what pattern will unlock the secret.'

'Is there a secret?' Juliet turned the piece over in her hands, as though she might hear the click of some concealed mechanism.

'Thousands of them.' Ethan gave her a conspiratorial smile. 'Unless you mean the kind where you move your bishop to the right square and the board slides away to reveal a hidden room. In which case, no, it's not quite like that.' His smile sharpened into a grin. 'Even in the actual hidden rooms. And speaking of hidden things . . .' He took the knight and replaced it on the board, before pulling the drapes aside, revealing a door. 'I didn't bring you here to talk about chess. There's someone you need to meet.'

The air hardened into something brittle, that might break if Juliet made too sharp a move. There was something she'd kept pushed down inside, not letting herself look straight at it. That phone call – *Stephen Stephen* – and the tear-stained letter. Those pictures and accounts in the Shipping News.

'Who?' Her mouth was dry.

'Conrad Danes,' Ethan replied. 'The Director.'

*

Crumbling plaster. Scuffed panelling. Worn floorboards. The occasional curl of paper hanging from a rusted tack. The odd glimpse into an empty room, furniture stacked against the walls. Juliet had thought the backstage areas would be full of bustle and clutter, with performers and stagehands colliding as they hurried about the place. Instead, the corridors were deserted, the only sound the muffled rumble of the Show's music. They reached a panelled hallway, and Ethan led her up a flight of wide steps and along a gallery to a heavy door in a carved frame. When he knocked, a voice spoke from the other side.

'Enter.'

Ethan pushed the door open and ushered Juliet into an office, carpeted in grey and gold. The bookcases that lined the walls were crammed full of hefty tomes with peeling spines. A large, brass-framed mirror hung above a carved fireplace, and in the centre of the room was a heavy desk, topped with dark-red leather, and strewn with papers.

The man sitting behind that desk – fountain pen raised, as though he'd been interrupted mid-task – had grey hair flecked with silver, and was wearing an old-fashioned smoking jacket in a shade somewhere between black and purple. He gave Ethan a nod of greeting, but his gaze stayed on Juliet.

'Director.' Ethan placed his hand on the small of Juliet's back. 'This is . . .'

'I know exactly who this is.' The man got up and came towards her. 'It would be hard not to.' When he reached for her hand, Juliet had to make herself unclench her fingers. 'I'm Conrad Danes. Director of the Theatre District. And you're Stephen's girl.' He tipped his head. 'I can see him in you. It's taken you a long time to find your way back here.'

'I didn't know.' The words sounded more defensive than she'd intended, and Juliet steadied her voice. 'He didn't talk about the district.'

'Never?' There was an intensity to that question.

'He wouldn't tell me anything about his past.' Juliet took a hard breath in, before stepping over the edge. 'Not even who my mother was.'

Was. The past tense had slipped out, and Juliet wanted to snatch it back.

'But you worked it out.' Danes leaned against his desk. 'How?'

'He said her name, just before he died. And he left me some things.' He hadn't, but she couldn't bring herself to admit that Stephen had departed the world without a single thought for her. 'A mask, some charms, a photo. And there was some paperwork – a letter about my birth certificate, and something from . . . something I couldn't read properly.' She took another deep breath. She didn't want to ask the question that had drawn close, but she had to know the truth. 'My mother. He said she was dead, but . . .' Unable to finish, she broke off, pressing her lips together.

'I'm sorry.' The Director shook his head, as she'd known he would. 'Whatever else Stephen did or didn't tell you, that part was true. Your mother died when you were a baby.'

She'd known. She'd *known*. But not for the first time, Juliet realised how many different kinds of *knowing* there were. There was an aching hollow inside her, and she wanted to curl around it, to protect it from anything else that could hurt.

'People saw her.' Her voice sounded brittle. 'They wrote about her in the Shipping News.'

'People see what they want to see,' Danes said gently. 'They tell themselves the story they want to hear.'

'But a police officer came to the house after my father died,' Juliet said. 'He asked about my mother.'

'A police officer?' Danes lifted his head. 'What was his name?'

'DI Mansfield.'

'D*I* Mansfield.' There was a curl in Danes' voice. 'He's gone up in the world. I'm afraid the district is something of an obsession for the good Inspector.'

'What was he looking for?' Juliet asked. 'He wouldn't tell me.'

'Nothing rational,' Danes replied. 'There have been a few like him down the years. Convinced there's some deep, dark secret at the heart of the district. The problem with police officers is that they spend their lives looking for patterns – for motives and methods and meaning – until that's the only way they can see the world. When DI Mansfield looks at the district, he sees a thousand tangled threads of things he doesn't understand. He thinks if he just tugs at the right one, it will all unravel and the truth will be laid bare. Your father was one of those loose threads, and now he's come tugging, to see what he can draw out.' Danes shook his head, with something that looked like regret in his eyes. 'You've come here for answers, and you will have them, I promise. But we need to know each other much better before we can talk properly.' Before Juliet could formulate any argument, he asked a question. 'What do you think of the Show?'

The change of subject knocked her off balance, leaving her flailing for an answer.

'It's like nothing else,' she said. 'I didn't want to leave.'

'Tell me about it,' Danes said.

Juliet stumbled through a disjointed account, straining to recall every detail. It felt like a test, and she was terrified of failing.

When she fell silent, Danes asked another of those seemingly unconnected questions. 'Do you enjoy dancing?'

'It's the only thing I've ever wanted to do, but my stepmother wouldn't let me go to ballet school.'

The Director gave a small nod. 'Anyone trained by Eleanor Abbeline has already learned more than most ballet schools could teach.'

Something exploded in Juliet's head.

The way Miss Abbeline had looked at her. The way she'd been with Stephen.

'She was from the district,' she said. 'She left, like my father. Why?'

'She had her reasons,' Danes replied. 'But yes, Eleanor was once a resident of the Theatre District. I haven't seen her in years, but I knew she'd set up a school.' He glanced at Ethan. 'Would you go and see if the gallery studio is free, please?' As the younger man left, Danes turned back to Juliet. 'Tell me why you came to the district. What were you looking for?'

Juliet had the sense that the whole conversation, perhaps her whole life, had been building to this moment. There were all sorts of answers she could give to his question, but she didn't have time to test out each one in her head.

'The life that should have been mine,' she said, choosing the one she thought best fit the moment.

Before Danes could respond, Ethan returned. 'The studio is free.'

The Director gestured Juliet towards the door. 'Please.'

He followed as Ethan led her along the gallery and into a room lined with mirrors. There was a portable record player on the floor, and Danes walked over to pick up a small stack of records lying next to it.

'Here.' He turned to Juliet. 'There should be something here you can dance to.'

'You want me to dance for you?' Tension flared in Juliet's shoulders. 'Now?'

Ethan touched her back again. 'Go on. It's all right.'

There was a bloodless tingle in Juliet's fingers as she walked over to take the records from Danes.

'This one.' She picked the first familiar piece she found, then realised she couldn't remember how it began.

Danes was already bending over the record player. She shot a frantic look around the studio. She wasn't dressed for dancing. Was there somewhere she could change? Everything was happening too fast.

Ethan had stepped back to lean against the wall, arms folded. As her gaze fell on him, he gave her an encouraging smile. She breathed out slowly, trying to release her nerves, as she slipped off her shoes. She'd rather have danced in her bare feet, but she couldn't exactly take her tights off here, and the record player was already cranking into life. The opening bars of the music filled the studio, and there was nothing to do but dance.

Once she had begun, the steps came readily enough, but that brought little relief. This was the Theatre District. She had to be dazzling. Perfect. She felt as though she was balancing on one of those wires, but this one was stretched towards her future. If her foot came down just a fraction away from where it was supposed to be, there'd be nothing but the fall waiting for her. Juliet strained every muscle, stretched into every hold. Every jump was a leap into all the possibilities that had ever wound through her dreams, and when she turned on the spot, hope spun around her.

When the music faded away, she couldn't look at Danes. She was sure she'd catch a swiftly hidden flicker of disappointment in his face. But when she finally forced herself to meet his gaze, he was smiling.

'I might have been watching your mother dance.' Sadness tugged at the edges of his smile. He looked away for a long moment, and when he turned back to her, the set of his shoulders suggested he'd reached some decision. 'You said you came here for the life you should have had. I can give you that, if you're sure it's what you want.'

Everything fell away, leaving just the two of them and the echo of his words.

'It is what I want.' Juliet's voice shook. 'More than anything.'

'Then I need you to promise me something.' The Director's gaze was locked with hers. 'The Theatre District keeps its secrets close. If you are to be part of what we do here, then I need you to swear you won't tell a living soul about this meeting, or anything that happens from this moment on.'

'I won't, I swear.' It was an easy promise to make. She wouldn't be part of the outside world anymore. She'd be here in the district, where she belonged, and everyone around her would already know every secret there was to know.

'You have to mean that, Juliet.' There was a warning note in Danes' voice. 'You're not just keeping a secret – you *are* the secret. Do you understand?'

'Yes.' Juliet hoped she sounded clear and certain. 'I won't let you down, I promise.'

Danes studied her for a few more heartbeats, and then smiled. 'I believe you.' He glanced at Ethan. 'You'll make the arrangements?' He turned back to Juliet. 'I can give you the life you should have had, but I need you to be patient. The Theatre District has its own way of doing things. Trust me, and do whatever is asked of you, no matter how strange it may seem. Now, I'm afraid you'll have to excuse me. Ethan will show you out, and explain what happens next.' He gave Juliet a final smile. 'I'm glad you've found your way back to us, and I promise you, this is only the beginning.'

*

The journey through the warren of the theatre felt blurred and unreal. All of Juliet's emotions were tangled together, making it hard to unpick any single thread.

Ethan stopped at a door. 'Here.' He opened his hand to show her a silver charm shaped like a tiny cog, on a chain so fine it was barely visible against the creases of his palm. 'This belonged to your mother. Anyone who sees it will know . . .' He gave a quick smile. 'Well, you know.'

Juliet wanted to say she didn't think she *did* know, but she didn't trust herself to speak. Her throat was tight at the thought of the necklace waiting for her all these years.

Ethan stepped behind her to slip the chain around her neck, leaning in to fasten the catch. A shiver went through her at the unfamiliar closeness. He must have felt it, and he placed his hand on her shoulder, turning her gently around to face him.

'I'm sorry about your mother,' he said.

'I think I always knew, deep down.' It was true, she realised, with a brush of regret for that long-nursed hope.

Shaking it away, she looked up at Ethan. 'What happens now?'

'You come back here at noon tomorrow.' He pulled out a key. 'Here, swap this for the one I gave you. The barriers won't keep it when you leave. Don't let anyone see you have it. Come in through the brass door, then turn right and right again. A stagehand will be waiting for you.' He shot a look over his shoulder. 'I have to go. You'll be all right?'

Juliet had so many questions, but she'd promised to be patient. 'I'll be fine.'

'Good.' Ethan gave her a quick smile. 'Put your mask on. I want you to head straight out of the theatre. Don't stay on the set.' Juliet wanted to ask why, but, again, that promise held her back. *Do whatever is asked of you.* Ethan peered through some hidden spy hole, then unlocked the door. 'Quickly.' As she stepped forward, he touched her arm. 'I'll see you soon.'

The door closed silently behind her, leaving Juliet alone in a room she recognised. It wasn't far from the entrance, and she made her way straight out, as Ethan had directed. When her key disappeared into the barrier, she felt a spike of panic, but then a mechanism whirred, and the key emerged again. Juliet gripped it tightly, reaching up with her other hand to touch the necklace. Together, they were proof of her connection to the district, and a solid confirmation of Danes' promise.

This was the beginning of everything.

Chapter 17

Juliet arrived at the House of Doors a few minutes before midday.

On her way out, she'd found a note Sally had left for her. She must have missed it last night. A James Lambert had called, and there was a telephone number for him. It had taken her a moment to remember the younger of the two police officers who'd come to her stepmother's house. Her stepmother had clearly received Juliet's letter, with her address in the precincts. What did DC Lambert want with her? Surely he wouldn't have tracked her down just to berate her for not passing on their message.

She'd crumpled the note into the bin. The last thing she needed was the police asking questions now she had a new life stretching out ahead of her, bright and full of promise.

When Juliet made her way to the dead-end passage Ethan had described, she couldn't see a door, but then a section of the wall swung inwards, opening enough to let her slip through. A black-clad stagehand fastened it back into place, then set off without a word, leaving Juliet to hurry after him.

The high-roofed room he delivered her to looked as though it couldn't decide what it was supposed to be. The side walls were lined with bookcases, rising the full height of the space, with a rickety arrangement of ladders and platforms granting access to the upper shelves.

Overhead there was a curved, stained-glass roof, its colours glinting dully in the borrowed light of bulbs hanging from wires stretched beneath. Below those wires, a heavy joist ran the width of the room, with an assortment of ropes attached to it, their trailing ends looped around hooks fixed to the wall below. In front of a row of what looked like part-built dollhouses, a man was leaning over some papers on a trestle table. Juliet thought it was Danes, but, when he looked up, she saw he was older than the Director, with a sharp, stern face.

The cursory glance he gave her was followed by an equally cursory introduction. 'I'm the district choreographer.' He didn't ask her name. He presumably already knew who she was, but the lack of niceties was jarring. 'There's a costume for you through there.' He gestured towards a door. 'Get changed, and we'll start.'

He was talking as though Juliet knew exactly what was going on. There was a possibility starting to thrum deep inside her, but she didn't want to look at it too closely in case she was wrong.

The door opened onto a dressing room, with a light-blue chiffon dress hanging on a rail above a selection of worn-in ballet slippers. Juliet found a pair that fitted well enough, and changed into the dress.

Back in the studio, the choreographer was leafing through some notes. He gestured towards the middle of the floor.

'You have three dances,' he said. 'We'll go through the solo first.'

'Dances?' Juliet felt another tremulous stirring of possibility.

The choreographer raised an eyebrow. 'You're aware of the concept, I assume?'

She bit at her lip. 'Yes.'

'Then let's get started.'

*

Despite his brusque manner, the choreographer was a surprisingly effective teacher. The dance wasn't technically challenging, but it was physically demanding, and Juliet felt a fresh resentment towards her stepmother for stopping her ballet classes.

The choreographer gave no praise – a nod was the only indication he was satisfied – but neither did he show any impatience or irritation at her more clumsy efforts, correcting each error swiftly and clearly.

'Let's try it with the music,' he said, when she had the steps memorised.

Turning to the table, he flicked a switch on an old-fashioned gramophone. A scrape of sound filled the studio, yielding to a haunting melody that clutched at Juliet with vague fingers of familiarity. The choreographer counted her through the opening bars, falling silent when she'd caught the rhythm of it. At the end, he lifted the needle back to the outside of the record.

'Again.'

*

They'd run through the dance half a dozen times when the choreographer finally called a halt. As he stopped the gramophone, Juliet leaned on the table, lifting her foot so that she could slide a finger inside her ballet shoe.

'Is your shoe rubbing?' The choreographer had turned to look at her.

'I'm fine.' She straightened up quickly.

'I didn't ask if you were fine,' he replied. 'I asked if your shoe was rubbing.' When she nodded, he walked over to the shelves and rummaged in a box, returning with something in his hand. 'Here.' He handed her a small piece of gauze. 'This should help.' He watched as Juliet slid it into her shoe. 'Better?'

'Yes.' She gave him a tentative smile. 'Thank you.'

His nod was curt. 'We'll take a short break.' He gestured towards the end of the table, where there was a plate covered by a cloth, and a copper jug with a glass next to it. 'Have something to eat. We've still got a lot of work to do.'

Underneath the cloth, Juliet found a couple of fresh rolls with butter and cheese. Nerves had taken her appetite, but she forced one down. She'd just finished when the door opened and a vaguely familiar man walked in.

He was older than her, perhaps around forty, with the lean, muscled frame of a dancer. His gaze raked over her briefly, and then he looked away.

'You're late,' the choreographer said.

'Better get on with it then.' The man's tone was tight.

Juliet thought she saw the choreographer's ribs lift, as though he'd taken a careful breath, but when he turned to address her, his voice was level.

'Arlen will be your partner for one of your dances. Let's get started.'

Juliet made her way to the centre of the floor. The choreographer rattled off a run of steps, repeated them twice more, then nodded at Arlen, who stepped in close. Goosebumps brushed the backs of Juliet's arms. She'd only ever danced with other girls at the Academy.

The choreographer repeated the steps a final time, and then, without any preamble, counted them in. Caught off guard, Juliet stumbled into the first turn, colliding with Arlen, who stiffened but didn't break stride. Stepping around behind her, his hand trailed from her hip to the curve of her collarbone, then round to the nape of her neck. His cool, impersonal touch made Juliet think of a diligent executioner, trying to work out where it would be best for the axe to fall. She gave an inadvertent shiver, and Arlen muttered something, and stepped back.

'I'm sorry.' Juliet put her hand to her neck. 'I'm not—'

'Again.' The choreographer cut across her, then counted them in once more.

This time, Arlen led aggressively, giving her no chance to step or turn the wrong way. Despite her discomfort, his bullish tactics were effective. By the time they'd run through the sequence half a dozen times, Juliet had caught the shape and rhythm of it.

'Next section,' the choreographer said, then reeled off another sequence.

As the rehearsal went on, Juliet picked up the steps more easily but grew ever more tense and self-conscious. It might have been easier if her partner wasn't giving the impression that dancing with her was an ordeal. Their bodies were close, but it felt as though he was trying to touch her as little as possible. When she stumbled again, he made no attempt to steady her, stepping back from her clumsiness, irritation etched into every line of his expression.

'Sorry.' Juliet shoved her hair back. 'I don't—'

'Again.'

As the choreographer's voice snapped out, Juliet saw Arlen's jaw tighten, and her stomach knotted in response. She couldn't work out what she'd done to deserve such hostility.

He pushed her unceremoniously into the starting pose. 'I lead, you follow.' It was the first time he'd spoken. 'And try not to look as though you can't stand me touching you.'

Juliet took a sharp breath at the unfairness of that accusation, but the choreographer was counting them in again, and she had to focus.

A thought formed. What would *Olivia* do? She'd take everything Miss Abbeline had said about what it meant to be a young lady, and turn it on its head with a secret smile, with the curve of an arm and a lilt in her steps. As Juliet explored these thoughts, she could feel something beginning to beat beneath the rhythm of her movements. A contained energy, a low, slow pulse.

This time, when they reached the end, Arlen stayed close, staring down at her for a few seconds, his expression unreadable. The moment was broken by the opening of the door. Arlen moved back abruptly, and Juliet turned to see Ethan stepping into the room. When their eyes met, he gave her a quick, almost conspiratorial smile, before rearranging his expression into something more serious and looking over at the choreographer.

'How is it going?'

'Could be worse.' The older man glanced at Arlen. 'Could be a lot better as well. Let's try it with the music.'

As Arlen moved into position, Ethan leaned against the wall, arms folded. Juliet's heart had given a leap when he'd walked in, but now she was conscious of a nervous need for him to see the best of her.

The melody was different from her solo piece, but with hints of the latter. The choreographer counted them in, and Juliet stepped around, only to collide with Arlen who hadn't moved. As she began a fumbled apology, he spoke over her.

'Why has the music changed?'

'Director's orders.' It was Ethan who replied.

'Director's orders.' There was something low and dangerous in Arlen's voice, and Juliet wanted to wrap her arms across her body against the almost palpable hostility.

Ethan tipped his head slightly, but made no other response. The music was still playing, and Arlen caught Juliet's wrist in a hard grip she thought might leave a bruise, pulling her into the dance. He'd picked up the right point with effortless accuracy, but Juliet was caught off guard, searching for the steps. As she found her place, she tried to relax, but it was impossible. Arlen's tension scraped against her like an over-tight bowstring, and she was relieved when the music gave way to the rumble of the final grooves on the record.

The silence that followed was broken by the choreographer. 'I think that will do for now, Arlen.' There was something in his tone that might have been understanding, or even compassion. 'You can go.'

As Arlen stalked out of the room, the choreographer gave Ethan a long, hard look. The younger man responded with the barest of shrugs, pushing himself away from the wall and over to Juliet, who was biting her lip against an urge to cry.

'Are you all right?' She nodded, swallowing the threatening tears. Ethan didn't look convinced. 'Do you want a break?'

'I'm fine.' She managed to keep her voice steady. 'I'm not tired.'

She knew that wasn't what he meant, but she wanted to pretend there'd been nothing challenging about rehearsing with Arlen other than the physical demands of the dance.

Ethan studied her face for a moment more, then turned to the choreographer. 'Let's do an hour, and see how we get on.'

As the older man picked up another sheath of notes, Juliet's heart gave another leap, and she looked up at Ethan.

'Are we dancing together?'

He nodded. 'If that's all right with you.'

'Yes.' She said it too quickly, then felt the heat rush to her cheeks. 'That's fine.'

'Good.' He gave her another of those swift smiles.

'If you're quite ready,' the choreographer said pointedly, then shook out his notes and ran through a sequence of steps.

*

Dancing with Ethan was an entirely different experience. As he guided her through the movements, calmly managing any errors, Juliet found her confidence growing. She began to extend herself, pushing beyond simple mastery of the steps, in an effort to match his easy skill. While they danced, there was no trace of *Ethan* – only the Shadow Man. His focus was complete, his gaze intent and seeming to hold all sorts of unspoken things, but at the end of each run-through, that mask fell away, and he was back, his smile warm with approval. Juliet found herself looking for the line between the two versions of him, for the moment when one gave way to the other, but she couldn't catch it. It might have been unsettling if it hadn't been for that smile, which set something fluttering inside her, and she had to fight not to let her thoughts run away, chasing all sorts of possibilities.

After a few successful run-throughs, the choreographer put the music on. Again, there were echoes of the other melodies. It was nothing clear or definable – just a brush or a hint of something shared, like a resemblance passed down through a family. As Ethan led her through the dance once again, Juliet felt another lift of confidence. She knew the steps and, despite her aching back and feet, could feel the certainty of her body responding to her every command. She had that sense she'd had before when she danced – that she was where she was supposed to be, with the whole world turning around her. But this time, she wasn't there alone.

The music was drawing into its final bars, and there was only one short sequence of steps remaining. Juliet went up on her toes and stretched her hand towards Ethan.

Instead of taking it, he moved close, placed his hands on her waist and lifted her off the ground. She felt a jolt of disorientation – this wasn't how the dance went – but there was such certainty in his touch that she suddenly knew just what to do. As he turned, still holding her, she curved her arm above her head, and stretched out her leg. He completed the turn, then lowered her back to the floor. Her balance held as he stepped behind her, ran his hand down her arm, then bent to press a light kiss to the inside of her wrist. A shiver went through her, but if he felt it, he gave no sign, wrapping his fingers into hers, and drawing her into the final steps of the dance.

The last notes faded, and the choreographer flicked the gramophone off, before addressing Ethan. 'Forget what you were supposed to be doing?'

'Just a small change.' Ethan appeared untroubled by the older man's caustic tone. 'She's good enough.'

'Good enough isn't what we're aiming for,' the choreographer replied. 'Simple steps performed perfectly are better than more advanced movements sloppily done.'

'Nothing's ever perfect,' Ethan said.

The older man narrowed his gaze. 'Maybe you need to spend more time rehearsing. Unless you have other things taking up that time, of course?'

It seemed to Juliet that there was something sharp and targeted in his words, but Ethan gave a one-shouldered shrug. 'A few,' he said easily. 'But that's by-the-by. The Show isn't about perfection. The audience don't notice mistakes.'

The choreographer gave a contemptuous snort. 'That's because they have no idea what they're looking at.'

Ethan shook his head. 'It's because it's not what they're looking *for.*' He glanced towards the door. 'Speaking of the audience, are we done here? If we go now, the stagehands should be able to get us some time on the set before the evening crowd come in.'

'Fine,' the choreographer said shortly, then looked at Juliet. 'Same time tomorrow.'

Musings on Moonshine and Memory

The Show goes on. That is the central tenet of the Theatre District, and an article of faith for those of us who have dedicated ourselves to uncovering its secrets. The Show never stops, never sees a curtain call or interval. It is unceasing. What it is not, however, is unchanging. If you delve into the vast repository of records in these rooms, you will notice recurring references to certain characters and storylines that are used to define particular eras of the Show. Where world history is defined in terms of its rulers and major events, the history of the Show is defined in terms of its stories.

As we know, the Show runs through cycles, the length of which vary from a few months to several years. Each culminates in a peak – usually an evening performance on a larger scale than usual – after which there are always changes. New storylines might emerge, or existing ones come to greater prominence. Previously itinerant or nomadic performers might join the cast, possibly replacing incumbent principals.

An era can contain any number of cycles, but the peak that precedes a new period in the Show's history is usually significant, with that era's defining storylines and characters brought into sharp focus. These changes are always foreshadowed in the build-up to the relevant peak – although this may not be clear until afterwards.

There has been only one notable exception to this. Twelve years ago, there was an important change to the Show with no apparent foreshadowing and no indication of any imminent peak. The sudden departure of the Moonshine Girl – and the strange circumstances of her penultimate performance – remains one of the Show's greatest unsolved mysteries, coming *only a few weeks after a significant peak that appeared to establish her as a central storyline. Indeed, there is an argument that her story, with its references to earlier characters and events, was the key to understanding much of what had gone before. (The echoes of the Wasteland storylines and those of the Seven Sisters are particularly interesting, and are discussed at some length in David Edmond's pamphlet, for those who are interested.)*

Following the disappearance of the Moonshine Girl, it was some time before a new central storyline emerged. At this point, the Show seemed to settle back into its usual pattern – which still holds to this day – although the cycles now tend to be shorter, with no character remaining centre stage for more than a year or so. What is notable is how frequently the Moonshine Girl is referenced within other storylines; her memory shines as bright as ever.

Chapter 18

OUT IN THE CORRIDOR, Ethan gave a rueful smile.

'Sorry about that. He's not my greatest fan. Long story. More than one, in fact.' He tilted his head. 'You impressed him, though.'

'Did I?' Juliet felt a brush of pleasure. 'He didn't say.'

'No.' Ethan gave her another of those wry smiles, as he ushered her through a door. 'He wouldn't.' His smile faded. 'Don't worry about Arlen.'

'Did I do something wrong?' Even as Juliet asked the question, she was remembering his expression when he'd stepped into the room. That was the first time he'd laid eyes on her.

'Of course not,' Ethan said. 'He can be . . . tricky. Just pretend it's part of the scene. The lines aren't always clear, anyway, so you can take it and put it in your performance.'

Your performance.

She wanted to ask him what that meant, but everyone was behaving as though she should know exactly what was going on. She thought perhaps she did, but she was afraid to reach for certainty, in case it all fell away. Right now, she had the possibility, and it was *everything*.

They were walking along a gallery, and to distract herself, Juliet looked down into the room below, which was full of dust-sheeted mounds.

'Why are there so many unused rooms?' she asked.

'The Show used to be much bigger than it is now.'

'What happened?'

'The war.' Ethan sounded surprised she had to ask. 'People still came, but not in the same numbers.' He opened a door at the end of the gallery. 'But the Show is growing again. Perhaps these rooms will be opened again one day.'

As she stepped past him, through the doorway, he suddenly caught her wrist in a loose grip. Juliet followed his gaze to see the bruise she'd anticipated already beginning to bloom. His lips tightened, but he didn't say anything, brushing her skin with a light fingertip, in what felt like an apology, before letting her go.

There was a stagehand waiting for them in the next corridor. He let them through onto the set, then closed the door behind them. Ethan led Juliet across a courtyard and into a small room, lit by a clutch of candles in jars. The walls were formed of vines and branches woven together, a few withered leaves still clinging to the stems.

A bed with a faded patchwork quilt stood in the centre of the floor. Leaning against the wall nearby was a full-length mirror. There was something odd about it, and it took Juliet a moment to realise she couldn't see herself in it. The surface was curved, catching strange angles of the room. It was disorienting, and she turned away.

'You'll start your loop lying on the bed,' Ethan said.

Juliet walked over to perch on the edge. 'What if someone comes in?'

'They won't,' Ethan replied. 'The stagehands will keep our route clear. A locked door here, a light turned off there – most visitors won't even realise they're being steered away.' She must have looked doubtful, because he gave her a swift smile. 'The Show never stops. If we didn't have ways of managing the audience, we'd never get to rehearse on set.' He stepped close to the bed. 'Lie on your side.' As Juliet complied, Ethan took hold of her hand, drawing it up to rest beside her face. 'Close your eyes.' He brushed a tendril of hair back from her cheek. 'Listen to the music. You're waiting for the first crescendo. There. Now you wake. Stretch your arm out. Slower. That's it. Now turn your head. Look around the room. You're somewhere unfamiliar, somewhere strange.'

His voice was low and compelling, and Juliet tried to let go of everything else. There was a strange pleasure in surrendering yourself to someone, letting them tell you what you should be. You didn't need to think. You just had to follow the steady pulse of their voice, moving from space to space, along hallways, up and down stairs. Her loop took her through parts of the theatre she'd visited, and through rooms she'd never seen before. A gallery lined with empty display cases. A dizzyingly high platform suspended above a ballroom where two shadowy figures pirouetted far below. A room full of music boxes. A square lit by a single spotlight. Ethan's voice led her through room after room, scene after scene, only falling silent for their dance together in a wide, paved space, cloistered round the edges.

Her scene with Arlen took place in a studio filled with scattered wooden blocks, and there was also a fleeting interaction with the Rose Singer – the girl whose picture Juliet had seen in the Shipping News and whose real name, she learned now, was Jemima – who waited in a fire-blackened room to lean close and whisper a warning.

Three times, Juliet played that loop. On the second, Jemima wasn't there, and on the next, Arlen was missing too. Each time, Ethan talked Juliet through solo versions of those scenes. At the end of the third run-through, he held his hand out to help her up from the bed.

'Well done,' he said. 'You're a natural.'

Gathering herself, Juliet looked up at him, and asked the question that had been shifting inside her since she stepped into the choreographer's studio.

'What's happening? Am I . . .' She swallowed against a sudden dryness in her mouth. 'That felt like a role. Am I . . . am I going to be part of this? Part of the Show?'

'Do you want to be?' Ethan asked.

'Yes.' Juliet answered so swiftly that she almost tripped over the end of his question. 'Yes.'

Yes yes please yes.

'That promise you made to the Director.' Ethan's expression grew intent. 'I need to be sure you understand what it means. You can't let slip a single word, a single breath of this. Not even if there's someone you think you can trust.' Eugene drifted through Juliet's mind, trailing a cobweb-fine thread of regret. 'Don't let people get too close to you. Don't get drawn into conversations about the district or the Show. Don't go to the Shipping News.' He gave a slight smile. 'If one day you're . . . not around anymore, it would be best if you didn't leave too many loose ends behind.'

'I won't.' *Not around anymore.* Juliet's pulse quickened at the implication of that. 'I promise. I'll do whatever you need me to.'

'Then, yes,' Ethan said. 'The Director is offering you a role. It will only be at quiet times, until he's sure of you. But you'll be part of the Show.'

The lift of joy that Juliet felt was dizzying in its swift ascent, but the fall that followed was equally swift. This was everything she'd wanted, except in all the ways that it wasn't. The doors weren't being flung open. The other residents weren't crowding around, smiling, telling her they'd never stopped hoping she'd come home. The stagehand who'd let her in hadn't so much as acknowledged her presence. The choreographer had barely spoken to her, save to bark instructions.

'I thought . . .' She broke off, realising that there was no way to voice any of that, without sounding like a petulant child who'd opened the wrong present on Christmas morning.

Ethan placed his hand on her shoulder. 'This is your chance, Juliet.' His voice was gentle. 'You just need to prove that you'll give everything to the district. You need to show everyone that they can trust you.' His hand slid down her arm, in what might almost have been a caress. As it brushed over the bruise he'd forgotten was there, Juliet smothered a wince. 'And you need to trust *me*. I'll help you as much as I can, I promise.'

Juliet found a smile. He was right. She'd been given an incredible chance. It was up to her to seize it.

'What happens next?' she asked.

'More rehearsals,' he replied. 'But you've done enough for today. Come on.'

A stagehand let them off the set. Once Juliet had changed, Ethan took her back to the door where she'd come in.

'Put your mask on.' As she tied it in place, he reached into his pocket. 'Take this.' He handed her a note. 'Details of the rehearsal slots.' Stepping close to the door, he peered through the spy hole. 'Coast's clear. When you're through, head straight out of the theatre.'

'Can I watch some of the Show?'

Ethan gave a sharp shake of his head. 'You can't go to the Show at all. No performer ever goes into the audience. It's . . . well, it's stronger than a superstition. It's a rule that's never broken.' He gave her a close look. 'Are you sure you want this? You could walk away now, find an ordinary job, where you go home to your ordinary housemates and talk about ordinary things.' When he smiled, there was something wistful, almost sad, about the shape of it. 'It's completely your choice. You know that, don't you?'

'I do want it.' Juliet pushed her regret firmly away. 'More than anything.'

This time, Ethan's smile was more straightforward. 'I'm glad.' He put his hand on her shoulder, his thumb rubbing at a tense spot that he instinctively seemed to know was there. 'You're going to be wonderful.'

*

When Juliet got home, the house was empty, but she still closed her bedroom door before reading the note. There was no preamble – just a list of days and times. No one else who read it would have any idea what it was about. Ethan and Danes had both been at pains to emphasise the need for secrecy, as though it was something difficult. But Juliet had never been on the inside of something like this, and she'd never imagined there could be such a biting thrill in it.

Lying down on the bed, she closed her eyes. Her thoughts drifted back to the theatre. She was masked again, and in the audience, listening to the whispers running through the theatre.

The Girl in the Silver Shoes. The Girl in the Silver Shoes. Have you seen her?

As the images began to fray, Juliet felt a tremor of doubt. Wasn't she supposed to be on the other side of things? But sleep was already wrapping about her, and she turned her head on the pillow and let herself slip away.

Chapter 19

SEVERAL DAYS PASSED, IN a blur of sleep and rehearsals and trying not to talk too much about her old life, even when Ethan asked.

Juliet didn't mention her father's funeral, just a couple of days away now, or her reluctant decision to return for it. She wanted it over, and then that life would be completely behind her.

After the third rehearsal, Ethan told her, almost casually, that the next time would be the real thing. She froze, gripped by the absolute certainty that she wasn't ready, but he squeezed her shoulder, and told her she'd be wonderful. She was due on set at midnight, by which time the theatre would be emptying out. She just had to do exactly what she'd done over and over in rehearsals. She might not have an audience at all, but if she did, she shouldn't be afraid. She could just pretend they weren't there.

Now, as Juliet stood in a tiny dressing room, she wasn't sure how she felt about the prospect of performing to no one. The idea of a masked crowd was terrifying, but there was something lonely about the thought of moving through her loop entirely unseen.

Pull yourself together. This is what you wanted, isn't it?

Ignoring *Olivia's* caustic tone, Juliet lifted the familiar blue dress off its hanger and slipped into it, her pulse a swift stutter. Nothing had ever mattered as much as this.

The silver ballet shoes Ethan had given her at their last rehearsal still pinched slightly at the toes, but they'd soften soon enough. As she put them on, her throat tightened. She was the Girl in the Silver Shoes again, and tonight she was coming home.

The door opened, and a grey-haired woman stepped into the room. She gave Juliet a quick, unsmiling glance, then stepped past her, gesturing at the narrow shelf crowded with make-up pots that served as a dressing table. Juliet sat down in a rickety chair, closing her eyes.

The woman's deft, impersonal touch reminded Juliet of stories an old classics teacher had told, about initiates being prepared for the sacred mysteries – and when she opened her eyes, someone else's reflection was staring back at her from the cracked mirror. The make-up had changed the whole shape of her face, creating shadows where there were none before, darkening her eyes and sharpening her cheekbones.

Olivia?

The reply was swift. *Who else?*

The woman finished arranging Juliet's hair. With a last appraising look at her subject, she turned towards the door.

Juliet twisted around. 'What happens now?'

'Someone will come for you.' She stepped out.

Juliet turned back to the mirror. It was hard not be unnerved by the transformation, but that was what the theatre was about, wasn't it?

The door opened again, and a stagehand looked in. He jerked his head at her, and she followed him to a door, which he opened just enough for her to slip through. As the Show's music swelled, sending her heart thudding against her ribs, she wanted to say *wait, stop, I'm not ready,* but the door had already closed behind her. For a panicked moment, she couldn't remember anything – not her loop, not her dances, not even how it had felt to want this. Her breathing was fast and shallow, and she tried to steady it, as she crossed the courtyard to open the far door.

The room with the woven walls was empty, and, as the music gave way to silence and the whole theatre seemed to hold its breath, Juliet lay down on the bed and closed her eyes. As the slow build of the opening notes filled the room, she realised she hadn't asked Ethan if he would be performing tonight. She wished she had his voice as a steady thread to guide her. Then her cue came, and, like falling, she felt the pull of the role.

As she moved through the theatre, each step felt a little more sure than the one before. It was strange at first, playing her scenes with no one there to see them, but the awkwardness of it eased as the loop played out. When she reached the burnt room, the Rose Singer was just stepping through the far door. Juliet was a little behind where she should have been, but only by a few seconds, and the other girl's swift steps were the only sign she had even noticed the error. Her timing in the room with the wooden blocks was perfect, but Arlen's hostility was still palpable, pushing her away, even as he held her close.

When she stepped into the cloistered square and saw Ethan walking towards her, Juliet felt a lift of joy, so swift-leaping it was almost frightening. For a moment, it was just the two of them and the dance and the dust-drift of the spotlight and the taste of the theatre on her tongue. Then a shift of movement at the edge of the light resolved itself into three masked figures, intent upon the unfolding scene. Juliet felt a fresh shiver of nerves, but Ethan tightened his grip on her waist. As he placed her back on her feet after the lift, he held on to her a fraction longer than usual, a message clear in his touch. *I'm here.*

Juliet breathed out slowly. *I can do this. I was born to do this.*

The dance was drawing to a close, and Ethan stepped behind her, pulling her against him, one hand resting on her ribs, the fingers of the other winding into hers. As the last notes of the accompanying melody gave way to the lower rumble of the Show's music, she felt a pressure in the hand he held in his. Again, the meaning was as clear as if he'd murmured it in her ear.

Well done.

Then he was gone, crossing the square with swift steps, the audience following, leaving her to gather up the thread of her loop. As she moved on, she realised, with another clench of nerves, that not all the audience members had followed Ethan. He'd lost one to her – a tall man in a decorated mask whose gaze was locked upon her.

Pretend they're not there. Ethan's advice echoed in her head, but it wasn't easy. Her awareness of the man's presence was acute, the scrutiny of that singular gaze unnerving. But as the scene played out, something else stirred, tugged into life by the way every tiny movement she made drew an answering reaction, the mask doing little to hide the intensity of his watching. There was a power in it, making her remember how it felt to be the one standing there, yearning for something just out of reach.

At the bottom of the staircase leading up to the roof space above the ballroom, a shadow slipped behind her, and the door closed, shutting the man out. Juliet climbed the stairs alone, played out her scene on the high platform, then made her way back down, only to find him waiting for her at the bottom of those steps. He was clearly a regular visitor, with enough knowledge of the theatre to have guessed where she would emerge.

He stayed with her past the end of that loop and into the next one, only leaving when a grey-haired woman joined them. Three more visitors arrived over the course of the next few scenes. Juliet hadn't expected to encounter this many audience members in the early hours, but she wasn't afraid anymore – not even when Ethan didn't appear in the cloistered square – and as she moved through the theatre, she found herself making small changes. A pause. A slight turn of her head. A glance over her shoulder, as though almost sensing the presence of the audience. Tiny things, but each one designed to bind them more tightly to her, to make them love her more.

*

It was on the fourth loop that she made the mistake.

By that time Juliet was alight with an almost reckless pleasure, barely aware of the growing ache in her feet. She'd let more and more of her focus slip to the audience, relying on instinct to guide her through the loop. It was only when she stepped through a door – one of several leading off a corridor – that she realised it was the wrong one.

The shock that ran through her was like ice breaking, revealing, in a swift, cold instant, what a brittle thing her confidence had been. She tried to steady herself. She could get back on track. She just needed to retrace her steps, hurry the next scene a little. But as Juliet turned towards the door, she found her way blocked. Her audience had crowded through behind her, pushing for the prime spot at the front. There seemed to be more of them than there should have been. She could feel their taut anticipation, and knew what lay behind it. This was something different. They didn't know what it meant, but it might be the thing they all sought.

She was so close to one man that she could see the lift of his ribs as he took a sharp, expectant breath in.

Too close.

Juliet's pulse was beating in her head as she took a step back. The audience followed, and a panicked pressure built inside her. In that moment, she was both more vulnerable than she'd ever been in her life, and also strangely untouchable, invisible behind the painted face of the Girl in the Silver Shoes. She could fall to her knees, cry, claw at the floor until her nails were ragged, and they'd all just watch. If she let them, they'd taste her tears to see what the salt could tell them.

I could die here, she thought, with a chill certainty. *You'd watch as the warmth went out of my body, and then you'd watch a little longer to see if I'd get up and dance for you again.*

There was a sound behind her, and she twisted round to see the wall opening up. She stumbled through, and it snapped shut. It was dark on the other side, save for a muted glow, which suddenly blared into the brightness of a stagehand's torch as he directed Juliet along the corridor.

Ahead of her, a door opened and a familiar figure stepped into view.

There was a terrible compassion in Ethan's eyes, and Juliet felt a drag of dull misery.

'I'm sorry,' she said. 'I tried. It was—'

'You're not the one who should be apologising.' Ethan's voice was sharp. 'The Director should have given you more time. Everything always comes back to his obsession with the Moonshine Girl. It would have been your mother he was thinking about when he rushed you into this role.' He gave a sharp shake of his head. 'I'll talk to him, make sure you get the time you need.'

'Time?' Juliet felt a limping hope. 'I'm not . . .' She swallowed. 'I thought I'd be sent away.'

Ethan reached out to take her chilled hand in his. 'You made a mistake. Everyone in the Show has made hundreds of them. And you were unlucky. At this time of night, there's rarely much of an audience. It's been busier recently for various reasons. That should have occurred to me. I'm sorry.'

'But it went so wrong.' Juliet's voice broke.

'And the Show went on. The Show *always* goes on. You're a part of it, and a first-night mistake doesn't change that.'

Juliet tried to choke back a sob of relief, but failed.

'It's all right.' Ethan stepped close, drawing her against him. 'It's all right.' The kindness of the gesture was Juliet's undoing, and she leaned into him as she cried.

Eventually, her tears subsided, and Ethan released her.

'I'm sorry,' she said, wiping her face.

'There's nothing to apologise for.' He looked down at her. 'You did so well. If the Director hadn't left you on set for so long, you would have come away from that performance full of confidence.'

There was an edge to his tone again, and Juliet felt a faint brush of unease, just like when she was young and realised for the first time that adults didn't always get along; that they sometimes made the world less safe, more complicated.

'It wasn't his fault,' she said.

'It was,' Ethan replied flatly. 'The thing you need to understand about Conrad Danes is that nothing will ever be more important than the Show.' He gave a swift shake of his head. 'It doesn't matter. I'll speak to him, get him to change the schedule so we can have more time to rehearse.'

He led Juliet to the dressing room, and waited outside as she changed. There was still a faint tremor in her hands as she wiped off her make-up, but the chill of failure was fading. There'd been such warmth and gentleness in Ethan's eyes as he'd looked at her. It was still there when she stepped out into the corridor to join him. His hand was warm too, resting on her back as he steered her through the theatre to the door where she'd come in.

'Come back here at nine tomorrow,' he said. 'We'll have a good few hours to rehearse before I have to be on set.' He smiled at her. 'And don't worry about the Director. I'll deal with him.' He opened the door. 'Get some rest and I'll see you tomorrow.'

Chapter 20

When Juliet returned to the theatre, it was Ethan who met her at the stage door, his smile easing her nerves a little.

He led her up several flights of stairs to a bare-boarded attic passage, and into a studio that didn't look as though it had seen much recent use.

'Sorry it's a bit shabby,' Ethan said, glancing up at the skylights set in the slant of the roof. 'But I thought we should make the most of the sun while it lasts.' He gave a rueful smile. 'I sometimes forget it's even up there.' He gestured towards a door in the corner. 'There's a costume in the dressing room.'

Juliet wound her fingers together, remembering the panic she'd felt when everything slipped out of her control.

'What if I can't do it?' she said. 'What if I'm not good enough?'

'You are,' Ethan said, with certainty. 'But it's not just about how well you dance. It's about how you make the audience feel. The moments they'll remember are the ones where you gave them something real. Go on. Get changed and we'll get to work.'

*

It was noon by the time Ethan called a halt.

They'd run through Juliet's scenes several times, polishing her dances, and she could feel her confidence slowly returning. They ate lunch on the studio floor, while Ethan sketched out her loop on a large sheet of paper, pointing out the connections with other storylines, marking the places where she was most likely to pick up audience members. Juliet was surprised how close her route brought her to several other performers. As she followed the pencil line of her loop, it crossed with another, and she leaned closer.

'That's you.' She touched the connecting line. 'But we don't have a scene in that room.'

Ethan reached over to scribble out the intersection she'd indicated. 'Old loop.' He smiled. 'See? I told you, even those of us who've been performing for years can make mistakes.' Juliet didn't smile back. Looking at all the winding threads of the Show, she felt a heavy certainty that she'd only ever achieve a stuttering grasp of the district, rather than Ethan's instinctive fluency. He laid his pencil down and took her hand.

'I know how difficult this must be for you. For those of us who've grown up here in the district, our roles are part of us. They're closer than our parents, our children. Our lovers.' He flicked her a quick, conspiratorial look on that last word, leaving Juliet with a flush of not-quite embarrassment. 'They're part of us, but they have their own existence too. Sometimes they feel things you don't, or want things you'd never choose, but you can't pack their bags and tell them to never darken your door again. Other times, when there are changes in the Show, you have to get to know them all over again. It's like . . .' He glanced around the room, as though searching for the right words. 'It's like waking up one day, next to a stranger, and finding that you're expected to make their breakfast and listen to them talking about their day.' He shot her another of those hooded looks, then grew serious again.

'The board don't really understand how it works. They have their roles, of course – everyone does – but they don't play them for long, if at all. They're brought up to manage the district, not perform in it.' He shook his head. 'Danes thought he could make you the Girl in the Silver Shoes instantly. He expected you to take just days to find something that the rest of us have had our whole lives to reach.' His voice was gentle. 'You're not the Girl in the Silver Shoes.' Even as Juliet tensed, a smile lifted the corners of his mouth. 'But you can be. I'll help you, I promise.' Relief flooded Juliet's lungs, and he tipped his head. 'What are you thinking?'

She couldn't answer truthfully without voicing things that made her shiver at the thought of saying them out loud. Things that had to do with the promise he'd just made, and how it sometimes felt when she was with him.

'I just . . . I wish I could remember her. The Moonshine Girl.' She'd intended it as a distraction, but she found the words tumbling out in a rush that had truth behind it. 'It's as though she's still here. As though . . .' She bit at the inside of her lip, afraid of sounding foolish or petulant. 'As though she's more real than I am, even though she's gone.'

'She is still here,' Ethan said. '*Real* isn't just about now. The Moonshine Girl was a bright thread in the tapestry of the Show, but you can be just as bright.' He hesitated, before continuing with what looked like a rush of honesty. 'Although I'm not sure that's what the Director wants. In fact, I'd say he's doing everything he can to make sure they're looking at you, but thinking of her.'

'What do you mean?'

'Your dress.' He touched the skirt. 'Your hair. Your dances, and the music that accompanies them. He may not be trying to pretend that you *are* the Moonshine Girl, but he's certainly ensuring that her ghost is haunting your every step.' He gave a small shrug. 'It's not surprising. I told you, she's always been an obsession of his. He spotted the potential in the way the audience responded to her, and he spun her story into what it remains today. A few hints scattered through the set, a handful of rumours let loose to wind their way through the district. An echo of something lost.' He brushed Juliet's hair with his fingertips. 'He knows you don't draw people in by giving them everything they want. You bind them to you by giving them a glimpse, then pulling it away just as they're reaching for it.'

'So what do I do?' Juliet wasn't sure she understood what he was telling her. 'How do I make them see *me*? I can't change what I've been told to do.'

'No,' he said. 'But there are places where you can push at the edges a little.' He gave her a secret smile. 'You discovered that last night, I think. It's about deciding what you want the audience to think and feel when they watch you. You make them see the Girl in the Silver Shoes by making them *want* to see her. There's no point going into battle with the memory of the Moonshine Girl. Danes has done his work too well with that story. You need to reach an accommodation with her. You need to take all those scattered fragments, all those glimpses of what was, and wind it into what *is*. Take her memory and make it part of you. Turn it into something new, something the audience will never forget.'

Juliet felt the ache of all she'd lost once again. 'If I could just remember. Something, anything, from before.'

Ethan tipped his head. 'I thought you said you remembered the wires.' When Juliet gave a cautious nod, he took her hand, wrapping her fingers into his. 'Come on.'

'Where are we going?'

He smiled. 'To find that girl.'

Chapter 21

AT THE TOP OF a steep flight of stairs, Ethan set his shoulder against a sloping trapdoor and pushed, the hatch swinging upwards to reveal a sky that had grown heavy and cloud-bruised.

Climbing through, he reached down to help Juliet up beside him. As she straightened, she felt a rush of vertigo. They were standing on a narrow ledge, with the great sweep of the roof falling away below them, and the glass dome rising behind them. There was another dome across the river, where the famous shattered roof of St Paul's rose above the city, a sad monument to the war, patchworked with scaffolding that had been there for years.

'It's all right,' Ethan said, as she clutched his hand, as though he was the only thing stopping her tumbling off into that great expanse of sky. 'You won't fall.' He gestured. 'Look.' The roof wasn't the unbroken curve it appeared to be from below. There were narrow pathways, jutting sills and old chimneys. A few feet away, the ledge gave way to a ridge pole. Ethan drew Juliet towards it, then turned to face her. 'Up high and looking down.' Twining his fingers into hers, he stepped back, without even a glance to check his footing. As Juliet tried to tug away, he gripped her hand more firmly. 'You won't fall, I promise.'

'I can't.'

'You can. Trust me. Just take one step.'

Trust me. He kept saying it, but she didn't know how.

This is how. It was *Olivia* again, impatient but certain.

Juliet's fear was a clenched knot, but somehow she found the first cautious step, curling her feet around the curve of the ridge. It was impossibly narrow, but Ethan's hands were steady on hers. As she inched towards him, he moved back, drawing her along, then gently extracted one of his hands, dropped it to her waist and stepped into their dance.

Juliet stumbled, but Ethan held her tight. *Trust me.* Mustering all her courage, she followed his steps. As she found her balance, and the rhythm of the dance, she felt a sudden lift of elation, her fear loosening its grip. Somewhere out there, beyond the city's grey sprawl, there was still a muffled, muted house, with walls like a strait jacket. But she was here, dancing on the roof of the Theatre District, beneath the great sweep of the sky.

'Look,' Ethan said. 'Across the river.'

A throng of tiny figures was visible, and Juliet could see arms upraised, pointing.

'They can see us.' She faltered, but Ethan's arms tightened around her.

'It doesn't matter,' he said. 'They'll think it's part of the Show. They'll watch for us tomorrow, and the next day. Maybe they'll try a week from now, or come back in a year. If they never see us again, they'll find a way to fit us into whatever story they want to believe.' He looked down at

Juliet, his eyes a much darker grey than usual, reflecting the heavy clouds. 'What do you think they'll say? That we're in love?'

As Juliet's breath caught, Ethan drew her arm above her head, pressing her into a turn. She'd forgotten to be afraid, she realised, joy sparking through her again. With a surge of reckless courage, she went up on her toes and turned again, once, twice, a third time. It wasn't part of the dance, but they weren't in the theatre, following a loop. They were up here, with nothing but the heavens above them, and no one to tell them what to do. When she stepped back into his arms, he smiled at her, and a glow of warmth wrapped out the chill of the evening air.

Drawing the dance to an end, Ethan placed his hands on either side of her face, thumbs stroking her cheekbones, then leaned down and pressed a kiss onto her lips. For a moment, Juliet was frozen, unable to breathe. Then, driven by some instinct, her lips parted. For the briefest of instants, his tongue brushed hers, the strange intimacy of it jolting through her, and then he stepped back and smiled. It was a tilted, mischievous smile, accompanied by a swift look at those tiny figures across the river.

'That will give them something to think about,' he said.

That warmth was swept aside by a cold rush of embarrassment. The wind pressed its advantage, chilling a shiver from her bare shoulders. He'd been playing a role, but she'd kissed him back as though it was real. Desperately, she cast around for something she could say to show him that she knew it hadn't meant anything. Her gaze fell on the figures across the river.

'Why do they keep coming back?' She tried to keep her voice light. 'Surely at some point they'll have seen everything there is to see.'

Ethan shook his head. 'That would take more time than any of them have. And it's about more than that, anyway.' His expression was contemplative. 'I think a lot of them – the ones who come back over and over – are lost in some way. Wanting to belong. They think if they can just get close enough, some hidden door will open up and let them in. They'd unzip us and climb inside us, if they could.' He was silent for a moment, looking out across the river, and then he turned, abruptly, towards the hatch. 'We should go back down.'

*

Back in the attic, Ethan was brisk, running through what would happen next. The Director had agreed to give her a couple of days off before she tried another performance. She'd be sent a schedule. Then he was gone, leaving a stagehand to show her out.

As Juliet walked home, she couldn't work out how to feel about anything that had happened. All her emotions seemed to come with a *yes but* attached to them. The one straightforwardly good thing was that the time off meant there was no need to mention the funeral; she hadn't been sure whether Ethan would approve of her dipping back into her old life.

Back at the house, she found an envelope addressed to her on the hall table. Inside was the list of days and times Ethan had mentioned.

A voice spoke from behind her. 'That's the second one. He must be keen.' Sally was standing in the kitchen doorway, her hands wrapped round a mug.

'He?' Juliet's thoughts leaped to Ethan.

'That nice young man with the enticingly broad shoulders who called by a few days ago. I assume that's from him.'

'Oh, yes.' Juliet felt around for a lie that wouldn't come back to bite her. 'He's just someone I used to know. I'll get in touch when I have a chance.'

'Quite right,' Sally said. 'Keep him hanging. It'll make him keener.' She took a sip of her tea. 'You're in demand at the moment. Eugene was asking about you earlier.' She nodded towards the kitchen. 'Kettle's just boiled if you fancy a cup of tea and a natter.'

Juliet was on the edge of accepting when she remembered the warning Danes had given her.

You are the secret.

'I've got a few things to do,' she said. 'Sorry.'

Chapter 22

THE TRAIN WAS LATE, and Juliet got to St Augustine's just before the service began.

The church was full of people she was sure her father couldn't have named, and a black-suited usher directed her to the back row. From there, Juliet could see her stepmother and half-sisters at the front. On the train, it had occurred to her that Miss Abbeline might be here. There was no sign of her old teacher, but Juliet did see two familiar faces. DI Mansfield and DC Lambert were sitting on the other side of the church, the senior officer seemingly looking for someone. Juliet's heart gave a guilty thump, and she dropped her gaze, pretending to study the hymns on the sheet.

The minister spent some time talking about death in general terms, before moving on to the specific death of Stephen Grace, extolling his wife's virtues, and holding his daughters in God's love and light. Juliet wondered if she would be mentioned, or if her stepmother had decided to quietly sweep her existence under the carpet. There was an odd almost-pleasure to that idea. When they all filed out, she'd go over to her stepmother and offer her condolences, as calm and polite as any other mourner. Everyone would see, and they'd take away the memory of her graciousness in the face of her stepmother's petty spite.

'. . . and we pray for his daughter, Juliet, and ask that God grant her solace.'

Juliet was brought up short, and as the minister moved on, she felt a flicker of resentment. Her stepmother couldn't even allow her the satisfaction of not being cared about in a suitably dramatic and public way.

After the minister had assured the congregation that Stephen would live forever in the glory of God, Juliet slipped out of the church, ignoring the usher as he hissed at her to wait until the family had left. She'd been intending to go to the reception afterwards, to collect her things and say goodbye to Rebecca and Elizabeth, but now she was here, she couldn't imagine setting foot in that house again.

*

The Academy looked different now Juliet knew where Miss Abbeline had come from. When she rang the bell, there was a swift clip of footsteps, then the door opened.

One of the assistants looked out, her expression of courteous expectation giving way to slightly startled recognition. 'Juliet. Mrs Grace said you'd moved away.'

'I did,' Juliet said. 'I'm just back for the day. Is Miss Abbeline here?'

'Come in.' The young woman held the door open. 'She's doing paperwork, but I'm sure she'll want to see you.'

She led Juliet upstairs. 'Juliet Grace to see you, Miss Abbeline.'

Juliet caught the sharpness of the teacher's glance, before Miss Abbeline smoothed it into milder lines of polite surprise.

'Juliet,' she said. 'How lovely. Do sit down. I didn't expect to see you back here. I understood you'd moved to London.'

'I'm just back for the funeral.' Juliet took the indicated seat. 'I thought you might be there.'

'I don't think your stepmother would have liked that.'

'Because you came from the Theatre District,' Juliet said. 'Like him.'

'Yes.' The reply was calm.

'I'm living there now.' There was a certain power in speaking openly like this. 'In the precincts.'

Miss Abbeline nodded. 'And how are you finding the district?'

She might have been asking about a seaside holiday.

'It was strange at first.' Juliet settled on a neutral answer. 'But I'm starting to understand how it works.'

'Are you.' It didn't sound like a question, and was accompanied by what seemed like a sceptical tip of Miss Abbeline's head.

'Yes.' Juliet met her look for look. 'I am.'

Miss Abbeline glanced down at her desk, brushing her hand across the polished wood. 'Why are you here, Juliet?' she said. 'What do you want from me?'

The direct question knocked Juliet slightly off balance. 'My parents,' she said, eventually. 'I want to know what happened to my mother, and why my father took me away.'

'What did the Director tell you?' Miss Abbeline took a small sip from a glass of water, before replacing it beside a small brass clock Juliet didn't remember seeing there before. It had multiple dials, all showing the wrong time and date. It was out of character for the principal to allow such imprecision. 'I assume you have asked him.'

'He won't tell me.' Miss Abbeline had clearly guessed that Juliet's association with the district went beyond living in the precincts. 'He said not until we know each other better.'

Miss Abbeline gave a tight smile. 'Yes, that sounds like something Conrad would say.' She tilted her head. 'What do you think of him?'

There was something in the way Miss Abbeline was watching her that made Juliet think of the fencing classes she'd taken here at the Academy. She could still remember what the instructor had said about the opening seconds of a bout.

You're not trying to score points. You're just trying to see where there might be points for the taking when the time comes.

'You've known him longer than I have,' she said.

Miss Abbeline nodded. 'Yes, I knew him. But I haven't seen him in years. There was little he wasn't prepared to do to secure the directorship. I've often wondered what he's done to hold on to it. After all, there's always someone waiting in the wings to step into that particular spotlight. A Ballard, perhaps. That's the usual pattern.'

'The usual pattern?'

'You know how the directorship works?' Miss Abbeline turned her head. 'No? In theory, any resident can put themselves forward, but there's never been an appointment from outside one of the five Director families. The Blythes are cautious, methodical. They'll build, but in a careful, brick-by-brick way that takes years to be noticed, and they don't care if they're remembered. The Carlyles are all about legacy; their name is what counts. The Thackerays are real showmen. It's the spectacle for them, the dazzle and illusion. Then there are the Ballards. They're businessmen, the ones who count the pennies, and turn them into pounds. They're ruthless, cold as ice, but they've seen the district through some of its hardest times. The Danes have always been the storytellers, the dreamers, the ones with the greatest affinity for the Show. They're responsible for many of the district's most enduring storylines. They're not always financially astute, but when the district is tired of being cautious and inward-looking, the Danes family comes into its own. It was always going to be a Danes this time round. Old Phineas Ballard steered the district through the Great War and the years that followed. A quarter of a century of that sort of austerity was long enough for people to start thinking it was time for something different. Something more hopeful.' When she smiled, there was something Juliet couldn't interpret in the curl of her mouth. 'It just wasn't clear which form of hope they'd choose.'

'What do you mean?'

'The board was split over his appointment,' Miss Abbeline said. 'In theory, all residents can vote, but, in practice, it's always left to the Directors and the heads of the various departments. Conrad only won by a single vote. His rival was a member of the Danes family too, although she didn't carry the name.'

She.

A flare ignited in Juliet's head. 'You. You're a Danes.'

'My mother was,' Miss Abbeline replied. 'My father was a distant cousin, but he didn't have the Danes name. It shouldn't have mattered. I'd shown I could lead the district.' She gave another of those cynical smiles. 'Of course, there's never been a female Director. The very idea was enough to put a cat very firmly among certain directorial pigeons.' The smile faded. 'I knew I had a fight on my hands, but I could have won it. I just didn't anticipate having to fight Conrad. We'd planned it for years. I'd be Director, and he'd be my right-hand man. But, in the end, it was Conrad who convinced them I wasn't what they needed. That he was.' Her expression was neutral, but Juliet thought she could glimpse another story behind Miss Abbeline's tale of political scheming. 'So much for the loyalties of youth.' Her tone grew brisk. 'Anyway, Conrad secured the swing vote, and, with it the Directorship.'

'So you left.' Juliet was feeling her way around this revelation, trying to work out where it fitted with everything else she'd learned. 'You just walked away.'

Miss Abbeline raised an eyebrow. 'Could you have stayed and watched someone else in the role you thought would be yours? I had it all planned out, everything I'd do, the changes I'd make.'

'To the Show?' Juliet asked.

Miss Abbeline glanced away. 'That too.'

'But why . . .' Juliet made a vague gesture, indicating the office, and the school beyond it. 'Why . . . this?'

'It's the same thing, when you come down to it.' Miss Abbeline gave a small shrug. 'Just with higher necklines and longer skirts. I teach them to play the roles they need to play. I teach them how to tell a story, and how to spot the stories other people are telling them. The world is what it is, but if they understand how people work, then they have some control.' She smiled. 'It's a tiny rebellion, I suppose, but who knows? Maybe it will change that world one day.'

'You mean you're teaching them to lie,' Juliet said. 'To put on a performance.'

'Yes, that's exactly what I'm doing,' Miss Abbeline replied calmly. 'All the world's a stage, after all.'

It sounded like a quote, but Juliet didn't recognise it. 'Who said that?'

'A young poet called William Shakespeare,' Miss Abbeline replied. 'He could have been great, I think, but he tried to set up as a rival to the Theatre District. He ended his days as a pauper, having sold every word he wrote to the district.' She returned to her previous point. 'Everybody lies. Everybody, everywhere, every day. People decide what they want the world to think, and that's what you see. I just tune that instinct until my girls can wield it at will.' She tilted her head. 'I'm not sure how well I managed with you. But then you were always looking elsewhere, weren't you?' There was a hint of compassion in her expression. 'I don't blame you. It couldn't have been easy, growing up in that house.'

'You knew my father,' Juliet said. 'Back in the district, I mean.'

Miss Abbeline nodded. 'Yes, although it was a few years before he turned up here. He did some work for me, and I gave you a place here.'

'Do you know why he left?'

'Yes.' Miss Abbeline's gaze was steady.

Juliet took a hard breath in. 'What happened?'

The older woman shook her head. 'I can't tell you that.'

'Can't?' Juliet felt a stab of angry frustration. 'Or won't?'

'You say that as if they're two distinct things.' Miss Abbeline reached for her glass and took another sip, the precision of the gesture irking Juliet. 'It was a long time ago, and there's no reason to revisit it.'

'I'm the reason,' Juliet said heatedly. 'I can't trust my own memory because he lied about everything. And no one will tell me the whole truth.'

'No one ever tells the whole truth,' Miss Abbeline said. 'They just give you their version of it – if they give you anything. I can't help you. Not with that. But I can offer you some advice.' She fixed Juliet with another level gaze. 'Walk away from the Theatre District. Whatever promises Conrad has made you, walk away and make a life for yourself somewhere else.'

'Why would I leave?' Juliet stared at her teacher. 'The district is where I belong.'

'It isn't,' Miss Abbeline said sharply. 'No one belongs anywhere. It's just something we tell ourselves so we can dig in a bit harder to whatever piece of the world we've decided to call home.'

'Home.' Juliet's voice shook on that word. 'I've never *had* a home.'

'And that's what he's promised you,' Miss Abbeline said. 'Isn't it? He's dangling it in front of you, so you'll dance to whatever tune he chooses to play. And I know exactly what tune that is.' When she smiled, it was a bare twist of her mouth. 'But you should be careful of Conrad's promises. He doesn't give them freely.'

She glanced at the clock on her desk as she spoke, and Juliet felt another flare of anger. 'I'm sorry I'm taking up your valuable time.'

'I have plenty of time,' Miss Abbeline said. 'But you don't, Juliet. Every day you stay in Conrad's district, there'll be a little less of you, and a little more of whatever he's decided you should be.'

'He wants me to be the Girl in the Silver Shoes,' Juliet said. 'It's who I was always meant to be.'

'That's true enough,' Miss Abbeline said. 'In a sense, at least. But you don't have to do what he wants. You could go anywhere, be anything.'

'Why are you so set on me leaving?' Juliet demanded. 'I belong there, no matter what you say, and the Director will tell me the truth one day.'

'One day will never come,' Miss Abbeline said. 'But by the time you realise that, it will be too late.'

Juliet shook her head. 'I shouldn't have come here.' She gathered herself, drawing on the chilly courtesy she'd learned in this very building. 'I'm sorry to have troubled you, Miss Abbeline.'

Chapter 23

JULIET EMERGED FROM THE Academy to find DC Lambert leaning against a nearby wall.

'Miss Grace.' He straightened up. 'I didn't manage to catch you at the funeral. You'll have to forgive me for following you.' He paused. 'I left a message at the address your stepmother gave us.'

'I'm sorry.' Juliet didn't meet his eyes. 'It wasn't passed on.'

'Seems to be a lot of it about.' His tone was wry, and Juliet stiffened. He made a conciliatory gesture. 'It's all right. I gathered there were good reasons you hadn't been back for cosy Sunday lunches. Your stepmother wasn't terribly forthcoming.'

'About what?'

Lambert glanced away. 'Can we find somewhere for a cup of tea?'

'I need to get the train to London,' Juliet said.

'So do I.' His smile told her he knew perfectly well that he'd side-stepped an intended brush-off. 'The DI has taken the car.'

'Why didn't you go with him?' Juliet asked bluntly.

'Because he wanted me to speak to you,' he replied, equally bluntly, pushing his hands into his pockets. 'We can find somewhere near the station, or maybe you'd prefer to talk on the train?'

Juliet very definitely did not want to field questions all the way back to London.

'Fine.' She shoved her hands into her pockets, before registering her unconscious imitation of him, and taking them back out. 'Let's go.'

*

There was a pub round the corner from the station, its frosted windows etched with the name of a brewery, the elaborate lettering giving a promise of grandeur that the interior failed to deliver. The walls were covered in peeling wood chip, and the carpet almost certainly hadn't started life that mottled yellow-beige. There was a row of scratched wooden booths to one side and, through the door opposite, Juliet could see a mismatched selection of tables and stools.

Lambert nodded towards the door. 'Grab a table. I'll go to the bar. Tea or coffee?'

Juliet wanted to refuse – this wasn't a social outing – but she was cold. 'Tea, please.'

She sat down at a corner table, and shortly afterwards, Lambert appeared, holding two chipped and steaming mugs. He passed one to her, and took a sip from the other, before grimacing. 'I don't think they get many requests for hot drinks. They've probably been using the same teabag all week.'

His casual manner grated on Juliet. She put her mug down and looked straight at him.

'What do you want, DC Lambert?'

Lambert gave a small nod. 'Cards on the table. We know your father was once a resident of the Theatre District. The last time we met, you said you'd never been there, but just days later, you turn up living in the district precincts. So, what do you know?'

'You first.' Juliet met his gaze. 'You came looking for me, after all.'

Lambert gave another – reluctant – nod. 'I suppose that's fair. Twenty years ago, DI Mansfield went to the Theatre District after an actress was seen to fall from a gallery. He was met with the usual obfuscation and citing of rights and privileges.' His mouth twisted. '*Powers to investigate crimes committed by persons not resident, or against persons not resident.* That's the legal position. Beyond that, you get what the district authorities choose to let you have. Mansfield pushed the matter as hard as he could, crossing all sorts of lines, and probably doing irreparable damage to his career in the process. Eventually the Director, Conrad Danes, produced a young, red-haired actress who said her name was Madeleine Austin . . .'

Austin. Juliet seized upon that snippet of information. 'And she played the character known as the Moonshine Girl. She confirmed she was the performer involved in the incident, but declined to answer any questions about what had happened. Conrad Danes also refused to give further details, stating that he couldn't reveal district secrets to an outsider. DI Mansfield wanted to continue investigating, but instructions came from higher up that he was to close the case. And that was the end of it.'

'But it wasn't,' Juliet said. 'Why did he come looking for me after all these years? And why are you so keen to talk to me?'

'Your father was there that night,' Lambert said. 'He was toeing the party line – smoke and mirrors and so on – but Mansfield thought he was hiding something. To be fair, he was convinced everyone in that place was hiding something, but there was more of that *something* about your father.' He swirled his tea around his mug. 'Why did the DI come looking for you? There's more than one answer to that question. The simple one is that we have an ongoing interest in the Theatre District, and it's almost impossible to talk to anyone connected with the place. The other answer is because he's a police officer.' There was a hint of sadness in his expression. 'Most officers have something they can't let go of – unsolved cases, things they think they got wrong.'

'But it wasn't unsolved,' Juliet said. 'The Moonshine Girl was alive.'

'It's not just about that specific investigation,' Lambert replied. 'There have been a number of other cases over the years. Deaths – mainly young women – going back centuries. The bodies were all found near the district, many of them in the river, and the ones who were identified all turned out to have spent time there.'

'I've heard this story.' Juliet injected a note of scorn into her voice. 'What do the police call him? The Knockerman? The Lambeth Stalker? Or something else?'

Lambert shook his head. 'There's never been any official suggestion of a link between the cases.' He swirled his tea again. 'But the Theatre District is a strange place. And while *strange* doesn't automatically mean *guilty,* there have been plenty of officers over the years who thought there was a pattern to the deaths. There's even supposed to be a stash of papers in the archives – statements, reports, information about the district.'

His words summoned up an unsettling image – a dark passageway, lined with filing cabinets filled with the work of men who hated the Theatre District, like a shadow version of the Shipping News.

'I don't see what any of this has to do with . . .' Juliet tripped over a near disclosure '. . . with the Moonshine Girl. She didn't die.'

'No, she didn't.' Lambert didn't seem to have noticed her stumble. 'But Mansfield was convinced she was part of the pattern.'

'Why?' Juliet asked.

'I think it had less to do with the circumstances of the . . .' Lambert hesitated, as though searching for the right word '. . . incident, and more to do with the way the district *is*. There was something about that night that niggled at him. That niggle bedded in deeper when he was told both Stephen and Madeleine had left the district. He tracked Stephen down a couple of years later. He was working as a stage manager for a dance company in the midlands, and living with one of the principals. He denied his reasons for leaving had anything to do with the incident, and claimed to have no idea where Madeleine might have gone. He also made no mention of having a daughter. A few days later, he disappeared again, and the DI couldn't find any trace of him. Not until a contact on the local force sent him the notice of your father's death, which was the first he knew of your existence.'

Juliet took a sip of her tea, not tasting it. She was trying to make sense of the timeline. When Mansfield spoke to her father, she'd been in the district, walking the wires, and writing herself into the stories of the place. Stephen must have come back for her. But why?

'What about Madeleine Austin?' she said. 'Did he find her?'

Lambert shook his head. 'Not a trace.'

'Could she still have been in the district?'

'She could,' Lambert said. 'But she apparently disappeared from the Show not long after the incident. If I had to come down on one side or the other, I'd say it was likely she did leave.'

'Or died.' Juliet curled her fingers around her mug.

'Perhaps,' Lambert said. 'But if she did, it doesn't seem to have had anything to do with the incident Mansfield was investigating.'

'So why are you here?' The conversation was going round in circles.

Lambert didn't reply straight away, and when he eventually spoke, there was a pinch of determination about his lips. 'DI Mansfield is a good officer. I've worked with him since I joined the force, and I don't want to see him drawn back into something I don't think will ever be solved. That's why I volunteered to come and talk to you. Which, of course, brings me back to my original question. What *do* you know? Just now, when I mentioned your father being from the district, that clearly wasn't new information. Either you were lying when we spoke to you the first time – and doing a very good job of it – or you've figured it out since.'

'I did some digging after your visit.' It was almost true. 'I found some things he'd kept – an old mask and a necklace.' She didn't mention the photo. 'And there was a letter from the record office.'

'A letter?'

'It said my birth was registered in the Theatre District. That's why I went to London. To try and find out what happened.'

'And have you?' Lambert said.

'No.' Juliet tightened her grip on her mug.

'Have you spoken to anyone?' he asked. 'In the district, I mean?'

'No.' The lie was a chill in her fingertips. 'I didn't know how to find anyone to ask.'

He gave a slight smile. 'You're not the first to have that problem.' The smile faded. 'You said you didn't know who your mother was. Was that true?'

'Yes.'

'Is it still true?'

'Yes.'

'Could Madeleine Austin have been your mother?'

Juliet hesitated, trying to work out the safest fork to take.

'Possibly,' she said eventually. 'I don't know how I'd ever find out.' She made herself shrug. 'I'm probably not going to stay in the precincts much longer.'

Lambert raised his eyebrows. 'So, that's it? You're just going to walk away?'

'What else am I supposed to do?' Juliet pushed into an attack, hoping to steer the conversation onto another topic. 'I don't understand what we're doing here, DC Lambert. You say you don't want DI Mansfield to keep investigating the Theatre District, and you don't think there's anything to investigate anyway. What do you want from me?'

'I said I wasn't sure,' Lambert said. 'Not that . . .' He rubbed at his face with his hands. 'Sorry. I'm not doing a very good job of this. When you're training to be a police officer, they talk about motive, method, intent, like you're measuring out ingredients in a cake. But it's not like that. Some crimes are never solved. Some are solved, but with loose ends. Sometimes you can't even work out if they're crimes at all.' He looked down at the table where his tea had left a damp ring. Drawing his finger across it, he flicked the edges out into a symmetrical sunburst. 'If you go through old cases, you start to notice how often the Theatre District is mentioned. It's always in passing, never at the heart of things. But if you spend enough time looking at it, you begin to think you can see the shape of something.'

'Something that isn't there,' Juliet pressed. 'That's what you're saying, isn't it?'

'Maybe,' Lambert said. 'There's no evidence linking the Theatre District to any of those deaths. No resident of the district has been arrested in the entire history of the Metropolitan Police. No crime has ever been recorded in the district.' He gave a cynical smile. 'That, in itself, is enough to make me wonder about the place.' He hesitated, clearly picking his words carefully. 'All I'm saying is, if there is nothing, it's a *nothing* that's felt awfully like *something* to a lot of people over a lot of years.'

'Including DI Mansfield.' Something occurred to Juliet. 'Should he even have come to the house that day?' DC Lambert lowered his gaze. 'I didn't think so. So now we've spoken, what will you tell him?'

'What you told me,' he replied. 'That you don't know any more than we do. That's right, isn't it?'

'Yes.'

'And if that changes, you'll be in touch.' Lambert gave her a steady look. 'That's also right, isn't it?'

'Yes.'

Lambert drained the last of his tea, setting the mug down on the table. 'There was another reason I wanted to speak to you,' he said. 'I want you to be careful, while you are living in the precincts.'

Juliet raised an eyebrow. 'The Knockerman?'

'A dead girl.' His voice was sharp. 'Pulled out of the river not far from where you're staying. And others before her.'

'I thought you said the cases weren't linked.'

'They're not,' he said. 'Not officially. But I'm not *officially* warning you to take care. I'm just . . . asking.'

Juliet shrugged. 'From what you've told me, the district might just be the safest place I could be. No residents ever arrested. No crimes committed.'

'Reported,' he said sharply.

She ignored him. 'It sounds considerably safer than the rest of the city you're supposed to be protecting.'

'I apologise for the failings of the Metropolitan Police.' His tone was cool. 'We do our best with the resources available.'

Juliet felt a twinge of guilt. He'd been more open with her than anyone else, and his concern seemed genuine.

'I have to go.' She put her mug down. 'There's nothing more I can tell you.'

He nodded. 'All right. There should be a train in a few minutes.'

'I'm going to wait for the next one,' Juliet said. 'There are a few things I need to do.'

Outside the pub, they said a stiff goodbye. Juliet was just about to turn away when Lambert reached into his pocket.

'I don't know if you still have the card the DI gave you, but here's mine.' He handed it to her. 'If anything worries you, get in touch.'

As Juliet watched him walk away, she felt a little pang, not quite of loneliness, but of something not too far removed. There was still so much she didn't know. Yes, he'd given her some more pieces of the puzzle – her father was there when Madeleine didn't fall, and he'd met DI Mansfield a couple of years later – but it felt like one of those mathematical equations she'd never been able to solve, where you had x and y and had to work out what z was.

Then there were those vague stories of decades-long police suspicions. He'd as good as admitted it was nonsense, but it had left her with a low churn of unease, particularly coming so hard on the heels of that conversation with Miss Abbeline.

Pushing the card into her pocket, Juliet turned and walked along the street. She'd probably never see him again, and if he thought of her, it would just be with a flicker of professional curiosity.

Oh yes, that girl from the district. What was her name again? I wonder what happened to her?

Chapter 24

JULIET'S SECOND PERFORMANCE PASSED without incident, despite her nerves.

None of the other performers were there for their shared scenes, and she had no audience for the first two loops. In the third, she picked up a single follower who only stayed with her until the stairs to the platform, leaving her torn between relief and a sense of abandonment.

The fourth loop was the last. As she crossed the little square, a door opened, and she slipped off the set. A stagehand led her to her dressing room, and waited while she changed, then showed her out.

As she walked home, Juliet felt oddly flat. She'd thought Ethan might be there to meet her when she finished. He'd known how much this meant to her. She'd imagined herself talking it through with him, analysing every detail. The way the audience member had looked at her. The way she'd felt as the loops played out. She'd pictured him smiling and taking her hand and saying, *See? I told you, you can do this. You belong here.*

*

Another three days came and went. Her performances were all late – from around midnight until the deserted pre-dawn hours – and, while she might have an audience during the early loops, she tended to finish her shift entirely alone. Arlen only appeared a couple of times, and Jemima and Ethan not at all. She hadn't seen the latter since the day after her first disastrous performance, and she knew she probably had to resign herself to rarely encountering him on the set. He was a popular performer, and most of his shifts no doubt ended after the evening peak.

On the fourth night, Juliet had a slightly earlier performance, with the set only just starting to empty out as she stepped onto it. Near the start, she picked up a sizeable group, and, after her initial nerves, began to enjoy the attention. They fell away, one by one, as the night tipped over into the early hours of the morning, but three men stayed with her. Their masks were undecorated, but it clearly wasn't their first time at the Show. There was a confidence to the way they moved through the set, seeming to know exactly where to position themselves, and showing no reticence about coming close.

Slightly unnerved, Juliet started altering her scenes slightly, trying to put space between her and the men, but they simply positioned themselves so she couldn't. Through her discomfort, Juliet felt a lick of anger. She was the one who decided how close people were permitted to come, how much of her attention they would receive. As she finished the solo version of her burnt room scene, another masked figure joined the group. The newcomer was small and plump, her mask standard-issue. As she hesitated just inside the door, one of the men glanced at her, and Juliet saw his lip curl beneath his mask. It reminded her of the way Esme looked when she talked about people who weren't as deserving of all the Show had to offer as she was.

Pushed into a swift recklessness, Juliet moved towards the girl, who took a nervous step back, one hand fluttering up apologetically. Stepping in close, Juliet slid her fingertips under the edge of the girl's mask and lifted it up. Brown eyes stared back at her out of a pale face. The girl looked naked, vulnerable, and Juliet felt an unexpected stirring of tenderness. She'd seen other performers touch the faces of those they picked out, or whisper in their ears, but with that tender feeling pressing behind her ribs, it seemed like the most natural thing in the world to lean forward and press a slow, gentle kiss onto the girl's lips.

Some prudish, suburban part of her was rigid with shock, but Juliet didn't care. The only rules here were the ones you wrote for yourself, the only boundaries the ones you chose. Remembering how Ethan's mouth had felt against hers, she let the kiss linger, until the girl's lips begin to part in what might have been a sigh, or something else entirely. Then she pulled back, holding the girl's gaze as she replaced her mask, before turning away with a small, knowing smile.

The men were still there, watching. As Juliet moved towards the door, she thought there was a stiffness in their stances that looked less like disappointment, and more like something close to anger. With a little lift of triumph, Juliet stepped through the door, glancing back over her shoulder, to see the girl standing still where she'd left her. Her arms were wrapped tightly around her body, as though if she let go, the moment might slip away and never have happened at all.

The men stayed with Juliet as she moved on, speeding up the next scenes slightly to make up the lost time, but they no longer came as close. That triumph was still sounding in Juliet, and when a new visitor found them, she saw the glint of another opportunity. Moving close to the fair-haired woman, Juliet lifted her mask and looked straight into her eyes.

Cold flooded her lungs, her chest clenching.

Ethan's voice sounded in her head, twisted into a discordant alarm.

Keep yourself a secret. Don't let anyone close.

But Esme was standing *so* close that she couldn't fail to identify Juliet, even through the stage make-up. The flash of recognition came swiftly, followed by a flare of shock. Juliet froze, and then, with an effort, dragged herself into movement. Leaning forward, she brushed a cold kiss to the other girl's cheek before replacing her mask with trembling fingers.

Juliet turned away, the men parting grudgingly to let her through. She didn't look back to see if Esme was following. Her heart was a staccato thud, and she could barely remember what came next in her loop.

Focus.

She had to be perfect. She had to be the brightest and best thing on this set, so that if the Director found out what she'd done, he'd forgive her for the sake of the Girl in the Silver Shoes and the Moonshine Girl and the story he was weaving and he wouldn't send her way, he wouldn't . . .

Focus, for God's sake.

Olivia's voice was whip-sharp.

Juliet tried, but the next scene was a blur, her dances ragged. The three men were still there, but Esme had gone, and there was a high-pitched buzzing in Juliet's head as she considered all the things the other girl could be doing, all the people she could be telling.

As she stepped into the cloistered square, her heart gave a thump. Ethan was walking towards her, flanked by two audience members in decorated masks and flowered dresses. The forlorn hope that tried to tear free was swiftly dragged down: he'd promised to help, but he hadn't meant this. When he reached her, he didn't take her hand and step into their dance. Instead, he stood still for a long moment, looking down at her. His face was expressionless. Then, with a swift, almost violent movement, he stepped forward, pulling her against him, so she had to lift her head to look up at him. As their gazes met, he tipped her back, arching her spine around the press of his hand. His lips grazed her neck for the barest of instants, and then he drew her up again, and turned to lead her across the square to a small door.

Juliet's men didn't follow, but the girls in the flowery dresses almost tripped over one another in their haste. They would give anything to be in her place right now, and in that moment, Juliet would have gladly yielded it. Ethan knew something had happened. There'd been no warmth in his eyes as he'd looked at her, and there was a slight ache in her back where he'd bent it too far. It felt like a punishment, although she knew he couldn't have meant to hurt her.

Ethan let go of her to open the door, and she stumbled into a room hung with tapestries, the floor covered with woven rugs. He locked the door, then turned to look at her. Behind him, the handle twisted.

'Why did you go off-script?' He kept his voice low, but his anger was clear.

'There were some men.' Juliet's mouth was dry. 'They were too close, and I—'

'Everyone wants to be close. I told you that.'

'But they kept getting in my way,' Juliet said. 'I thought the stagehands—'

'The stagehands intervene when there's a need for it.' Ethan cut across her. 'If they don't, then it's for a good reason.'

'I'm sorry.' Juliet was trying to unwind the panicked coil of her thoughts. He had no idea that Esme knew Juliet. He would have said so, surely. 'I promise it won't happen again.'

'It can't,' he said sharply. 'You have to follow the rules, or this won't work.'

'I'm sorry,' she said again. When his expression didn't soften, she took a couple of faltering steps towards him, hoping he would relent and hold her. Then she could cry, as she had that other time, and he'd forgive her and everything would be all right. 'I will, I promise. I'll do whatever you want me to do.'

He hadn't moved, but something stirred in his eyes as he looked at her. With desperate recklessness, Juliet stepped in close, going up on her toes, and tilting her head back. For a moment, he didn't respond, then, with a swift wrench, he pulled her against him, crushing his mouth to hers.

This wasn't like the kiss on the roof, and it wasn't like the kisses Juliet had imagined when she was younger. Those fantasies had been chaste, unthreatening things, bearing as much resemblance to the real thing as illustrations in some textbook. But there were no accompanying instructions. Juliet had no idea how to kiss him back. She didn't know where to put her hands. She felt weak – not weak at the knees, like the heroines in books – but shaky all over, as though she might pass out. She almost wished she *could* faint: it seemed like the only way out. She'd wanted him to kiss her, but not like this. His mouth was hard on hers, and one of his hands was winding into her hair, the other against the base of her spine, forcing her closer to him.

This was passion, she thought. There must be something wrong with her if she couldn't feel it. Perhaps it was just because it was the first time. If she let him keep kissing her, maybe she'd start to feel how she was supposed to feel. She had no choice, anyway. She couldn't tell him to stop when she was the one who'd started this.

His hand had moved round to find the top button at the front of her dress. That tiny button swelled in her mind, until she was sure he wouldn't be able to fit it through the buttonhole. But it came undone, as did the next one. The third button snagged, and she wasn't sure if she'd imagined the tiny clink as it fell to the ground. Every sound, every breath, every sensation seemed heightened and stretched out, giving her time to examine each detail. It should have given *Olivia* space to tell Juliet what she thought – *This is what you wanted*, she'd say. *This is everything you wanted from him* – but there was silence in her head. A vast, loud silence. *Olivia* wasn't here. The Girl in the Silver Shoes wasn't here. There was only Juliet, intensely, starkly alone, despite being closer to someone than she'd ever been before.

As Ethan laid a line of kisses down her exposed breastbone, Juliet was cold, almost shivering. His mouth reached the fabric of her dress, and he kissed his way back up again. As he did, his lips just grazed the edge of her breast. That cold grew sharper, more acute, and this time the shiver broke through.

Ethan lifted his head and looked at her. Whatever he saw, it made him take a slow breath in, and he stepped back, lifting his hands to rub at his face.

Juliet reached up to tug the fabric of her bodice across. The movement felt clumsy, too big for the little room. Ethan turned away, and she felt a stab of guilt. She wanted to tell him she hadn't meant it; she just hadn't known what else to do. But then he'd think she was some stupid little girl who had no idea how these things worked. Tentatively, she reached up and touched his shoulder.

'Ethan.' There was no response. 'I'm sorry. I thought . . .' As she searched for words, he gave a small sigh, and reached over his shoulder to take her hand, holding on to it as he turned back to her.

'It's all right.' He gave her a lopsided smile, but there was a bruised hurt in his eyes. 'I just thought . . .' He shook his head. 'It doesn't matter.' Juliet desperately wanted to tell him that it did matter, that it mattered more than anything. For a moment, she considered leaning up to kiss him again, in the hope she could get it right this time. But

Ethan had let go of her hand. 'We need to get back to the set,' he said. 'But listen to me first. You have to stay on-script. I know I told you there's room to make the role your own, but you're trying to run before you can walk.'

'I'm sorry.' Juliet wasn't sure which part of it the apology was for.

Ethan's expression softened again. Dipping his head, he dropped the barest brush of a kiss onto her mouth, before reaching for the door. Juliet wanted to cry. There'd been something like regret in that kiss, making it feel like an ending. Swallowing against the tightness in her throat, she quickly fastened her buttons.

Ethan led her to a room near the end of her loop, and left her there, with a last sweep of his fingertips over hers. Juliet didn't know whether that fleeting touch had come from *him* or the Shadow Man, and she couldn't think about it now. Somehow, she found the rhythm again, playing out the last scenes of that loop in empty rooms. Then the usual stage door opened, and she stepped off the set. The stagehand who met her gave no sign of knowing that anything had happened, although it must have been one of them who'd alerted Ethan.

They're always watching.

The stagehand led her to her dressing room, and then, when she was changed, back to the little dead-end passage, leaving her to make her way out of the theatre. With those airless moments in that too-small room playing over and over in her head, she'd almost forgotten what had led to them in the first place, when Esme stepped out of the shadows of a narrow alley, blocking her path.

'Well,' she said. 'That was very . . . enlightening.' As Juliet stared at her, she raised her eyebrows. 'Cat got your tongue?'

'Please.' Juliet forced the words out, her mouth dry. 'Please don't say anything. I promised I wouldn't tell anyone.'

'You haven't told me anything,' Esme said. 'But you're going to. All of it.'

Juliet gave a sharp shake of her head. 'I can't.'

Esme shrugged, as though none of this mattered. 'Fine. I'll just head back to the house and tell Sally and Anna everything I saw tonight. It will be all round the district tomorrow.' She smiled. 'I mean, you won't mind that, will you? It's not as though I saw you go white, even through all that make-up, when you recognised me.'

'You can't.' Juliet was fighting to keep control of her ever-rising panic. 'You can't tell anyone. Esme, please.' It was humiliating, having to beg, but the alternative was unthinkable. 'I'll do anything you want. Just don't tell anyone.'

'What I *want* is to know how this happened.' Esme's gaze was flint-hard. 'Either you tell me, or I tell everyone.'

Juliet was thinking frantically. She had to tell Esme something that would satisfy her, if she was going to have any chance of persuading the other girl to keep her secret. It couldn't be the truth, of course, but she couldn't risk constructing some complicated story that didn't hold up.

'Something happened at the Show,' she said. 'That night I—' Her half-forgotten lie almost tripped her up. '—the night the Wanderer gave me the tickets . . .'

'Oh, come on.' Esme's voice was scornful. 'We both know that never happened. You bought them, didn't you?' As Juliet gave a humiliated nod, the other girl smiled, cat-satisfied. 'I thought so.'

It took longer than it should have done to give Esme the bones of it. Juliet kept skirting round things she couldn't say, then having to work in some vital piece of information elsewhere. Esme listened in silence, although her gaze narrowed every now and again, as though she was considering some particularly flimsy element of the account.

When Juliet finished, the other girl gave a small nod. 'All those rumours. I always knew there was something real behind the rubbish about hidden doors and secret codes.' She studied Juliet. 'And it was all because the Shadow Man saw you dancing? There was nothing else?'

'That's what they told me.' Juliet could already feel regret winding about her. Was there some easy lie she could have told? Had she rushed into a disclosure she hadn't needed to make? She had a sense of everything spinning away from her and didn't know how to pull it back.

'Did they say how it usually happens?' Esme asked.

'It doesn't,' Juliet said. 'This was . . .' She stopped, once again teetering on the edge of something she couldn't say, but her near-slip was covered by Esme's scornful laugh.

'Don't be ridiculous,' the other girl said. 'You really think you're the only one in the whole history of the Show to be chosen?' Her mouth twisted. 'You're not that special. Which brings us back to the question of how they select someone. I mean, how many people would be arrogant enough to try and insert themselves into the Show like you did?'

Juliet felt a flare of anger. 'And look what happened.'

'Don't speak to me like that.' There was an answering flame in Esme's eyes. 'You need something from me, or have you forgotten?' She gave a tight smile. 'And I want something from you in exchange.'

'All right.' Juliet tried to steady her voice. 'I'll tell you what I can about the Show. Or if it's private scenes you want, maybe I can—'

'Private scenes.' Esme's laugh was sharp with contempt. 'You think I'd be satisfied with more of what I've already had when I know what else there is for the taking?'

'I don't understand.'

'Then let me spell it out for you,' Esme said. 'I want to meet the Director.'

Juliet stared at her. 'The Director doesn't meet people.'

Esme gave her a withering look. 'Yes, I know. That's why I need an introduction. I want to be in the Show, like you are.' Steel glinted in her eyes. 'And you're going to make it happen for me.'

'I can't,' Juliet said. 'You don't understand. The Director isn't like some manager in a shop, where you just walk in and ask for a job. You can threaten all you like, but I can't do what you want. And if you tell everyone, they'll throw me out, and then I'll be no good to you.' A thought took shape, and she steadied herself. 'Besides, do you really want everyone to know?' As Esme's gaze narrowed, Juliet pressed on. 'Look, I might be able to get you what you want.' *Over my dead body.* 'But you need to give me some time. I'm still new to this myself.'

Esme considered this for a long moment, during which Juliet barely dared to breathe. 'All right,' she said, eventually. 'I'll keep your secret. For now.' Her expression hardened. 'But don't think I'll forget about it.'

Juliet's relief was edged with the cold knowledge that she'd only postponed the problem, and perhaps not that far. There was something shifting behind Esme's eyes – some thought or idea that she hadn't voiced. But even a temporary reprieve was better than the unthinkable alternative.

She felt weak and shaky as she nodded. 'I will. I promise.'

'All right.' Esme turned away, as casually as though they'd been chatting about nothing more than what they'd seen in the Show. 'I'll see you back at home, I suppose.' As she walked towards the end of the alleyway, she glanced back over her shoulder. 'You might want to be careful, out and about this late. You don't want to run into the Knockerman.'

Then she turned the corner and was gone, leaving Juliet brittle with anger, regret and a low thrum of fear.

To whom it may concern,

Further to the recent – somewhat *ahem* animated – discussion about the places in the district where the usual audience-performer roles are reversed, I thought it would be useful to put together a list of locations/descriptions. Please feel free to add anything you think qualifies, whether recurring or one-off. Everyone appears to be in broad agreement that there is some purpose to these events, and if we can compile a full list, perhaps we'll see a pattern.

The Lily Theatre (Behind the Penny Arcade)
Timing – not specific
The scene requires two audience members but the presence of a performer appears to be random/optional. There is a selection of scripts in the ante-room, or you can improvise your own. As long as the door is unlocked, you are free to enter the theatre and perform your scene. If a performer is present, it's usually in the centre of the back row of the stalls, and often the Capetian (although stage lights make identification difficult).

There is a rumour that one Follower was given a token after playing her scene, but no one seems to know the full details.

The Lark Hall
Timing – approximately six minutes into the loop
During the magic show, the Lighterman will pick a member of the audience to come up to the front and

assist in a trick. Once this trick has concluded, he will take the audience member's seat, leaving them to carry on with the show. If they choose not to, he will get up and take over once again. If they do attempt a performance of some sort, he will watch for around four minutes, before returning to the front, bowing to the stand-in, and offering them their choice of a selection of origami models.

The China Vaults
Timing – possibly once a day
If the Sackcloth Geisha is present when an audience member enters the central vault alone, she will take their hand and demonstrate a short series of dance steps. If the audience member attempts to repeat them, she will watch intently, before making any small corrections that are necessary. This 'lesson' will continue for anything up to fifteen minutes, but will end if any other audience member appears. The end of the encounter is abrupt, signalled only by the Geisha walking away, with no indication being given as to her satisfaction – or otherwise – with her pupil.

Please add your own experiences, and let's see if we can crack this!
   Jack
   PS As regards the theory that these scenes represent an audition of some sort, I think we're all looking forward to an announcement of the performance everyone has been auditioning for, and to seeing some of our number pirouetting in tutus.

Chapter 25

A WEEK PASSED, THEN another.

Most days ended with a late-night or early morning performance, all uneventful. Twice, she was summoned to the choreographer's office for tweaks to her loop, small changes to her dances. The second time, her brief solo on the platform was extended slightly, and, to her relief, her dance with Arlen removed altogether. She found it easy enough to pick up the new versions. Performing was becoming instinctive, the role fitting around her like a well-made dress. Sometimes, just for a moment, she'd have the sense that she fitted too, and a feeling of something like peace would settle around her, as she pirouetted between the smiling images of her mother, with the spotlight drifting down to halo her hair. If she could have stayed in the theatre forever, playing out her loop, she might have been happy. But sooner or later the stage door would open, and she'd have to shed the Girl in the Silver Shoes, and shrug on Juliet, with all her worries and fears once again.

She only saw Esme a few times – fleeting encounters in the hallway when her smile glinted, tight and knowing – but she was never far from Juliet's thoughts. She found herself listening for the other girl's footsteps, the sound of her bedroom door or the hard-centred lilt of her laughter. She even went into her room once, opening drawers to touch the smooth satin of her camisoles, the soft cotton of her blouses, as though she might be able to read her intentions in the weave of the fabric she wore against her skin.

Esme wasn't the only thing playing on Juliet's mind. She hadn't seen Ethan since he'd walked away from her on the set that night. She spun myriad imagined scenarios around his absence, all ending with him finding her, telling her he'd wanted to see her but something beyond his control had intervened. But no matter how hard she tried to believe those stories, *Olivia* was always ready to point out the weaknesses and inconsistencies, and Juliet couldn't find a way to silence her. It felt as though the more tired and anxious she became, the stronger *Olivia* grew.

Late one afternoon, she was alone in the house when there was a knock at the door. When she answered it, Eugene was standing on the doorstep.

'Hello, stranger,' he said. 'I got away from work early, so thought I'd call by on my way to the Shipping News, and see if I could persuade you to join me. We haven't seen you there for ages.'

'I've been busy.' Juliet's heart had lifted at the sight of him, only to tighten swiftly into the nervous flutter she so often felt now. *Don't let people get too close.* 'Sorry, I can't make it tonight. I have something to do.' As his face fell slightly, Juliet felt a pang of regret, and found herself saying, 'I've got a bit of time now. Would you like a cup of tea?'

Eugene brightened. 'I've got a better idea. There's a rare bit of sun out there.' He jerked his head in the direction of the river. 'Why don't we go for a walk? Get some colour in your cheeks.' His own face flushed. 'Sorry, I don't . . . I'm not saying you're pale. It's just . . .' He broke off, giving her a close look. 'Actually, you do look a bit pale.' His blush deepened. 'Not in a bad way. I mean . . .' He made a nervous gesture. 'I'm sorry.'

Juliet felt a surge of affection for his good-intentioned clumsiness. She'd missed him, she realised. He was the first person in her life who'd seemed to think she was worth befriending.

'I've got time for a quick walk.' Even as she made the decision, however, the familiar anxiety reared up, and she found herself glancing along the street. She couldn't risk them being seen together. 'Why don't you head to the river, and I'll meet you there? I need to leave a note for Sally about something.'

'I'll wait for you,' he offered.

'Really, I'll be right behind you.' Juliet forced a smile. 'I'm a dab hand at navigating the precincts these days.'

'And I'd only slow you down?' He grinned and gave her one of his trademark bows. 'See you there. If I get there first, I'll leave a chalk mark on the pavement. If you get there first, you wipe it off.'

As he headed off, Juliet ducked back inside the house and leaned against the wall, trying not to regret her decision. It was probably just tiredness, and the situation with Esme, but for the first time, she felt resentful at the restrictions tied around the bargain she'd struck. She'd agreed to them readily enough, but hadn't envisaged feeling so *trapped*.

After she judged enough time had passed, she picked up her coat and headed out.

Eugene was waiting by the river, leaning against the railing. She thought she saw relief in his smile, as though he'd feared she might not come after all.

'Which way?' he said.

Near the bridge, Juliet could see two police officers talking to a tall man in a dark coat. She turned away quickly.

'This way.' As she set off, Eugene fell into step beside her.

'So, what have you been up to?' he asked. 'I thought you were going to join the ranks of the obsessed, but you seem to be managing to maintain a life outside the district. Care to share your secret?'

Juliet took a swift breath before his meaning caught up with her.

'Oh, nothing terribly interesting. What about you?' Better to keep the conversation turned away from her. 'Have you been to the Show recently?'

He shook his head. 'I've had a bad run of luck with the ballot. I wondered about booking a ticket, but then people started talking about the clocks, and I figured I might need all my money.'

'The clocks?' Juliet said.

'The build-up,' Eugene said. 'You really haven't been keeping up with things, have you?' He tilted his head. 'I thought we talked about the clocks once before.'

Juliet dredged up a memory of walking to the Show with him. She'd been entirely focused on her discovery of her old identity as the Girl in the Silver Shoes, and he'd gone off at a tangent about cycles and peaks and countdowns. 'Yes, we did.'

'Well, it looks like it's happening again,' he said. 'There was some disagreement when people first started to notice things, as it's not that long since we had a big peak, but the Followers who know how to do the calculations were adamant. Adamant – and smug when all sorts of other hints started popping up.' He glanced at Juliet. 'You really should come to the Shipping News. I remember how fascinated you were with the Moonshine Girl that first time I took you there.'

'The Moonshine Girl?' Juliet was struggling to follow, and conscious of a chill of exclusion. She was the one on the inside, but it was Eugene telling her things she didn't know.

'People think the coming peak has something to do with her story,' he said. 'There are more references to it appearing all the time. Particularly in the loop of the Girl in the Silver Shoes.'

Juliet felt a little catch of breath. She desperately wanted to ask him more, but she was terrified of making another mistake.

Eugene was still hypothesising, talking about rooms where the Moonshine Girl had once had scenes, about references to her story. He was jumping about – catching at something that occurred to him, before snatching at another snippet – but his excitement was clear. Juliet could feel the sharp bite of irony: if she'd been on the outside, she'd have been as thrilled as he was by the prospect of something new. She'd have been at the Shipping News every night, leaning into the avid discussions. She'd have been part of something joyous. But right now, she felt lonely and cold. She was always stiff and aching – not just from the effort of dancing every night, but from a constant sense of straining after something beyond reach.

'I should get back,' she said abruptly.

Eugene gave her a close look. 'Are you all right?'

'I'm fine,' she said, not looking at him. 'I'm just tired, that's all.'

Eugene didn't push the point. As they retraced their steps in silence, Juliet found herself wishing she could tell him everything. The miracle of the chance she'd been given, the promise of it all, but also the way she felt – as though she was walking one of those wires with every step she took, frightened of a fall that would shatter everything. And Esme; she could tell him about Esme and the impossible promise the other girl had extracted from her.

Tell him then. See what happens.

Juliet gritted her teeth against *Olivia*, and kept walking.

As they approached the bridge, the tall man was still talking to the police officers. He looked up, and Juliet's stomach tightened as she recognised DC Lambert.

'Miss Grace.' He walked over. 'I thought it was you.' He glanced towards the district. 'You're still living in the precincts?'

'For now.' She was conscious of Eugene listening curiously. 'Sorry, this is . . . James Lambert.' She turned back to Lambert. 'Eugene is a friend of mine. We were just out for a walk.'

'Nice day for it,' Lambert said neutrally. There was an awkward pause, while Juliet tried to work out how she could extract herself, and then the young officer spoke again. 'I wonder if I might have a word with you.' The unspoken *in private* was clear in the way his gaze flicked to Eugene.

An instinctive refusal shaped itself, but she bit it back. She'd give Lambert a few minutes to say whatever he wanted to say, and that would hopefully be the end of it.

That's what you thought last time.

Juliet turned to Eugene. 'Sorry, would you mind . . . ?' She made a vague gesture. 'I should . . .'

'Yes, of course.' Eugene had been giving Lambert a covert – and faintly suspicious – once-over, but he smiled at Juliet. 'Perhaps we could do this again sometime?'

'Yes, that would be lovely,' she said swiftly.

'I'll see you soon, then.'

Lambert waited until Eugene had disappeared before turning back to Juliet, who was already regretting her decision. She was uncomfortably conscious of how close to the district they were. That thin man walking past – she was sure she'd seen him in the precincts.

'Is everything all right?' Lambert asked.

'I'm fine.' A woman had emerged from a narrow passage to the side of the bridge. It led through to a small square near the edge of the precincts. Juliet pushed her hands into her pockets. 'What did you want to talk to me about?'

'Well, right now, what I want to talk about is how edgy you are about being seen with me.' He studied her. 'In fact, I'd go as far as to say that you're scared of being seen with me.'

'I'm not scared. I just . . .' Juliet bit at the inside of her lip. 'You're a police officer. People might talk.'

'About what?'

'About me being seen with a police officer,' she said sharply. 'It's the kind of thing that gets noticed.'

'I'm not in uniform,' he said.

'They are.' She jerked her head towards the other officers.

'Would you like to move?' Lambert asked politely.

'I didn't...' Juliet broke off and took a steadying breath. She should never have agreed to this conversation. 'I'm sorry, DC Lambert. I'm not sure what you want from me. There's nothing more I can tell you than I already have.' She started to turn away. 'I need to go.'

'Wait.' He caught hold of her arm. 'Juliet, what's wrong? Has something happened?'

'No.' Juliet tugged at her arm. 'Let go of me.'

Lambert loosened his grip slightly, but didn't release her. 'Tell me what's wrong.' His tone was urgent. 'I know there's something. If you tell me, I can help you.'

'There's nothing.' They were garnering glances from passers-by. 'I came to see what I could find out about my mother. I'll be moving on soon. That's all there is to tell.'

'I don't believe you.'

Juliet shook off his hand. '*I'm sorry about that.* That's what DI Mansfield said to me, wasn't it? That first time, when you came asking questions and refusing to answer mine.'

'This isn't tit-for-tat, Juliet.' There was frustration in Lambert's voice. 'We pulled another body out of the river a few nights ago.' His gaze narrowed. 'Hadn't you heard?'

'What does that have to do with me?' That chill was deepening, and she raised her voice. 'What do you want from me? I don't *know* anything.'

'What does it have to do with you?' Lambert said. 'Maybe nothing at all.' He rubbed at his face. He looked more tired and drawn than when she'd seen him last. 'Because that's what we always finish up with in these cases – nothing. No suspect. No theory. No official link with any of the other deaths. But that doesn't mean that—'

'*These cases.*' Juliet cut across him. 'You told me you weren't even sure there was a pattern. Now you're talking as though there is.'

He looked away for a moment, out across the river, and when he turned back, there was what looked like resignation in his expression. He made a swift gesture. 'Those papers I told you about, the ones in the archives, I've seen them. Or enough to understand why so many people have spent their whole careers trying to work it out. There have been clusters of deaths. Years have gone by – decades in some cases – with nothing at all, and then there'll be a rash of them.' He shook his head. 'None of it goes anywhere. *Nothing* to do with the district goes anywhere. It's like a black hole. But there's something at the heart of it. I can see the shape of it, even if I don't know what it is.'

'The shape of something.' Juliet's voice was rising. 'Patterns. Shadows. That's all everyone talks about when it comes to the district. There's nothing—'

'Everyone?' Lambert's expression had sharpened. 'Who else have you spoken to?'

'No one.' Juliet knew she needed to calm down. 'Look, it's awful about that poor girl, but you said there's never been any evidence connecting the district to any of this.' She shook her head. 'Do you even know who she was?'

'We're still working on that,' Lambert said. 'We spoke to a local resident.' His mouth twisted. 'The ordinary kind, from the part of Lambeth the district has never tried to claim. He'd seen a girl matching her description coming and going in the direction of the Theatre District at various times of the night. He last saw her a couple of days before the body was found. We're running an appeal in the newspapers tomorrow. She had a distinctive tattoo on her shoulder – a hummingbird. We're hoping someone will recognise it.' As Juliet went very still, his face changed. 'What is it?' Juliet didn't answer. She was trying to remember when she'd last seen Jemima. There was ice water in her veins. 'Juliet.' Lambert took hold of her shoulders. 'Look at me.' When she lifted her gaze to meet his, she could see concern fighting with professional urgency. 'Have you seen a tattoo like that?'

'The hummingbird.' Her voice seemed to be coming from a long way away. 'What did it look like?'

'It was hovering in front of a mirror.'

Juliet wanted to close her eyes, to shut it all out, but it wouldn't do any good. The memory of the tattoo she'd seen on that picture in the Shipping News was clear and sharp. The curve of the mirror. The reflection of the little bird. The lift of its wings.

'Juliet.' Lambert gave her a little shake. 'For God's sake, talk to me. Where have you seen that tattoo?'

Panic stabbed through her, and she wrenched herself free, staggering and almost falling. 'I haven't seen it. I don't know anything.' This wasn't his fault, but she felt an irrational blaze of anger. 'Leave me alone.'

'What's going on here?' A man in a suit had stopped a little way away. 'Are you all right, miss? Do you need help?'

Juliet turned back towards the district, breaking into a stumbling run. Behind her, Lambert shouted her name, but as she looked back, she saw the other man step forward to block his way. It wouldn't be long before Lambert revealed his badge but the district wasn't far and Lambert had told her that the police authority ended at the district gates.

Near the entrance, she ducked in among a small crowd of visitors, tying her mask in place as she made her way in through the barriers. Once safely inside, she turned off the main route and into a narrow side street, trying to drag her thoughts under some semblance of control. It felt as though she was freezing from the inside out, ice crackling around her ribs with each swell of her lungs. Lambert had told her that none of the victims had been district residents. She'd used that against him, to counter his vague warnings about the place. But Jemima *was* from the district.

Jemima.

She hadn't known the other girl beyond a few brief encounters, but she was real, not some stranger, staring out from the pages of a newspaper.

Walk away. Miss Abbeline's voice echoed in her head. *Be careful of Conrad's promises.*

A wall rose up in front of her – a dead-end. Caught by a sudden lurch of dizziness, Juliet leaned forward, pressing her palms against the cold stone, until the nausea receded. As she straightened up, something caught her eye – a narrow opening behind the corner of the building to her right. If she'd stumbled across it when she'd first come to the district, she'd have slipped through with a thrill, following the promise of the hidden, the secret. But now, with Miss Abbeline's and Lambert's warnings sounding inside her, it felt like a threat.

With a horrified wrench, Juliet realised that she was teetering on the edge of a terrible possibility. If Jemima was the girl in the river, then someone in the district must know that she was missing. *The Director* must know – and if Danes knew, what did that mean for all those other lost girls? What did it mean for those papers Lambert had told her about, tucked away, like something dark and dangerous?

No. She gave a hard shake of her head, as though there was someone there to see it. *No.*

Terrible things happened all the time in the world outside the district's gates. Perhaps Jemima had gone out one night. Perhaps she'd just been unlucky.

Juliet drew in a hard, shuddering breath. As she exhaled, a face rose in her mind, and she felt the faintest drag of hope.

Ethan.

He'd told her to trust him. He'd promised to help her. She could go to him, tell him about Lambert, about the girl with the tattoo, and he'd say, *We had no idea. We didn't know what had happened to her.* Danes would call the police, tell Mansfield that this time he was right and they had to work together to make sure nothing this terrible could ever happen again; she'd know there was nothing wrong at the heart of the district, and it would all be over and she could still be happy here.

A memory surfaced – the wariness on Ethan's face as he'd talked about the Director. What if . . .

Perhaps. What if. It was *Olivia*'s voice, sharp with impatience. *What are you actually going to* do?

With another ragged breath, Juliet turned back along the street.

She'd find Ethan, and tell him everything, and then, no matter what the truth of this was, she wouldn't be alone with it.

For a moment, Lambert's face hung in her mind. *Tell me what's wrong. I can help you.*

Juliet shook the thought of the young officer away.

Ethan would help her.

He would.

Chapter 26

Juliet kept her head down as she walked towards the entrance of the House of Doors.

She'd tucked her hair under her scarf, and turned her mask the other way, hiding the decorative trim. Once inside, she headed up to the third floor, following her memory of Ethan's loop from the sketch he'd drawn her. The evening build-up was just beginning, but the theatre was already busy.

Ethan didn't appear in the first couple of hours, and when the Show reset for a third time with no sign of him, Juliet could feel herself beginning to unravel. All the dark thoughts she'd been struggling to keep at bay were pressing close about her, like an audience refusing to keep their distance. Something occurred to her, and she pushed her hand into the pocket where she kept her father's key, closing her fingers round the cool metal. The backstage passages were a tangled maze, but she knew where Ethan started his loop. If she could find her way there, perhaps she could intercept him.

And if someone sees you?

Juliet ignored *Olivia*'s question, her thoughts too much of a frightened snarl for her to follow any single possibility to its conclusion. All she could think of was finding Ethan and unburdening herself. Making her way back to the room where his loop began, she waited until it was empty before walking the length of the wall, searching for any hidden handle or keyhole. When she found nothing, she moved to the next room, and then the next. In that third room, she found a door, tucked around a corner. Her key turned smoothly and silently, and she stepped quickly through the door, closing and locking it behind her.

She was in an odd, unfinished space, like the back of something not meant to be seen. The walls were made of rough boards, and there was no ceiling, just a dark cavity through which she could see the vague shapes of roof beams. A mismatched clutter of sconces and lanterns had been fastened to the wall anywhere there was a suitable support. Only a few of them were working, casting scattered pools of low light, like stepping stones through the gloom. They led away from the room where Ethan started his loop, but there was just a blank wall in the other direction.

Juliet navigated those patches of light, hoping to find a way back to where she needed to be. She'd only gone a short distance when she caught a shift of movement up ahead and stopped dead, her heart thumping. The movement came again, but there was something muted about it. Juliet took a few cautious steps and saw a dark gleam. As she moved closer, she found herself looking through a two-way mirror, onto the set. The room on the other side was familiar from her loop, with a model city inside a central glass case. No, it was a mirror-image room – plaster streaked and crumbling, the glass cracked around a shattered miniature London. Beyond it, she could just make out the lines of the *real* room, rendered ghost-vague through the blurring of the two mirrors.

Juliet was about to turn away when something brushed through the tarnished haze of the glass. A pale arm raised, and a glint of muted red.

A thought slid in, irrational, but, in that moment, terrifyingly plausible. *Olivia* had broken through into the real world, forcing Juliet into the shadowland in her place. Now *she* was the unreal one, trapped behind the glass in a faded echo of the world. Perhaps she'd been there for a long time, without knowing. Perhaps that was why nothing made sense.

As her head spun, she pressed her fingers against the mirror. The glass was cool and hard – *real* – and it steadied her. She was here, in her own skin, and when she peered through the mirror once again, there was nothing there. It was just her overwrought imagination playing tricks on her. She had to keep going. She had to find Ethan.

Juliet moved on, following the pools of light along the edge of the set. She passed other mirrors, but didn't stop to look through them. When she found a door, it was locked, but opened with her key. A blank-walled corridor on the other side led to a narrow flight of steps, which she followed down to a hallway, lit by a flickering bulb hung from the rafters. Another door opened onto a miserly scrape of a passage, so narrow she had to twist sideways. Her pulse was picking up, the first staccato stutterings of what could swiftly accelerate into panic. She wanted to turn back, but she'd seen no other way out.

The passage grew tighter still, the darkness lifted only by thin shafts of light breaking through chinks in the roof boards. Juliet had no sense of where she was in the theatre. There could be anything in front of her – broken floors, a dangerous drop. She was teetering right on the edge of that threatened panic as she pressed on through the dusty confines, tilting her head up to each slant of light like a drowning swimmer seeking pockets of air. The passage had to lead somewhere.

Olivia? she thought.

Even the abrasiveness of her other self would be some reassurance right now. But *Olivia* seemed to have deserted her, and that irrational fear dragged at her again. What if the dark version of herself *had* taken her place, leaving her trapped in a never-ending loop of passages and tiny spaces?

She rounded another sharp turn, then stopped, muffling a cough with the back of her hand. She could hear a voice, too faint to make out the words, then again, louder. A response came, brief and curt.

Juliet began to move as quietly as she could. As the voices grew clearer – two men, close by – Juliet saw a grey glimmer of light.

A window?

No, she realised, as she edged towards it. Not a window but another two-way mirror. Through it, she could make out a room, and two figures, blurred and featureless.

'. . . a risk,' one of them was saying. 'You've known that from the start.'

When the other man spoke, his voice was familiar.

'It was a risk worth taking,' the Director said. 'And I'm managing it.'

'Yes.' The other man gave a sharp laugh. 'I can see that.'

'We've been here before,' Danes replied. 'Nothing came of it last time, and nothing will come of it this time.'

'The Inspector will never let it go,' the other man said.

'The district is his obsession.' The Director's shoulder moved in a slight shrug. 'Like I said, nothing will come of it.'

'You'd know something about obsession, wouldn't you?' The other man's voice was hard. 'Yours almost cost you the directorship all those years ago, and yet here we are again.'

'Yes, here we are again,' Danes said levelly. 'That's the point, isn't it? The Show isn't only about what the audience sees playing out in front of them. It's about everything that's gone before as well. All those old stories, everything loved and lost and longed for. You know this, Kellan.'

'The audience? Or the Backers?'

'Both,' Danes replied. 'The same considerations apply. It's just the management that's different.'

'Management.' The other man – Kellan – gave another harsh laugh. 'That's what we're calling it, is it? We've had this conversation over and over. Only the language changes. You used very different words when you made a certain promise to me.'

'A promise I still intend to keep,' Danes replied.

'You'll forgive me if my credulity is wearing somewhat thin.'

'And you'll forgive me for reminding you that the office I hold is bound with all sorts of promises.'

Juliet hardly dared breathe. She didn't understand the nature of the dispute, but this wasn't the kind of conversation anyone could know she'd overheard.

The other man's head snapped up angrily. 'You think I need you to tell me how this whole thing works? I'm at the very heart of it.'

'Yes, you are,' Danes replied coolly. 'Which means you know full well what a balancing act it all is.' He paused, and when he continued, his tone was more conciliatory. 'You've been at my side as Stage Manager throughout my Directorship. I *owe* you my Directorship. And no, I haven't forgotten what I wrote in the debit column of that transaction. But I have other debts to worry about. You know what the war did to us. We're still clawing our way back.'

'Us, and the rest of the world,' the other man said.

'The rest of the world is only my concern insofar as it keeps coming in through those gates.'

'And its money with it.'

'Of course,' Danes said. 'I'm no Ballard, but there's not a Director in the history of the district who has had the luxury of disregarding that particular duty.'

'The Ballards.' Kellan shook his head. 'It all goes back to them, doesn't it? Back to that old . . . what was the word you used? That old *transaction*.' He paused. 'I say old, but your nephew is working hard on polishing it up.'

'We all play to our particular skills.'

The other man gave a low laugh. 'Oh, he has no shortage of those.'

Danes tilted his head. 'What are you saying, Kellan?'

'I'm saying that we're circling back to the same place again,' the Stage Manager said. 'How do you see this ending?'

'Nothing ends,' Danes said. 'We—'

'Who do you think you're talking to here? Some clueless punter who's wandered in off the street? *The Show must go on. Nothing is lost, nothing forgotten.* I've heard them all. And you know damn well what I'm talking about.'

'It won't be like that,' Danes said. 'You've seen how they respond to her. They've never forgotten the Moonshine Girl.' Juliet's swift breath almost triggered a betraying cough. 'No other story has come close to the draw of that one. And I'd barely got started. Now I have another chance. I can make the Show into what I always intended it to be.'

'A new golden age for the district.' Kellan's voice was heavy with cynicism. 'What a time to be alive, eh?' He shook his head. 'You're putting a lot of stock in the power of a single story.'

'With good reason,' the Director said. 'If there wasn't power in the stories we tell, this place would have dwindled into a penny sideshow centuries ago. Stories are our currency. The question is what exchange rate we can command for any given one.'

'But it's not just the exchange rate,' the Stage Manager said. 'It's not about how much you can extract from the Backers. The temptation was too great, wasn't it? The Moonshine Girl. The Girl in the Silver Shoes. Who could resist the symmetry of it?'

Juliet could barely breathe. *You've seen how they respond to her.* They were talking about her. Danes had been watching her, analysing the way the audience reacted to her performances. And he was pleased with what he'd seen. For a moment, she felt a swooping lift of joy, then her heart clenched as she remembered what had brought her to this dusty passageway.

'An imperfect symmetry,' Danes said. 'The Moonshine Girl's story was broken off before its time.'

The Stage Manager shook his head. 'You should never have involved her.'

'You know why I did,' Danes said. 'It's a delicate situation.'

'And if the board doesn't agree with how you've managed it?'

'Then there'll be another Director in this office.'

'And we both know who that will be,' the Stage Manager said. 'He knows it too. Do you really think you can trust him?'

'Trust means many things,' Danes said. 'I trust him to have his eye on the district's future. I trust that he's seen the merit in supporting me as I work towards that future. And he is my nephew.'

'Whatever that means.'

'It means shared blood,' Danes said. 'And that means everything. It's what ties us to this place, and to each other.'

'Not all of us share blood,' Kellan said. 'Your people. My people. That's how it's been since your forebears and mine first came to terms. That's exactly why we are where we are.' His voice darkened. 'The wars should have taught us that, if nothing else.'

'Kellan . . .'

'No.' The Stage Manager made a sharp gesture. 'Tell me this, *Director.* How many of your young men went off to the trenches? How many did the inner district . . .' His voice tightened. '. . . the *real* district, lose to those guns?'

'You're as much part of the district as I am,' Danes said. 'Whatever our bloodlines.'

'Sisters beneath the skin. Is that what you're saying?' There was a curl in the Stage Manager's voice.

'You're part of this,' Danes repeated. 'And so is Ethan.' *Ethan.* 'It's in all our interests for the district to thrive. That's what trust is, when all is said and done. Something in common, something precious and shared.'

'You talk about blood,' Kellan said. 'You remember, don't you, whose *blood* she has?'

'I remember,' Danes said. 'And I will keep my promise, Kellan. Just give me time.'

'Two hundred and fifty years in the shadows.' The Stage Manager's voice was low. 'Doing the work that can only be done in the shadows.'

'I know,' Danes said steadily. 'But right now, I need you on my side. The Show—'

'The Show.' Kellan cut across him. 'The Show before anything. That's how it's always been, and how it always will be.'

'You make that sound like an accusation,' Danes said. 'But that's the promise that underpins the offices we both hold. It's the promise we make, the legacy we leave.'

'And it's all about *legacy*, isn't it?'

'What else is there?' Danes said. 'So, I'm going to ask you, does the promise *you* once made to *me*, Stage Manager to Director, still hold?' There was a long pause, and then Juliet saw the other man nod slightly. Danes mirrored the gesture. 'Thank you, my friend.'

'I have to get back.' The Stage Manager turned abruptly away.

His outline faded, and she heard the door open and close.

The Director stood still for a moment, then turned and walked towards the mirror. Her breath caught as his gaze seemed to meet hers, and then she saw that he was focused on his reflection. This close, she could see his expression, and there was something tired and heavy there. Then he pushed his shoulders back, and smiled his showman's smile, his whole bearing seeming to lift and lighten.

'The Show must go on,' he said, then turned away.

Chapter 27

Juliet drew in a slow, deep breath.

Turning away from the mirror, she continued along the tight passageway, replaying the conversation she'd just heard. They'd been talking about her – that much was clear, even if little else was. Broken promises, obsessions, blood and belonging. DI Mansfield and his suspicions. The Moonshine Girl. Ethan, who'd never told her he was the Director's nephew. All of it was tangled together with other things she could sense, but not see clearly.

The passage took a final sharp turn, then ended abruptly at a door that opened onto a steep flight of stairs, with more corridors beyond it. The Show's music had grown louder, so Juliet knew she was close to the set, but beyond that, she still had no sense of where she might be. She'd abandoned any attempt at stealth when she turned a corner and came face to face with a stagehand.

The sharp lift of Juliet's ribs was mirrored by the swell of a frightened thought. No one could know what she'd heard.

'I'm sorry.' Her voice shook. 'I . . . I was looking for Ethan. I . . .' She broke off, trying to gather herself. 'Something's happened. I couldn't find anyone.'

When the stagehand motioned at her to follow him, there was nothing to do but fall in behind. Her heart was a hollow thud behind her ribs. Where was he taking her? To the Director? She still had no idea if Danes knew what had happened to Jemima, or if he'd—

'What's going on?' A familiar voice spoke from behind her, and Juliet twisted round to see Ethan crossing a small hallway towards them.

The relief that washed over Juliet felt colder than it should have done, sending a hard shiver through her.

'I found her backstage,' the stagehand said.

Ethan glanced at Juliet, then back to the other man. 'You can go. I'll take this from here.'

The stagehand gave a curt nod, and made his way through one of the doors leading off the hallway. When it closed behind him, Ethan turned to Juliet.

'What are you doing?' His voice was cold. 'How did you get backstage?'

'I was looking for you.' Juliet's throat was tight. 'I had to . . . I mean, I heard something. About the girl in the river.'

'The girl in the river?' Ethan stared at her.

'She had a tattoo.' Juliet had to force the words out. 'A hummingbird.'

'Why are you telling me this?' Ethan said, then understanding dawned. 'Did you know her? Is that why you're so upset? Juliet, I'm sorry, but—'

'I didn't know her.' Juliet gave a sharp shake of her head. 'Or I did, I mean . . .' She made an effort to drag herself together. 'Ethan, it's Jemima. The girl in the river is Jemima.'

'What are you talking about?' There was blank incomprehension on Ethan's face. 'Who told you this?'

'A police officer,' Juliet said. 'He told me about the tattoo, and I remembered it from a picture I saw of Jemima.'

'You told him her name?' Ethan's voice was sharp.

'No.' Juliet gave another hard shake of her head. 'I didn't tell him anything. He kept asking me if I'd seen it. I told him I didn't know anything, to leave me alone. Then I came to find you, to tell you that Jemima was . . .'

As she broke off, fighting back tears, Ethan reached out and gripped her shoulders.

'Juliet,' he said. 'Listen to me. Jemima isn't the girl they found.'

'No, they did, they found her.' He didn't understand what she was trying to tell him. 'She had the hummingbird tattoo, and then I remembered I hadn't seen her. Not since that first night.' The words were tumbling out, driven by her confusion and fear. 'People keep saying there's something wrong here, but I thought it was just stories, because none of those girls were from the district, but Jemima is, and I thought . . . I didn't know . . .' She was crying now, shuddering sobs that she could no longer fight back. 'I thought there was . . .'

Ethan let go of her shoulders. 'Come with me.' When she didn't move, he reached for her hand, holding it firmly. 'I need you to see something.'

He moved through the backstage passages with swift certainty, Juliet stumbling at his side, desperately trying to get herself under control. At a stage door, he let go of her hand, and peered through the spyhole.

'Here. Look.'

'What . . .'

'Just look.'

Juliet stepped up to the door and pressed her eye to the spyhole. There was a vaulted hallway on the other side of the door, and at the far end, a girl was dancing.

Jemima.

The thought didn't make sense. Jemima was dead. How could she be here, dancing in a drift of light, watched by a half-circle of masked figures?

'You see?' Ethan spoke from behind her, his voice gentle. 'Jemima is fine. You haven't seen her because her role has been scaled back. It wasn't working as it was before.'

Jemima finished her dance and moved on, disappearing through a door and out of sight.

'I don't understand.' Juliet's hands were shaking as she looked up at Ethan. 'The tattoo . . .'

'Jemima doesn't have a tattoo,' he said. 'Where did you get that idea?'

'I saw a picture in the Shipping News,' Juliet said. 'I remember it.'

'Are you sure?' That gentleness was still in his voice. 'Juliet, you've been through a lot. Your father dying. Coming here. Joining the Show. And don't think I don't realise how much strain the Director has put you under. It's easy for our memories to play tricks on us.' He paused. 'Or maybe you did see a picture. But how would you ever know who put it there, and why? Perhaps someone wanted to pretend they were part of the Show.'

'But that would mean they spent time here.' Juliet's heart gave another thud.

'Along with half the population of London,' he said, then lifted a hand. 'I don't know what you saw – or didn't see – but there's no mystery to solve here, Juliet. You've seen Jemima with your own eyes. She's safe. Whoever that girl is, whatever happened to her, she's not from the district.'

'I was so sure it was her.' Juliet wrapped her arms across her body. That chill should have been easing, but it still had her in its grip. 'I thought . . . I was afraid something was wrong. In the district, I mean.'

'Because of what people have told you.' Ethan's voice was steady. 'That's what you said a moment ago. Who have you been talking to?'

'Just DC Lambert.' Her voice was too high. 'He's the one who came to the house with DI Mansfield that time. I went for a walk and he saw me. He recognised me. He wouldn't—'

'You said *people*.' Ethan's gaze was locked with hers.

'There's stories.' Juliet dug her nails into her palms. 'My housemates told me. Stories about dead girls. That's what I meant. DC Lambert is the only one I've talked to.'

'And whatever he told DI Mansfield was enough to set him on the warpath again.' Ethan rubbed at his face. 'This explains the call the Director had, from someone in the police. Mansfield is talking about court warrants, raids on the district, getting our liberty status suspended to allow an investigation.'

'What?' That chill sharpened. 'That can't happen, can it?'

'No,' Ethan said. 'But that doesn't mean the board will look favourably upon the Director for giving Mansfield reason to dredge up every old grudge the police have ever held against the district.'

'But he could show Jemima to the police.' Juliet snatched desperately at that possibility. 'He could tell them that—'

'Tell them what?' Ethan said. 'Show them what? A girl who *isn't* the one they found in the river? A girl with no tattoo? What would that achieve?' He shook his head. 'No. We'll just have to weather this.'

'I'm sorry.' Juliet was shivering again. 'I thought if I listened to what he had to say, he'd leave me alone.'

'He'll never leave you alone,' Ethan said. 'Not if he thinks you know something. You can't talk to him again. You can't talk to *anyone* about the district. I told you, you have to guard yourself.'

'I'm trying,' Juliet said. 'I'm so sorry. What will . . .' Her voice shook and she tried to steady it. 'What will the Director do?'

'Nothing,' Ethan said. 'Because I'm not going to tell him this had anything to do with you.'

Juliet felt a faint flicker of hope. 'But what if he finds out?'

'He won't,' Ethan said. 'But Juliet, listen to me. Everyone has something they'd save if their house was burning down. This secret has to be the thing you'd save. You cannot make any more mistakes. If you do . . .' His mouth tightened, and he glanced away, before continuing in a swift, urgent tone. 'You need to promise me that if anything, *anything*, else happens to make you afraid or unsure, you'll come to me. Don't speak to anyone else. Come to *me*.'

'I didn't know how to find you. No one speaks to me.' Juliet looked down at the floor. 'I don't think anyone wants me here. It sometimes feels like . . .' She swallowed. 'Like I don't really exist.'

'Listen to me.' Ethan tipped her chin up, making her look at him. 'You need to stop worrying about anything but proving yourself to the Director. That's the only thing that matters.'

'I will.' Juliet tried to drag herself together. 'I know he didn't have to give me this chance.'

'He's not doing it for you.' There was a warning note in Ethan's voice. 'He doesn't do anything unless he can see it helping the Show, or the district. Don't ever make the mistake of thinking he's your friend, or on your side. He's not on anyone's side – we're all on his.' His mouth tightened. 'Or not, as the case may be.'

'You don't trust him?' Juliet said hesitantly.

'Oh, I trust him,' Ethan said. 'I trust him to ensure the district's survival. I trust him to protect himself, and, by association, all of us.' It was a mirror image of the conversation she'd overheard. 'I suppose you could say I trust him to be exactly what a Director is supposed to be.' He gave a swift shake of his head. 'I shouldn't be talking like this.' He let go of her. 'Come on. I'll take you out.'

Juliet tried to drag her scattered thoughts together as she followed Ethan down through the theatre to a stone tunnel with a gate at the end.

'This brings you out south of the theatre,' he said. 'Have you got your mask?' When she pulled it out, he opened his hand. 'Your key, please.'

'My key?' Juliet felt a leap of panic. Had he changed his mind? Was he going to tell Danes to dismiss her? 'How will I get in for my performances?'

'Not the key I gave you,' he said. 'The one you used to get backstage. Your father's, I assume.'

Reluctantly, she reached into her pocket and pulled it out. As he tucked it away, his expression was unreadable. The distance between them seemed to be opening up once again, after that brief moment of intimacy when he'd spoken about Danes, and Juliet stumbled into a decision.

'I heard something,' she said. 'When I was trying to find my way through the theatre. There was a mirror, looking onto the Director's office. I didn't want to listen, but I was scared they'd hear me if I moved.'

'They?' Ethan turned back, hawk-swift.

'The Director,' Juliet said. 'And the Stage Manager. They were talking about you. Danes said he trusted you because you both wanted the same thing.'

'Did he say what?' Ethan's gaze was fixed on her face.

Juliet shook her head. 'I didn't understand much, but they talked about my mother.'

'Your mother?'

'The Moonshine Girl's story. The Director said it was valuable. But the Stage Manager said he shouldn't have let me be part of it. I suppose he thinks I'm not good enough.' She thought Ethan might reassure her, but he stayed silent. 'There was something else. Danes said you would be Director after him.'

'He said that.' Ethan's voice was low, and it held something that made the air feel tight around them. 'He said I'd be the next Director.'

Juliet wasn't sure if it was a question, but she answered it anyway. 'Yes, that's what he said. They talked about the board being angry with the Director if something went wrong, and that's when he said it.'

'And what did the Stage Manager say about that?'

'He didn't seem to like the idea.' Juliet was conscious that she was in uncharted territory, trying to navigate the unseen currents of relationships between people she barely knew. 'I think he was angry with Danes about something.' She hesitated. 'You never said he was your uncle.'

'We're not close.' His expression shut down. 'Did they talk about anything else?'

Juliet shook her head. 'That was all I heard.' It had felt as though there were all sorts of things shifting between Danes and the Stage Manager, but none of it had made any sense, and she didn't want to blunder into saying something she shouldn't. 'Will you . . .'

She stopped, not sure whether she could risk the question she wanted to ask.

'You want to know if it's true.' Ethan gave a small smile. 'I'm not the only candidate, by any means, but yes, if the district has such a thing as an heir apparent, I suppose that would be me.'

'Do you want it?' Juliet asked hesitantly.

It was a long moment before Ethan answered, and when he did, there was something shadowing his face. 'I'm not sure *want* is the right word, but there are things that need to change, and only the Director has that power.' He gave a quick shake of his head. 'We can't be talking about this. Don't tell anyone what I just said.' He glanced away, and when he turned back, he looked as though he'd reached some decision. 'I'm going to ask Danes to give you a place to stay in the district. He doesn't like being pushed, but the way you're living now – half-in, half-out – it's not fair. It might take me a while to persuade him, but you'll need that time to wind in those trailing ends we talked about. Your housemates will need to know you're thinking of moving out. Drop a few hints, and be ready to move when you hear from me.' He glanced back along the passage. 'You need to go. Put your mask on.'

While she tied it in place, he unlocked the gate. When she looked up, he was staring down at her, with an expression that made her heart beat harder. Stepping close, he brought his hands up to her face, brushing his thumbs over her cheekbones. His kiss was gentle this time, almost tentative, and it was Juliet who moved towards him, drawn by the threads of the thousand possibilities the kiss was spinning into being.

He pulled back. 'Go on,' he said. 'Get some rest. And Juliet, no more mistakes.'

*

Juliet's thoughts were a confused shift as she walked away from the theatre.

That kiss – she put her fingers to her lips as though some trace of it might still be lingering – it should have had her heart leaping, but there was too much tangled about that moment for her to feel anything as straightforward as joy. It was as though her fear was a tide that had receded, leaving dark stains and twisted debris scuffed across her emotions.

She could still see that picture of Jemima so clearly in her head. Where had that certainty come from?

Her thoughts moved to the irrational terror she'd felt, as she'd imagined herself replaced by a dark mirror-version. For a few brief seconds, it had been all-consuming and starkly possible. Was her mind unravelling? Was that why nothing seemed to make sense? A chill went through her as she realised there was no way to dismiss that possibility. If you were going mad, you wouldn't know, would you?

Remembering the letter she'd found in the desk at her stepmother's house, with its almost unreadable smear and scrawl, she thought she could see the shadow of something dark and painful. Had the Moonshine Girl lost her mind? Was that what no one wanted to tell her? Juliet felt something tightening around her skull, forcing her thoughts into a small, hard knot. There was a tension around her ribs too, each breath harder than it should have been.

Olivia? she thought, as she turned onto her street, wanting her other self to tell her how stupid she was, to shake her out of her unease.

No reply came.

Chapter 28

THREE DAYS AFTER THAT fraught, confusing night, there was a knock at the door.

It had come twice before, and, both times, Juliet had stood very still in the empty house, until he – she knew exactly who it was, and had no intention of speaking to him ever again – had given up and gone away.

'I'll get it.' Sally's voice floated up.

Cold adrenaline flooded through Juliet, but before she could stop the other girl, she heard the door open. There was a muted exchange of voices, then Sally called up the stairs again.

'Juliet. It's for you.'

*

Lambert was waiting on the doorstep.

'What do you want?' Juliet closed the door and leaned back against it, tucking her hands behind her so that he wouldn't see the tremor in her fingertips.

'To talk to you,' Lambert replied levelly. 'About the way you reacted when I told you about that tattoo. You've seen it. I know you have.'

'I thought I had, but I was wrong.' That quiver had transferred to Juliet's voice, and she pressed her lips together before continuing. 'I made a mistake.'

'Pretty big mistake,' Lambert said. 'Care to enlighten me as to how you came to make it?'

'I was wrong,' Juliet repeated. 'I thought I'd seen a picture, but—'

'A picture?' Lambert cut across her. 'What picture? Where did you see it?'

Careful.

Juliet didn't need that warning from *Olivia*. She could see it clearly. The police descending on the Shipping News, upending cabinets, ripping everything off the walls in search of anything they could use against the district.

'At the Show.' She pressed her palms against the door. 'It was dark. I must not have seen it properly.'

'Where was it?'

'I can't remember.'

'You're lying,' he said flatly, then gave a hard shake of his head. 'No, don't bother with the outraged denials. I've been a police officer long enough to know when someone is hiding something. And to be frank, you're not doing a very good job of it.' He paused. 'Unless, of course, that's what you want me to think.'

'What do you mean?' Juliet stared at him.

'This place.' Lambert glanced up at the broken roof. 'How are you supposed to know what's real, and what's not?' He looked back at her again. 'I told Mansfield you knew something. I shouldn't have said anything. He was sure that this time we'd finally get something on the district, on Danes. There was no talking him down. I think he was close to storming the doors of the Show, with anyone he could drag with him.' His expression darkened. 'Then he was called in before one of the superintendents. The appropriate investigations had been carried out, he was told. The Director had been *most* co-operative, but knew nothing at all about a girl with a hummingbird tattoo.' Lambert gave a small shrug. 'And that was that. End of investigation. No appeal in the newspaper. No more time spent on a nameless girl who doesn't matter enough for anyone to have noticed she's even missing.' There was a bitter note in Lambert's voice, and Juliet's heart twisted with an unidentifiable emotion as he gave her a weary look. 'Juliet, what the hell is going on here?'

'Nothing.' The denial sounded thin and unconvincing. 'I don't know anything.'

'What about Danes?' Lambert said. 'He claimed to have had no idea that Stephen Grace's daughter was living in the district precincts.' He gave a cynical shake of his head. 'I don't believe a sparrow could fall in this place without the Director knowing, which very much begs the question, why would he lie? Have you talked to him? Has he told you why your father left?'

'He wouldn't . . .' *Careful.* The voice in her head was sharp, and Juliet lifted a trembling hand to her brow. 'I haven't talked to anyone. I thought I'd seen the picture, but I was wrong.'

'How do you know?' Lambert's gaze narrowed.

'What do you mean?'

'I mean how do you know you made a mistake?' As Juliet stared at him, he made an impatient gesture. 'It was almost the first thing you said to me. When I told you about that tattoo, you were terrified. So, what made you decide that actually you'd never seen it?'

Juliet's lies were tangling tighter and tighter about her. She had to find a way out – a way that meant he went away and forgot about her. 'I went back,' she said. 'To the Show. It wasn't there.'

Lambert raised an eyebrow. 'I thought you said you couldn't remember where it was.'

Something caught Juliet's eye. Had that been a movement at an upstairs window across the street?

She raised her voice. 'I want you to go, DC Lambert. You have no right coming here and harassing me. I haven't done anything wrong.'

Lambert had followed her gaze up to the window, and when he turned back, the coldness in his eyes had been replaced by concern.

'What is it, Juliet?' He said it quietly. 'What are you afraid of?'

Out of nowhere, Juliet found herself wanting to step close to him and lean against his chest. She could gather up every fear and doubt, everything she didn't understand, and say *Here, take it and make sense of it*. That was what the police were supposed to do. They unravelled all the messy, hidden things that people did, and wrapped them into neat skeins of meaning.

Fool. That's why he's here.

The impulse fell away, and Juliet lifted her head. 'Did Mansfield tell you to ask me that?'

Lambert's expression closed down. 'DI Mansfield is retiring at the end of the month.'

'Retiring?' Something cold wound its way around Juliet's lungs. Lambert had told her he didn't want to see the older officer's career destroyed. She shook her head, trying to throw off the guilt that was threatening to dig its claws into her. 'That has nothing to do with me. I can't tell you anything, and I'm not afraid.'

'You are,' Lambert said. 'And you're right to be. This place isn't safe.' He took a step towards her, stopping when Juliet threw up a hand. 'I don't know what's going on, but I'm telling you, there's something very wrong in the Theatre District. And I think you're in over your head.'

'I don't want to hear any more.' Juliet's voice was rising. 'All those years, all those cases, and it's still just stories and rumours and things that could mean something or nothing.'

'That's what most police work is,' Lambert said. 'But you keep looking at those things, and at everyone and everything around them, until you work out which ones are something.'

'And what if none of them are?'

'There's a girl on a slab,' he said sharply. 'The same slab where others have lain, waiting for us to figure out what put them there. There is something, and I wouldn't be much of a policeman if I just shrugged and thought, *Ah well, we'll probably never know. Anyone for a beer?*' He glanced away, and when he turned back, there was something heavy, almost sad, in his expression. 'I used to wonder why the DI couldn't let it go, even when his career was on the line.

Now I'm starting to understand. Every time something else happens, you think of those girls and wonder if this is the time you'll find that crucial clue, that vital piece of evidence. It would be like putting it to rest for all the other officers it's haunted over the years.'

A picture formed in Juliet's mind. A greying DI Lambert, working on another investigation into the death of another girl, telling another young officer about the Theatre District and that *something* he'd never been able to work out.

Another girl.

The thought had slipped almost casually into her mind, as though she'd entirely accepted the fact that there *would* be another dead girl, and that the district *would* be at the heart of the subsequent investigation.

It's just a show, she thought desperately.

The district was a bright and glittering thing in a world that held very few bright, glittering things. A world in which girls were found in rivers, and the police had to wade through the mud and misery and mess of real life to try to work out how they'd met their end.

'I want you to go,' she said. 'I can't help you.'

Lambert looked at her for a long moment. 'All right,' he said eventually. 'But if there's ever anything—'

'There won't be.' Juliet folded her arms across her body. 'I'm leaving soon. Perhaps in the next few days.'

Lambert stepped back from the door. 'Goodbye, Miss Grace,' he said, polite and formal, then turned and walked away.

In the narrow streets around the Theatre District, evil stalks the night!

November, 1891. Three years have passed since Jack the Ripper plied his grisly trade on the fallen women of Whitechapel, and the citizens of Old London Town sleep safe in their beds once more.

But across the river, a dark force is stirring. Soon fear will have a new name . . . or perhaps an old one . . . as the hunt for a ruthless killer tests the brave men of the Metropolitan Police past the limits of human endurance. Are they facing a mortal man or a fiend from the pits of hell?

The truth is still to be uncovered. The truth about the killer they call . . .

. . . the Ripper of the Southern Hallows.

Chapter 29

Juliet went to the theatre, performed, and walked home alone.

She was always tired, never able to hold on to sleep for long enough to wake refreshed. She felt thin and insubstantial, like the ghost she'd briefly thought she'd become, fading from one life and haunting the edges of another.

She didn't hear from Ethan, although she did encounter him on set a few times, early in some of her shifts. Each time, she searched his face, the way he moved, the way he touched her, looking for hidden messages, but she could never see past the Shadow Man.

The set was growing busier, night by night. She'd heard Sally and Anna talking about the build-up Eugene had mentioned, bemoaning the crowds. A couple of times, she heard the other girls mention the Girl in the Silver Shoes, but nothing that told her how close she was to being what Danes wanted – or how far.

One day, she was summoned back to the choreographer. He was, if possible, even more tight-lipped than before, as he taught her a new solo. When she had it memorised, he released her to a stagehand who took her up to the platform above the ballroom for her to rehearse.

When she'd first joined the Show, Juliet had loved the scene on the platform. The open space around her, the heat of the lights – it felt like being at the very heart of everything. She wasn't sure when that feeling had started to fray, but she did know when it had given way to something much colder. The fear she'd felt when she'd thought Jemima was dead still hadn't left her. It was as though it had been stained into her skin, like a layer of shadow, just beneath the surface.

Now, when she stepped onto the platform, with its almost imperceptible sway, she was conscious not of the space around her but the drop below. Her thoughts kept going back to that newspaper story of a fall, a scream, a shock of panic and confusion. *A gallery*, the clipping had said, but when the scene played out in Juliet's head, it was the platform she saw, suspended from its metal joists, and linked to the edges of the roof space by connecting bridges.

She didn't fall. Olivia had been quiet recently, with only the odd, half-hearted dig to remind Juliet she was there. *You know she didn't.*

But Juliet didn't feel as though she knew anything at all.

Walking back through the district after the rehearsal, Juliet saw someone coming the other way. She kept her head down as they drew closer together, but then she heard her name and looked up to see Eugene in his feathered mask.

'There you are.' He smiled at her. 'I've just been round to your place, but no one was in. I was hoping to catch up with you.' His smile faded. 'Are you all right? Sally says they hardly see you. She seemed a bit worried.' He flushed. 'Sorry, it's not my place to pry.'

'I'm fine.' Juliet felt around for a change of subject. 'Are you on your way to the Shipping News?'

'I am,' he said. 'I've got a bit of a project on the go. We're as sure as we can be that whatever the Show is building to, it has something to do with the Moonshine Girl. I've been collating all the references to her that I can find.' He gave Juliet a hopeful look. 'You could come and see.'

Juliet shook her head. 'Sorry, I'm really tired. I'm going to head home.'

Eugene looked disappointed. 'Well, if you want to see what I've been doing, my papers are in the filing cabinet that doesn't close properly. The one in the back left room. There's a cardboard folder at the front of the top drawer.' He smiled. 'Although, if you do come by, there's at least a fifty-fifty chance I'll be there. I'm running out of time, after all.'

'What do you mean?' Juliet asked.

'To figure out exactly what this peak will involve.' He grinned. 'Maybe I'll be ahead of the game for once.' He tilted his head. 'Are you going to come on Friday? Most of the Followers have bought tickets. Come on, you don't want miss the peak, do you? It could be a couple of years before it happens again.'

'I'm not sure.' Juliet's throat felt scuffed and sore. Her current schedule ended with a performance in the early hours of Thursday morning. Surely, if she was part of this coming peak, someone should have told her *something*. 'I'll let you know.'

'Yes, do. I'll be at the Shipping News till late most nights in the run-up. It would be nice to go together, given that

I took you to your first ever Show.' He cleared his throat, another flush shading his skin. 'There's something else. When it's over, I may not be around quite so much.'

'What do you mean?'

'I've been thinking about things recently,' he said. 'This is the third time I've seen the Show peak, and when all is said and done, it's just a show.' He was talking fast, as though embarrassed about what he was saying. 'All the things we spend so many hours arguing over and trying to figure out, they've been made up by someone so that people like us will come and look at them. And if we crack the code or find the hidden door, then there'll be something else, then something else. There's never going to be that moment we all dream of, when we've somehow won.' He glanced along the street. 'Don't get me wrong, I love all this as much as ever. It's not real, but you can pretend it is, and that's good and exciting and *joyful*. But only for so long.' His flush deepened. 'What I'm trying to say is that I've sort of met someone.'

Juliet was surprised at the tug of regret she felt at his words. She wasn't jealous. She didn't feel that way towards him. But she'd thought of him as someone who would always be here if she needed him, caught in an endless orbit around the dazzle of the district.

'That's good.' She pushed her lips into a smile. 'Does she come here?'

'She came once and quite liked it. She said she might come with me sometimes.' He shook his head. 'It's strange, but I like that she's not a Follower. I'd like to take her to the Show, then go home and talk about it in a different way to how we talk about it here. I think it would just be the fun, without any of the . . .' He frowned. 'I'm not sure what the word is. It just feels as though I need to find a way to fit the district into my life, rather than trying to make myself fit into the district.' He gave Juliet a slightly anxious look. 'You don't mind? Me not being around so much after this peak? I didn't think it would matter to you.'

He sounded worried, and Juliet realised she'd let her smile slip away.

'Of course not,' she said. 'I'm happy for you. It's just that . . .' Her throat tightened, and she looked away as the tears broke through. She didn't know where they were coming from. The district held everything she'd ever wanted, but the idea of spending time with an ordinary someone had scraped something away inside her, revealing an odd longing.

'What's wrong?' Eugene's voice was sharp with concern. 'Juliet, what is it?'

'I'm fine.' She wiped her face on her sleeve. 'I'm just . . . I've been waiting to hear about something important, and it's taking a long time.' She needed to get away. 'Everything is fine, Eugene, I promise. I should get home.'

'Don't go.' Eugene put his hand on her arm. 'Come for a drink with me.'

'I can't,' Juliet said sharply. 'I mean, I'm tired. I need an early night.'

'Well, I'm here if you need to talk.' He took his hand away. 'Like I said, I'll be at the Shipping News most nights until the peak. You can always come and find me.'

'Thank you,' Juliet said. Then, remembering what Ethan had told her to do, she added, 'I may not be around after the peak, either. I'm moving on soon.'

'Where will you go?' Eugene's brow was creased.

'I'm not quite sure yet. I'm still waiting to hear.'

'All right,' he said cautiously. 'But you'll let us know before you go?'

'Of course,' she said. 'I'll see you soon.'

*

Another performance came and went. Then another and another. On the Thursday, she finished at the theatre around eight in the morning, collapsed into bed, and slept through till late afternoon. She was woken by Anna walking into her room, carrying two mugs.

'I've had about enough of being alone,' she said. 'Sally's been doing a load of overtime. You're either out or sleeping. Esme's off doing . . . well, I don't know what she's up to. She's so secretive at the moment. Jan said she was dropping hints about having had some extra-special private scene a while back, but when I asked her, she wouldn't tell me anything.' She handed Juliet one of the mugs, and plonked herself down on the end of the bed with the other. 'I'm starting to feel like it's me.'

'A special scene.' Disquiet was scratching around the edges of Juliet's thoughts. 'Did she say who with?'

Anna shook her head. 'Most unlike her.' She looked wistful. 'One of these days, something special will happen to me, and I'll be able to tell everyone all about it. Or not tell them, while telling them just enough to make sure they know how extra specially special it was.'

Juliet took a sip of her tea, not tasting it. Every day that had passed without Esme ramping up her threats had felt like a reprieve. But what if her apparent patience had been something else entirely? Esme didn't belong to the district. She never could, no matter how hard she might try to find some gap to squirm through. But Juliet couldn't stop an image playing out across her thoughts. The other girl, smiling up at Ethan, going up on her toes to press a kiss to his lips, arching herself into his touch as he—

'Are you all right?' Anna's voice broke into her thoughts.

'I'm fine,' Juliet said quickly.

'Are you sure?' Anna gave her a narrow-eyed look. 'Like I said, I've hardly seen you recently. You come and go at odd hours. You've been so vague about this mysterious job of yours that Sally and I have been seriously contemplating the possibility of you being a spy.' Her gaze ranged over Juliet. 'You've lost weight, too. What's wrong?'

'Nothing's wrong.' How many times could you say that before the teetering stack of denials grew top-heavy and flipped over into an admission? She pushed back the covers. 'Thank you for the tea. I'm going to get dressed.'

'Do that, then come to the Shipping News with me,' Anna said. 'Quite a few people are planning to get there early today. It's been heaving for the last few days, and I'd imagine it will be the same tonight, given tomorrow is the big day.' Juliet's stomach twisted. She still had no idea whether or not she would be involved tomorrow – or what it would mean if she wasn't. 'I'm almost looking forward to it being over,' Anna went on. 'If it's the same as last time, once the fuss dies down, there'll be a couple of weeks of blissful quiet, before things pick up again.'

'What happened at the last peak?' Juliet asked.

'Honestly?' Anna said. 'I can't remember many of the details. There was a big evening performance, with a full cast on set. A couple of the storylines wrapped up, some new ones appeared, and then the Show carried on.' She smiled. 'Sorry, that's not a lot of help, but my memory is awful. I couldn't swear to which bits of it I actually saw, and which bits I've heard other people talking about – or just made up in my own head.'

'Does that often happen?' Juliet asked. 'Not being sure what's real? I mean, do you think you could forget something big?' She was treading close to dangerous ground, but she found herself desperate for reassurance. 'Something important?'

'Like what?' Anna asked. 'Juliet, what's this about? I'm worried about you.'

'Like a whole part of your life,' Juliet said. 'Do you think someone could ever persuade you things were different to how you remembered them?'

'I don't know,' Anna said. 'I wouldn't have thought so. I think you'd know, deep down at least, that what you were being told wasn't right. But seriously, what's going on?'

'Nothing.' Juliet forced a smile, although she found herself wanting to cry. 'I forget things too sometimes. I wondered if it was just me.'

'Come to the pub,' Anna said gently. 'Whatever it is, I bet it will feel better with people around you and a beer inside you.'

Juliet looked away. 'Another time.'

'Well, if you change your mind, you know where we are,' Anna said, getting up and walking out of the room, leaving Juliet with an ache of loneliness.

*

Juliet waited until she heard Anna leave before heading downstairs to make a sandwich, which she found she couldn't eat. As she was washing up, she heard the front door open, then voices and footsteps on the stairs. A few seconds later, Sally walked into the kitchen, followed by a little crowd of people. Macy was there, and Jan, and some other Followers Juliet vaguely recognised.

Macy gave Juliet a little wave. 'Hello, stranger.'

Anna squeezed through the door behind them. 'Our usual table was occupied,' she said. 'There was *outrage*. We decided to come here instead.' She gave her housemate a slightly lidded look. 'So you don't need to drag yourself to the Shipping News. We brought the Shipping News to you.'

Juliet could feel the back of her neck growing clammy.

Keep yourself apart.

There was a thudding from the hallway, and Eugene appeared, followed by another man, both carrying chairs.

'Well done,' Sally said. 'If anyone else turns up, they'll have to sit on the floor.'

'So where have you been hiding away?' Macy said to Juliet.

'I've just been busy.' Juliet moved so Anna could rummage in a cupboard for glasses.

'Juliet has a new job.' It was Esme's voice from the doorway, but when Juliet looked up, she almost didn't recognise her. Her blonde hair was dyed red, only a tone or so lighter than Juliet's natural auburn.

The shock that shuddered through Juliet didn't come wrapped up in any coherent thought. It was just an instinctive, gut-deep dread.

'A new job?' Macy said. 'Sounds interesting.'

'Yes, why don't you tell everyone about it, Juliet?' There was a glint in Esme's gaze.

'It's only temporary.' Juliet dredged the answer from somewhere, her voice echoing oddly in her head. 'I'm waiting for something permanent to come up.'

'I didn't have the impression that was likely any time soon.' Esme raised her eyebrows. 'From what you said, I mean.'

When Juliet didn't answer, Macy gave her a swift look, then addressed Esme. 'Nice hair. What prompted that?'

'I just fancied a change,' Esme said lightly. Her gaze hadn't left Juliet. 'Have you been to the Show recently? I haven't had a chance to ask you if you've seen anything new.'

'Not recently.' Juliet tried to keep her voice steady.

'Have *you* seen anything new?' Macy seemed determined to distract Esme. 'What about this new private scene you're supposed to have had? Are you going to spill the beans?'

'Now that would be telling,' Esme said, a smile curling about her lips. She turned to the young man next to her. 'On the subject of private scenes, why don't you tell us about the Girl in the Silver Shoes? Didn't you get picked by her recently?'

Despite her tension, Juliet felt a tiny flicker of satisfaction. In her eagerness to keep needling Juliet, Esme had tripped herself up. Any minute now, someone would point out that the Girl in the Silver Shoes didn't have a private scene.

'Did you?' Macy looked at the man Esme had addressed. 'You're the first person I know who's had that. It seems very hit and miss as to whether she does it.'

'As far as I can tell, it's fairly hit and miss as to whether she's there at all,' Jan said. 'She doesn't seem to do as many peak-hours performances as you'd expect, given how popular she is.' He looked over at the young man. 'You must be in a fairly small and privileged minority.'

'I think I just had the sharpest elbows,' the man replied with a grin. 'I had to resort to near-violence to get close enough. It was mid-evening on a Saturday night, and the crowd was about four deep around her.'

'I can imagine,' Jan said ruefully. 'I did try to follow her once, but gave it up as a bad job. It's always a feeding frenzy in the early days of a storyline.'

'Not forgetting all the call-backs to the Moonshine Girl,' Macy said. 'That's like catnip to the older fans. Hopefully, we'll see a lot more of her after the peak. Everything seems to be pointing that way.'

There was a high-pitched buzzing in Juliet's ears. Through it, she could make out the scratch of a voice, like someone trying to get her attention. There was an ease and familiarity to the way they were all speaking about her role, as though this was something they'd discussed many times before, but what they were saying didn't make sense. She'd never performed during peak hours. She'd never had a four-deep crowd clamouring about her. She didn't have a private scene.

Over by the door, Esme was speaking, but Juliet couldn't focus. With a last sly smile, the other girl put her hand up to touch a fine silver chain around her neck, then turned and walked out of the room, as distant and untouchable as something viewed through the wrong end of a telescope. A moment later, the front door opened and closed, the sound of it seeming to echo inside the hollow that had formed in Juliet's chest.

'Are you all right, Juliet?' Macy said. 'You look awful. What's wrong?'

'I . . .' Juliet's hands were shaking so hard that she had to dig her fists against her thighs to force them still. 'I'm sorry, I'm not feeling well.' Nausea clutched at her, bringing a lurch of dizziness with it. 'I'm going to go and lie down.'

Before anyone could respond, she walked swiftly out of the kitchen and upstairs to her room. Closing the door, she leaned against it and shut her eyes. Her thoughts were slipping away from her, rearranging themselves in ways that didn't mean anything.

It does mean something. There was a merciless implacability in *Olivia's* voice. *You know what it means.*

I don't, Juliet thought back, desperately. *I don't know anything.*

You know everything, the answer came. *You just won't let yourself put it together.*

Shut up shut up shut up.

An image rose in Juliet's mind – a ghost-thin glimpse of a girl with red hair, moving through the set just as Juliet would have moved. She gave a violent shake of her head, trying to dislodge that picture. There was an explanation for all of this. There had to be.

Opening her eyes, Juliet pushed herself away from the door and walked over to her wardrobe. Taking out the blue-grey dress, she changed quickly. It was the closest thing she had to her costume, and it was irrational, but she desperately needed to hold on to the certainty of her role. She covered her hair with the same scarf she'd used when she went looking for Ethan, and pulled on her coat, tucking her mask and key into her pocket. Then she slipped downstairs and out of the house.

On her way through the precincts, Juliet passed one of the high-fronted workshops that was usually locked and shuttered. The doors were open, revealing a row of decorated steam fair wagons, with stacks of crates and sacks beside them, as though someone was readying them to leave. For a moment, she wished she could climb into one and tuck herself away where she wouldn't be found until they were miles from here.

The queue for the House of Doors was almost to the corner, but it moved quickly. The theatre was busier than Juliet had ever seen it, and she wove her way round the edges of the crowds, pressing herself against walls to let performers hurry past, trailing their individual audiences behind them.

Everything was just as it should be, and, as she made her way up to the lumber room, Juliet felt a faint shifting of hope. Perhaps it was nothing after all. Perhaps someone had just started a rumour about a private scene, and none of the Followers wanted to admit they didn't know what everyone else was talking about. Perhaps—

Juliet's thoughts broke off in a dizzying lurch of vertigo. It was as though she'd fallen out of herself. She was there, dancing in the dusty light between the pictures, beneath the massed gaze of a yearning crowd. Putting her hand out, she clutched at the door-frame. The contact steadied her slightly, bringing everything back into focus. This wasn't a hallucination. She wasn't going mad. The girl in the spotlight looked like her, but she didn't dance like her. There, on that pirouette, that wasn't how Juliet would place her foot. And she didn't turn her hand like that as she raised her arm above her head.

Esme.

There was something off-key about the note of recognition that sounded in Juliet's head, but the swell of rage she felt was too hard and blazing to come from any rational place. She was several steps into the room before she realised she was even moving. The spotlight lit up the other girl's face, lending a dusty brilliance to her smile. In that moment, it didn't matter how the other girl could possibly be here, such a short time after taunting Juliet at the gathering at the house. It didn't matter *why* she was here, dancing in Juliet's place. She was everything that had made Juliet afraid, a dark and multiple presence. She was the girl in the mirror. The girl from the river. Doppelgänger, chimera, changeling. She was every girl who had watched Juliet dance and wanted it for herself. She was the ghost of the Moonshine Girl, the broken promise of the Girl in the Silver Shoes. She was *Olivia*, and Juliet knew, with a sudden jagged-edged certainty, that she had always hated *Olivia*, and *Olivia* had always hated her.

With another jolt of fury, Juliet pulled off her mask and her scarf. Letting her coat fall to the floor, she pushed through the crowd, with only one thought in her mind.

Mine.

When she stepped into the hazy circle of the spotlight, the other girl stumbled, losing the rhythm of the dance. Juliet felt a lift of triumph as she turned to face the audience. It was all hers – the crowd, the spotlight, the dance, all of it – and she would never give it up.

For a few seconds, there was nothing but the dance, *her* dance. Then she caught a glimpse of the girl's face, white under the lights.

It wasn't Esme.

As Juliet faltered, there was a blur of movement, then arms came round her, dragging her back from the spotlight, and out of the lumber room. In the corridor, she was pushed hard into the wall. A hand fumbled at something beside her, then that section of wall swung away, sending her stumbling through into a dusty, unlit space. As she whipped round, the hidden door closed again, plunging her into near-darkness.

'What—' That was all she managed before a hand clamped down hard over her mouth, forcing the furious words back down her throat, where they twisted into a tight panic.

All the dark possibilities that had haunted the edges of Juliet's fears crowded close. She struggled in her unseen assailant's grip as she was dragged through the darkness. She could hear the Show's music fading behind her, and her fear grew into a desperate clamour. As she fought harder, trying to twist free, she landed a kick on her captor's leg, and he swore, harsh and low.

There was something faintly familiar about his voice. The smell of him was familiar too, sweat and dust and something bitter, like spice. It had been on her skin sometimes after they'd shared a scene, even though he'd always seemed to be trying to touch her as little as he could. Even as that recognition glinted, Arlen dropped her back onto her feet again. Fumbling at another door, he opened it to reveal a flight of steps, lit by a single bulb.

'Down the stairs.' His voice was terse, and when Juliet didn't move, he gave her a push, sending her stumbling against the door-frame. 'For God's sake, go.'

Juliet wanted to scream at him, to demand that he tell her the truth, but there was something in his voice, and the accompanying look he threw over his shoulder, that kept her silent. Heart thumping, she set off down the stairs, with him close behind. The steps went down a long way – two or three floors, at least. The lighting was poor, and when they reached the bottom she stepped down too far, sending pain jarring up through her knee.

Arlen pushed past to a heavy door. Unlocking it, he pulled it open a little way and looked out.

'This brings you out in an alleyway behind the theatre.' He shoved her mask into her hand. 'Go home, get whatever you need, then get as far away from the district as you can.'

'What?' That buzzing was back in Juliet's ears again, making it impossible to think clearly. 'No. I'm not leaving. What was—'

Arlen swore again, cutting across her. 'We don't have time for this. You should never have come here.'

'I *belong* here.' He'd always hated her, and she'd done nothing to deserve it. 'I belong in the district.'

'You don't.' Arlen pushed the door wider. 'I'm telling you to go. Walk away, and don't look back.' When Juliet didn't move, he gave her another hard push, almost toppling her. 'For God's sake go, before it's too late.'

Then he yanked the door shut, leaving her alone outside, with shaking hands that she couldn't force still.

Chapter 30

JULIET'S MIND WAS LIKE the kaleidoscope she'd had as a child, a decorated tube with scraps of coloured cellophane between two pieces of glass. You turned it, and the pieces moved, drawing close to a pattern, only to split apart and spiral away again.

She was afraid, and not just that she might not get what she wanted. This was much deeper than that, and had been lurking inside her for a long time. Lambert was right. There was something terribly wrong in the district, and it had to do with another red-haired girl who looked like her, just as the girl in the river had looked like Jemima.

She thought of Ethan, smiling down at her, his hand warm on her shoulder.

You need to trust me.

She shivered, and the image reshaped into the Director.

I promise you, this is only the beginning.

A third voice echoed. *Be careful of Conrad's promises.*

But Miss Abbeline had lied too. How did you know who to ask for help if you couldn't work out who to believe? Lambert had said something like that, hadn't he? Something about how were you meant to know what was real and what wasn't?

Lambert.

Juliet felt a desperate flare of hope. He'd never asked her to trust him. He'd never asked anything of her but the truth. She set off along the alleyway, leaning heavily on the wall as she went. At the end, she turned into the street that led towards the main gate, and her heart thudded. There was a figure coming towards her. A girl, unmasked.

Jemima.

Juliet crossed the space between them in a few swift steps, catching the other girl's arm. 'I need to speak to you.'

Jemima pulled away. 'You shouldn't be here.'

'I saw a girl,' Juliet said. 'A girl with red hair and silver shoes, playing my role. A girl who looked like me.'

'Leave me alone.' Jemima's hands were curled into fists. 'I don't . . . I can't . . .' She broke off, her face so white Juliet thought she was going to faint – but as she reached out again, Jemima shrank back. 'Don't touch me,' she hissed. 'This is all your fault. If you'd never come here, she . . .'

'She? Who?' As Jemima shook her head, lips pressed together, Juliet realised, with a strange, cold calm, that she already knew the answer. She knew exactly what this was, just as *Olivia* had told her she did. 'There's more than one person playing each role.' Her voice sounded as though it was coming from a long way away. 'The girl in the river, she was your . . .' She stopped, not sure what name to give to her revelation.

Jemima sagged against the wall, all resistance draining out of her. 'She was my Night Version,' she said dully.

'Night Version?'

'It's what we call them.' Jemima was dry-eyed, but there was a rasp in her voice that sounded as though she'd already shed all the tears she had in her. 'They're from outside, and they play our roles in the Show during quiet times, or if we can't. They look like us, and they dance like us, and no one ever realises they're not us.'

'Who are they?' Juliet's own mouth was dry. 'How do—'

'We're not supposed to know. We don't meet them. We don't know anything about them.' Jemima's face tightened, as though her words had jolted her into the realisation of what she was doing. 'I can't be here, talking to you.'

'You did meet her, though,' Juliet said slowly. A memory had surfaced – two fair-haired girls, kissing in the shadows. 'I saw you with her.'

Raw fear blazed across Jemima's face. 'You didn't tell? We're not supposed to talk about them. They're our ghosts, and they always go away, sooner or later.'

Juliet went still. 'Go away?'

Jemima shook her head mutely, her fingers twisting into a fold of her dress.

'Jemima.' There was a tremor in Juliet's voice. 'What happened to her?'

The look Jemima gave her was sharp with something close to hatred. 'You did. How can any of us compete with the Director's beloved Girl in the Silver Shoes?'

There was something off-key about what Jemima was saying, but Juliet couldn't spare a thought for what it might be. There were too many other things crowding close about her, and the darkest of them wore a familiar face.

Don't trust Conrad. Miss Abbeline's voice echoed once again. *Walk away before it's too late.*

'Jemima . . .'

'She's dead.' As she said the words, Jemima curled inwards, arms wrapped across her body, as though she was trying to hold all her pain and grief inside. 'I thought if I was good enough, she'd be safe, because they'd need her. But I wasn't, and now she's dead.'

Juliet's mind was a black, shifting void. As she stared at Jemima, the other girl's head suddenly jerked up. When Juliet followed her gaze, she saw a Wanderer watching them from the end of the street, in the dull glow of a streetlight.

With an incoherent sound, Jemima pushed Juliet away and lurched into a run, disappearing round the corner, leaving Juliet staring at the cloaked figure. The metallic gaze was unreadable, and her fear thinned to a tight wire.

As the silent figure took a step towards her, the moment broke, and she tore free, throwing herself down the alleyway. It was a reaction of pure, panicked instinct, with no thought beyond the next step. As she rounded the corner, there was no sound of pursuit, but she had no idea what secret routes the Wanderer knew. He could already be flanking her, ready to cut her off.

A figure rose up ahead of her, and Juliet swerved, stumbling against the wall. She was vaguely aware of a voice, but it was several stretched, panicked seconds before she recognised her own name. Her vision cleared slightly, and the face looking down at her came into focus.

Ethan.

Juliet felt a bare breath of relief, but it swiftly snapped off. He'd known. They'd all known.

She wrenched against him. 'Let me go.'

'Juliet, stop. Listen to me.'

'No.' She was crying now, great heaving sobs of fear and desperation. 'Please, let me go. I'll walk away. I won't tell anyone.'

'Juliet, listen.' He gave her a sharp shake. 'You have to come with me now.'

'Please. I—'

'You're not safe out here.' His voice was low and urgent. 'Please, Juliet, just come with me.'

There was nothing in his face but concern, yet this was the Theatre District, where everyone was schooled in the art of telling the brightest, most glittering lies from the moment they could smile or speak.

'The girl,' Juliet said. 'That girl in the theatre. She—'

'I know. I'll tell you everything, but we have to go. There are people looking for you right now.'

'The Wanderer.' With a fresh surge of fear, Juliet twisted round. 'He was watching me and—'

'That's why we have to go.'

'Out of the district?' She felt a flicker of hope.

He shook his head. 'They'll be watching. But somewhere safe.' As she opened her mouth to say *no, no she couldn't stay here, she had to go now and get as far away as she could*, he suddenly dropped his head and kissed her, quick and hard. 'Juliet, please trust me. I promise I will answer any question you ask me, but not here.' He shot a look along the street. 'We have to go. Please, Juliet.'

Her mind felt as though it was splintering apart. Perhaps it was all those different versions of herself deserting her, leaving her alone to face the dark and twisted wreckage of her dreams. There was too little of her to stand up against the enormity of what she'd discovered, but no one else was coming to help her. All she could do was hope against thin, brittle hope that Ethan was somehow the one true thing in the darkness.

Juliet let him take her hand in his, leading her through the back streets of the district. At each corner, each doorway, he stopped to peer out, before hurrying her across yet another street or up another flight of steps.

At the end of a low-roofed arcade, lined with shuttered shops, he stopped to unlock an iron gate. The passage on the other side was dark, and Juliet felt as though a vice was tightening around her lungs. She took a small step forward, straining for any warning from *Olivia*, but there was just silence. Another step, and she was through. Ethan closed and locked the gate behind them, and they set off again, along the passage to yet another flight of winding stairs. They'd passed several landings when realisation swelled inside Juliet, forcing all the air out of her lungs. There was only one place in the district with this many floors.

He'd brought her to the House of Doors.

Chapter 31

Juliet thought about leaning back and letting herself fall.

There'd be a second or two of nothing but the lurch of her stomach, and then she'd hit the stone edge of a step and tumble on, down and down, until there was nothing but a bloody, bruised mess of unconsciousness, slumped on the floor at the bottom. There'd be nothing more they could do to her.

The moment passed, and she kept walking, as though she was made of clockwork, wound up and set on some course. At the top of the stairs, a door opened onto a familiar passageway. Juliet felt the crushing tightness in her chest ease very slightly. He wasn't taking her to the Director. They were up in the attic where they'd rehearsed.

Ethan climbed the steps to the roof and pushed the hatch open. Scrambling through, he reached down to help her up. It was a cold, clear night, and the sky was scattered with more stars than she could remember seeing in a long while. Somewhere in the distance, she could hear the rise and fall of sirens. She wanted to close her eyes and imagine that they were coming to save her. Instead, she made herself turn and face Ethan.

'Why have you brought me here?' She was surprised at how calm she sounded.

'Because it's one of the few places we won't be overheard.'

'Are you going to lie to me again?' It was as though Juliet was on the wrong side of a pane of glass, cut off from her emotions.

He shook his head. 'It's too late for that. The truth is the only hope for us now.'

'Us?' She gave a harsh, high laugh that made her throat feel the way it did just before she was sick. 'There is no *us*. You're part of all of this.'

'It's not that simple,' he said. 'Yes, I'm part of the district, and that means I never had a choice about—' He broke off, and looked away for a moment. 'Tell me what you know,' he said, turning back to her. 'Or rather tell me what you think you know, and I'll tell you the truth of it.'

'All those dead girls.' The words still didn't feel real. 'They were Night Versions. And they . . .' Juliet clenched her lips against another pitch of nausea. She'd spent so long trying to draw the scattered pieces together, and now all she wanted was for them to stay separate, so she wouldn't *know*. But it was too late. The fragments were coming together, and they formed a dark, brutal picture. 'You knew. All this time, you knew what was happening.'

Ethan's hand came up, but Juliet stepped back out of reach, and he let it drop to his side.

'I'm a monster,' he said bleakly. 'We're all monsters. We see the Night Versions on the set. We perform with them, rehearse with them, but they're not real. We don't know their names, or where they came from, or who loved them – if anyone ever loved them at all. But then . . .' His mouth was tight with pain. 'Then one day they're gone, and suddenly it's there, everything you've pushed away. It's pressing about you, and you hold your breath, because if you don't, you'll break. And then it passes, and you breathe and let yourself pretend. Because perhaps they've just moved on. Perhaps they wanted something else. Perhaps it wasn't . . . *that*.'

Juliet wanted to cover her ears. When Ethan had brought her up here the first time, to dance with her, and kiss her beneath the great stretch of the sky, everything had felt like a possibility. Now he was telling her that none of it had ever been real.

'All those girls,' she said again. 'How long has it been going on? And *why*?'

'There was a deal,' Ethan said. 'Struck a very long time ago. The country had been through some hard times and the district was struggling for the first time in its history. I can't imagine Byron Ballard was fool enough to think there wouldn't be strings attached, but I don't suppose he realised what he was starting. The first Backers poured money into the district in the expectation that it would become their playground.' His mouth curled in a cynical smile. 'But the Directors aren't inclined to share their toys, so once they realised what kind of games some of those rich men liked, they found something else for them to play with.' The smile fell away. 'And some of those toys ended up broken.' Revulsion twisted in Juliet's stomach. 'But there were always more where they came from – drawn from the never-ending stream of young hopefuls coming through the gates, looking for work and dreaming of a place in the Show. Something to be used for a while, and then discarded.'

'You mean murdered.' Juliet was shivering, and she saw Ethan move slightly, as though he was thinking of reaching for her again. If he was, he thought better of it.

'Not all of them,' he said. 'We're talking over two hundred years. Not every Director was as transactional as Byron Ballard, and not every cohort of Backers had the same . . . predilections. For the most part it was a simple enough transaction. Money and connections in exchange for extra access. Special performances, guaranteed private scenes, exclusive events attended only by them. A few hints of what was coming. Storylines twisted to their whims. Years might go by without incident. But, sooner or later, there'd be tough times, or the district would elect a Director who had greater plans than most, and it would start again.'

Juliet's thoughts went to that group of men who'd moved through the theatre as though they owned it, and the look on Ethan's face when she'd protested. 'The Backers. Who are they?'

'I don't know,' he said. 'Names aren't exactly shared freely. I just know they're wealthy enough to afford whatever they desire, and powerful enough to ensure that the darkest of those desires never come to light.'

'All those dead girls.' The stark horror of those words wasn't fading with repetition. 'All those years. How has no one ever realised?'

'Because this is the Theatre District,' Ethan said. 'It's full of fragments and illusions and distortions.' He shook his head. 'The Night Versions are just another half-glimpsed story, and that's no accident. The Directors deal in stories. They understand how they work. If you bury a secret, and it finds its way back to the light, the truth is there, stark and unmistakeable. Better to give people a glimpse of that truth, let them spin tales about it, until it's so tangled that no one remembers there's anything real at the heart of it. When they pull another body from the river, the old stories are dredged up too. The rumours of taunting letters sent to the police. The names – the Knockerman, the Lambeth Stalker, the Ripper of the Hallows. When you have a Show that goes beyond the walls of the theatre, how do you know how far it stretches? Perhaps the stories of dead girls and police suspicion are part of it too.' His mouth twisted. 'Perhaps those girls never existed at all, because how can anyone ever be sure what's real?'

All the world's a stage.

Juliet gave a sharp shake of her head. 'The Night Versions were real. And they're dead.'

'Not all of them. It isn't all of them.' He'd said that before, and Juliet had a sense that he was clinging to it, like someone hanging on to any bit of wreckage to keep from drowning. 'But when the district needs money, or when close isn't close enough for some of the Backers, that's when another strand is wound into the district's darkest stories.' Shadows shifted behind his eyes. 'And there's a power in darkness. Danes understands that.'

'Danes.' Juliet's thoughts had gone back to that overheard conversation. 'The Stage Manager wanted him to keep a promise he'd made. He said . . .' She stopped. Somewhere in the memory of that conversation, she could hear an off-key note, like a warning, but she couldn't work out what had set it sounding.

'He promised Kellan Grey he'd put an end to it,' Ethan said. 'In exchange for his support in the election.' He gave a brief smile. 'It took me a while to work it out.' He shook his head. 'He'll never keep that promise. He intends to write his name into the history of the district, even if he has to do it in blood. Night Versions are just part of the machinery for him. I'm not even sure he sees them as real.'

'And what about you?' The anger that rose inside Juliet was mired in fear, but it was directed straight at Ethan. 'You knew everything. Why didn't you tell someone?'

'It should be simple, shouldn't it?' He sounded bone-weary. 'Something bad is happening, so you tell someone and they make the bad thing go away and everyone lives happily ever after. But what happens when everything you've ever known, everyone in your world, is bound so tightly to that bad thing that it would drag them all down with it?' His voice was bleak. 'The Show must go on. That's what we're told from the moment we're old enough to listen. And by the time we understand what it means, we're part of it too. Every single one of us is culpable. If this secret ever got out, it would bring the district down. Would you have the courage to be the one to cause that?'

'But it's not just that,' Juliet said. '*You* made me part of this. *You* took me to Danes.'

'I thought it would be different for you. You were part of the story of the Moonshine Girl, and I knew what that meant to him. And then there was what I wanted. I was selfish; I wanted you so much that I couldn't see straight.'

As he moved closer, Juliet's hands came up to push him away, but somehow she found them curling against his chest. 'I'm sorry, Juliet.' His voice was low. 'I put you in danger, but I did it because I'd fallen in love with you. I thought I could keep you safe.'

'And what about the girl I saw on the set?' Juliet said. 'What about my Night Version?' Would she *go away* one day, if Juliet wasn't good enough, if she couldn't live up to the Director's obsession with her mother? 'I thought it was Esme but . . .' She broke off. Ethan had turned his head slightly, the gesture catching at something hidden inside her and drawing it into the light, in a long painful scrape.

'No.' She shook her head. '*No*. I'm the Girl in the Silver Shoes.' She took a step back from him. 'I'm the Girl in the Silver Shoes. I was born here.' The missing entry in the little book in the record office. 'I belong here.' *You don't.* The hardness in Arlen's voice as he spoke those words. Juliet took another step, fighting against the knowledge she didn't want. 'I walked the wires. People saw me. They told stories about me.' She gave another hard shake of her head. 'No. It's not true.'

You know it's true. You've always known.

'Juliet.' Ethan had gone very still, and Juliet realised she'd stepped onto the ridge, narrow and precarious, with the great curve of the roof falling away below her. Her head spun with a vertigo that had as much to do with the emptiness inside her as the knowledge of the fall that lay just a step away. How much of yourself could you lose before the earth let you slip free and you fell away into the sky?

'No,' she said again. 'No.'

'Juliet.' Ethan raised his hand slowly. 'Come towards me.'

The dizziness receded, leaving Juliet feeling clear and sharp and brittle as glass.

When she spoke again, her voice was steady. 'Tell me who that girl was.'

'Juliet.' Ethan risked a step forward, putting a note of command in his voice. 'Take my hand. Now.'

'I'm not the Girl in the Silver Shoes.' The words sounded in the hollow place inside her, setting off mocking echoes, as though a whole chorus of *Olivias*, of Esmes, of other selves and dark reflections, were taunting her for ever thinking she could belong here. 'I'm her Night Version.'

'Juliet, please.' Ethan took another step. 'Just take my hand.'

As Juliet lifted her head to look up at the stars, glinting in that clear, cold sky, wishing she could just float away and never have to think about any of this ever again, Ethan lunged for her, wrapping his arms tightly around her and dragging her back onto the ledge. Pressed to his chest, Juliet could feel his heart thumping, and the frightened beat of it seemed to restart her own frozen emotions. A hard shudder went through her. She wasn't the real Girl in the Silver Shoes. She was the mirror image, the shadow version. The Night Version.

That thought wrapped around another, drawing it out, and she pushed against Ethan's arms, to look up at him. 'My mother wasn't the Moonshine Girl, was she?' The words brought a dragging pain with them. 'She was a Night Version too.'

'Yes.' Ethan's voice was low. 'She was a Night Version. From what I've heard, it was a perfect match. Her resemblance to the Moonshine Girl was striking, and she was every bit as talented as the real version. And she wanted it so much. Danes told me that, the only time he spoke openly about her. But he thought he could manage the situation.'

'I don't understand,' Juliet said. 'The Backers . . .'

'The Backers had nothing to do with what happened to your mother,' Ethan said. 'The rules around the Night Versions were put in place for good reasons, but the Director thought he was above those kind of restrictions.' He paused. 'No, that's not quite fair. For centuries, this place has taken what it can from anyone offering anything of value, but still we look at people who aren't *district*, and see them as lesser, as *other*. Danes, for all his faults, is surprisingly egalitarian when it comes to blood. For him, it was simple. There was a complication, and he saw a solution.'

'What complication?' Juliet was struggling to follow.

'A performer in the Show was taken ill,' Ethan said. 'A tumour in his spine. His condition deteriorated very suddenly, leaving him unable to manage more than a couple of hours on set. His storyline was closely tied to that of the Moonshine Girl, and, like her, he'd become very popular. With no time to unwind that story from the Show, Danes broke the rules and let someone else take over.'

'His Night Version,' Juliet said.

Ethan shook his head. 'There are very few male Night Versions. With a small number of exceptions, the most popular characters have always been female.' His face darkened. 'And that's not entirely down to chance. The Backers have more influence over which storylines come to prominence than most Directors would ever admit, and their tastes tend towards the conservative – in some senses, at least. No, this wasn't a Night Version. It was a replacement.'

'I didn't know performers were ever replaced.'

'They aren't,' Ethan said. 'But Stephen Grace had that in common with the Director – both of them believed rules were for lesser mortals.'

'My father?' Juliet stared at him.

Ethan nodded. 'He grew up in a stagehand family in the precincts, with the usual expectation that he'd spend his life in the shadows, keeping the Show running. But he'd found his way into the affections of a young performer who persuaded Danes to use him in the Show. They'd spent time together in secret since they were both very young. She'd taught him to dance, and he turned out to have a natural talent for it, as well as the kind of charisma that shines through. It created a furore when it came out. But what Danes' beloved Moonshine Girl wanted, she got. Danes railroaded the board into granting Stephen the full privileges and duties of a performer. From what I've heard, the Moonshine Girl was transformed by love and happiness, shining so brightly that people practically fought for a glimpse of her.'

'What happened?' Juliet had spent so long believing that her mother was the Moonshine Girl, it was hard to remember the dazzling, transformed-with-love girl he was describing was someone else. 'What went wrong?'

'She fell pregnant,' Ethan said. 'It was a difficult pregnancy, and her Night Version took on more and more of her performances. I would imagine Danes was under considerable scrutiny from the board at this point. Not only a stagehand stepping into a performer's shoes but the relationship between Principal and Night Version turned on its head – it must have looked as though he was hell-bent on breaking the rules. Still, I suppose he had little choice, and he would have expected Catherine to take back her role once the baby was born. But that didn't happen.'

Catherine. The real Moonshine Girl now had a name. 'Why not?' Juliet asked.

'She became more and more unwell,' Ethan said. 'She said she couldn't dance, couldn't face the audience. She spent hours crying in a dark room, barely even looking at her newborn daughter – and she wanted Stephen at her side every minute of every hour.'

Juliet could see the shape of the unfolding story. She'd seen it before, trailing along in Stephen's wake. 'He left her, didn't he?'

Ethan nodded. 'It turned out he'd never cared that much about her. She was just a step from somewhere he didn't want to be, to something different. The forebears of the stagehand families were travellers, and Danes told me he thought that was still in Stephen's blood. He was always looking for the next thing, and the next. And it didn't take long for him to move onto the Moonshine Girl's Night Version. That should have been the end of your mother, of course. Not only had she crossed a boundary that should never have been crossed, but she'd stolen Stephen away from the Director's favourite, who was completely broken by the betrayal. Ironically, though, it was Catherine's decline that saved Madeleine's life. Of the two Moonshine Girls, she was the only one who was still performing. Even when she became pregnant, she carried on dancing.'

'Did no one notice?' Juliet's throat was tight. She'd been carried through the theatre, curled under her mother's heart as Madeleine had danced and shone and believed she had everything she'd ever want.

Ethan gave a small shrug. 'A slight change of costume, some tweaks to the loop to keep the audience further away; it's been done plenty of times before. The difference here was that, in those final weeks, when the Night Version would usually step up, it was the real Moonshine Girl who was coaxed back onto the set.'

'She reclaimed her role?'

'She tried,' Ethan said. 'I can't be sure, but I think Danes persuaded her Stephen might return to her if he saw her as the wonderful, dazzling Moonshine Girl once again.' He shook his head. 'But she wasn't dazzling. She was a shadow of what she'd once been. Madeleine, on the other hand, had her baby, and was dancing again within days, as beautiful and perfect as ever.'

Two Moonshine Girls. Two babies.

If Juliet had imagined this before she arrived in the district, her mind would have been full of the miracle of her sister's existence. She would have dreamed of them meeting: the initial awkwardness, with them both speaking at once, and then finding they couldn't think of anything to say. But they'd find their way through that, and notice they made some of the same gestures, spoke in the same way. They'd talk late into the night and when the moment came for Juliet to leave, her sister would put out her hand and say, *Don't go. Don't ever go away again.*

Instead, the slice of envy that went through Juliet was so sharp and jagged it felt as though she was tearing open around the injustice of it. They were the same, the two of them, just an accident of maternity apart. But her sister had been given everything that had been withheld from her.

'She's the real Girl in the Silver Shoes,' Juliet said dully. 'My sister.'

'Yes,' Ethan said. 'I'm sorry.'

That was why she hadn't been allowed onto the set apart from her performances. They couldn't risk her seeing another red-haired girl playing her role. Snatches of conversations replayed in Juliet's mind – things the Followers had said about recent changes, a new cast member. How many times had she let some piece of the truth drift by because it didn't fit the picture she thought she could see?

Another realisation hit her.

Olivia.

For all her fractured, conflicted relationship with that imagined other half, Juliet found herself aching with loss and an irrational sense of betrayal.

'What happened to my mother?' She knew the answer was going to hurt, but she had to know.

'It limped on like that for a while, and might have gone on indefinitely – perhaps, in time, people would have started to forget that Madeleine, shining like the moonlight her borrowed role was named for, wasn't the real Moonshine Girl – but Catherine's jealousy and hatred grew stronger and stronger. And then someone else got involved. Another performer. He saw Stephen with Madeleine and reported back to Catherine. He was very young, and thought he was in love with her. I suppose it was the only time she paid him any attention, and he probably hoped she'd turn to him eventually.' *He was very young.* How old would Arlen have been back then? Was this the reason why he could barely look at her? 'One night, Catherine put her baby down to sleep, put on her costume and made her way to the set. Then she waited until her Night Version was up on the platform above the ballroom, and – pushed her.'

Juliet closed her eyes. She'd wanted the truth, but now she wished she could unwind everything that had happened and slip back into not knowing. Her mother had kissed her goodbye and gone to the House of Doors, where a woman who hated her had pushed her off a ledge to break on the theatre floor. Had the audience watched as she died? Had she looked up at them, through her blurred and darkening vision, and seen their masked stares?

Something else occurred to her, and she opened her eyes. 'My father was there.' There was a stark horror to the realisation. 'He saw her die. He was the one who shouted her name.'

Ethan nodded heavily. 'He was waiting for her down in the ballroom. They had a scene together.'

'Why didn't he tell the police?' Juliet said. 'If he cared for my mother at all—'

'You don't understand.' Ethan cut across her. 'You don't know how it feels to be part of this. The stagehands are deeper in it than most of us. Stephen might have felt little loyalty to the Show, or to Danes, but betraying them would have meant betraying his own people.' He shook his head. 'Oh, I suppose Danes might have come up with some story or other, but it all happened too fast. The Director is used to having all the time in the world to sit back and ponder over every move before he pulls on someone's strings. The police arrived so quickly.'

'He showed them the Moonshine Girl,' Juliet said. 'He told them she was Madeleine.'

'He didn't have to,' Ethan replied. 'Danes said Catherine was frighteningly calm. When she looked at Mansfield, he thought she was going to confess, but then she smiled and said her name was Madeleine. She never used the name Catherine again. Maybe it was a penance of sorts, or perhaps some part of her believed that if she said it enough, she could make it true, make Stephen love her instead, I don't know.'

Juliet felt a painful glint of understanding. She knew how easy it was for your own edges to blur and shift, so that you felt like a chain of paper dolls, unfolding to reveal other selves, other lives that could have been yours if just one cut of the paper had been different.

'My father,' she said. 'What happened to him?'

Ethan shrugged. 'You know as much as I do. He just walked away, leaving everything behind.'

'Not everything,' Juliet said. 'Why did he take me? He didn't want me.'

'Danes mentioned some deal they struck between them,' Ethan said. 'Perhaps you were part of that. Or perhaps he only realised he'd made a mistake when it was too late.'

Juliet dug her fingernails into her palms. A mistake. A deal. Was that all her life had been? A picture came into her head – her stepmother sitting at her father's old desk with the solicitor's letters she'd taken from Juliet, tallying up old accounts, offsetting all those years of payments against the costs of raising Stephen's unwanted child.

'Why did Danes let me come back?' she asked. 'After all these years, he must have thought it was over.'

Ethan shook his head. 'This is the district. Nothing is ever over. The Show is full of echoes of what's gone before. Even the Night Versions are there, scattered through the theatre. If you knew where to look, you could piece every one of those lost lives back together. The Moonshine Girl was one of Danes' greatest obsessions. He had such plans for her story, but after your mother died, Catherine only performed a few more times.'

Juliet thought she could see the shape of the final piece in the story. 'She killed herself.'

'Not exactly,' Ethan said. 'She drank every trace of herself away, until all she had left was the bottle and the memory of loving Stephen. She used to talk about him as though he'd just gone away for a while, and sooner or later he'd come back. She died still waiting for him, just days before you arrived.'

'But why make me a Night Version?' Juliet said.

Ethan gave her another of those cynical smiles. 'Because Danes is the consummate storyteller, and it was such a perfect story, such a beautiful, perfect symmetry. The Moonshine Girl and her Night Version. The Moonshine Girl's daughter and her Night Version's daughter. I can only imagine the pleasure it gave him, to gather up those broken threads and weave them into something new.' His smile dropped away. 'But I have to take some responsibility too. The other Night Versions, they all know what they are, even if they don't know their full purpose. I assumed Danes would tell you, but when he realised you hadn't seen the Girl in the Silver Shoes, that you thought you *were* the Girl in the Silver Shoes, he decided to keep the truth from you.'

'Why?' Juliet said.

'To ensure a great moment in the Show,' Ethan said. 'The Moonshine Girl's story playing out once again, through the Girl in the Silver Shoes.'

'I'm supposed to die in the Show.' The words barely seemed to mean anything. It was impossible that she was speaking them, impossible that this was her, up here with the city stretching away beneath her, remote and unknowing. 'I'm supposed to fall, like she did.' She looked up at him. 'Why? Why would he want it to happen again?'

'I would never have let him do it.' Ethan's face was taut with emotion. 'You have to believe me, Juliet. As soon as I worked out what he was planning, I realised we could use his own plan against him.' He gripped her shoulders. 'We can bring him down. We let him put on his great performance, but we take control of the ending. We use it to expose him.'

'I don't understand,' Juliet said. 'You said if you told anyone, it would be the end of the district.'

'Which is why no one will be telling anyone anything. Not a single word.' When Juliet stared at him, uncomprehending, he dropped his head to kiss her. It was just a warm brush of his mouth on hers, lips barely parted, as though this was the early stages of an ordinary courtship. 'It's better if you don't know everything.' As she started to protest, he shook his head. 'I can't, Juliet. It's safer if you know just enough to play your role.' He gave a small smile. 'And that's all you have to do. Play your role tomorrow night. Be the Girl in the Silver Shoes. Give the performance of your life. You don't have to worry about anything else. The stagehands will make sure you get where you need to be.'

'No.' Juliet gave a convulsive shake of her head. 'I can't. I have to get away. You have to help me.'

'We can do this.' Ethan tightened his grip on her shoulders. 'Everything is in place. I promise you, Juliet, you won't be in any danger from the Director or the Backers. Not for a moment.'

'But I'm not the Girl in the Silver Shoes,' Juliet said. '*She* is. My sister. She'll be the one performing tomorrow.'

'No, she won't.' Ethan's voice was low.

'But—' Juliet broke off. Of course. It couldn't be Olivia, because of how this was supposed to end.

It couldn't be Olivia because Olivia mattered.

Ethan gave her a gentle shake. 'Juliet, we can do this. If you help me, we can finish him.'

'And you'll be Director,' Juliet said slowly.

He nodded. 'I told you – things have to change. *We* can change them. *We* can make a different future.' He kissed her again, then turned her in his arms to face the city. 'The district is the light that keeps shining, through war and plague and famine, and the hardest of times. That's why we have to do this, to make sure nothing can extinguish that light.' His arms tightened around her. 'We only have one chance at this, and it will only work if you help me.'

His breath was warm on her neck, his voice soft against her ear. 'I love you.'

Juliet desperately wanted to believe, but she was cold to the bone, despite his arms around her, with everything he'd told her, everything she'd seen and heard and tried not to know, all jangling in her head.

A voice rose from that off-key scrape. *Your nephew is working hard at polishing up that old deal.*

Ethan brushed his lips along the curve of her jaw, then murmured in her ear. 'Trust me, Livvy. We can do this.'

A tiny crack opened up inside her, growing and spreading, like the first fissure in a frozen lake sending out a deadly spider web across the ice. She was acutely aware of how high up they were, how narrow the ledge on which they were standing. If she fell, she wouldn't float away into the sky. She'd break on the stones below, and that would be the end of her.

She closed her eyes. She only had a few heartbeats to find her way into the role she had to play. It was a role she knew well, even if it felt as though she'd left it behind a long time ago. It was the girl she'd once been. Starry-eyed, brittle with hope, terrified of it all slipping out of her grasp. And believing, beyond everything, in stories where love was real.

Taking the slowest, most careful breath she could find, Juliet turned to look up at Ethan, meeting his gaze with no deception in her eyes.

'I'll help you,' she said.

Chapter 32

IT WAS COLD ON the roof, with a brittle fog turning to drizzle.

As the attic door closed behind Ethan, Juliet sank to her knees and gave in to racking sobs.

Olivia.

She wasn't another version of Juliet, or the girl in the mirror, or some story an old man had made up. She was flesh and blood, and part of this place in a way Juliet could never be. All those almost-memories, of the wires, of being the Girl in the Silver Shoes, they weren't real. Or if they were, they weren't *hers*. They were Olivia's.

And Ethan was hers too.

Livvy, he'd called her, and she'd heard the tenderness, the intimacy wrapping about his voice. *Trust me.*

Had he spoken those words so many times that the memories had blurred and merged into one, making him forget which girl he was holding in his arms? Juliet didn't know what else he'd lied about, but it didn't matter. What mattered was that none of it was meant to end with her walking away from the district. She'd learned too much for that. She'd *wanted* too much for that.

The Director had told her that *real* didn't mean what she thought it did, but the truth was that it didn't mean anything at all. Even the stars up there in the sky . . . how could you be sure that they meant what everyone said they meant? You could try to do your own calculations, work out all those complicated angles of light and distance and the way the Earth turned. Or if you couldn't do that, you could make up stories about them, telling yourself that their purpose was to hold their place in the skies, so that you could look up and always know they were there. But, in the end, you couldn't *know*.

So if you couldn't know, and couldn't trust, and couldn't believe, what did you have left? An answer came to her, bleak and cold, but bringing with it a certain calm.

Me.

She was all she'd ever had, her only certainty in all of this.

Juliet stood up, cramped and clumsy with cold. Behind her, the glass dome rose, smooth and glistening, offering no escape. Below her, the roof curved down towards the embankment, its criss-cross of ridges and chimneys like a network of old scars. Through the darkness, she saw a faint glint a little way off. A skylight, like the one in the attic room below her. Her pulse picked up. She had no idea if the window would open, or what lay beneath it, but if she could just escape the prison of the theatre, there was a chance she could find a way out of the district.

As Juliet stepped onto the ridge where she'd danced with Ethan, she found herself listening for *Olivia*, but the voice in her head was silent. There was no *Olivia*, and the real

Livvy was probably lying in Ethan's arms right now. The ridge felt narrower than it should have done as Juliet edged carefully along to one of the wooden roof joists.

The beam was smooth and slick as she inched her way downwards. Her foot slipped a couple of times, sending cold flares of adrenaline through her, but she gritted her teeth and kept going. She'd almost reached the comparative safety of another ridge when something shifted beneath her. With the sound of splintering wood, a joist broke away, leaving Juliet teetering off balance. As her foot came down on a roof board she felt it sag, before it, too, gave way. Juliet threw herself forward, landing on another joist, her breath catching behind her ribs in a swell of panic.

When she recovered enough to look around, there was a ragged hole in the roof, through which she could see the glint of lights below. A fresh urgency wound into her fear. Forcing herself to a crouch, she moved on, inch by careful inch again, until she reached the ridge. The old tiles were scraped with lichen, but they felt solid as she scrambled along. When she got to the end and straightened up, she could see the skylight more clearly. The ridgepole above it ran to within a couple of feet of where Juliet was standing. Gathering every scrap of nerve, she inhaled, that drag of air snagging on an incoherent prayer, then leaped across the gap.

The tiles were ice-slick as she landed, and she flailed, one foot sliding out from under her. Somehow, she wrenched herself back, sprawling across the ridge. For a few seconds she lay there, letting the white blaze of fear subside, before crawling the final distance to the skylight. The glass was murky with dirt, but when she rubbed at it, she could see the hazy outlines of an attic room with an empty fireplace and a half-open door. She pushed at the window, but it didn't budge. As she leaned forwards, putting more force into her effort, a tile slid beneath her. When she eased her fingers underneath, it came away in a crumble of mortar. She had no idea if there was anyone in the building below, but what other option did she have?

Juliet swung the tile at the skylight, sending jagged shards crashing to the floor. Her heart was pounding, her instincts screaming at her to *hurry hurry*, but she made herself run the tile carefully around the edge of the window, knocking away the remaining razor-sharp pieces of glass. Resting her arms on the frame, she lowered herself as far as she could, and hung there for a moment, panic tightening around her, before letting her weight tear her free.

The impact knocked the breath out of her body, and for a moment, she could do nothing but lie there, struggling for air. As her lungs filled again, she felt the bite of glass, and scrambled to her feet. There was blood beading on a dozen or more cuts on her arms and legs, and a sharper pain in her hand. She turned it over to see a shard of glass sticking out of her palm. As she yanked it out, her vision swam and a shiver broke through her. She gave a hard shake of her head, fighting against the dizziness. She had to keep going.

When she tried the door, the handle turned, and with a sag of relief, she pushed it open. The stairs on the other side were reassuringly dusty, and she smothered a cough with the back of her hand as she made her way down to a hallway with paint peeling from the walls. Two of the doors leading off it were locked, but the third opened onto an empty room, with a pair of threadbare curtains pulled across the window. When Juliet moved them aside, she found herself looking down onto a cobbled street. Sliding the window up, she could see a ledge running along the front of the building and disappearing into a gap between the roofs at the end. It was narrow by most standards, but wider and more solid-looking than the ridges she'd just negotiated, and she eased herself out.

Keeping tight to the wall, Juliet edged along, holding on to windowsills and pipes where she could, curling her fingers into the cracks between the stones where there were no better handholds. She reached the gap and squeezed through, emerging onto a narrow path that wound between a haphazard tangle of rooftops and upper floors. Relief flickered when the path ended at a flight of steps leading down, but it was short-lived. The steps stopped at a small platform; at her feet, a wire stretched across the street to another rooftop gap.

A memory presented itself – being that little girl, stepping high above the street in her silver shoes. Then Juliet remembered she'd never been that girl. She was about to turn back, when she heard a scuff of sound behind her. When she twisted round, there was no one there, but she caught a shift of shadow, as though someone had paused, just out of sight at the top of the steps.

Juliet felt a strange calm settle upon her. Turning back to the wire, she looked across the street. It wasn't far – perhaps a dozen steps – but the smallest error would send her crashing to the cobblestones below. The image of her broken and bloody body gave way to another – the white face of a girl, her dark hair wreathing about her, as she sank, blank-eyed, into the murk of the river.

There was a ringing in Juliet's ears as she stepped forward, spread her arms and stepped off the ledge.

The shock of that first step was like nothing she'd ever felt, but the wire was taut beneath her foot, and her balance held. She breathed out, a slow release of the air caught behind her ribs, then took another step, and another, past the middle and on, across the last few feet.

She didn't waste time looking back. Ducking under a low hang of guttering, she squeezed along the gap. It ended at a flight of steps leading down into a narrow passage, which she followed to a cobbled street, crossing it swiftly to dive into an alley on the other side. An idea had taken shape. It was a desperate hope, but it was all she had.

The alleyway took Juliet to a street she knew. From there she wound her way through a series of passageways, emerging close to the Shipping News. There was no sign of pursuit as she pushed open the door slightly, peering into the bar-room. It was empty and she crossed, swiftly and silently, to the stairs.

The Followers' rooms were also deserted, shattering the brittle hope she'd had of finding Eugene. Hurrying through to the far room, she opened the top drawer of the cabinet he'd described, and found his folder tucked at the front. Grabbing a pencil, she scribbled his name on a scrap of paper, followed by the words *Call DC Lambert*. It was only when she reached down that she registered the missing weight of her purse with Lambert's card inside, and remembered her coat falling to the floor as she'd moved towards Livvy.

Before she could work out what to do, she heard a tiny sound from the next room, barely there, but unmistakeable. Juliet froze, her hand gripping the cabinet, the sharp metal digging into her fingers. She didn't hear anything else, but knew, with terrified certainty, that someone was moving towards her, stepping carefully to avoid another tell-tale creak. Pushing back against the fear that was threatening to smother her, she wrote two more words – *help me*. Then she dropped her pitiful attempt at a message into the folder, and turned away from the cabinet, treading as lightly as she could, through to the other back room. If she could just make it to the door, then there might be a chance.

Again, it was the softest slip of a sound.

As she started to turn, an arm came around her. The explosion of terror was blank and soundless, blotting out all thought. A cloth was pressed against her face, and a bitter sharpness filled her lungs. As her head spun and her legs gave way, a thought echoed in her head.

I'm dying.

That idea had a surprising clarity and hung, spotlit in her mind, as the darkness rose. She stopped struggling; the tightness in her chest eased.

There you go. Not so bad if you just don't fight.
Olivia?

Juliet's thoughts stretched and narrowed, before fading to a thin line of regret and disappearing into the darkness.

Chapter 33

THERE WAS AN ACHE in Juliet's shoulder as she came back to herself.

Not just her shoulder. Her whole body was sore, and everything felt muffled, as though her head had been stuffed with cotton wool. She struggled against the haze, uncovering a vague memory of falling, and of blood. Had she been in an accident? When she opened her eyes, there was darkness around her, and she felt a catch of fear. Then the memories rushed back.

The Night Versions.

Her mother's death at the hands of the Moonshine Girl.

Her own failed attempt at escape.

She was lying on a stone floor, somewhere cold and dark. Panic scraped at her, and she pushed herself up to sitting. She couldn't see a thing. She might as well have been blindfolded.

A sound from nearby sent Juliet's heart slamming against her ribs. A slat of light glinted and widened, as a door opened. A figure was outlined briefly before it closed again. As Juliet bit down against a whimper of fear, another sound came, smaller this time – a scratch – and a tiny flame flared. Shadows stretched as the figure turned, sliding the match into a lantern which guttered brighter, casting a ruddy light across a tiny, cell-like room. His face was still obscured, but Juliet knew, with leaden certainty, who it was. She could see the fluid grace in his movements as he stepped forward and crouched beside her.

Juliet shrank against the cold stone wall. There was a terrible tenderness to Ethan's touch as he reached out to brush her hair back from her face. For a moment, she wished she could fall into the illusion of that gentleness, but she'd ignored the truth too many times.

As she met his eyes, he gave her a small smile. 'When did you know?'

'You called me Livvy.' Juliet had to swallow against the bile of her hatred. 'Up on the roof.'

'Did I? That was careless.'

'Was anything you told me true?' Juliet was almost grateful for the loathing she felt for him. It was stronger than fear right now. 'Or was it all just what Danes told you to say?'

'Danes?' Ethan raised an eyebrow.

'You're on his side,' Juliet said. 'You've been working with him all along.'

'You really haven't listened to a word I've said, have you?' Ethan said. 'You still think it has to be straight and simple. You should have been a police officer, compiling your neat list, deciding what fits the story you want.'

'I don't want a story. I want the truth.'

'No you don't,' he replied. 'You came here with whole armfuls of hopes and dreams and possibilities, desperate for something to weave them into. I barely had to do anything. You did it all yourself.' He smiled. 'That's the trick, of course. But for what it's worth, I've never lied to you.' His smile tilted. 'Well, about one thing, perhaps. But then, I'm not sure there wasn't some truth in that too.'

'How can you say you didn't lie?' Juliet said. 'You told me you wanted to save the Night Versions.'

'I said I wanted to bring the Director down,' Ethan said. 'I said I was going to change the ending, and that's exactly what I intend to do.'

'But you're—' Juliet broke off as a horrified realisation spread through her. 'You're not working with him,' she said dully. 'You never were. And he never meant for me to fall. That was *your* plan.'

Ethan nodded. 'I've told you more than once, for Conrad, nothing matters as much as his vision for the Show.' His voice was contemptuous. 'If you can call it a vision, given he can't see past his own obsession with a story that was over a long time ago. That's what tonight is about for him. A chance to continue the story that ended when Catherine pushed your mother off that ledge. The return of the Moonshine Girl. There's nothing – no one – he wouldn't sacrifice in her name. Not even the Girl in the Silver Shoes.'

'But you said . . .'

'Not you.' His gesture was sharply dismissive. 'I'm talking about the real Girl in the Silver Shoes. I'm talking about Livvy.' He shook his head. 'I told you once, we're closer to the roles we play than to any living soul. Whatever demands might have been made of the residents of this place down the years, no Director has ever sought to interfere with that bond. No Director until Danes.'

'He was going to take her role from her?' Juliet was struggling to understand.

'He wanted to turn that role into something else,' Ethan said.

Understanding dawned. 'The Moonshine Girl. He wants her to become the Moonshine Girl.'

'In all but name.' He shook his head again. 'She deserves better. Better than a second-hand role that the Director has been hawking around like a market trader, calling in the crowds.' His expression darkened. 'And better than a replacement waiting in the wings.'

'A replacement.' Juliet stared at him. 'You mean me.'

Ethan nodded. 'It's been circling in his head since he first found out you'd returned to the district. I've seen it, although I didn't know what it was at first. Livvy has her troubles. Given who raised her, it would be surprising if she didn't. Danes assumed that, once she was part of the Show, she'd fall into line like everyone else.' His smile was cold. 'Like all his other puppets, like every other cog in the machine. He was wrong. He's spent more time trying to control her than she's spent on set. You, on the other hand . . .' Juliet flinched as he brushed her cheek. 'You were the perfect clockwork toy, so desperate to be *real* that you'd do whatever he asked. It was inevitable he'd start wondering what it would be like if you were the Principal. He's never admitted it, of course. When he's touched on it, it's been all about Livvy's *difficulties*, about the *delicacy* of the situation, and how it might be *wise* to *consider other options*. The truth is, he wouldn't have cared if she'd drunk herself to death like her mother, as long as there was someone else willing to play her role in the way he wanted it played.'

There was a hard gleam in his eyes. 'If I'd realised right back at the start how this would go, you'd never have walked back out of the district that first day.' Juliet shuddered, and he gave another of his small smiles. 'As it turned out, I had another use for you. Once Conrad outlined his plan for his big performance, I could see it all so clearly. The Girl in the Silver Shoes dancing just where the Moonshine Girl danced, ready to take up the latter's mantle. But what if it didn't work out like that? What if history truly repeated itself? Conrad barely survived the backlash last time. When your mother fell from that platform, it was the closest the district had ever come to having their darkest secret exposed. He won't survive a repeat performance. No matter what he tells the board, he will be finished.' He tilted his head. 'He can take some comfort, though. There'll still be a symmetry to it all. The Moonshine Girl will still fall. But this time, the Director will fall with her.'

'How?' Juliet said. 'They'll know it was you. The stagehands will see.'

'The thing about loyalty is it's not always unconditional. Sometimes it's only yours until a higher bidder comes along.'

'How do you know it will work?' Juliet was desperately searching for something she could use against the merciless certainty in his voice. 'Danes will still have Livvy, like he had Catherine. If the police—'

'The police.' Ethan made a dismissive gesture. 'Oh, they'll come calling at some point, but this isn't about them. I'm bringing him down, not bringing him to justice.

By the time they arrive, I'll be the one dealing with them. Telling them it was just smoke and mirrors, and, as you say, Livvy will be there, alive and well. No crime to investigate, no body to find. The Show will go on, as it always does.' He gave a little shrug. 'And it never hurts to have a bit more darkness wound through the stories people tell about us.'

'How do you think you're going to make me go along with this?' Juliet's voice was tight with hatred.

'I don't need you to go along with anything,' Ethan said. 'Oh yes, it would have been perfect theatre – and I have to admit that I'm no more immune to the pull of that than Danes – but look at you.' His voice was as gentle as her stepmother's when her youngest sister had fallen down the stairs. But if her stepmother was here, she wouldn't be looking at Juliet with tenderness. She'd have been regarding her coolly, with judgement in her gaze. *This is what happens to girls like you.* Ethan ran his hand over Juliet's leg, and she stifled a cry as his fingers brushed one of the deeper cuts. 'You can't go on set like this. Or knowing what you know. Fortunately, I have another option. One you delivered straight to me.'

An awful understanding dawned. 'Esme.'

'Esme,' he agreed. 'I hope she's the only one who knows how you brought yourself to my attention. It will get tedious if there's a never-ending stream of hopefuls lining up to dance between those pictures. She's not quite as pliable as you, but that won't matter soon.'

'Why . . .' Juliet's voice broke. 'Why bother with the charade? Why pretend to love me?'

'What better way to secure your full and dazzling cooperation?' His expression turned contemplative. 'But it's more than that. You've danced before an audience. You know the power of binding them to you. On set, you only ever get to exercise a fraction of that power. With more time, you can take someone apart, piece by piece. There's a pleasure in it most people can't even imagine.' His eyes were like flint. 'And the greatest part of it is that, deep down, most of them want you to do it.'

'That's not true.' Juliet was shivering so hard that she didn't think she would ever stop. 'How could you think I want this?'

He shook his head. 'People come to the district wanting all manner of things. Once you know what that is, they're yours. You came here wearing your wanting on your sleeve. You were scraped so raw with all the things you'd never had that there were times I wished I could find Stephen and make him pay for every one of those hurts.'

Juliet's laugh was wrenched out of her. 'You think I believe that? That you ever cared about me in any way?'

He gave another small shrug. 'I already told you – loving you wasn't entirely a lie.' He paused. 'Or maybe it wasn't you I was drawn to. Maybe it was the man I would have had to be to love you.' There was something twisted and unreadable in the smile that lifted the corner of his mouth. 'I think about it sometimes. All the other people I could have been if I hadn't been born here. Everyone has them, you know, those might-have-beens. The trick is to leave them in the shadows, where they belong, and that's a trick you never learned.' His smile faded as he leaned closer. 'I could make you want it again, you know. Part of you still does.'

His gaze moved, as though he was looking inside her, picking through the rubble of her hope, examining each sharp shard of regret, each dull, broken dream. 'Despite everything I've told you, part of you still wants to see my face change, hear me say that you're different, more special than every other special, special girl who I've touched, and kissed, and stripped naked, and fucked . . .' Juliet flinched. That crudeness was like a flash of bone through skin. '. . . while they tried to smile and pretend that it was their desire, their choice.' His breath was warm on her cheek, and as she turned her head away, he brushed his lips down the curve of her neck. 'I could do it,' he murmured. 'I could make you believe it was all a mistake, or that your love had saved me, or that the things I'm saying to you right now are just part of a plan to save you, to save all of them.'

In that moment, Juliet realised how fine the line between hope and belief really was. It was only the briefest stutter of possibility, of *what if*, but it made her breath catch.

He felt it and lifted his head to look at her. 'There it is. And you ask me why I do this? It's because I can.' He stood up. 'And it's why I'll be the kind of Director this place hasn't seen in a long time. It's the same thing, but on a different scale. The audience, the police, the people who read about us in the papers, they have their own stories about the district. Wind them all together in just the right way, and they'll make something no one will ever forget.'

'You don't care about anything, do you?' Juliet looked up at him with hatred.

'There are plenty of things I care about.' There was something in his expression that looked almost like regret, but colder, more distant. 'But people only ever care about the things closest to them. For me, that's the district and its legacy – which is something the Director and I have in common. We just don't quite agree what shape that legacy should take.'

'The whole place is built on blood,' Juliet said.

'That's true,' Ethan said. 'But not in the melodramatic way you mean. The district – the Show – is made of the blood and bone and memory of everyone who has ever been part of it. The Night Versions, too. It's our history, our purpose, and we need it to survive.'

'The Show must go on,' Juliet said dully.

Ethan nodded, the shadows brushing across his face again. 'You're part of it too. You always have been, even before you understood what that meant. And you always will be, even when you're no longer here.'

Something inside Juliet grew brittle, drawing into itself, the first sob knocked aside by a whole dragging heave of them. She had to stop. As long as he was here, there was still time to change his mind. If she could just find the right words, the right way to look at him, she could still undo this. But the only thing she could force out, in between her tears, was, 'please.'

Ethan watched as she cried. When exhaustion and despair had slowed her sobs to sporadic shudders, he gave a small shake of his head. 'I'm sorry. This is brutal. It wasn't like this with any of the others. They did what they loved, right to the end. You could have had that too.' He paused, considering. 'Or perhaps not. You were different, Juliet. You were special.' He smiled again. 'That's the story you wanted. Not with this ending, perhaps, but that's something, isn't it?'

He placed his hand lightly on her hair, like a priest performing a benediction. His touch made her want to claw her own skin off, but, somehow, she made herself reach up and take that hand, drawing it down to her cheek.

'Ethan, please.'

He extracted his hand gently from her grip and stepped back.

'Goodbye, Juliet,' he said, then turned and walked towards the door.

DI James Greenland, Serious Crime Division

I have read the report you sent me. You have carried out an extremely thorough and meticulous analysis, as I would expect of an officer of your experience and standing. It was, however, unauthorised, and I cannot permit you to proceed any further with these unsanctioned lines of enquiry.

I am ordering you to deliver your files and the evidence upon which this report was based, as well as any other copies of the report itself, to me, and to desist from any further investigations of this nature. In the circumstances, I believe it would be inappropriate for you to continue as lead officer on the Charlotte Brodeur murder investigation, and I have asked DI Langton to take over the case.

I now consider the matter to be closed.

DCI Matthew Longwell, Head of Serious Crime Division

Chapter 34

ETHAN HAD BEEN GONE for what could have been an hour or a day – the darkness, and the fractured drift of Juliet's thoughts, made it hard to hold on to any sense of time.

When a key scraped in the lock, it took a few seconds for the sound to register. By the time she realised what it was, the door was opening. As someone stepped across the light, a blaze of fear went through Juliet, and she scrambled upright.

Backs straight, knees together. Miss Abbeline's voice echoed in her head. *Young ladies don't slouch.*

As the figure moved towards her, Juliet made an incoherent sound, her fear greater than her power to hold it back.

'Shut up.' The words were harsh, but the voice behind them was undeniably female. Red hair glinted in the light from the door. 'And get up. You need to get out of here.'

For a moment the words were meaningless, echoing in the hollow Ethan's deception had dug out inside her. Then Juliet felt a crack of hope, so thin and sharp she thought it might cut her if she tried to take hold of it. Her legs were cramped from the cold floor, her whole body aching and weak, but she dragged herself to her feet, and stood face to face with the real Girl in the Silver Shoes for the first time.

Olivia.

Livvy.

They were almost the same height, their eyes on a level, and Juliet wondered what she would see if they stood side-by-side in front of a mirror. But this was no tender reunion between long-lost sisters, and Livvy clearly had no intention of wasting time.

'Come on.' She turned towards the door. 'We need to go.'

Juliet didn't move. 'Why are you helping me?'

'You'd prefer that I didn't?' Livvy's voice was like stone.

'No, I—'

'Then shut up and follow me.' She was already moving towards the door, leaving Juliet no choice but to limp after her, out into the low light of a stone-roofed passage.

'What if someone finds us?' she said, as Livvy led her through a swift series of twists and turns.

'Then we have a problem,' Livvy said. 'Or rather, you do.' She glanced back. 'Can't you move any faster?'

As Juliet tried to pick up pace, the passage opened out into a high-roofed hallway. They approached a flight of stone steps at the end, and Juliet could just make out the thrum of the Show's music overhead.

'What about Ethan?' Juliet felt bile rise in her throat. 'What if he comes back? He said—'

'I don't want to hear.'

'But—'

'I said I don't want to hear it.' They'd reached the bottom of the stairs, and Livvy stopped to look at Juliet. 'I don't *need* to hear it. I've lived with him since I was seventeen. Believe me, after three years in his bed, there's nothing you can tell me about Ethan Ballard.'

'Ballard.' Juliet stared at her. 'I thought he was a Danes.'

Livvy gave a hard laugh. 'That's a whole mess that neither side likes to talk about. His mother was the Director's sister, but he's a Ballard, with all that comes with that. There's a fair bit of the Danes flair in there as well, but he turns that to his own ends. As I suspect you know all too well.' She reached into her pocket and pulled out a key and a mask. 'Up here and along the passage at the top. There's another flight of stairs, then a door that will take you onto the lower level of the set. That room isn't in anyone's loop, and visitors rarely find their way there, so there'll be no stagehands watching it.' She pushed the key and mask into Juliet's hand, then pulled off her wrap and handed that over too. 'Find a crowd and stay hidden in it, until you can make your way out. Your best chance is to surround yourself with people.'

'What about you?' Juliet said. 'What will happen if Ethan finds out you let me go?'

'Not what you're thinking.' Livvy gave a dark smile. 'Oh, he'll make me pay for it – I have no doubt about that. But there's only so much he can do to me.' Her smile twisted. 'You, on the other hand, are a different matter. You need to leave right now. Otherwise there'll be another body in the river.'

'Another body.' Juliet felt a brush of loathing. It was a muted copy of the hatred she'd felt for Ethan, but the hues of it were the same. 'Just another Night Version who doesn't matter. How can you stay here? How can you live like this?'

Heat flared in Livvy's eyes. 'What do you know about it? Our father took you away. You grew up free.'

'Free?' Juliet gave an incredulous laugh. 'You have no idea—'

'No, you're the one who has no idea,' Livvy shot back. 'No idea what it was like, living with someone who died twenty years before their heart stopped beating.'

'She killed my mother.'

'And I saw what it did to her,' Livvy said. 'She might as well have jumped off that ledge herself and been done with it. She couldn't close her eyes without seeing it. She couldn't sleep without dreaming about it. It only got worse over the years. She stopped me walking the wires. She wouldn't let me leave the enclave. She barely let me leave the house.' She shook her head. 'Is it any wonder that when Ethan offered me a way out of that, I took it? I pretended it was what I wanted.' She gave a cool smile. 'He likes that, you know, when you play along with him.' The smile faded. 'When she died, the only thing I felt was relief. I could stop feeling guilty. I could finally take my place in the Show without her threatening to cut her wrists or throw herself off the district roof. I don't know how she found out Stephen was dead.' Juliet knew, though. She remembered that voice on the phone. *Stephen Stephen.* 'She just kept saying he was gone. The next morning, she was too.' She shrugged, but her mouth was tight with what looked like pain. 'I thought it was over, that the Moonshine Girl would finally rest.' She gave a bitter twist of a smile. 'But Danes had other ideas. He wanted me to have her place in the Show. And if I refused, well, he had another option, didn't he?'

'Me,' Juliet said.

Livvy nodded. 'You'd have thought he'd have learned his lesson, wouldn't you? Ethan told me he'd dealt with *the problem*. That's all he would say, but it didn't take much to work out what he meant.'

'Why would you care?' Juliet said.

'Why?' Livvy's expression darkened. 'Because I don't want to have to live with the knowledge that they took my sister, turned her into a puppet with my face, then cut her strings and threw her in the river.'

'So you can live with what happens here, as long as it doesn't touch you too closely.'

Livvy nodded. 'Yes, I can. Because I don't have a choice.'

'We have to go to the police,' Juliet said.

'The police?' There was an odd, too-high note in Livvy's laugh. 'The district pulls their strings too.' She shook her head. 'Walk away, and thank any god you might believe in that you're still breathing air and not river water.' As Juliet started to speak, Livvy made an impatient gesture. 'We don't have time for this. You have to get out.'

'Come with me,' Juliet said, urgently. 'We can leave together.'

Livvy laughed again. 'Leave? I can't leave. There's no place for me outside the district.'

'And when Ethan is Director?' Juliet asked. 'Will your *place* be at his side?'

Livvy shrugged. 'I'll worry about that when the time comes. I don't think Conrad will be handing over the reins anytime soon.'

Juliet stared at her. 'Don't you know what's happening? Ethan's trying to bring him down. There's another girl – Esme – she's going to die tonight. She's going to fall, like my mother fell.'

Livvy stared at Juliet for a moment, and then her face shut down. 'Better her than you.'

'It's not better.' Juliet's voice rose. 'We have to help her.'

'No.' Livvy's voice was hard. 'You have to go, and I have to get to the set. Your friend—'

'She's not my friend. But that doesn't matter. I can't let her die.'

'And what exactly do you think you can do?' Livvy said. 'Don't be a fool. I'm giving you the only chance you'll get.'

'I have to find her.' Juliet made a last appeal. 'Help me. Please.'

Livvy was backing away. 'You're a fool,' she said again, then turned and ran down the hallway, disappearing around the corner.

Chapter 35

THE TEMPTATION TO RUN as Livvy had was so strong Juliet thought something in her would snap with the effort of not giving in – but with a wrench, she pushed away thoughts of escape, and plunged onwards, the Show's music growing louder and closer.

She headed along a short corridor and took another flight of stairs two steps at a time, emerging onto a tiny landing with a single door leading off it. Tying on the mask Livvy had given her, and pulling on the wrap, she slid the key into the lock. She didn't try to compose herself. There was no point. Her fear was closer than her own skin, mixed into the blood running through her veins, riding each breath in and out of her lungs.

When she opened the door, the room on the other side was empty, save for a mirror propped against the wall and a scatter of dead roses on the floor. The petals rustled beneath Juliet's feet as she crossed the room and stepped out into a long hallway. There was another flight of stairs at the end, and she hurried up them, emerging at the edge of the dead forest.

A flood of relief rushed through her as she saw the crowds of black-masked visitors weaving through what was usually a quiet space. The Show was building to the peak everyone had been waiting for, and they'd all come to watch. She could draw the audience around her, like a cloak, let them carry her through the theatre and, eventually, out onto the streets and away from the district. Livvy had left to go and take her place in the Show, which meant that Esme wouldn't be on set. Not yet, anyway. Juliet had no idea how the deadly finale would be managed, but at some point, Esme would have to appear on the platform above the ballroom.

And what are you going to do? The question came from the place where *Olivia* used to dwell, but it was Livvy's voice. *Fool.*

As Juliet made her way through the theatre, every room was a close throng of bodies, making progress painfully slow. Focused on getting to the upper levels, it took her a while to realise that something had happened to the music. It seemed to be splintering, breaking into two distinct strands of the same melody, as though two loops of the Show had somehow become entwined. It was disorienting, making Juliet feel as though she, too, was splitting apart.

A performer she recognised came into sight. A name flickered in her memory – the Dust Singer. Juliet pressed herself against the wall as the woman walked swiftly past, her following crowd hurrying to keep up. When the way was clear, she set off again, climbing the winding stairs at the end of the passage to a gallery above a mosaic-floored room. Glancing down, she saw something that made her falter. A performer – the Capetian – was on his knees, arms spread like a supplicant, face upturned to a balcony where the Dust Singer stood looking down at him.

Juliet felt another lurch of disorientation. Her grasp of the theatre's layout was imperfect, but she couldn't see how the other woman could have reached the balcony that quickly. She shook the confusion away and hurried up a flight of steps and along a corridor. The room at the end was the one where she'd danced with Arlen. As she crossed the floor, her gaze was caught by a spotlight in what was usually a dark corner. It was lighting a heavy-framed picture of a young woman with silvery-blonde hair. She was kneeling, hands crossed in front of her, as though in the final pose of a dance.

The next room was usually empty, but when Juliet stepped through the door, there were masked visitors ranged along the walls, watching a dance of ghosts at the centre of the space. The projections were hazy, drifting down on dusty beams of light, oblivious to their audience, and to each other.

They're our ghosts.

No. Juliet gave a sharp shake of her head. Why would Danes let everyone see the shades of those lost girls? *Focus.*

But the Show's splintered soundtrack made it hard to concentrate. She tried to take hold of one of the two strands, clutching at a familiar phrase and using it to anchor herself in the loop. Livvy should be making her way to the lumber room right now. At some point, Esme would need to take her place, and Juliet had to be there when it happened.

The artist's studio was just ahead, and beyond it was the passage that led to the lumber room. As she stepped through the door into the studio, Juliet stopped dead with a jolt of confusion. On the dais at the end of the room, the Girl in the Silver Shoes was dancing, but Juliet could still hear the music that told her that Livvy should be further on in her loop – and she'd never danced in this room.

A memory surfaced – Ethan scratching out a pencil line on his sketch of the theatre. *Old loop – I forgot.*

He hadn't forgotten. He'd slipped up, drawn the full loop, the *real* loop of the *real* Girl in the Silver Shoes. If tonight was an ordinary performance, he would have been here with Livvy. Was he already up at the platform? How was he going to make the switch? And why was Livvy here when . . .

Realisation flared.

Two Dust Singers.

Two lines of music.

Two red-haired girls with silver shoes.

Livvy and Esme were *both* on the set, bound by their shared role, their shared face, but held apart by everything the Night Versions could never be. And it wasn't just Esme. There were other Night Versions on set too, haunting the steps of their counterparts. This couldn't be what the Director had intended. The Night Versions were the district's darkest secret. Was this Ethan's plan? But what would he gain by it?

Focus.

It didn't matter whether it was Danes or Ethan behind this sundering. Only the ending mattered, and Juliet knew what that would be.

Skirting the edge of the crowd, she slipped out of the room, pushing her way through to the lumber room. There was too tight a press inside for her to get close, but as she strained to catch a glimpse of the girl beneath the spotlight, the crowd shifted slightly, briefly giving her a clear view.

Esme's smile was a glitter of a thing, triumph etched into every line of her body. In that moment, the other girl had everything she'd ever wanted. This vast crowd with its jostling and clamouring and longing. Every face turned towards her. Despite the urgency of the situation, Juliet felt a sharp twist of envy, trailing away to an ache of regret for all the things she'd almost had.

Esme's dance drew to a close, and Juliet watched her step out of the spotlight and towards the door. The crowd shifted again, and she was lost from view, but Juliet could trace her movement across the room from the way her audience turned to follow. As they made their way out of the room, she fell in behind. Somehow, she had to get both Esme and herself out of the theatre.

They reached the next room, the crowd fanning out, and Juliet edged forward until she could see Esme. As she watched, her attention was caught by a ripple of movement on the far side of the wall. A section had slid open, revealing a lit room beyond. The visitors nearest to it were turning, craning their necks to see inside. A girl in a jade-green dress stepped through, and others followed. Elsewhere in the room, more heads turned, drawn by the promise of something new. The tight press of the crowd had eased, with about a quarter of the audience drawn away. Then, without warning, the door slid back once again, leaving a man, who'd been just too slow, scrabbling uselessly for a hidden handle.

Juliet's tension notched tighter.

She could feel the audience responding to that delicious sliver of a promise, but to her, it was the quiet click of some hidden mechanism, the jaws of an invisible trap inching closer.

The dance was coming to an end, the audience already starting to move, anticipating the rush for the door. Juliet was carried along as they jostled out of the room and through to the gallery on the other side, slowing to a shuffle at the door to the burnt room. Just before Juliet stepped through, there was a disturbance behind her, and she turned to see one of the empty display cases swinging inwards, revealing the enticing glow of yet another hidden room. More people turned aside this time, most of the crowd behind her abandoning the crush of the gallery for the lure of the unknown.

As Juliet stepped through the door into the burnt room, her stomach was a tight knot. The stagehands were drawing the audience away. Had Ethan prised their loyalty away from Danes? She didn't know, but soon Esme would be alone. The other girl was dancing – a solo Juliet had never been taught. She had no idea of the danger she was in.

As another section of wall slid back, and yet another group broke away, pressure grew inside Juliet. It felt like inevitability. Her fear drew back to the edges of her mind, leaving a spotlit certainty, just waiting for her to step into it. Somewhere, a voice was screaming at her to run away and not look back; she didn't have to do this – it wasn't her fault, none of it was her fault.

Better her than you. Livvy had twisted into *Olivia,* that darker self, the one who knew Juliet was a desperate fool who was always going to end up here.

I barely had to do anything at all, Ethan agreed. *You did it all.*

Juliet silenced the voices and reached up to pull off her mask. None of them were real. Not here, not in this moment. There was only her, and the choice she was making. As she stepped forwards, letting her wrap drop to the floor, a few faces turned towards her. Juliet stretched out her arms, pinned on the most glittering smile she could find and stepped into her solo from the lumber room.

It only took a second or two for her presence to ripple through the audience. Faces turned towards her and stopped in their tracks, as they stared, uncomprehending, at the two girls.

Yes, Juliet thought. *Stay. Stay with us. Don't leave us alone.*

On the other side of the room, Esme faltered. As Juliet turned on the spot, she saw fury and hatred in the other girl's eyes. Then Esme picked up the steps of the dance once again, and Juliet imagined she heard a thought echo between them.

Mine.

This wasn't a battle, but Esme didn't know that. She was answering the perceived challenge, calling on all her ballet school poise as she stretched into the dance. Some part of Juliet was watching from a distance, noting the precision of the other girl's movements, recognising with cool dispassion that the other girl was the better dancer. But, for once, it didn't matter. There was no prize here, no role to win. The only hope lay in using their shared allure to keep the audience close.

With that thought in mind, Juliet directed her steps to bring her into view of the crowd in the other room. Heads turned, and turned back, caught by the dilemma Juliet remembered from her first visit – that sense of too many things to see, too many scenes unfolding.

On the other side of the opening, Esme's would-be defectors were retracing their steps. Juliet leaped, landing, perfectly balanced, on one foot. Her shoulder screamed in protest, and she could feel blood running down her leg from a reopened cut, but she ignored the pain. Stepping into a turn, she heard the music changing, a new melody grazing through. It was the Moonshine Girl's, winding into the tune that belonged to the Girl in the Silver Shoes, the two wrapping round one another.

Ethan ran through her thoughts once again, spinning on twisted threads of truth and deception.

Take everything she was and everything you are and turn it into something they'll never forget.

Juliet let go of the familiar, and let the music lead her into something else, drawing on the memory of that film playing endlessly in the depths of the set.

Everything you are.

Ethan thought he knew her. He thought he'd tested her limits, worked out which parts of her he could take and fold into a shape of his own devising. He'd thought he could use all those empty years, when she'd taught herself that any love was better than none; that any pain was worth bearing if it meant you were wanted, chosen, seen. Now *she* would use it instead. All the aching, the loneliness, the never-having, the longing, and the *rage*, all wound together and forged into something stronger than steel.

Juliet spun, using the movement to look for Esme. When she found her, fear surged inside her. The other girl was moving away, towards the far door. Juliet moved after her, catching some of those masked gazes as she went.

Follow. Follow.

They obeyed her unspoken command eagerly, pressing close.

Relief flickered as she cleared the door, the quickest audience members tight on her heels. As Esme moved towards the stairs at the end of the passage, Juliet glanced back, just in time to see the door beginning to close. It snagged briefly, as a last masked figure managed to push through, then snapped shut, locking the rest of the crowd out. Only a handful had made it through. They couldn't afford to lose any more.

From somewhere, Juliet dragged a secret smile for those who remained, tightening the bonds tying them to her. They stayed close as she followed Esme up the steps – but it wasn't close enough. As she stepped through the door at the top, it swung shut behind her, leaving just the two of them, in the square where Juliet had so often yearned for Ethan.

Panic flared, white and hot, and she twisted round, scanning the cloisters, terrified he'd be watching her with a cool smile curling his lips. There was no one there, and her pulse steadied slightly. Of course he wasn't here. Esme wasn't the real Girl in the Silver Shoes.

Juliet crossed to Esme in a few swift steps, catching her arm in an urgent grip.

'Esme, listen to me.' Her voice sounded thin and unreal. 'We have to go. You're in danger.'

The other girl dragged free, her face furious. 'Get away from me. You're not going to spoil this for me.'

'Esme, please.' Desperation was pulsing behind Juliet's ribs. 'We have to get out of the theatre. They're going to kill you. They're going to kill both of us.'

Esme's laugh was sharp with incredulity. 'Is that the best you can do?' She shook her head. 'This is mine now. Ethan told me about all the mistakes you made. He said they should never have picked you.' Her eyes gleamed. 'The Show peaks tonight, and they've given it to me. A special scene, with everyone watching.'

'Why would they do that?' Juliet said desperately. 'Think about it. Why would they use you, and not the real Girl in the Silver Shoes?'

'Why? Because I'm better. Better than you, better than her.'

'Esme, you have to believe me.' Juliet could hear the fear in her voice. Surely Esme could hear it too. 'We need to get out. Please.'

But Esme gave Juliet a hard push, sending her staggering back. As she caught her balance, she saw the other girl run across the square to disappear through the far door, which closed behind her. Juliet lunged after her, grabbing at the handle, but the door was locked. As she hauled in a ragged breath, she felt temptation swell once again. She could go, find another crowd in which to lose herself. She'd done everything she could.

There was a pinch of pain in her hand, and Juliet realised she was still clutching the key that Livvy had given her. It had dug lines into her palm, like a brand. Hope lancing through her, she fumbled it into the lock. It turned and the door opened. The passage on the other side was empty, as was the hallway beyond it. She needed the key again to get through the door at the bottom of the stairs, which she took at a run.

When she reached the corridor at the top, there was still no sign of Esme, but Juliet knew where she would be. It felt as though there wasn't enough air to breathe. Through all her panicked determination, she'd thought only of getting to Esme, but now that question echoed in her head again.

What are you going to do?

It wasn't *Olivia's* voice, or Livvy's. It was her own, heavy with something perilously close to resignation. How had she ever thought she could stop this? She was alone, with all the might of the Theatre District ranged against her.

Her steps were weary as she walked to the double doors, pushed them open and stepped through into the roof space of the ballroom. In front of her, the central platform stretched across to the far side, spanning the sheer drop, down through the levels of the theatre to the ballroom floor, and the gauzy drapes that must have hidden her mother from view as she drew her last broken breaths.

Juliet could feel, rather than hear, the rustle of the audience, packed into the galleries below, straining to catch a glimpse of what was happening above. The highest balconies, with the clearest view of the platform, contained only a few dark-clothed figures.

A cold calm settled over Juliet.

Such a perfect symmetry.

The music that was playing was the Moonshine Girl's. And ahead of Juliet, her movements causing the platform to sway very slightly, Esme was dancing her last dance.

Chapter 36

JULIET FELT SLACK AND empty, as though everything that made her who she was had been scooped out, leaving her hollow.

Esme was blazing with joy and triumph once again, her smile a sharp dazzle, but Juliet's gaze went past her to the far side of the roof space, as Ethan stepped onto the end of the platform.

She knew she should be terrified, but her fear was remote and muted; a weary sadness, tinged with regret for all the things she'd chosen not to know.

As Ethan began to make his way towards Esme, Juliet moved to stand between the two of them. She felt as though she was following a script, written for someone much braver and more determined.

Ethan's steps were unhurried, and there was a small smile curling at the corner of his mouth. Juliet wanted to close her eyes, but she was afraid of what she'd see in the darkness. Below her, the balconies were still filling up. She'd never imagined the theatre could hold so many people. It was the cruellest thing, the presence of that vast audience. All those witnesses to what was about to happen, and not one of them would lift a finger to help her: she was trapped behind the glass of her role. Whatever she did, they would just watch, and then they'd take it away with them and weave it into whatever story they thought they knew about the district.

They were still coming. And not just onto the balconies and galleries. There were people thronging onto the floor of the ballroom, pushing through the drapes, almost tripping over themselves in their haste to see everything. But the ballroom floor was where it was all supposed to end, just as it had ended for Madeleine, all those years ago.

Ethan had stopped and was looking down at the crowd, his expression unreadable. Esme had dropped out of her dance and she too was standing still. In her face was confusion, and something that might have been the first stirring of fear.

The platform shifted slightly, and Juliet turned to see Livvy making her way towards them. Behind her, black-clothed figures were slipping through the double doors, spreading along the outer ledge to form a silent ring around the unfolding scene.

As Livvy stepped past Juliet, Ethan turned to look at her.

'You shouldn't be here,' he said, his voice low. 'This isn't how it was supposed to play out.'

'So how was it supposed to play out?' Livvy nodded towards Juliet. 'Were you going to do it yourself?'

'I don't know what you're talking about,' Ethan said calmly. 'Danes was the one who planned tonight's performance. Whatever has happened, I'm sure the stagehands will have it under control very soon, and the Show can go on.'

'And then what?' Livvy said. 'You bide your time and wait for another opportunity?'

Ethan shook his head. 'I don't know what you think you know, Livvy, but I'm just playing my role here, the same as everyone else on the set tonight.' Something glinted in his eyes. It was gone so swiftly that Juliet might have doubted she'd seen it if it hadn't been for the shiver it sent through her. 'We can talk about this later.'

'And wouldn't that be an interesting conversation?' There was something hard in Livvy's voice. 'Almost as interesting as one I had just before I came on set.' She nodded towards Juliet. 'What do you think she told me?'

'I have no idea,' Ethan said. 'And this isn't the time.'

Livvy tilted her head, studying him. 'You don't know what's happening on the set, do you?' She gave a low laugh. 'Let's just say it's a slightly bigger cast than usual.'

Juliet saw a flare of understanding in Ethan's eyes. 'The music,' he said. 'I wondered what that was about.' He regained his composure swiftly. 'All the more reason to get things moving. We can work out what's gone wrong later.'

'The Show must go on,' Livvy said. 'Of course. But I think we're all asking the same question. Whose script is this?' She looked down at the ballroom floor. 'Not yours, clearly. You'd struggle to sell that old *smoke and mirrors* story to people who've just had *real* land on their heads from several floors up.' As Juliet flinched, Livvy glanced over. 'Sorry.' She turned back to Ethan. 'The Director's?' She shook her head. 'No. Why would he? Whose, then?'

Before Ethan could reply, there was a scuffle of noise from below, then an urgent lift of voices, a few rising clear above the rest.

There. Secure the doors. No one leaves.
The platform. Get up there now.
Police. Everyone stay where you are.

Juliet froze, an almost painful hope tightening her lungs.

Livvy gave another low laugh. 'The plot continues to thicken.'

Ethan gave her a sharp look, and moved closer to the edge to look down. The masked faces below were turning back and forth, their confusion evident. The occupants of the upper balconies, however, were already moving, disappearing into whatever hidden passages led to those usually inaccessible vantage points.

As though tipped into action by their example, Esme turned and ran for the doors. Juliet caught a glimpse of her face as she went, white even beneath the stage make-up. She felt a stab of fear for the other girl, but before she could call out to her, there was more shouting, closer this time. Down below, a group of men stepped through the door onto one of the upper balconies. As one of them looked up, Juliet's heart gave a thump of recognition, followed by a hard rush of relief.

Lambert was tense, his face grim, but as he saw Juliet, there was an answering flicker of relief in his eyes. Mansfield appeared behind him, following his younger colleague's gaze up to the platform. Turning to his men, he snapped out an instruction, and they disappeared back through the door. The Inspector turned back, then stilled, staring across the vault of the ballroom to a gallery on the far side. Conrad Danes was standing there, hands resting lightly on the rail in front of him, surveying the ruin of his perfect story. As

Juliet watched, he looked up at Ethan, then nodded towards Mansfield, the question clear.

Your doing?

Ethan gave a small shake of his head.

Mansfield spoke. 'I'm terribly sorry. Am I interrupting something?'

'You are, I'm afraid,' Danes said calmly. 'Hopefully, we can resolve whatever the problem is and get on with the performance.' He glanced down at the ballroom floor, where officers were herding reluctant audience members through one of the open doors. They craned their necks as they went, desperate for a last glimpse of the incomprehensible events playing out above them. 'Perhaps we can hurry. I can't imagine our visitors will be terribly co-operative if your officers try to evict them from the Show they've paid to see.'

'You'll have that in common with them, then,' Mansfield said.

'Not at all, Inspector,' Danes replied. 'You will, of course, have my full assistance as you investigate whatever crime it is you think you've uncovered here. Although I fear you will be disappointed once again.'

'Disappointed?' Mansfield glanced up at the platform. 'Not this time. Smoke and mirrors – that's what you told me twenty years ago. Well, I can see the mirrors now.' He gave a sharp shake of his head. 'One performer, one role. Everyone knows that's how it works, so no one ever thought to look behind it.'

The Director's calm was unshakeable. 'Tonight is a special performance, with some changes to our usual routine.' He didn't look round as the door behind him opened, and two police officers stepped onto the balcony. 'Everything would have become clear, had we not been interrupted.'

'Everything is entirely clear,' Mansfield said. 'Murder. Concealment. A conspiracy going back generations.'

'How terribly dramatic.' Danes' voice was perfectly polite. 'Almost worthy of the Theatre District itself. But tell me, Inspector, do you have evidence of these heinous crimes? Witnesses?' He raised an eyebrow. 'For that matter, do you even have authority? You're aware, I assume, that your powers end at the district gate.'

'We covered this last time,' Mansfield replied. 'For all you like to think yourselves untouchable, the terms of the King's Gift are clear.'

Danes tilted his head. 'So which is it? Crimes against persons not resident, or crimes by persons not resident? Because, once again, it seems to me you have a jurisdictional problem.'

'That won't work, Danes,' Mansfield replied. 'Even if I were minded to fall in line with a game no one but the district has been playing for hundreds of years, the rules you've quoted give me clear jurisdiction.' He nodded towards Juliet. 'Crimes against persons not resident.'

Danes raised his eyebrows. 'Murder, you said. But I see a reassuringly living girl. As for her residence status, I think you may find that in dispute. The precincts have a long and somewhat debatable history.'

'So you are aware she's been living in the precincts,' Mansfield said. 'She sent us a plea for help.'

Juliet's heart thumped. That brief, incoherent scrawl of a message. Eugene.

Danes shrugged. 'People will tell you what they believe to be true, but I can assure you no one was in any danger. It was all part of the Show.'

Juliet's fear should have abated once Mansfield swept in with such certainty – the cavalry charging to the rescue – but she had an awful sense of his authority slipping. She was terrified that, any moment, there'd be a tap on his shoulder, and he'd step off the balcony, followed by his colleagues, never to return. There'd be nothing for her to do but move into the deadly dance Esme had vacated, following the music that was still playing, low and ominous. Then Ethan would step forward, and the Show would indeed go on – to the ending he had planned for it.

A voice spoke from behind her, and she turned to see a grey-haired man stepping onto the central platform. She recognised him, even from the blurred view she'd had through that mirror.

'Lily Carter.' The Stage Manager crossed the platform, stopping at the edge to look down at Danes. 'Elspeth Graham. Matthew Blair.'

'Kellan . . .' The Director's voice was low.

'Miriam Essen.' The Stage Manager continued as though Danes hadn't spoken. 'Evelyn McAllister. Phoebe Ward.'

'Ward.' Mansfield had gone very still. 'McAllister.'

'Katya Vinski.' The Stage Manager looked over at Juliet. 'Madeleine Austin.' A painful realisation twisted inside Juliet. It was a litany of the lost. 'Charlotte Brodeur. Lakshmi Rahman. Millicent Davis.'

As he finished speaking, there was a long, stretched silence. It was broken by Mansfield, who turned to look across at Danes.

'Still think you're going to walk away from this?' Triumph blazed in his eyes.

'They're just names.' The Director's voice was steady.

'Not just names,' Kellan said. 'Nothing is lost. Nothing is thrown away. You've told me often enough that the Show is the history of the district, written by generations of Directors, generations of your people. Well, there's another history in there too, stored up by generations of *my* people. I don't know why it started – penance, perhaps – but the pieces of those lost lives are scattered through this theatre, and I will give the police every fragment.'

'Is this a confession?' Mansfield had moved forward to grip the rail of the balcony.

'It's an invitation to one.' Kellan didn't take his eyes off Danes. 'I think the Director has forgotten how much knowledge he entrusted to me. Better it comes from him than being dragged from me, piece by dangerous piece.' He addressed Danes directly. 'There's another thing you've told me over and over. About the hierarchy of promises – which you have to hold to, and which can be allowed to slip away.'

'Kellan . . .'

'I'm giving you a chance to keep them all. The one you made to me, and all those you've made in service of the district.' The Stage Manager's voice was entirely level. 'You can keep your promises, or I can break every one of mine. Your choice, *Director.*'

There was a twist in his voice, but it wasn't as straightforward as hatred. There was something there that sounded like regret, frayed deference and a painful letting go.

'What promises?' Mansfield looked between Kellan and Danes. 'What is this?'

Neither answered him. Their eyes were locked, and Juliet thought she could feel all sorts of things passing between them, shivering on bow-tight lines of tension. It was Danes who broke away, turning his head to let his gaze range around the ballroom, passing over the assembled performers and stagehands and moving up to the beamed roof, as though he could see through it, out to the great glass and steel dome. His expression was as composed as ever, but there was something about the slow turn of his head that told Juliet exactly what was about to happen.

Danes turned back to face Mansfield across the vault of the ballroom. His chin lifted as he pinned on the showman's smile Juliet had seen once before.

'Such drama,' he said. 'Very well, I confess. You've caught me at last, Inspector. If I had a mask, you could snatch it away, to the appropriate gasps from the onlookers.' He pantomimed flicking a cloak over his shoulder, then dipped into a bow. 'Time to exit stage left.'

'Mock all you like, Danes.' Mansfield's voice was hard. 'It's over. Phoebe Ward. Evelyn McAllister. Charlotte Brodeur. Their bodies were all found in the river near here.'

'I can assure you, Inspector, I'm entirely serious,' Danes said. 'You're right. It's over. You've won. To the victor, the spoils.' He gave a small smile. 'But before I am dragged away in chains, there is the matter of the succession.' He looked up at Ethan. 'You know what to do.'

'No.' Kellan shook his head. 'He's part of this.'

'So I have an accomplice.' The Director's voice was light. 'I wonder who else is going to be unmasked.' He looked across at Mansfield. 'Perhaps one of your officers will turn out to be harbouring a dark secret. Or maybe there'll be an eleventh-hour bait and switch, and you'll find yourself in the frame.' He shook his head. 'I'm your villain. You have my confession. You're not looking for anyone else.'

Juliet started to shake again. She knew what this was. Danes couldn't risk letting fault lines spread through the whole district. He couldn't risk exposing the Backers. She had to speak up, but fear was wrapping tight hands around her throat, choking back the words she needed to say. Ethan was a consummate performer, a poised master of deception, and she was the stupid little fool who'd told Lambert so many lies she could barely remember them all. And there were so many things at play here, so much culpability and betrayal, that it felt as though she was at the centre of a maze of mirrors, reflecting an endless shimmer of suspicion. Point to one of those reflections, and you'd leave another free to step out from behind the glass. And when everyone had gone and you were alone again, he'd smile and say, *See? I told you I could make them all believe it,* and you'd be dragged back to that dark room and never see the light again.

'We'll decide who and what we're looking for.' Lambert's voice was calm and level, breaking into Juliet's spiralling thoughts. As she caught hold of it and clung on, she felt a desperate longing to have him beside her, with all his steady certainty. 'This conversation can continue at the police station. The scene will be secured, the witnesses identified and their statements taken. All necessary investigations will be carried out, and all suspects will be interviewed.'

'Of course.' It was Ethan's voice. When Juliet looked round, there was the ghost of a smile playing about his lips. 'You have a job to do, and I am sure we will all be happy to co-operate.'

Mansfield gave a bark of laughter. 'Will you.' It wasn't a question. His gaze narrowed. 'Who are you, anyway?'

'Ethan Ballard.' Another flicker of a smile. 'Fifty-seventh Director of the Theatre District.'

Juliet was struggling to take a breath, certain she could see how this was going to play out. It didn't matter what she – or Kellan – said or didn't say. Nothing would be as powerful as the Director's confession, so nothing would stop Ethan. Juliet didn't know whether Danes had worked out his nephew had intended to betray him, and she didn't know if he would even care. *There are different kinds of trust*, he'd told Kellan. *I trust him to have his eye on the district's future.*

'I was rather under the impression there needed to be an election before anyone could assume the title of Director.' Lambert spoke up again, his tone cool.

'There will be an election.' Ethan gave a small smile. 'Should any other candidate present themselves. In the meantime . . .'

Before he could finish his sentence, there was a rustle at the edge of the platform, and a group of stagehands moved aside to let a slim, upright figure step through. Juliet's heart gave a thump of startled recognition.

Down on the balcony, Mansfield stared up at the newcomer, who met his gaze calmly.

'Eleanor Abbeline,' she said, pre-empting the inevitable question. 'Fifty-seventh Director of the Theatre District.' She glanced at Ethan, whose smile had fallen away. 'Elect.'

'Any more?' Mansfield spread his hands, shooting a sardonic look at Lambert. 'You fancy throwing your hat in the ring? No?' He shook his head. 'I've heard enough. This isn't part of your bloody Show, and we're not your audience.' He glanced over his shoulder. 'Somebody get up there, for God's sake, and let's have an end to this.'

Lambert shot a swift look at Juliet, then made his way off the balcony, leaving Mansfield to fire a series of instructions at another officer who'd arrived.

'You think they'll choose you over me?' Ethan's voice was close, and Juliet twisted round, heart thumping in instinctive reaction. He'd moved near enough to address Miss Abbeline without anyone beyond the platform hearing. 'A woman? One who turned her back on the district over twenty years ago?'

'The district turned its back on me,' Miss Abbeline replied. 'And yes, they'll choose me, for that precise reason. Nothing that happened during Conrad's directorship can be laid at my door. Not by the board, and not by the police.'

Ethan looked between her and the Stage Manager. 'Quite the unholy alliance, the two of you. And quite the show you put on tonight. Lift the curtain on the magic show, let the world see the sleight of hand behind the trick, and wait for the board to tear Danes apart for it.' He tipped his head. 'As a plan, it's not without merit.'

'Well, this is interesting.' Livvy had moved closer to listen, and she addressed Juliet. 'You know, I'm almost starting to feel sorry for Conrad.'

'Are you?' Miss Abbeline hadn't taken her eyes off Ethan.

Livvy considered the question. 'No. Perhaps not.'

'Livvy.' Ethan's voice was steady. 'I want you to walk away right now. Find a way out of the theatre and go home.'

'I don't think the police would like that,' Livvy replied.

'I don't care.' Ethan turned to look at her. 'Do what I'm telling you.'

'No, I don't think I will,' Livvy said calmly.

Ethan stared at her for a long moment, then returned his gaze to Miss Abbeline. 'Fine.' Juliet had a sense of something shifting beneath his calm – the first threat of a crack in his perfect composure. 'So, you bring Danes down. What about me? I'm the obvious successor.'

'And there it is,' Kellan said. 'The Danes arrogance. The certainty of your own value to the district.'

Ethan's eyes flashed. 'I'm a Ballard.'

'If you were all Ballard, you might have been more careful,' the Stage Manager replied. 'I knew about your approach to the first of my people within minutes of you making it. And that's just one of the things I know about you.' He shook his head. 'You forget, all of you, what we see from the shadows.'

'I don't think Conrad will forget again,' Ethan said. His eyes darkened. 'They'll burn you for what you just did. That's if they get a chance after the police have finished with you. That was quite a speech you gave, but did you not think about what you were doing by making it? You won't walk away from this.'

'I don't intend to,' Kellan said. 'I've put an end to the burden my people have been shouldering for generations. I'm ready to pay the price.'

'Your people,' Ethan said. 'How much blood is on their hands? How do . . .' He broke off, staring around the ranks of assembled stagehands. Juliet noticed for the first time how young they all were, and she remembered that glimpse of wagons, getting ready to leave the precincts. How much dark knowledge was packed in amongst those crates and sacks? 'Oh, you've thought of everything, haven't you? A clean slate for a new era. But then I wouldn't expect anything less of the Stage Manager of the Theatre District.' He tilted his head. 'Tell me, have you appointed a successor? I'd like to know who I'm going to be working with in this brave new world.'

'You won't be part of that world.' Kellan's expression was hard.

'Oh, but I will.' There were no cracks in Ethan's calm now, that faint shiver of doubt long gone. 'I'll admit, the mechanics of the plan were flawless. And the theory is sound enough. Putting it all in the Show guarantees the audience will never be entirely sure. There'll already be a thousand versions of tonight's events winding their way through the district. Give it a month and each of those accounts will have frayed into a thousand more. Give it six months and what happened here will have been woven into the mythology of this place, and everyone – the audience, the police, even people who've never been near the district – will choose the story they prefer, as they always do.' He glanced down at Mansfield who was firing orders at another group of officers.

'Oh, he'll try to unpick it all, but in the end, he'll take what's been handed to him.' He smiled again. 'The holy grail of this long quest of his. Proof that he was right all along, that Conrad Danes is the villain he just proclaimed himself to be. You think you can sweep me off the board alongside him, drag our names through the mud, while she—' He jerked his head towards Miss Abbeline. '—steps over us, holding her skirts clear of the filth. But Conrad has given them a story that'll dazzle them all, so they won't see the dirt. He's the only one they'll be looking at.' His smile faded. 'And everyone else here will have to tell that story if they want to survive. One villain. That's how it works. That's how the Show goes on.'

'I won't tell your story.' The words were wrenched out of Juliet, as anger wound into her fear. 'You were going to kill Esme. You were going to push her over that edge, and then you were going to kill me.'

'You?' His eyebrows went up as he turned to look at her. 'Tell me, Juliet—' His voice caressed her name with a tenderness that set her stomach churning. '—how do you see that working out?'

The look in his eyes made her feel as though he'd closed his hand across the sensitive spot at the base of her throat, but she held his gaze. 'You're a monster. You were telling the truth about that. You can't be Director.'

'He won't be,' Miss Abbeline said. 'Whatever he may say, I'm the only option.'

Ethan laughed. 'I can be whatever the district wants me to be. I can play whatever role is needed. Hold your election, by all means. I'll win, because I'm the better performer, and the role of District Director is just that – a role, like any other.'

'A role.' It was Livvy's voice. As everyone's gaze went to her, she smiled and took a step back towards the edge of the platform. 'You play so many of them, Ethan, I'm surprised you even know who you are anymore.' She took another step. 'I certainly didn't, did I? Not the depths of it, the depths of *you*.'

She'd reached the side of the platform, but took another baby step until her heels tipped over the edge.

'Livvy.' Real fear brushed across Ethan's face. He moved towards her, hand outstretched. 'Come away from the edge.'

'Why do you care?' Livvy took another of those tiny steps. It left her on her toes, right on the very edge, where the smallest shift of weight would see her plunge to the ballroom floor far below.

Juliet's head spun, as though she was the one hanging over that deadly drop. The two of them had somehow swapped roles: it was Juliet who was supposed to die, so how was Livvy teetering there, a breath away from a fatal fall?

Such a perfect symmetry.

Down on the balcony, Danes had shaken free of the officers holding him and was gripping the railing, watching Ethan move towards Livvy in small, cautious increments.

'Livvy.' Ethan was only a couple of feet from her now. 'Please. Take my hand.'

Livvy laughed, low and breathless. 'You're right. You can be anything you want to be, tell any story you want. You'll find your way out of this and into the Director's seat.' Her face hardened. 'And I don't want to see what you have planned for the district. Or for me.'

'Livvy.' There was a plea in Ethan's voice. 'Don't.'

'Why not?' She looked down. 'Why shouldn't it end in one last, perfect performance?'

'What performance?' He was working hard to sound calm. 'Livvy, this isn't the Show. The audience have gone.'

As he took another step, Livvy's smile flashed again. 'This performance.'

She threw up her hands, her voice a terrified scream. As she swayed, Ethan made a desperate grab for her, but even as his hand closed on her wrist, Livvy wrenched it away, pulling him off balance. For a heart-tearing second, the two of them hung suspended over that deadly fall, and then Livvy pushed off her toes in an impossible, contorted leap that Juliet was sure would be her last. As she landed in a graceless sprawl on the very edge of the platform, Juliet had a brief glimpse of Ethan's face twisting in shock, before he disappeared from view. Her heart thumped once, twice, and then there was a sickening thud.

There should have been silence after the impact, but music rumbled on, low and unceasing. *The Show must go on*, Juliet thought blankly.

Chapter 37

BEHIND JULIET, SOMEONE SWORE, a shocked rattle of profanity.

She looked round to see two officers by the door. Lambert was just behind them. Her head spun once again, and this time she felt her legs giving way.

Someone caught hold of her, lowering her to the platform.

'Put your head down.' It was Lambert.

Breathing in slowly, fighting against the threatening darkness, Juliet was vaguely aware of the young officer issuing curt orders from his place beside her, and of people moving. A glint of silver as Livvy passed, as easy-footed as if she was playing out her loop. Heavier steps followed, as Kellan Grey was led away.

'I'm all right.' Juliet tried to push herself upright, but Lambert's arm tightened around her.

'Steady,' he said. 'Give it a moment.'

'I'm all right,' Juliet repeated, making another attempt.

He gave up trying to stop her, and helped her to her feet. Down on the balcony, Danes was sitting in a velvet-backed chair. Even at this distance, Juliet could see his grey-tinged pallor, but he sat like a king surveying his realm.

The king is dead, thought Juliet. *Long live the queen.*

Miss Abbeline was standing a few feet away, her expression neutral. As their gazes met, she gave her old pupil a small nod. Beside Juliet, Lambert stirred as though he was about to speak, but then someone by the door called his name. More officers had found their way to the platform.

'Will you be all right for a minute?' he asked Juliet.

She nodded, and he went over to his colleagues. As he reached them, there was a commotion on the other side of the door, drawing his attention. With a swift glance over his shoulder, he disappeared. Realising this might be the only chance they got, Juliet walked over to Miss Abbeline.

'You knew,' she said. 'You knew about the Night Versions, and you let me come back here.'

'I advised you to walk away,' Miss Abbeline replied. 'I couldn't exactly tell you the truth. And given what I'd learned about Conrad's plans for the Girl in the Silver Shoes, I had no reason to believe you were in any immediate danger.'

'And what about *his* plans?' Juliet looked over at the spot where Ethan had gone over the ledge. 'He was going to kill me. I was locked up in the dark, wondering when he was going to come back, how he was going to do it. And you let that happen.'

'I didn't know,' Miss Abbeline said. 'Not when you came to me. It was only when he approached some of the stagehands that his intentions became clear. If everything had played out as it was supposed to, you would never have known what he had planned for you. The Show would have reached the peak *we* had planned, Danes would have been quietly removed from office and I would have stepped into his place.'

'And what about Ethan?' Juliet said.

'He would have been . . . managed.' Miss Abbeline gave a cool smile. 'That doesn't matter now. The script changed. *You* changed it.'

'I'm sorry I spoiled things for you,' Juliet said coldly. 'I was rather busy trying to save Esme's life – and mine.'

'That was an observation, not an accusation.' Miss Abbeline's voice was gentle. 'I know it's probably little comfort, but he would never have been allowed to lay a finger on either of you.'

'You're right,' Juliet said. 'It isn't much comfort.' She shook her head. 'It was all about the directorship. You never intended Danes to face any sort of justice.'

'We never thought justice – whatever that means – was within reach,' Miss Abbeline said. 'We planned for what we thought we could achieve. To drag the Night Versions into the light. To put an end to the centuries of secrecy surrounding them. And yes, to put me in the Director's seat.' As Juliet started to speak, her old teacher held up her hand. 'That list of names – almost all young women. How many stories are there about the dark things that the world does to women and girls? It's as though we're made to be broken. The district may pride itself on how unfettered it is by the conventions that govern the rest of society, but it's still a place where men decide what use they can make of women.'

'And you're going to change that, I suppose,' Juliet said. 'You're going to leave the Academy, with all its rules and courtesies and *conventions*, and you're going to turn the district into, what? Some sort of paradise for all the mistreated women of the world?'

'I told you when we last spoke, I taught more than manners and dancing.' Miss Abbeline's voice was steady. 'Trust me, Juliet, the district is going to be a very different place from now on.'

'Trust you.' Juliet gave a bitter laugh. 'I've heard that too many times. And look where it got me.'

'Ethan Ballard was one of the district's finest actors,' Miss Abbeline said. 'How could you have seen through that?'

'I didn't let myself.' There was a bitter taste in Juliet's mouth. 'He showed me everything I'd ever wanted.'

'Oh yes, he knew exactly what he was doing.' Miss Abbeline gave a faint smile. 'The irony is that he would have been a great Director. Of a certain kind, anyway. But he's gone. It's over. DI Mansfield has solved the case, caught his white whale. Hopefully, he will find some peace in his last years, and that young officer of yours won't spend his life searching for the missing pieces of the puzzle, or blaming himself for not being able to put a stop to it.'

'He's not mine,' Juliet said.

'Really?' Miss Abbeline gave her a tiny smile. 'In any event, he will be free of the district, and so will Mansfield. And that is due, in no small part, to you, Juliet.'

'And what about the Backers?' Juliet glanced at the upper balconies where those dark-clad figures had been waiting to see the return on their investments. They were gone now, perhaps mingling with the rest of the audience, or already long gone from the theatre, hustled out by some private route. 'Do they just get away with what they did?'

'Their dealings with the district are over,' Miss Abbeline said. 'I'm not Conrad. I don't want or need their blood money, and with the Night Versions no longer a secret, there is nothing they can hold over us. But you need to understand that powerful men support one another. To bring them down, you'd have to snap everything binding them to each other, expose every dark truth, everything they've ever been part of. If I tried, I would fail. They'd survive, but I'm not sure the district would.'

'I don't care,' Juliet said.

'Oh, I think you do,' Miss Abbeline replied. 'I know this place, and I know you. Are you really telling me that you didn't find anything here to love?' She shook her head. 'I don't believe that. Not for a moment. The district isn't the creation of the Directors alone. It's not even the creation of the performers. It's built from the hopes and dreams and wishes and beliefs of everyone who has ever walked in through the gates. It holds the memory of everyone who has ever performed here – resident or Night Version. Your mother is here, and your father, and you'll be here too, long after you're gone. A single villain is a story that the world will understand – and forgive. And no more lives will be stolen. No more of our people will spend our days haunted by ghosts whose names we daren't speak. The district will be what it should always have been – what it *has* been at various times in its history. Not a paradise, but a place where there's more light than darkness.' There was a hint of sadness in her smile. 'And some might say that's far, far more than most of this world can offer.' That sadness was replaced by something harder. 'I'll keep my promises, Juliet, but I came back to change the district, not to preside over its end.'

There was steel beneath Miss Abbeline's skin, but the picture she was painting was a compelling one. Juliet found herself thinking about the performer she'd seen hiding with an audience member, both of them helpless with laughter. About the promise in the smile of the fortune teller who'd beckoned to her on her first visit. The old man in the record office, lost in the maze of years. The young couple in the residents' enclave, leaping across the gap above her, their hopefulness still untarnished.

And then there were the visitors who'd come to the district and found something they'd never known was missing, the people for whom this place was acceptance, joy, belonging. An image formed – the same one that had haunted her as she'd told Lambert she wasn't afraid. The Shipping News ransacked. Eugene, Macy, Jan – all the Followers – distraught, as those countless years of history were swept away, along with the many futures they'd ever imagined for the place they loved so much.

The Moonshine Girl. The Night Versions. Danes. Broken promises, and broken faith. Kellan Grey, stepping out of the shadows and into the spotlight, with the ghosts of the lost in a slow dust-dance around him. It was a web of stories and lives as complex as the Show itself, and Juliet was part of it.

A perfect symmetry.

It was, in a way. She was standing in the last place her mother had stood. Something had been set in motion when Madeleine fell, and now her daughter had seen the end of it – and perhaps the start of something new.

With a feeling like falling into something that was already there, Juliet made a choice she suspected she would question any time she found herself awake deep in the night.

'All right,' she said. 'I'll tell your story. But I want something from you in return.'

'Which is?'

'You said everyone is remembered in the Show,' Juliet replied. 'Does that include Ethan?'

'Yes,' Miss Abbeline said. 'He's part of this place, however much you might wish otherwise.'

'I want every trace of him erased,' Juliet said. 'Every picture, every reference, every storyline that's ever touched his. I want everyone to forget he ever existed. Can you do that?'

'It will be difficult,' Miss Abbeline said.

'I didn't ask if it would be difficult.' Juliet held her old teacher's gaze. 'I asked if you could do it.'

Miss Abbeline studied her for a moment and then nodded. 'Yes, I can.' She gave a small smile, coloured with something that might have been approval. 'He underestimated you. I think I did too. Maybe you learned the lessons I taught better than I realised.'

'I learned more lessons than yours,' Juliet said, with a flicker of resentment.

'I know that.' Miss Abbeline made a conciliatory gesture. She paused for a moment. 'You don't have to leave, you know.'

'What?' Juliet stared at her. 'I can't stay here.'

'You could,' Miss Abbeline said. 'You could have a place in the district, just as you wanted.'

'How?' Juliet said. 'I'm not the Girl in the Silver Shoes. I never was.'

'You don't have to be,' Miss Abbeline replied. 'Things will be changing, and there are many ways you could be part of that.' As Juliet opened her mouth, Miss Abbeline lifted her hand. 'You don't have to decide now. But there'll be a place for you, if you ever want it.' She paused again. 'There's something else – something in the theatre that belongs to you.'

'In the theatre?' Juliet said. 'What?'

'A memory,' Miss Abbeline said. 'Hidden away in the Show, like everything else. Kellan told me to tell you. The room with the film of the Moonshine Girl – if you take out the top drawer of the cabinet and look underneath it, you'll find a name. Of a man who came to the district looking for his daughter. His red-haired daughter who'd once told him she wanted to be the most famous dancer in the world.'

Juliet's chest grew tight.

'The Night Versions were chosen because they were people who wouldn't leave too much of a gap in the world. Kellan thought Madeleine was a mistake. He said the reason she shone as bright as she did was because she was loved.' Her voice was soft. 'And he told me to tell you she loved you. So very much.'

Juliet blinked back tears. Her body was tensed, expectant, waiting for the hurtle of *and then and then and then and on into a happy ever after.* But she wasn't sure she'd ever feel that reckless again. From now on, she'd always test the ground before she stepped.

Something occurred to her. 'What about Esme?' she said. 'Ethan promised her all sorts of things. I think . . .' She paused, feeling her way round what she wanted to say. She'd never liked the other girl, but now realised she'd always understood her. 'I think she was looking for somewhere to belong. Like I was.'

'A lot of us are,' Miss Abbeline replied. 'And that's what the district should be. Even if it's just for a little while for most people. I'll make sure Esme is looked after.'

Before Juliet could reply, a voice spoke from behind her.

'What exactly is going on here?' Mansfield threw a look back along the platform. 'Is there any particular reason why two witnesses have been left to have a private conversation in the middle of a murder scene?'

Miss Abbeline raised a polite eyebrow. 'A murder scene, Inspector? I was under the impression the crimes you were investigating were historical.'

'Historical?' Mansfield's voice was incredulous. 'I've got a dead body under a sheet down there, and a young woman refusing to say a word about it.'

'A deeply unfortunate accident, Inspector,' Miss Abbeline replied. 'But entirely incidental to your investigation.'

'You'll excuse me if I don't take your word for that,' Mansfield said, then gave a sharp laugh. 'Right now, I'm not taking anyone's word for anything at all.' His expression hardened. 'We'll see if the young lady is more talkative once we get her to a police station.'

'I'm afraid that won't be possible,' Miss Abbeline said coolly. 'The incident involved only district residents. I am entirely content for you to question her here in the district – and in my presence – but I cannot consent to more intrusive methods of investigation.' As Mansfield opened his mouth, Miss Abbeline held up her hand. 'I do not wish to begin my directorship with a fight, DI Mansfield. I understand the value of compromise, and I'd like to find a way to exist alongside external authorities rather than setting myself against them at every turn. But if I have to set myself against them, I am prepared to start right now, by picking up a certain jurisdictional discussion where Conrad left off.'

'By all means, let's have that *discussion*,' Mansfield said. 'But in the meantime, I have more pressing concerns.' He walked over to look down at the ballroom floor. 'Is there any prospect of me getting some help up here?'

'The theatre is difficult to navigate,' Miss Abbeline said smoothly. 'Please, allow me.' She gestured to the nearest group of stagehands. 'Please go and assist the police in any way necessary.'

Mansfield glared at her, then turned away to beckon to one of his men.

Juliet looked at her old teacher. 'Goodbye, Miss Abbeline,' she said.

As she reached the double doors, Lambert reappeared.

'Are you all right?' He made a quick gesture. 'I mean, as all right as . . .'

'I know what you mean,' Juliet said. 'And yes, I will be.' A group of uniformed officers had appeared at the door. 'You got my message. I didn't think I'd been clear enough, even if Eugene found it. I was . . .' She pulled her thoughts away from the terror of the ambush that had followed her abortive attempt at a note. 'I was interrupted. I only had time to write down your name.'

'One of your housemates was with him when he found it,' Lambert said. 'She remembered me leaving a note at the house. They turned your room upside down and found the DI's card, along with some letters and a photo of the Moonshine Girl. Eugene had apparently been harbouring all sorts of suspicions, but hadn't quite been able to pull it together. When he rang the station, he was speaking very fast, about a lot of things I didn't understand, but he kept saying it wasn't the Moonshine Girl who fell, and you were in danger.'

Juliet felt something that could only have been a sort of love. Eugene had told her he wouldn't be the one to figure out the secret at the heart of the district, but he'd done exactly that – or been part of it, at least.

'That was enough?' Juliet said. 'Weren't you taking a huge risk, coming here?'

Lambert shrugged. 'The last time we spoke, it was obvious that something was very wrong. And the DI had nothing left to lose. He would have stormed the place on his own if he'd had to.' He smiled. 'He didn't have to. As it turned out, a surprising number of officers were entirely willing to risk their necks – or at least their careers – in an unauthorised raid.'

'What if you'd been wrong?'

'We weren't,' he replied. 'Every now and again, the pieces *do* fit perfectly together, although I won't hold my breath for it happening again. I suspect there are a lot of pieces we still haven't slotted in, and we'll never find a place for some of them. But we've got enough.'

Juliet thought there was a question in his words – one she might answer some day. But not now.

'So what happens next?' she asked. 'Do I go home?'

'To the precincts?' Lambert said. 'I wouldn't advise it. There's a safe house we use.' He grimaced. 'That sounds terribly dramatic. It's not used for hiding witnesses from the mob or anything like that. In fact, it's mainly used for storing files. But we sometimes put people up there for a few days. We could go there now. I can find someone to collect your belongings from the house.'

When Juliet nodded, he placed his hand on her back, steering her towards the door. As they made their way down through the theatre, they passed officers stationed at various doors. Near the entrance, Juliet stopped.

'Wait,' she said. 'There's something I need to do.'

In the room behind the drapes, that film was still playing. The Moonshine Girl was dancing, her smile still in place. It wasn't her mother, but Juliet felt an unexpected brush of sadness for that smiling girl. This place had destroyed her, as surely as it had broken her rival.

The cabinet drawer came loose easily, and Lambert tore a page out of his notebook, so Juliet could scribble down the name and the few lines of writing below. Then she tucked the paper into her pocket, a little folded possibility to be taken out and considered at some point in the future.

The district was quiet as the two of them made their way towards the main gates. There were a few groups of visitors milling about, and the odd police officer hurrying past, but none of the usual night-time bustle.

Lambert glanced at Juliet as she turned to look at a small man in a decorated mask. 'Looking for someone?'

'I thought Eugene might be here. Did he say where he was going after he called you?'

'There wasn't much time for small-talk,' Lambert said. Then he smiled. 'I am a police officer, though. I took his details, and asked him to come to the station tomorrow. I can pass on a message if you like.'

Juliet nodded, her spirits lifting. 'Yes. Yes please.'

She'd tell him things were going to be different. That it was all right to come back here, that there would be new stories for him – and all the Followers – to love. The thought of him coming here with his girlfriend – Juliet didn't know what she looked like, but in her head, she had kind eyes – was appealing; the two of them walking hand in hand through the streets, letting the district's diversions brush lightly over them.

As they crossed the plaza, there was a flutter of wings overhead, and Juliet looked up to catch the black and white flash of a magpie. Without conscious thought, she saluted.

'Better make a wish,' Lambert said.

Juliet turned to find him watching her. 'A wish?'

'Just something my mother says. If it's bad luck to see a single magpie, then you're lucky if you manage to salute it in time to ward off that bad luck. So it's good luck, really, and you get to make a wish.' He gave a wry smile. 'She makes it up as she goes along, but in a good way.'

Juliet realised there was something she still hadn't said. 'Thank you, DC Lambert.'

'Call me James,' he said. 'I always want to look around for my father when someone uses my rank.'

'He was a police officer too?'

'Yes.' Lambert glanced away.

There was a story there, Juliet thought, but now was not the time to try to chase it.

'James,' she said. 'Thank you.'

'Just doing my job, ma'am.' His smile faded as he looked at her. 'How are you feeling?'

'I don't know.'

'Take it as it comes,' he said gently. 'One day at a time.'

One day at a time.

It was one of those things you heard people say, but there was comfort in the idea of just thinking about *now*, for a little while at least.

As they walked on, towards the gates, they passed more visitors. This far from the theatre, the place felt almost normal, albeit much quieter than it should have been. Juliet wondered how long it would take for the crowds to return. As she glanced down a side street, she saw a girl dancing, her fair hair loose. She was holding the hand of a masked man, who was trying and failing to match his steps to hers. They were both smiling, with a dust-drift of light from a lantern silvering their skin.

Juliet felt something inside her loosen and fall away. *The Show must go on*, she thought. For the first time in longer than she could remember, it felt like a promise.

The London Gazette   *13 March*

The Theatre District has confirmed the election of a new Director, following the resignation of previous Director, Conrad Danes. Eleanor Abbeline's appointment as fifty-seventh Director of the district comes during the ongoing Metropolitan Police investigation into the criminal activities of several of her predecessors. A police spokesman has confirmed that Miss Abbeline is not being treated as a suspect and has fully co-operated with all enquiries.

Acknowledgements

Ah, the acknowledgements. Home of the intense and slightly sweaty paranoia that you will forget to mention someone really, really important, and they will turn out to be, not only important, but also incredibly well connected within the book world, and you will be shunned and despised for the rest of eternity. Or, if it's a member of your family, all babysitting favours will be withdrawn, and you won't be invited to Christmas – even if you're hosting it. There's more scope than usual for making that kind of mistake with these particular acknowledgements, as this book was a long time in the making.

I should start by thanking everyone on the Bath Spa Creative Writing MA who encouraged me in the very early stages of this project, despite it being, at that point, somewhat heavy on setting and concept, and light on actual story. Particular thanks go to my manuscript tutor, Maggie Gee, and to course leader, Richard Kerridge, for not responding with 'no, you bloody well can't' when I emailed him to say I wanted to put this aside to write a completely different novel in the final 2 months of the course.

Thank you to all the other authors who supported me when I thought this book would never see light of day.

I need to start with Katie Khan – she knows why. Then there's the Bath and Bristol SFF massive who still invite me to things, despite my inability to recognise people if they're remotely out of context – you know, like a writer who lives in Bristol, and regularly attends book events in Bristol, at a ... book event in Bristol. Sorry, sorry, sorry. I'd say I won't do it again, but you all know perfectly well that I will. Thanks also to the members of a certain Facebook group, without whom this book definitely *wouldn't* have seen light of day, and to my online writing group for all their support. We began meeting during lockdown, as an offshoot of an online events series I organised, and we're still going strong. I am more grateful to every one of them than they will ever know.

Thank you to all the friends who've supported me along the way. To Anna, for feeding me many, many cups of tea, and occasionally saying 'no, just no' to my proposals for solving stubborn plot holes. I should probably also apologise for dragging her to an immersive show without warning her that there was a real risk of her being sacrificed to the great god Apollo by a sake-swigging barman. Sorry, Anna, these things happen. To Debbie for yet more tea, and for the endless support with this book and everything that came before, as well as the company on yet more theatrical expeditions. Oh, and Debbie, I'm not going to apologise for the whole locked room and hugging thing because I definitely *did* warn you. Thanks to Helen, for tea (yes, there's a theme emerging) for the best of hospitality, and for the ongoing one-woman mission to bring my books to the attention of each and every resident of Scotland. I think there's someone in the vicinity of Inverness who hasn't heard of me, so if you could just pop up there and sort it out, I'd be ever so grateful. Thank you to Chris, for accompanying me to my first ever immersive show, and many more since then, and for delving through the history of London corporations to generate names for fictional organisations that didn't actually make it into the final draft. I fought for the Guildable Manors, Chris, I fought hard.

On the subject of fictional or unofficial organisations, particular thanks must go to one of the members of the impromptu Difficult Decisions Committee, which held its one and only meeting in the middle of a cow field in Somerset. The answer to the question 'what would it look like on the other side?' is this book. Thank you.

Thank you to all our lovely local booksellers, with special mention to Harry at the Oldfield Park Bookshop. He has cheered this book on throughout its rollercoaster journey, and I am beyond grateful for his support.

I'm grateful to the theatre company, Punchdrunk for all the vast, multi-layered worlds they've created over the years, and to the lovely community of immersive theatre appreciators who have come together to explore those worlds. It's hard to imagine a more inclusive and welcoming group of people. This book wouldn't exist in its current form without that community, their joy in discovery, and their love of all the possibilities that exist within theatre. My particular thanks to Seb, Maya, and Peter of Sleepwalk Immersive, supported by Alexis and Charles, for bringing some of my characters to life and giving the book the most incredible and immersive launch any author could have asked for.

The biggest of thank yous to my wonderful agent, Laura Williams. When we first met, you already had pages of meticulous notes, containing some rather tricky questions like 'this scene in chapter 11, what's it for exactly?' You were right, it had no purpose. None. I think I said something like 'hmm, yes, interesting point.' What I was thinking was 'YES.' Thank you for everything, and I promise I won't ever subject you to 160,000 words again. Probably.

To Sam Humphreys, thank you for your faith in this book. I think I knew as soon as we met, that I wanted to work with you. It has been an absolute joy and privilege. Even the bit where you said 'We could do with getting the word count under 100k.' Turns out less really is more. Who knew? And thanks to the whole team at Bonnier, with particular mention of Lucy and Flora for everything they've done to launch this book on an unsuspecting world.

Thank you to my family for their support and belief. At least, I think they believed. They might have thought the whole thing was a load of twaddle, in which case thanks to them all for not saying so. To Margaret for all the babysitting. To Simon, again, for everything, always. And to Thomas, Ben and Sam, even though their plot and title suggestions are almost never helpful and generally ludicrous, and they're neither impressed nor particularly interested in the fact that I have Written A Book.

Finally, thanks must go to someone who shall remain nameless. I am intensely, endlessly grateful. Thank you, thank you, thank you.*

* Yes, this is a blatant attempt to protect myself from the wrath of anyone I've forgotten. If you can't find yourself in these acknowledgements, please give consideration to assuming that you are Shall Remain Nameless, and don't shout at me.